Praise for *Better Than I Know Myself*

"I laughed, I cried, I identified!!!"

—Sybil Wilkes, *The Tom Joyner Morning Show*

"Become absorbed in the lives of these three complex and talented young women."

—*BookPage*

"A wonderfully enriching tale . . . though it has its dark moments, through it all shines friendships that nothing can destroy."

—*Romantic Times BOOKclub Magazine*

"A touching and compelling work about life, love, mistakes, survival, and the powerful connection with those in our lives who anchor us through our greatest joys and our darkest hours."

—*New Pittsburgh Courier*

"*Better Than I Know Myself* is a novel of heartache, triumph, tears, and the impenetrable bonds of three sisterfriends. DeBerry and Grant remind us that life is fragile, that tomorrow is not promised to anyone, so we should live each day to the fullest."

—*ReadinColor BOOKclub*

"Tremendously powerful . . . a true testament to the writing genius of DeBerry and Grant."

—*Real Times*

Also by Virginia DeBerry and Donna Grant

Far from the Tree
Tryin' to Sleep in the Bed You Made

Better Than I Know Myself

Virginia DeBerry *and* Donna Grant

ST. MARTIN'S GRIFFIN
NEW YORK

This is a work of fiction. All of the characters, organizations, and events portrayed in this novel are either products of the author's imagination or are used fictitiously.

Published in the United States by St. Martin's Griffin, an imprint of St. Martin's Publishing Group

 For information, address St. Martin's Publishing Group, 120 Broadway, New York, NY 10271.

www.stmartins.com

The Library of Congress has cataloged the first St. Martin's Griffin edition as follows:

DeBerry, Virginia.
Better than I know myself / by Virginia DeBerry, Donna Grant.
p. cm.
ISBN: 978-0-312-34136-7
1. African American college students—Fiction. 2. African American women—Fiction. 3. Female friendship—Fiction. I. Grant, Donna. II. Title.

PS3554.E17615B47 2004
813′.54—dc22

2003069768

ISBN 978-1-250-84664-8 (trade paperback)

Second St. Martin's Griffin Edition: 2024

10 9 8 7 6 5 4 3 2 1

For our school friends—

Patricia Lancaster and Beverly Houston
Lorraine Braithewaite Harte and Ana Henry
Pearl Tsang and Ruth Marquis

Lawrine Childers, Barbara Malone Saxon,
Barbara Hairston, Nancy Helms Dodd, Natalie Marcus Whitlow,
Patricia Martin Fontenot, Adrienne Fraioli Klein

Without you life wouldn't be the same; neither would the memories.

We Gratefully Acknowledge

Hiram L. Bell III: Thank you, Bear. For everything—D.G.

And for being my angel brother—V.D.B.

Andrea Cirillo for her encouragement and advice, even through the fire (XOXOXO).

Always Gloria Hammond Frye, Juanita Cameron DeBerry and the late John L. DeBerry II for the right stuff.

Alexis, Lauren and Jordan, Brian, Christine and Arielle, the future.

And all of our friends and family members whose continued love and support is surely the grace of the Creator at work.

In life, all we really have is the moment
—and the memory.

Prologue

"...side by side by side."

Present Day
North Brunswick, NJ

I can't sit here all day. She'd been in the car at least ten minutes, squeezing the door handle, unable to budge. She stared through the windshield, careful to overlook the precise rows of engraved plaques dotting the grass. There were no massive headstones or memorial statues, so if she let her eyes skim the tranquil landscape she could pretend it was a park, and not a cemetery.

It was never supposed to be like this. The three of them, Carmen, Regina and Jewell, were going to be together until they were old ladies—side by side by side. Maybe deaf, toothless and half crazy, but still together, laughing, fussing, swapping stories, being there for each other, the way they had been since sophomore year of college, since 5D—the "fifth dimension," they used to call it. That apartment had been like the fourth friend, the one that kept them all together. They hit some rough patches, especially in the beginning, but for two decades they had been part of each other's lives—through joy and pain, sunshine and some really funky weather. Then suddenly, randomly, that all changed, and only two remained.

She rocked for a moment, building momentum, summoning her strength. Finally she flung open the door, stepped out and marched along the road, clutching a bouquet of creamy white roses edged in a froth of green as alive as the late spring day. For the three of them, white roses had become a symbol of celebration and success. How could these sit on one of their graves?

As she left the road and stepped onto the manicured lawn, the heels of her suede pumps sank into the soft ground and came out muddy. Not so long ago, she would have been annoyed about ruining her shoes, but now she realized that didn't matter. Neither did a lot of the crap she used to get so worked up about. She would gladly wear army boots every day for the rest of her life if that would change what happened. *Okay, maybe not gladly.* A smile curled her lips. They had been friends so long she had an answer for the comment she knew would have come her way. *But you know I'd do it for you, if only...*

Her chest heaved and tears leaked from the corners of her eyes. She looked up at the cloudless sky to drain them back into place and wiped at her face with her shirt cuff. She'd been through a million "if onlys." None of them could change what already was. *Okay. Get it together*. There had been so many tears in the months since it happened, but she had promised herself she'd hold them back today. The grief had finally subsided enough to allow for conversations that started "Remember the time..." and ended with laughter, because among the three of them there had always been laughter. Nothing would take that away. She suspected there would always be an ache, though, prone to flare up at a remembered phrase, the glimpse of a photo, the scent of roses.

In the distance she could see the other alumna of 5D, already kneeling by the newly installed marker, tracing her fingers over the raised engraving—the name, the dates—so official, so formal, so final. The two of them had talked about the old days on the ride to the cemetery, staying focused on the beauty of a wonderful life, not its tragic end.

Since they first met, they had shared enough moments for a lifetime of memories, but all those years ago Carmen, Regina and Jewell could not have been more different from one another. So different that their paths would not have crossed had it not been for the one thing they did have in common—a letter—that introduced them to a different world, and to each other.

1
"I made it."

April 15, 1981
Brooklyn, NY

I wish they'd all go to hell. Carmen felt the throbbing bass of her brother's stereo vibrate the steel fire door as she shoved her key in the last of four locks.

"How you gon' throw that card down? You's about a dumb mother—"

"Shut ya ass and pass the cheeba."

She knew Z and some of the fools he hung with were in there, playing pinochle or dirty hearts, eating greasy egg rolls and pork fried rice. That's why she went to the library every day after school, stayed there studying until it closed. She was never in a hurry to get home.

Carmen slipped into the dark hall, eased the door shut. Her stomach did its usual flip-flop, bracing for the crap that would greet her. A cloud of menthol and marijuana smoke hung in the air, stung her nose and eyes. She ducked into her room, eased the overstuffed backpack onto her beat-up desk and rubbed her shoulders. She hauled a big load of books, especially for someone her size. From the first day her parents brought her home her father called her Li'l Bit. At seventeen she still shopped for jeans and shirts in the children's department, and sometimes had to speak twice as loud to keep from getting stepped on.

Carmen's stomach growled, reminding her she hadn't eaten since the jelly doughnut and bottle of orange-flavored quarter water she grabbed for lunch. *If I can just get the mail and some Spaghetti-O's it'll be fine.*

Well, not exactly fine. Carmen Webb's life hadn't been fine for as long as she could remember. Two weeks before she started kindergarten her dad bought her that pine desk and painted it glossy white, so she'd have a place to study, he said. So she could get good grades and go to college. "You get to college Li'l Bit, you got it made," he said. Two weeks later police found Zachariah Webb Sr. near Lincoln Terrace Park, slumped over the steering wheel of his gypsy cab, killed for defending a grand total of twenty-three dollars in fares. Her mother, Geraldine, took to her bed, Z, a teenager by then, declared himself man of the house and Carmen learned to fend for herself.

And by the time she was ten, her mother was gone too. Carmen was ready for school that May morning. She came into the kitchen and found that Geraldine had pulled every jar, can and box out of the kitchen cabinets. Leopard-print nightgown stuffed into awning-striped bell bottoms, Geraldine balanced, one foot on the windowsill, the other on the edge of the sink, and scrubbed the shelves to the rhythm of a song she sang to herself.

"You're gonna fall," Carmen had said.

"Am not." Geraldine hopped down, light as a cat. "Can I get a hug from my Love Bug?" she'd asked and Carmen gave her a big one, even though she felt a little old for the "Love Bug" stuff. "I love you, Mommy." Then she was out the door, glad to see Geraldine so full of energy. Sometimes she sat in the dark, staring at the TV like a zombie for days, even weeks.

Geraldine wasn't around when Carmen got home, but she was glad her mother had gone out. That really meant she was in a good mood, one that might last for a while, except she didn't make it home that night, or the next. By the end of the week the rash that always broke out on Carmen's neck when she was worried itched like fire. She tried not to scratch, and to convince herself it would be all right; Geraldine had wandered off before. Sooner or later she'd show up wearing strange clothes and talking like she'd seen you just yesterday. The first time it happened Z had called the police, but then a social worker came and took Carmen away. Geraldine was back in a few days, but there was a court hearing and a lot of trouble before Carmen could come home. So they stopped calling when Geraldine disappeared on one of her walks, but this time six weeks passed without a sighting.

Carmen did her best to act normal in school, but she was scared. Her mother was flighty and confusing, but Carmen missed her chirpy voice, her good-night kisses, even her bad cooking. Besides, her father was gone; Geraldine was all she had.

One night Z appeared in her doorway, caught her sobbing into her pillow. "Look, I ain't your mama or your daddy. You need to stop that cryin' shit or I'ma call that social worker and have her carry your ass outta here." Z's tone turned Carmen's tears to dust—she knew he meant it. Once, when she was four and he was twelve, she drew a duck in yellow crayon on his basketball. He shook her until she got dizzy and threw up, and from that moment Carmen understood that her presence was not part of his program. And if he was blood, she figured strangers had to be worse, so she learned to keep out of his way.

After a year Geraldine still hadn't returned, and little by little Carmen gave up expecting her to unlock the door.

For the last six years Z had taken the Social Security check Carmen received every month toward her share of the rent. He drove a truck part time for a meat packing plant, and on the side he fenced hot steaks, or worked one of his other hustles—driving carloads of untaxed cigarettes up from North Carolina, stripping copper and aluminum from abandoned buildings—Carmen didn't stick her nose into the details. He managed to keep the lights on most of the time and gave her an allowance for food, toothpaste, personal stuff.

And since Carmen had no intention of following in her brother's footsteps, she concentrated on her grades. As far as her schools were concerned, Geraldine Webb still lived on Montgomery Street, so Carmen signed her mother's name on report cards and other official documents. She wasn't a problem kid, so nobody questioned it. Carmen kept classmates and teachers at a distance—less to explain that way. She excelled at her studies, always guided by her father's dream of college for her. He had died trying to make it come true.

It must have come today. Carmen peeled out of her peacoat. *If I just ask him for the mail and go about my business what can he say?* Most of the time Z got to the box before she did and usually it didn't matter. Nobody sent her birthday greetings or postcards from their vacations, but there was one letter she was waiting for.

"Oooh-wee! I'ma have to take you sucker's money again!"

"Nigga act like he can play some cards 'cause he got lucky."

By the end of a night with Z's posse in the house, Carmen always felt beat down and bruised, but they weren't going anywhere so she adopted her battle-ready stance and marched to the living room. "Hey."

At first they didn't hear her over the music, then Z saw her. "Whatchu lookin' at?" He was taller than Carmen, but just as slight, wiry. They were both the brown of spicy mustard, but where Carmen's big eyes looked sad behind the hard-edge she put on, Z's pierced you like a street-corner challenge.

"Nothin'." She crossed her arms over her chest, looked past him sitting at the card table in the middle of the room and let her gaze rest on the broken console TV stacked with stereo equipment. "Where's the mail?" She tried to sound like it didn't matter, tried not to scratch her neck.

"Shit, what difference it make?" Z's hair was already thin, and what was left he slicked back with the stocking cap he slept in. "You gon pay the bills?" His buddies laughed.

"I'm waitin' for somethin', all right?"

"Damn, ain't you heard all that college shit? You can't go to but one." Arm slung over the chair back, Z slouched in her direction, picked his tooth with a matchbook corner. "Look on top of the refrigerator."

That wasn't too bad. Carmen flipped on the kitchen light and held her breath as roaches scurried from counters, the stove and the sink full of dishes. She pulled one of the dingy yellow vinyl chairs from under the table and dragged it to the refrigerator, but before she could step up she heard the swish-swish of a nylon track suit and Randy was behind her.

"Can't reach that high Li'l Bit?" Grease from Randy's Jheri Curl had turned the collar of his jacket from red to a murky maroon.

It made her skin crawl when he called her what her daddy used to. "I'll get it myself." Carmen shoved the chair between them. She didn't feel safe with Randy in the same apartment, much less in the same room. Since that day in the elevator the sight of him made her want to vomit, but before she could stop him he grabbed the stack of mail.

"Here's the Mays sale paper, you want that?"

Carmen rolled her eyes.

He flipped through some other junk mail, then stopped. "Lookie here. Lookie here. A letter addressed to Miss Carmen Webb. This what you want?" He dangled it in her direction.

Carmen could see the pale blue crest at the top left corner. She reached for the envelope.

Randy snatched it away. "Must be important, huh?"

"No biggie." She leveled a bored look at him.

"So you don't want it?"

Carmen seethed inside, but she just shrugged.

Randy unzipped his jacket pocket, came up with a disposable lighter and flicked it. "So if I burnt it up you wouldn't care?" He held the envelope over the flame, grinning at her.

Don't beg. "I don't care *what* you do." Carmen's face hardened into a stony mask.

Randy eyed her and waved the envelope closer to the flame, but Carmen didn't budge. Then, one corner caught fire. "Ooops."

Fists balled at her sides, Carmen stared him down, didn't flinch as the creamy paper slowly blackened.

Finally Randy laughed, let it fall to the floor. "Damn, you one hard-headed bitch."

As soon as he turned away Carmen stomped on the envelope to put out the fire. She snatched it and headed for her room.

Door closed, Carmen sat on her bed, shaking. She'd already been accepted to Brooklyn College and Hunter, which her guidance counselor treated like some kind of miracle. But this was the wild card.

She'd never thought of going to Columbia until her chemistry teacher spent half a period gushing about his twenty-year college reunion. When she asked her counselor about applying he said Columbia didn't accept women. Barnard, their sister school did, "But I wouldn't encourage you to apply. You'll never be admitted." Carmen had scored higher on the SATs than anybody at her school in ten years, and she decided that if her science teacher had gone there, it couldn't be that hard to get in. She ate boxed macaroni and cheese and skipped lunch for two months to save enough for the application fee. She knew she'd need a ton of scholarship money, but if anybody fit the bill for a hardship handout, she did. She figured it was time for her to catch some kind of break.

As far as Z was concerned, college was a waste. "I been carrying you since I was nineteen. When the hell you gettin' up offa me?" he had asked.

Carmen didn't care what Z said, she was going, and to medical school after that. And when she became a doctor she'd work in a place that was antiseptically clean, live in a place where there were no roaches and no neighbors like Randy. People would respect her and she'd make enough money so she wouldn't need anybody—not ever again.

For the moment, Carmen's world narrowed to the contents of that one scorched envelope. She dusted off the burned flakes, gingerly opened the flap.

I made it! Carmen rolled onto her back, clutched the paper to her chest, thought of her dad. *I'm on my way.*

April 16, 1981
Franklin, NJ

"'There's a party goin' on right here. A celebration to last throughout the year.'" Regina sang and danced through the unlocked front door, letting it bang shut behind her. "How come it's so dark in here?" She ended her ode to Kool & the Gang, dropped her loose-leaf binder and shoulder bag on the flowered hall bench, flipped the light and checked the banister. *No note so Mom's here somewhere, like I need to know where she is every freakin' minute of my life.* Regina caught the savory aroma of dinner. *Her world-famous lasagna again.* Her mother had stopped teaching long before Regina came along, and was always there after school. *Guess she can stop pretending to be mother of the year when I graduate.*

Regina hit the living room light, yanked off her purple-and-gold school jacket and dumped it on the sofa. She checked her 'do in the mirror over the fireplace. "Fox-y!" Then she fluffed the hair framing her face, satisfied she'd found the right setting lotion to keep it from drooping by third period. From kindergarten on Regina Foster was a ringleader. Hot-chocolate brown with sweet cheeks and a cute, round nose, her fast smile and eyes brimming with equal parts fun and mischief drew classmates to her and kept teachers from coming down too hard when she was a bit over the line.

Regina still wasn't used to how quiet it was at home, now that her brother Keith had finished grad school, vacated the holding cell, the apartment above the garage where each of her brothers had lived—summers, after college, between jobs or girlfriends. She was the only one left in the nest and she was counting the months until she would fly the coop and be free.

Her friends had always flocked to her house, but as far as Regina was concerned, life chez Foster was a bad fifties flashback, but so was the rest of her neighborhood. White, black, it didn't make any difference. Dads worked and moms mostly stayed home, except when they volunteered at the hospital or, worst of all, at school. Nobody even seemed embarrassed by the white picket fences that surrounded their well-tended colonials, like there could be a clearer stereotype. Her parents, Lonnie and Al were perpetually cheerful, responsible and solid, like King and Kennedy hadn't been assassinated, Vietnam never happened, Nixon hadn't been an accessory to burglary, or John Lennon hadn't been murdered right on the street by a maniac. Like they had been just thrilled about their midlife bundle of joy. It was all so fake as far as Regina was concerned.

"*Regina, would you come in here honey?*" her mother called from the kitchen.

Now what? Regina burst through the swinging door. "What are you all doing here?" Her parents, Keith, and the next-door neighbors who'd been like family her whole life all wore variations of the "I know something you don't know" grin.

"I heard you were crying yourself to sleep every night because you missed me, so I drove up." Keith, the youngest of Regina's three older brothers, and her favorite, was the only one still living at home while she was growing up.

"Hardly." She stuck her tongue out at him. "You got tired of Spam and Velveeta burgers and came home for some real food."

"Okay you two clowns." Lonnie, a round-faced butterball in a pink tennis shirt and chinos, came up behind her daughter, gripped her shoulders. "Let's go into the dining room."

"Dining room? It's Wednesday." Before Regina got an answer her mother steered her through the door and turned up the chandelier, revealing the table, set like Sunday dinner.

"Daddy get another promotion?" Regina asked, but when she looked up, all eyes beamed her way.

"Look at your place, Queenie." Keith had given her that nickname when she was ten and found out her name was Latin for queen. For weeks she reminded her family of her royal designation.

Regina zeroed in on the two envelopes beside her plate and her knees turned to rubber bands. She sent off college applications months ago, then put them out of her mind. She knew she'd get in someplace. In spite of her less than enthusiastic effort, she maintained a 3.8 average, had great SAT scores. She was class vice-president and yearbook editor—because she liked being out front, planning the fun and delegating the grunt work. The thought of four more years in school made her want to chew glass, but she applied to college anyway, because becoming the first Foster in three generations not to attend was not an option.

From the time she learned B followed A, Regina had heard the proud recitations. Her grandma and granddaddy Foster as well as both of her parents and her oldest brother, AJ, had graduated from Howard. Her dad earned his doctorate in chemical engineering from Columbia. AJ got his Ph.D. from Stanford. Her middle brother, Michael, completed his graduate work at Duke and Keith had just finished his master's at Rutgers. Regina was left to bring up the rear, although she couldn't see anything left for her to accomplish. Her parents never exactly said she had to follow the family academic legacy, but every time one of her mother's sorority sisters asked about her major, or a church member wanted to know what she was going to do when she finished college, she felt the pressure. "Be famous, or maybe infamous," she would answer, only half joking. Regina felt like her whole family was born knowing why they were put on the planet. She didn't have a clue what she wanted to be, except not like them.

"Isn't it wonderful?" Lonnie's eyes glistened with barely contained tears. "Howard and Barnard on the same day! I was so excited when the mail came I called your father and your brothers right away." She clapped her hands gleefully. "I called Gregory too, but he wasn't home."

"I'll be heading straight to the poorhouse now." Her father folded his arms across his broad chest. "Straight to the poorhouse." His eyes looked suspiciously watery too.

"You're all standing around waiting for me to open these?" Regina looked at her parents incredulously. "*And* you called my boyfriend? What if I didn't get in?"

"Of course you got in. You'll get into the other schools too. You'll have your pick, just like your brothers did." Lonnie fussed with the silk flowers on the sideboard. "AJ and Michael sent their congratulations. Oh Regina, we're so proud of you!"

"Are you talking about the same nutball I grew up with, or have you adopted some other child?" Keith rested his elbows on his chair back.

Regina rolled her eyes at him, picked up the envelope with the pale blue seal. College felt like her ticket to the same-old, same-old: graduate, have a respectable career, raise a model family, take her place as a credit to society, just like her parents. But if she had to go to school, she wanted to do it in New York, far from her hopelessly passé, perfect suburban world. She longed for a big, important, uncharted life, full of unexpected turns and fascinating people, not luncheons, pearls and a suitable spouse. For her, that dream began in magical Manhattan, back when she was five.

One summer afternoon, Al took Regina and Keith for a Circle Line ride around Manhattan. From her perch atop her father's shoulders she was mesmerized by the sun glinting off the towering buildings. It looked like Oz, and she ached to be Dorothy. Tucked in the '65 Bonneville on the way home, she leaned across the backseat and whispered to Keith, "I'm gonna live there one day, like the boat." He laughed, and with eleven-year-old worldliness dripping from every word he said, "A boat doesn't *live* anywhere! It's docked." Regina didn't care what he said. She had already made up her mind and with each subsequent trip into the city, her determination grew.

"Are you waiting for Easter? That's not until Sunday," Keith interjected.

"Later for you." Regina ripped the envelope open and her eyes widened to searchlights. "I made it." It was barely a whisper. "I made it!" She bounced up and down, waving the letter in her hand. Keith, Lonnie and Al moved in for a group hug. *New York City here I come.*

Sunday, April 18, 1981
Baldwin Hills, CA

"You haven't booked any more last-minute appearances for me, have you?" Jewell unfurled her long legs and stepped from the driver's side of the British green Jaguar. Her Jaguar, although it was the car Vivian drove. Jewell preferred her white TR7, a sixteenth-birthday present to herself, but Vivian complained the little convertible didn't have the right cachet for public appearances. She insisted that if they weren't going to hire a limo, at least the Jag made a better impression. Jewell nixed the limousine. After one of these events with all the handshakes, waving, flashbulbs and shouting, her head was abuzz and driving, even on the LA freeways, relaxed her. So since she chose her battles with her mother carefully, she agreed to use Vivian's car.

For five years Jewell had made weekly visits to America's living rooms as Tonya Gifford, the pigtailed, impossibly cute, wise-cracking kid with the husky voice on *Daddy's Girl*, one of a handful of sitcoms with a largely black cast. The show was canceled when she hit puberty, grew breasts, and shot up ten inches, making her no longer little-girl cute. In the years since, work had been sporadic—a few movies of the week, guest spots on sitcoms, a record that hit the charts for a few weeks, even a supporting part in a major movie, although to this day she wished she'd never read that screenplay—but now, at seventeen, *Daddy's Girl* was still her claim to fame.

"No. I promise." Vivian scurried past the graceful palms and unlocked the towering door to the gem of a thirties moderne house—Jewell's house. Vivian had had her heart set on one of the homes built by Paul Williams, the black architect who designed distinctive houses for early film stars. There wasn't one on the market when they were looking, but Vivian loved the house that they, well she, had chosen. Baldwin Hills had been *the* place for prominent blacks since Bill "Bojangles" Robinson made it his home in the thirties and it was a universe away from the rented Culver City bungalow they could afford when they first moved to California, on Jewell's father's sporadic earnings as a struggling comic. But with Vivian's push Jewell had shown him how stars really shine. "But you just sang the National Anthem at a Dodgers game, darling—a *nationally televised* Dodgers game—that's terrific exposure." She playfully bumped hips with Jewell. "Don't be unmanageable, darling. We have to keep your name out there."

Jewell hated when her mother called her that. "I'm not your only client anymore, Vivian. Maybe *we* could give *my* name a rest." She followed into the house.

While waiting in line at Ralph's with her mother, five-year-old Jewell had been playing, pretending the pineapple in her cart was the queen of fruit. She caught the eye of a casting agent. Jewell made a quick leap from local to national commercials and by the time she was seven she was tapped for *Daddy's Girl*. On their first pre-dawn ride to the studio, her mother suggested Jewell call her Vivian while "they" were at work. "It sounds more professional than Mommy." And since Vivian spent more time managing than mothering, it wasn't long before she was Vivian all the time. That's also when she had Jewell's last name changed from her ex's to her own.

"Of course you need your rest. That's why I'm here to look after you." Pumps clicking across the terrazzo tiles, Vivian stopped at the entry table and plucked a limp lily from the arrangement. Although Prescott Management now represented a choice few other child actors, Jewell remained Vivian's number-one priority and she had done a stellar job of looking after her daughter, at least business-wise. She had long ago given up her job as an assistant bank manager to make sure that Jewell's career would be no child star tragedy of squandered talent and misspent fortune. Before the end of the first season Vivian sought out the best financial advisors and Jewell's earnings had been invested wisely, some with great foresight and others with great luck, and as a result, Jewell was more than comfortable. "Now if you'll go retire your baseball jersey, we'll still be in time for lunch. There's a new Italian place in…"

"I'm not in the mood for Italian." Jewell took off her Dodgers cap and conferred it, like a crown, on her mother.

"All right." Vivian reached up and smoothed stray hairs off Jewell's cheek. No one would have cast them as mother and daughter. Vivian was a tiny golden sprite who navigated the world with the nonstop flutter of a hummingbird. Jewell was like a black swan, long neck and all, gliding gracefully along the surface of the pond with no visible effort, while in reality she paddled furiously below. "Then what do you want, darling?"

You wouldn't let me have what I really wanted. But right now Jewell was eager to hear from Barnard College where she had applied, over her mother's objections.

Vivian swore Jewell would detest dorm life in cold, dirty New York. "What if something great comes along? Another series? A lead in a movie? You'll be so far away," she had said. After all the years of positioning and planning, Vivian didn't want to believe Jewell would abandon her career. Their career.

"They have airplanes now, Vivian. And telephones," was Jewell's reply. In the last year she had begun to exercise her right to say no to her manager, which did not sit well with her mother. It wasn't easy for Jewell either. For as long as she could remember her job had been to follow direction, hit her mark, make people happy, and not cause any trouble, because after all, didn't she know how lucky she was? "There are a million girls who would do anything to be where you are," her mother would tell her. But now Jewell's heart wasn't in it. She wanted out of the set-designed life Vivian had orchestrated, where husbands were cancelled when their ratings weren't high enough, and children could be written out when they didn't fit the storyline. After going to class on the *Daddy's Girl* set, then on to the Hollywood Professional School, Jewell wanted to experience real school—real life. She didn't know what that entailed, except she was sure it meant you didn't feel washed up before most people got their feet wet. In Jewell's mind, New York was the capital of real, a whole continent away from Vivian's interference and cold calculations, a place where she could stop acting and just be.

The wait to hear if she'd been accepted had made Jewell more nervous than she had ever been about a callback, but she had only submitted the one application. If it was supposed to happen, it would. She knew competition for admission to any Seven Sisters school was fierce. They measured brain power, not star power. It was a new arena for her, but she wanted to be accepted on her own merit, without points for being a celebrity. Jewell had a driving curiosity and read voraciously: in her trailer between takes, in the car on her ride home, sometimes half the night. She wanted four years to study what intrigued her, not lines other people had written. She wanted to speak her own mind, make her own decisions, deal with her own mistakes.

Jewell twisted her blanket of black hair into a knot on top of her head and decided to give Vivian the short answer. "Right now what I want is a swim." The pool, surrounded by a lush garden, had been her favorite part of the house when they bought it after the first season of *Daddy's Girl*. When she was lonely she used to pretend it was an enchanted forest with fairies and elves and that one day her father would fly on his winged stallion to see her. Now she let her hair fall back around her shoulders. "After that, maybe I'd like a big salad, with avocado and sprouts and…"

"Sounds divine." Vivian took Jewell's hand. "But first, I have a little surprise for you."

The taupe-and-cream deco living room, complete with wet bar and white baby grand was very Hollywood. Jewell plopped into a club chair and smiled slyly. "Your surprises are never little."

Vivian opened a drawer in the burled walnut end table and removed a large gray envelope.

Jewell rolled her eyes. "Is that *it*?" She knew it was another script.

Vivian's face lit up as she did the pitch. "It's called *After Class*. It's about a group of high school wise guys who always meet in detention…"

"Great. *Welcome Back, Kotter* meets the Dead End Kids." Jewell twisted her hair into a loose braid.

"Give it a quick read." Vivian held it out. "I think it has potential."

"First, I'm not interested. Second, nobody's going to cast a six-foot sophomore girl."

"Fine." Vivian tossed the script on the sofa. "There's more." She pulled two envelopes out of the drawer, took a deep breath. "The benefit of being older is that you get wisdom. You can see farther down the road instead of getting distracted by…"

"Where is this going?" Jewell slouched impatiently in her chair. She didn't know what load of crap Vivian was selling this time, but it was a big one.

Vivian held her head high. "Congratulations. You've been accepted to UCLA Film School."

Jewell jumped out of her seat. "I didn't apply to UCLA Film School, so why would they accept me?" Her voice dropped to a growl. "And why were *you* notified?"

"I applied for you. I sent them the same information you sent to Barnard…"

"Except *you* changed my essay to why I want to go to UCLA. I don't believe you!"

"It's the best of all worlds, Jewell," Vivian pleaded. "You want to go to school. Fine. You'll be classmates with tomorrow's directors and screenwriters." She folded her arms over her chest. "And may I remind you that the last time you made a big decision when I wasn't around…"

"You had to save the day and clean up my mess, and you'll never let me forget—"

"It wasn't for me. It was your life. Your future. You were only fifteen, only a child yourself, even though you thought you were grown." Vivian took two steps back to keep from having to look up at her daughter. "You thought it wouldn't matter, that they would still send you scripts. But I'm here to tell you that you wouldn't have been America's little black darling anymore."

"Who says I want to be? That's what you're worried about, isn't it? It's not good for Prescott Management if my career tanks." Jewell was defiant. She knew she had made a mistake and she didn't need Vivian to remind her. She wasn't going to forget. Ever.

"That is not true."

Jewell shifted her focus to the other envelope in Vivian's hand. The one with the pale blue crest in the corner. She snatched it. "How long have you had this?"

"I wanted you to have options."

"You wanted me to do it *your* way." Jewell tore open the flap. *Dear Miss Prescott: We are pleased to inform you…*an angry smile curled her lips.

"Now you can congratulate me, Vivian. Because whether you like it or not, I made it, and in the fall I'm going to New York."

"I know what you're doing, but what's done is done, Jewell. Running away won't change anything."

2

"Three pieces from very different puzzles."

July 13, 1982
New York, NY

She must be ignoring me on purpose, because filing cannot be that interesting. "Excuse me?" Jewell's husky voice bounced off the walls of the cavernous library. The girl who sat in one of the cubbies behind the circulation desk continued to flip through a stack of folders, completely oblivious to her. Jewell had met her during freshman orientation weekend last fall and even though most of the black undergrads at the university had at least a nodding acquaintance, all Jewell knew about her was that she was a commuter and didn't hang around campus much. *Karen? Carla? I never remember.* She had even been in Jewell's Art History section first semester, along with a hundred other students, but she might as well have been a magician—now you see her, now you don't. *She's always so serious.* Always looked the same too. Overalls or Wranglers, with a T-shirt—long or short-sleeved depending on the season, always baggy, like she was trying to add bulk to her small frame. She wore her hair snatched back into a twig of a braid that she bobby-pinned in place, and her skin looked dull, like it was missing something—sunlight, vitamins or sleep. Whenever Jewell was in her presence she felt a "keep your distance" vibe, but the defiance was betrayed by the dark-rimmed sadness that never left her eyes.

Jewell tugged her ponytail up against the elastic band to tighten it, flung the length of thick black hair behind her back then leaned across the desk. "Hel-lo-o?"

Carmen finally looked up and was surprised to see Jewell, although she wasn't about to show it. They didn't know each other personally, but nearly everybody on campus recognized Jewell Prescott. Carmen was never a *Daddy's Girl* fan. It was way too silly, like anybody's problems worked out neatly in thirty minutes, and fathers were always there to save the day.

They'd had a class together, but Carmen had only taken Art History because it fulfilled a requirement, fit her schedule and seemed like an easy A, since her scholarship required her to keep her GPA up. So did going to med school, which was "The Plan." The class met right before she had to race to Brooklyn to make her shift under the Golden Arches and Carmen claimed a seat by the exit so she could be out the door as soon as the bell rang. And if she happened to doze off in the dark, stuffy lecture hall during the endless slide shows of Tintoretto, Rembrandt, and other ancient painters, at least the professor wouldn't see. After all, her schedule was tough. She left Brooklyn at dawn, didn't get home most nights before midnight. Even she had to sleep sometime.

Jewell, on the other hand, seemed to crave the spotlight. Always perky and eager to offer her two cents about the artist being considered, she sat dead center in the first row, like anybody could miss a six-foot black chick, especially one who wore an ever-changing variety of costumes from peasant blouses and clogs to sweater sets and circle skirts. On top of that she was famous.

Carmen glanced up at the clock on the opposite wall and caught the big hand click one notch closer to quitting time. "Can I help you?" she asked in a less than helpful voice, determined not to suck up. She half expected Jewell had shown up at the last minute looking for the Mandarin Chinese translation of *War and Peace*, or some other obscure book because she had a paper due. Not that Carmen thought somebody like Jewell actually wrote her own papers. "We close soon, you know."

"Yeah I know. That's the problem." *Does this girl ever lighten up?* "I was supposed to meet Regina Foster outside half an hour ago. You know her, medium brown, medium-sized, always talking? She's a sophomore too. Anyway, she hasn't shown up. Have you seen her?"

"No." Carmen chucked the folders in a bin. She couldn't imagine what Regina would be doing in the library anyway. From what Carmen had seen, Regina was majoring in social life with a minor in fashion. First semester she'd started sponsoring birthday parties for people in the dorm and charging a dollar a head, to cover supplies she said, but it sounded like a plain old rent party to Carmen and she wanted no part of it. Regina invited her once, but she didn't go and their paths rarely crossed after that.

"Well could you see if somebody else has?" *And maybe make this harder for me while you're at it.* Jewell tried not to roll her eyes.

"Yeah. Okay." Carmen disappeared through a door behind the counter. Jewell could hear muffled conversation and a minute later Carmen returned. "This guy thinks he saw her in the stacks on six, but that was a couple of hours ago."

"I'll go check."

"You have to hurry. Summer hours." Carmen went back to her folders.

"I know." Jewell screwed up her face in a fake smile. "You already told me."

When the elevator doors opened on six she stepped out and felt like she had entered a tomb. Jewell hated the desolate rows of musty volumes and spent as little time as possible in the stacks here at Columbia or across campus at Barnard's library. All that quiet made it too easy for her to hear the thoughts she'd come three thousand miles to silence. She peered down the dark aisles, looking for a light at one of the desks. Then she heard the muffled snore, shuffled toward the noise and found Regina, head on her arm, drooling on her notebook. Jewell watched for a few seconds, debating her options, then grinned as she snatched the soggy spiral-bound book from under Regina's head.

"Huh? What?" Regina sat up abruptly.

"I'm roasting outside, waiting for your behind, and you're here rehearsing for *Sleeping Beauty*." Jewell plopped the notebook back on the desk and dropped her hands on her hips.

Regina wiped her mouth with the heel of her hand. "Oh man. I musta just dozed off. How'd you find me in here?"

"What's her name, light skinned, little, dresses like a farmer and never speaks to anybody?"

"Carmen?"

"Yeah. Carmen was at the desk and she said you were here. Or rather, I had to practically beg her to ask if anybody'd seen you."

"I can't take her. She's too weird." Regina blinked, trying to focus. "What time is it?"

"Time to get outta here. The library's closing right now." Jewell folded her arms across her chest and tapped her foot.

Regina spoke through a wide open yawn. "I still don't know how you can study in Macintosh with everybody playing cards and yakking—"

"And watching soaps like you? The student center musta worked better than the library since I'm not the one trying to make up, how many incompletes over the summer?"

"Never mind." Regina stood up, stretched and re-tucked her white, sleeveless blouse into the waistband of her starched jeans, then jammed her notebook into her tote and slung the bag over her shoulder. "Guess we missed *E.T.*" She followed Jewell.

"Yeah, but if you move it we can catch this film downtown that I heard was pretty interesting." Jewell pushed the elevator call button.

"Interesting film?" Regina stopped short. "That means long and boring. I need a pit stop."

"Go at the theater."

"The bathrooms are always nasty. You comin'?"

"No. Just go."

Jewell smirked as she leaned against the wall. Early on she learned Regina was time challenged; that's just how she was. But she had always treated Jewell like a regular person. No butt kissing and back stabbing. "They don't like you. They like what you can do for them," is how Vivian used to put it and after ten years in Hollywood Jewell found that her mother was often right, but Regina had just been real. Her main mission was having fun and she could figure out how to broker her last five dollars into enough jug wine and cheap chips to start a party. After the last dance she'd be planning the next one. Regina was as outgoing in life as Jewell was when the director said, "Action," so after some hesitation, she gave in to the fun.

After a few minutes Jewell checked her watch, trotted down the hall and flung open the ladies' room door. "Come on!"

"Just a sec." Regina opened a bobby pin with her teeth and clipped her hair behind her ear.

"You're only spending the night. How can you haul all that crap around?" The counter looked like a drugstore cosmetics aisle, littered with bobby pins, sponge rollers, hair spray, deodorant, a family-size lotion, cologne, two blushes and three lip glosses.

"Never know what I might need. And you know I cannot be lookin' raggedy. Ever." Regina held her bag to the edge of the counter, swept her supplies on top of her nightie and two "just in case" changes of clothes, and took a last glance in the mirror. "Let's book."

Jewell led the way back to the elevator. "We need to move it if we're going to make…"

"Aw shoot!" Regina cried. "I left my other bag. I bought this bad shirt at…"

"Just go!"

Regina headed back to the rest room. She used to think famous people rode in limos with an entourage and were stuck up, but Jewell was never like that. When Jewell first arrived at the dorm with her mother, loads of boxes and matching luggage in tow, Regina almost choked. There hadn't been many black girls on television when she was young so Tonya Gifford, Jewell's TV persona, became her hero. For a year she took to wearing khakis, T-shirts and pigtails like the character and wishing that her own father was exciting like Dr. Jay, Tonya's dad, the handsome, widowed, exotic animal veterinarian, instead of Dr. Al, a boring old drug company chemist. During orientation Regina wanted to run over to Jewell and gush, but she checked herself and gave the star plenty of space just as other students did. And Jewell seemed to want to blend in. She took the number One local train and ate cafeteria food like everybody else. It puzzled Regina; with Jewell's money and connections Regina would have happily skipped the scholastics.

So at 7:15 one Tuesday morning when Regina traipsed down to the basement of Hewitt toting her pillowcase full of panties and bras so she could get dressed for her 9 A.M. biology lecture, she was shocked to find Jewell sitting in front of a spinning washer, highlighting passages in *The Theory of the Leisure Class*. Before Regina could muzzle herself she blurted out, "Doesn't somebody do that for you?"

Jewell shrugged and smiled. "That's why I left home, Regina. Sometimes you want to be the only one handling your dirty laundry." She raised an eyebrow for effect.

Regina was surprised Jewell knew her name. "I hear you, but if it's just some funky drawers, I sure wouldn't mind if Mom let me bring 'em home to her, 'cause sitting here waiting for the spin cycle is the pits." She had lifted the lid on the neighboring washer and emptied her sack.

"It's not so bad, and I'm really diggin' the city." Jewell scooted to the edge of the bench.

"Hey, Chaka Khan is at the Beacon next week. Wanna go?" Regina was surprised how easily the invitation rolled off her tongue and how quickly Jewell said yes. And what a night. A photographer from the *Amsterdam News* recognized Jewell in the lobby, brought them backstage and took their picture with the soulful diva. Jewell barely looked at the photo that ran the next week, but Regina was stoked—the picture was the first proof of the extraordinary life she would lead in New York, especially with a friend like Jewell.

Regina returned to the elevator, waving her bag. "Wait till you get a load of this."

"Don't open the bag. Don't show me anything." Jewell rang for the elevator. "Don't remember anything. Don't say another word until we're outta here."

"Fine." Regina mocked an attitude.

"That was another word!" Jewell put her finger to her lips. "Shhhh!" The elevator arrived and they crept inside silently, then giggled.

They stifled their laughs when the door opened and Carmen got on, an army green backpack slung over her shoulder. "It took you all this time to find her?" Carmen asked Jewell as she eyed Regina. The doors banged together.

"Long story," Jewell answered and grinned at Regina who sucked her teeth at Carmen then reached between them and jabbed the elevator button again.

And at that instant the car went black as it screeched and jolted to a halt.

"What the…" Carmen's pack thumped to the floor.

Jewell grabbed the wall to keep her balance. "If you didn't want to see the movie you should have just said so, Reggie."

"Very funny, smart ass." Regina cracked. "But this is kinda freaky. I can't see my own—"

"It's not funny. Somebody could get hurt." Carmen's voice sliced the dark.

"What, like we planned this get-together?" Regina snarled. "Maybe if we jump up and down a little—" She started to bounce.

"Are you crazy?! If this thing falls it could kill us!" Carmen shouted.

"You don't have to yell!" Regina felt her way to the front and poked at the buttons.

"Then quit playin'." Pinpricks of fear tingled Carmen's arms and despite the heat she tried not to shiver. "The emergency button is the red one on top," she snapped. "Think you can find it?"

"It would help if I could *see* red," Regina shot back.

"Just move." Carmen pushed to the front, away from memories of another elevator in the dark. "I'll do it." But a chilly trickle of sweat slid down her back anyway. She leaned in and smacked at the buttons until a piercing bell ripped through the silence.

When it stopped Regina peeled her hands from her ears. "Shit, I may never hear again."

"Do you have to curse?" Carmen asked, forcing herself back to the present.

And Regina lost her cool. "What is with you, Carmen?! Damn! You walk around with your nose in the air like you can't be bothered with anybody."

"I'm here to get an education. Period," Carmen shouted. "I've got a job, work-study, my classes and an hour commute. I don't have time to socialize, like some people!"

"La-de-freakin'-da. It's the same four-year sentence whether you talk to anybody or not. It doesn't mean you can't say hi, or crack a smile."

Jewell couldn't see their expressions, but she felt the heat of their angry exchange. "If you come to blows, tomorrow's *Spectator* headline will read, 'Barnard Blacks in Butler Brawl.' Hmm, that's good. Maybe I have a future in journalism." She sensed the tension ratchet down a notch.

"You're not well," Regina said finally.

"I have to get out of this box and go to work if that's all right with you two." Carmen struggled to bring her voice down from the scared shriek that had slipped out before. She fidgeted with the token in her pocket, trying to keep her hands from shaking, trying not to feel trapped. It wasn't just what happened with Randy, she'd mostly felt trapped all her life. Carmen truly believed school was the only way out and she could handle what was expected of her in class. But there was no syllabus for relating to the people, and from students to professors, they were a different breed from the folks she was used to—even the black ones, especially the black ones. They knew more, had more, expected more. She looked across the darkness toward Regina and Jewell, certain that she wasn't the one with her nose in the air.

Before the fussing started again, a muffled voice called from somewhere beneath them. "*Anybody in there?*"

"Yeah," they yelled.

"Sit tight. We're workin' on it. If we have to, we can lower you manually soon as the mechanic gets here."

"Great, I'll be late for work. Again." Carmen retreated to a corner, sank to the floor.

"The mechanic is probably home in the Bronx, watching TV." Regina headed for the opposite corner.

Jewell took a spot on the floor between them, felt around in her bag until she found her Virginia Slims and the monogrammed silver lighter her mother had given her when she was fifteen. The brief flash brought their faces into view, then they faded, their voices filling the void.

"I hate cigarette smoke," Carmen announced before the filter tip was out of Jewell's mouth.

Jewell took a big drag, blew a smoky plume up in the air. "Okay. You hate smoking." She stubbed the cigarette on the floor and thumped the butt to the corner. "Let's get this out while we're stuck in here. What else don't you like—about me?" It was matter-of-fact, the way she'd ask the director for comments on a scene. "Must be something. You never spoke to me in Art History. Not once."

"Guess we're in it now." Regina leaned back in her corner, waiting for the fireworks.

"I didn't have orchestra seats. I sat in the balcony." Carmen was surprised by Jewell's direct approach.

"Oh come off it," Jewell complained. "I sat in the first row because it was a two-hour lecture and I needed the leg room. And so I could answer enough questions to let the professor know I wasn't the stupid girl from the sitcom who got in because I could afford to pay tuition." She leaned toward Carmen. "That's what you think too, isn't it?"

"Why do you care what I think?" Carmen gave Jewell credit for being direct. If she wanted it straight, she'd get it.

"I hate when people judge me on what they think they know," Jewell replied. "Fair?"

Carmen knew what she meant. "Okay. Fair." Jewell wasn't at all like what she expected.

"What *did* make you come here?" Regina asked, while the truth serum was flowing. "I mean, you don't exactly need a degree to act."

"Maybe I don't want to act. Maybe I want to be a diplomat, or a drama critic, or an art historian." Jewell scooted back against the wall, stretched her legs. "What's your major, Carmen?"

"Bio-chem. I'm pre-med." Carmen always liked the way it sounded. She had staked out a future to obliterate her past and the present was what she had to go through to get there.

"Man. Pre-med! You really do have to study all the time," Regina lamented.

"What did you get in that art class anyway?" Carmen asked Jewell.

"An A. You?"

"Man, I only got a B."

"Guess you should have studied with the sitcom girl," Jewell announced.

Carmen let the comment dangle a while. "Maybe next time," she said finally.

The supercharged atmosphere in the small space calmed another level. The momentary lull was interrupted by loud growling from Regina's stomach which made them all laugh.

"I need a sandwich," Regina announced.

"You're always hungry," Jewell squawked.

"Not always. Just often. This'll be a great story over sausage slices at V&T. Somebody we know will be there."

"Somebody *you* know which means half the students here," Jewell teased Regina.

Regina rummaged in her tote. "I know I've got some Twizzlers—bingo!" She produced a package. "You want? They're strawberry."

"No they're not. They're corn syrup, food coloring and artificial flavoring," Jewell said. "Besides, I thought they went bye-bye along with your old boyfriend Greg."

"That was last month." Regina pulled out a piece of candy. "He deserved to be dumped—way too boring. My mom's more broken up about it than I am. But this?" She took a bite. "No way!" After a pause she added, "Carmen, you want, or are you like Ms. Bean Sprout Birdseed here?" She held out the package.

Silence.

Carmen hadn't eaten since her corn flakes, and like most days, she'd been too busy to notice she was hungry. "Okay." She followed the crinkling cellophane, grabbed a stick. "Thanks."

"It's a shame, but I haven't met anybody here I wouldn't trade for a Twizzler," Regina continued. "Except there *is* this fine specimen I've seen around campus this summer."

While Regina detailed how she planned to bump into him, Carmen bit a hunk of the gummy candy, and chewed on the fact that boyfriends were not part of her curriculum. She'd heard Z and his crew brag about getting over, taking what they wanted. Randy had taken what he wanted, but if Jewell and Regina hadn't learned that lesson, she wasn't going to teach it to them.

"Carmen, I guess we're gonna bag the movie, but I know we'll go for dinner when we get out of here." Jewell changed the subject before Regina started one of her "If I looked like you, the men would have to take numbers," harangues. Dating wasn't simple for Jewell. Twelve times out of ten, guys at school were convinced she was either stuck up or an easy lay. Older guys, a few professors included, wanted to show off—impress her, teach her, own her. So Jewell mostly avoided the whole dating scene. "We'll get pizza, Spanish, something—come with us."

"Yeah. That's cool," Regina added half-heartedly.

"Or I could cook," Jewell suggested. "My agent found me this great sublet for the summer, Carmen. I've had so much fun trying new dishes. That and having a sofa. Actually, I've been thinking about bailing on the dorm next semester and finding a place."

Regina sat straight up. "Tell me you want a roommate."

"I hadn't thought about it, but—yeah. Roomies. We can do what we want! Paint the walls orange, eat pizza for breakfast, go and come as we please. It'll be an adventure—"

While Regina and Jewell jabbered about neighborhoods to look in and how they would decorate, Carmen sweated being late for work and sulked about how unfair it was that Jewell and Regina could change whatever didn't suit them so easily. After she was accepted, Carmen had waited anxiously to hear if her financial-aid package covered campus housing, but first dibs had gone to girls from out of town. She ended up stuck on the IRT and in the dump she shared with Z. And since her Social Security benefit ended at eighteen her budget was as tight as a straightjacket just to come up with her half of the rent.

"Sorry, Carmen. We got way off the subject," Jewell laughed. "But we really are gonna get something to eat. Come with us! We'll have fun."

"Uh—thanks but I can't. Gotta get to work—remember?" Carmen clutched her backpack and reasoned away her disappointment at spending another Saturday night asking, "You want apple pie with that?"

Then, as suddenly as the compartment had stopped, it bumped to a start. They gasped and sat glued to their places until it lurched to a halt. The door slid open and one by one they handed their gear up to the security guard and crawled out of the car.

Regina dusted her clothes. "Don't *ever* put me in solitary confinement."

"That wasn't solitary. There were three of us." Jewell swiped at a smudge on her jeans, then looked over at Carmen. "Are you okay? You look…"

"I'm fine." Carmen was embarrassed to get caught looking as unnerved as she felt. "Glad to be on solid ground." She tried to put some tough girl back in her voice.

"Amen to that," Regina chimed in. "Now I can get some real food."

So, well after they started out, Regina, Jewell and Carmen finally left the library and walked into the warm summer evening, looking like three pieces from very different puzzles.

Jewell found a deli receipt and pen in her bag and scribbled her phone number. "It's only for the next month, but call okay? We'll get together and do something."

Carmen took the paper. "Sure." She shoved it in the bib pocket of her overalls.

"You have to be the first visitor to our new place since you were here when we hatched the plan." Jewell smiled.

"Yeah. We'll let you know when we move in," Regina added reluctantly.

There was an awkward pause, like they had said all there was to say, at least for now. Less than an hour ago they were barely speaking, now they were—what were they?

"I gotta go." Carmen waved, "Later," then melted into the night. She snaked her way through sidewalk traffic, praying the train would come soon, resenting that she had to leave and take her place at the fry station. Sometimes she felt like the only person at school who had to scrape and sacrifice, who didn't vacation in Provence or have someone to show her the ropes. She'd never admit it though, because one day it would be different. That's what kept her going.

As she crossed the avenue Carmen heard the underground rumble and raced downstairs in time to wedge her bag between the doors so the conductor had to open them again. She plunked down in the seat next to the handrail and dug the biology flash cards she'd made out of her pack, but she spent the ride reliving the hell she kept from Regina and Jewell in that elevator in the dark.

September 27, 1977
Brooklyn, NY

"Thought that was you, Li'l Bit." Randy had caught the elevator door with his big hand, just as it was closing. Carmen rolled her eyes and stared at the numbers above the door. "Think you can ignore me, huh?" He slapped the emergency button. The car jerked to a halt between floors and the alarm screamed, but nobody in the building paid attention to that. People stopped the elevators all the time to hold the cars until they were done with them. Before Carmen could complain Randy grabbed her by the hair, spun her around. "Scream if you want." His musty breath assaulted her. "Nobody's gonna hear you." He pushed her to her knees and the zip of his pants sliced through the incessant clanging. Carmen's heart raced like she was about to die, then Randy grabbed her head, jammed himself into her mouth and started pumping. "Ignore this." The sour taste made her gag and he slapped her so hard she saw an electrified flash in the darkness. "Don't throw up on me bitch." Randy pounded and started to whimper louder than his dog who paced impatiently beside them in the airless cube. Carmen couldn't breathe, or feel her life beyond the pounding. Then it was over in a wheeze and a sour dribble. "Tell and your ass is mine."

"Next and last stop, Utica Avenue."

Carmen shook herself from the memory and got off the train just before the door closed, wondering what Jewell and Regina were doing and how much lip she'd have to take from Alan, her manager, when she got to work.

Arms folded across his blubbery belly, Alan blocked her path as she tried to scoot into the locker room to change. "Don't bother. You're history. Pick up your last check next Friday."

"It's not my fault." Carmen's need for the job only slightly outweighed her disgust at having to beg him for it. "I got stuck in—"

"I don't care. Your shift starts at seven." He checked his watch. "You're two hours late." For all his bulk he had a high, whiney voice that got to Carmen like nails on a chalkboard.

She wanted him to shut up, but he kept going on about the importance of reliable employees. Suddenly, she imagined choking him with his short, greasy tie until his flabby arms flailed and he couldn't talk. She couldn't stop the hiccup of laughter even though she knew the situation wasn't funny. She'd just been fired, Z would be pissed, and Alan looked at her like she was an alien, but that only made her laugh harder. "You know what? Keep your stupid job. When I'm a doctor you'll still be pushing Happy Meals." She wasn't sure where the words came from, but they felt good.

Carmen plowed down Utica Avenue, propelled by the giddiness of standing up to Alan, standing up for herself. She wanted to tell somebody, thought of Jewell and Regina and the phone number in her pocket. *Like I could find them tonight. Like they'd care.* As she passed White Castle, the reality of rent day with only one more check on the horizon set in and she almost stopped to fill out an application, but decided fast food was too degrading for a future doctor and that she'd never flip burgers again.

Carmen trotted past the knot of men drinking beer and playing dominoes in front of her building. They were always there Saturdays after midnight when she got home. Z was always gone. She assumed he was with some woman since he wouldn't straggle in till Sunday. Carmen never cared where he was. It was her night to herself, and by the time she unlocked the door she was looking forward to the shower and hot dog she needed right now. *I'll check the want ads tomor...*Suddenly she heard bare feet slapping linoleum, and before she could speak, Z sprang into the hall, a gun leveled in her direction. A vein in Carmen's neck pulsed a frantic tattoo, pumping fear from her heart to her fingertips.

"What the fuck you doin' here?" Z relaxed his stance, lowered the weapon. "I coulda blew your head off." He yanked at the elastic waist of his briefs which were on backward.

"Are you crazy?" She knew he had a gun, but he'd never pointed it at her. "I live here!"

"*Come on back in here, baby,*" a woman's slurred voice called from the living room.

"Shut the fuck up!" Z hollered over his shoulder at his mystery guest, then turned back to Carmen. "Don't call me crazy! Your fuckin' mother was crazy. That's why she left your ass!"

"She left us both, Z!"

"I don't give a shit!" Z hollered. "Your ass belongs at your job."

"I got fired, all right! I didn't know I had to call." Carmen spent years keeping tight and tidy like a ball of twine, but now she was unraveling. "How could you point a gun at me?"

"Coulda been any fool comin' in here." He scratched his armpit with the gun barrel. "And you best be findin' another job if you plan on livin' here."

"Don't act like you doin' me a favor." For a moment Carmen wished the gun would go off. She imagined him sprawled on the floor, twitching. Then he'd be gone like everybody else.

"You'da been living with some foster freaks if I wasn't around!" Z patted at the spikes of hair standing all over his head. "You need to forget that college shit and get a real job. If you was smart as you think you are you'd be making some serious money."

"Serious money? Like you make?!" Carmen wanted to cry but she wouldn't give him the satisfaction. "You never had a job longer than six weeks! And your stinkin' drawers are on backward." She let the door slam behind her, heard him slide the safety chain in place.

Carmen stormed out of the building and furious momentum carried her to Eastern Parkway before her hands started shaking and her legs gave way. She dropped on a bench, overcome by the assaults of the day and feeling once again like she'd won the jackpot in Bad News Bingo. She hugged her backpack and rocked, trying to pull herself together and will herself to keep believing that she could climb out of the pit she'd been born into before the mud slide buried her alive.

3
"...flying solo in the naked city."

"Look Al! French doors!" Lonnie chirped as she flitted from room to room of 5D, Regina and Jewell's new apartment. Regina followed in her wake, rolling her eyes. The Fosters were the first to pay a visit to the apartment on 110th Street. "The place has so much potential!" Regina looked at Jewell and made gagging gestures behind her mother's back. "Fantastic view of the park," her father added cheerily as he raised and lowered the windows to make sure they worked.

Regina's parents brought her old bedroom furniture as well as some kitchen things Lonnie thought they might need. Regina took great pleasure in saying, "We have those already." Not that she thought of pot holders, can openers or kitchen towels, but Jewell had, and Regina claimed joint credit. Right now it just felt good to show Lonnie her motherly services were no longer needed, although she did accept the wad of cash her father slipped to her for odds and ends. Regina was too busy gloating to notice the worried look Lonnie gave Al, or his whispered words of comfort.

It had taken Regina a week to convince them their little girl was ready to live on her own. She argued that it would cost the same as the dorm, "But it'll be quieter, so I can study." She reminded them that her brothers had lived off campus, then she pulled out the big guns, pointing out that her parents had gotten married sophomore year and still graduated with honors. She wanted to add "and two babies," but knew the dig wouldn't help her case. They agreed to the move, but their cost stipulation, an obstacle Regina hadn't foreseen, pricked a hole in her fantasy of penthouse living with her famous, rich friend.

She and Jewell had combed the classifieds and pounded the pavement until they found 5D. At first Regina didn't believe Jewell was serious about the apartment or the neighborhood. Folks propped on pillows in open windows watched who came and went. Corner trash baskets overflowed with empty forty-ounce bottles and fast-food bags, and groceries with red and yellow awnings displayed dusty containers of Enfamil and roach powder in their windows. Five D was a far cry from Regina's sanitized, homogenized suburban world but escaping the ho-hum is what fired her New York dreams.

The apartment was in the budget, close to school, a block from the subway and Regina had to admit the view of Central Park was amazing, like having the Emerald City across the way. Jewell clinched the deal when she told Regina 5D reminded her of a flat she'd once stayed in on the Quai de Voltaire in Paris.

At the end of August, a week after the Fosters' visit, Vivian blew into town, Jewell had been in a touchy mood all day, wondering if her mother remembered what day it was, but she realized Vivian was too good at air-brushing her universe to let an unpleasant detail like that survive. And like old adversaries who knew the rules of engagement, the two of them started duking it out, right after the obligatory hello kiss.

"It's hot as blazes in here," Vivian said. "And what in the world do you have on?"

"Air conditioning feels so fake. This is more natural to me." There was a moist glow on Jewell's coffee-brown face, but she looked cool and serene in the flowing white caftan she had chosen for the occasion.

Vivian brushed by and headed down the hall, peering in the rooms she passed. Regina said hello, but stayed on the sidelines, out of the way. She'd never seen a mother like Vivian, a miniature commando in a powder blue Ultrasuede suit.

In the kitchen, Vivian frowned at the scarred bistro table and chairs Jewell had scored at the Salvation Army. "Nothing matches. It's a hodgepodge of junk."

"Any idiot can match. These are complementary. I find it much more interesting." Jewell folded her arms, stood her ground, liked the feel of her own turf under her feet. She had always enjoyed prowling through thrift shops and antique stores while Vivian made it clear she wanted no part of anything used, even if it was called antique. She did not need anybody's castoffs. Jewell, on the other hand, was drawn to beautiful old items with patina and a previous life. It was like they invited her to mine the memories they'd absorbed.

Vivian sighed and headed for the front of the apartment. "Okay. You've made your point. Now let me find you a realtor and we'll arrange to buy you a place."

"Not necessary." Jewell wasn't in the market for any more of her mother's arranging.

"My god, Jewell, you weren't raised like this." Vivian swooped through the French doors into the living room. "I was embarrassed to have the car drop me here."

The neighborhood was definitely not Baldwin Hills. This wasn't a movie set. It was the gateway to Harlem, the gateway to real life. Granted, the dingy lobby and hallways had seen better days, but 5D had two bedrooms, a big kitchen, dining and living rooms with French doors, parquet floors, a marble fireplace and a priceless view. Jewell could easily afford more lavish digs but she was caught up in the bohemian first apartment experience and this prewar building had real character, besides she already knew her mother's feelings.

Jewell had Leonard Penman, the attorney Vivian put on retainer when Jewell got her first contract, look over the lease. "You sure you want to do this, kiddo? Vivian's having conniptions." Through the years Leonard often functioned as an intermediary when she and Vivian were at odds, the way a father would—the way Ted Hampton would have if he hadn't chosen fame over fatherhood and walked out on them years ago. Besides, Leonard was cool. The day they moved in, he sent a gigantic arrangement of roses—pearly white ones with heads the size of a fist. And although Jewell had no proof, from the time she was a teenager she suspected that her mother and the very married Leonard shared more than legal affairs. "Vivian's always having conniptions about something," Jewell had told him. And today Vivian was true to form.

"That's your problem." Jewell's voice was sugary sweet. "We lived in Cabrini Green before we moved to LA. Did you think I was too young to remember, or did *you* forget?"

"Nobody moves backward if they can do better, and I made sure you'd never have to scrape and struggle." Vivian bent to sit on the ruby velvet chaise, noticed the worn fabric along the edge and reversed direction. Instead she stood awkwardly, her back to the glorious park view.

Jewell had spied the chaise longue in the window of a secondhand store on Columbus, convinced Regina it was just right for their living room and dragged her in to look. Regina wasn't a lover of period furniture, but she liked the sweeping curve of the lounge. "It's perfect for swooning." Jewell had climbed into the window and draped herself on the Victorian recamier in a dead-away faint. Regina ran outside to see. Then they switched places. Soon it became a swooning contest which drew an audience. After a bit of negotiating the chaise became their first piece of furniture. And Jewell didn't care if Vivian sat on it or not. Jewell flounced over to the lounge, sat cross-legged right in the middle, encircled by yards of drapey white linen, looking supremely content. "I'll make sure nobody ever points a finger at you for the choices I make."

"That's not what I'm talking about. Think of your safety. You're a celebrity." The taupe leather satchel on Vivian's shoulder looked heavy, but she wouldn't put it down.

"Casting directors don't pay me any attention." Jewell's big eyes sparkled. "Why should anybody else?"

"Jewell, you're being unreasonable," Vivian huffed.

"No, I'm being unmanageable. Isn't that what you call it?" She knew Vivian wouldn't play her dog-earred trump card because Regina was in earshot, and as far as the world was concerned, Jewell Prescott's big mistake had never happened. She was a special talent, who lived a charmed life. Knocked-up teenager had been officially erased from the record. They never talked about it directly, never uttered the "P" word, but that episode was a wedge between them, with Vivian declaring the case closed, and Jewell unable to get it off her heart.

Of course Jewell hadn't told anyone either, not even the father after she got it through her head he was history. Those were scenes she was supposed to cut, especially the part where exactly three years ago today a baby girl had come into her life, and almost as quickly was gone.

"Exactly darling, and if you'd just let me manage—" Vivian dug in her bag and produced a familiar large gray envelope. "It's a comedy called *All the Way Home*. They're hot on you for one of the leads, the middle of three daughters—"

"Not into daughters these days." Jewell bristled, just hearing Vivian say the word, with no hint of understanding that it might cut too deep. "And since you brought up the subject, I think the time has come for me to manage my own career, if I decide I want one." Jewell unfolded her legs. She hadn't planned for the conversation to veer in this direction, but as soon as she said it she knew she'd been thinking it since she'd been in New York. It was time for a change.

Vivian froze for a moment, then went off like an M80 with a short fuse. "You can't fire me! I'm your mother!"

Vivian's explosion seemed to make Jewell even calmer. "I'm not firing you as my mother. I'm firing you as my manager. There is a difference, isn't there?"

"I quit my job and devoted myself to making you a success—"

"And I appreciate your efforts. Last I heard Prescott Management has a roster of sparkling young talent, so you don't need me." She hadn't seen her mother so upset since that pregnancy test came back positive.

Vivian smoothed imaginary wrinkles from her skirt. "Is this the way you want it?"

"Yeah I do—Vivian." She thought about saying mom, but it just didn't fit.

Vivian's expression was frozen, trying to save face. She clutched her satchel to her side like she had to hold on to keep from blowing away. "Your attorney will receive an official termination of services notice." She headed toward the hall.

"My attorney is your attorney and it doesn't have to be this formal." Jewell got up to intercept her.

"I'll be forwarding your files to your attorney, which include all financial papers—"

"Will you stand still a minute—" Jewell had seen the indignant act many times, and she was determined not to fall for it.

Vivian shoved a card in Jewell's hand. "I'd appreciate it if you'd call me a car."

Jewell waited for Vivian to turn around, but she didn't, so she went to the kitchen and called a cab, feeling she was losing more than a business associate. "They said ten minutes. They'll call when the car is downstairs."

Vivian posed by the door, her foot tapping impatiently, holding herself close so not to touch the walls. Jewell leaned against the doorway, sad and empty because she had nothing else to say.

Suddenly Vivian dug in her bag. "I forgot. I have a message for you." She pulled out a neatly typed sheet of paper. "You got a call from Billy Roland—"

Goose bumps sprouted on Jewell's arms, despite the late summer heat, the same way they did the first time she laid eyes on Billy.

"I didn't know you knew him—"

You can't know. Jewell rubbed her arms to warm them, to keep ahold of herself.

"—but he said you met when he was in film school. Anyway, I took his number. He's a good contact for you and whoever your manager is. His father is well connected." She shoved the paper in Jewell's hand without looking at her.

Jewell jammed it in the pocket of her jeans, glad her mother was looking away.

"If I were your manager, I'd make sure you called. He's important," Vivian added.

"I can decide for myself what's important," Jewell snapped. Every word out of her mother's mouth this afternoon was some kind of torture, but for her to bring up Billy, today of all days, sent Jewell tumbling back to that movie set in New Orleans, back when he taught her to fly.

December 4, 1978
New Orleans, LA

"I want a ride." It bubbled out of Jewell's mouth before she could stop it. She hadn't seen Billy for two days, but she'd lain awake thinking about him, dreamed about him, looked for him around every corner, and now here he was, squatting by his motorcycle outside of the makeup trailer, and she had to talk to him.

Jewell knew who Billy was before she laid eyes on him. During her first few days on the *Hoochie Coo* set, she'd heard the wardrobe mistress and one of the production assistants raving about what a fine specimen he was and detailing his pedigree—his father was the award-winning black actor John Roland, who had come to Hollywood prominence along with Sidney Poitier and Oliver Oakes, the first black director of a major studio feature. His mother, Birgit Christensen, was a Danish actress and John's second wife just long enough for Billy to have cut his baby teeth. "You two sound like dog breeders," Jewell had said. "Hell, I'd have his puppies," the P.A. told her, then pointed to the wardrobe mistress. "She would too except he's only twenty and she's an old bitch." Jewell had been around enough sets to be blasé about the abundance of beautiful people, and even as a child she became familiar with the endless "who's doin' who" cast and crew gossip. Mostly she thought it was silly, immature, not how real people behaved.

But the first time Jewell spotted Billy, stationed beside a lighting tower in the cavernous warehouse on Tchoupitoulas Street where they were shooting, wearing raggedy cutoffs and a T-shirt, a spark shot up her spine and ignited her brain. He looked like a statue, cast in pure gold, but there was something more, something magnetic. Normally when she was on her mark getting set for a take, Jewell tuned out the hordes of crew, but she kept peeking at him, wanting him to look back, wondering if he saw her watching him. And then his gaze found hers. The room went still for her and they were locked, eye to eye, neither one willing to break the connection. The spell was snapped when goose bumps blossomed on Jewell's arms and the director called for somebody to bring in a blanket to warm her up. Fortunately her costume, a camisole, petticoat, and bare feet, gave her a good excuse to be cold, yet even as inexperienced in the rules of attraction as she was at fifteen—a few studio setups with juvenile boys for awards shows and benefits—Jewell knew it wasn't about the temperature. When the scene was over, she searched for him, but he was gone.

Now, Billy looked up from the gear bag on his bike, surprised. "Sorry. No helmet." His voice was smooth, spiced with the hint of his mother's

Danish, his hair, a confusion of brown corkscrews framing his face. Taller than Jewell, with wide shoulders that tapered to narrow hips, the rib-knit pullover he wore skimmed the muscles beneath. He'd been in the wind since the warehouse, running the errands his internship required, keeping Jewell out of his field of vision.

"So?" Jewell was taken aback by the color of his eyes. Even in the dusky, late-day light she could see they were amber, like tiger eyes, and she was glad she had on a jacket to cover the suddenly prickly flesh on her arms. "You planning to crash?"

Billy threw a leg over the seat. "Right. Like I would ride the talent through these crazy streets with no helmet. They'd serve my ass on a platter with powdered sugar and chicory coffee."

"Come on, I'm done for the day," Jewell pleaded. She walked down the stairs, stood beside him. She had no idea why she was compelled to be near him, talk to him, look at him. "I've been here a whole week and all I've seen are locations and my room." And while she wasn't exactly glad her mother had come down with bronchitis and flown home to see her own doctor, Jewell was glad to be on her own.

And there was something in Jewell's big, soulful eyes, that made him say, "Climb on."

Jewell felt awkward at first, as she straddled the seat behind him, then scooted forward and locked her arms around his waist, but once he sped off, the moist air parting around them, her hair trailing behind like streamers, she felt free. "It's like flying," she said close to his ear as they zipped through the French Quarter, past carolers, horse-drawn carriages, and row houses, their lacy ironwork balconies festooned with rainbows of Christmas lights.

"Don't fight the curves. Lean into them," Billy told her and she followed his moves, shifted her weight with his, thrilled and scared by the edgy pleasure of feeling out of control.

From then on they'd squeeze time from their jam-packed days to hang together. Jewell bubbled with energy, curiosity fascinated by the unique city; by Billy and his LA—Copenhagen life. They knew some of the same people, the same places, but he knew more and she soaked up his experiences. Jewell ran lines with him, and something about his presence made her feel comfortable enough, inspired enough to find new takes on her scenes and on her character, They'd talk late into the night in the lobby of her hotel, about his post—film school dreams, about her mixed feelings toward show business and how sometimes she felt like a trained seal, performing tricks, taking bows. Jewell loved the way Billy listened with his eyes as well as his ears and for the first time she really felt heard. He told her she was too young for him, but she still ached for his good-night kisses, chaste lips on her cheek, a hot hand on her arm, that left her smoldering for hours.

Before dawn Jewell would sneak out and ride with him, fly with him, arms wrapped around him through the empty streets to Café Du Monde for beignets and coffee and be back in her room to be picked up at her call time. One cloudy night when there were no stars they wandered Bourbon Street, side by side, among the good-time seekers and their paper cups of booze. Her hand would brush his, he'd move away, put it in his pocket. Then some gut-bucket blues over a guitar lament drew them into a smoky dive, with ancient Mardi Gras masks on the walls and jars of pig feet on the bar. They huddled around a lopsided table, neither of them drinking, intoxicated by the music and by each other.

"I want to see where you stay," Jewell announced when they strolled out.

"Not much to see. You've got the deluxe digs. I'm a lowly intern," Billy answered as he unlocked his bike.

"Oh come on. My call's not till noon. Just ride by it."

Billy turned, studied her face for a moment. "Do you always get what you want?"

"Hardly ever," Jewell said.

The drizzle started when they were halfway there and by the time they arrived it was pouring so they raced down Prytania Street to the huge yellow house where Billy rented a room. When they got to the porch they were soaked to the skin.

"That's the one problem with bikes. You can't hold an umbrella." Billy unlocked the door.

Jewell's attempt at a laugh was overcome by a shiver.

"Looks like you need to dry off. I'll find you something."

Jewell followed Billy up the wide front stairs to a room with a crooked number two on the door. Once inside he yanked the blanket off his unmade bed and surrounded her in it. But before he could move Jewell locked his eyes in an embrace and she wouldn't blink, wouldn't let go, and finally Billy gave in to her again, let her eyes draw him in until their lips met. Softly at first, they sampled each other in tender nibbles and Jewell's chill was replaced by a warmth that heated them both. She had enjoyed being pressed up against Billy's back on the bike, but for the first time they were face to face with his arms encircling her and she fell into him, into a kiss so deep there was no air, only his breath, then hers, and they inhaled each other. Oblivious to the rain pelting the windows, they kissed until the one breath they shared became too shallow. Dizzy from longing and lack of oxygen, Jewell tilted her head back just far enough to look into his amber eyes.

Then Billy pulled away. "We have to stop," he whispered.

Jewell knew they shouldn't—knew it was wrong, but this was her first time and she was sure there would never be a first time or a first man more right than Billy. She'd spent most of her life around adults who talked in front of her as if she was one of them so she heard plenty about sex. Good sex. Bad sex, Casual sex. Boring sex. Kinky sex. Anonymous sex. Noisy sex. She'd listen to women talk about being in love and talk about giving "it" up. And of course, when she was ten, Vivian had awkwardly given her the required "talk," full of dire warnings about boys and their single-minded pursuits and Jewell nodded dutifully like this was news to her. But Billy was no boy, and no one ever told her about what she was feeling right now. Not a word about the quiver in her stomach, the tremble in her legs. No mention of feeling so helplessly drawn to another human being that she wanted to melt into him—so drawn that becoming a part of him would be the only way she could breathe again, quiet the thumping of her heart, keep from exploding.

"Come on, don't stop," Jewell said, then buried her face in his neck, smelling him, kissing him, urging him to do what she wanted.

"Are you sure?" Billy asked, his head slowly surrendering to his own need for her,

Jewell yanked her wet sweater over her head, dropped it on the floor, untucked her T-shirt—but he stopped her.

"We've got all the time in the world," Billy said. He took her face in his hands, kissed her forehead, her cheeks, her neck, and she held onto his waist to keep from crashing to the floor. He eased her down on his twin bed, knelt beside her and undressed her slowly, caressing her, savoring her. Then he removed his own clothes and lay next to her on the narrow bed. Their long, lean bodies fit together, onyx and gold, molded together—like they belonged that way.

Billy was tender and patient and Jewell didn't feel pain, she didn't feel the loss of her innocence, she felt only the joy of finding her womanhood. Together they soared, finding in each other a place that didn't know time or gravity.

By the next day Billy had crashed to earth. "You're too young. We can't ever do that again." Except she'd look at him with soulful eyes. They'd get lost in deep conversation. And they did it again, and again—

The jangle of the phone brought Jewell back from New Orleans, to her 110th Street kitchen and to her mother, who couldn't wait to leave. She yanked the receiver from the cradle. Mercifully it was the car service and without another word Vivian left.

When the front door clicked shut Regina emerged from her bedroom. "You okay?"

"Yeah." Jewell turned the lock. "Wounded but still standing. This was only a skirmish, but I guess I'm flying solo in the naked city."

"That makes two of us, Bijoux," Regina said. "Living in the fifth dimension.

They saluted their freedom with high fives. "Yes!"

"Reg!" Jewell spat a mouthful of toothpaste into the sink. "You're going to miss your eight o'clock—again!" After three months Jewell had learned that Regina was a pain to wake up. Not Jewell—too many sunup call times with Vivian harping on punctuality. "*We* have a reputation for lateness." It took a while before Jewell figured out that "we" meant black folks.

Jewell left the bathroom and pushed open Regina's door. "You getting up today?"

"I'm dropping this class." Regina burrowed deeper under her covers. The white Formica furniture she'd brought from home took up so much floor space she had to scoot across the bed to get to her dresser. Piles of clothes decorated her desk and chair. "It's too early."

"I have an eight o'clock too, I get up." Jewell pulled gray sweats over her leotard.

"It's ballet," Regina moaned. "I have 'The Labor Movement in the Twentieth Century!'"

"And who didn't register *before* there was nothing left at what you call a civilized hour?"

Regina threw her pillow at Jewell. "Okay. Okay. I'm getting up." She dragged herself out of the bed. Regina was not a morning person. Never had been. "*Hurry up or you're going to miss the bus!*" Her mother would call upstairs and often as not, Regina would still end up sprinting to catch the bus at the next stop. Half the time, Lonnie ended up driving her to school anyway.

Regina shuffled to the kitchen, bathrobe belt trailing behind her. She pried open the freezer door and dislodged the ice tray from it's frosty igloo. Every time she yanked open the ancient Kelvinator, she missed the frost-free side-by-side with ice cube maker at home. Whipping 5D into live-in shape was more of a challenge than she had been prepared for—neither she nor Jewell had ever hand-and-knee scrubbed floors, or bathroom scuzz. But together they gagged and held hands to clean cockroach shells in the kitchen and dried boogers on the bathroom tiles. And now she was flying solo, charting her course to be anything but ordinary. She hadn't figured out what or how yet, so she wrestled the ice and wrangled roaches, deciding it was a small price to pay for freedom.

Regina whacked the metal ice tray on the counter to loosen a few cubes, dropped them in a tumbler and poured in orange juice which she downed in one long swallow.

Jewell shook the container, "You weren't planning to leave that? It's only a mouthful." She finished the rest. "Have you seen Carmen?"

"Yeah, for a sec yesterday. Said she got a job at Alexander's. She looks like shit on a Ritz, but she says she's okay, just swamped."

Since the elevator party, the three had crossed paths on campus, grabbed coffee a few times, but Regina and Jewell hadn't even been able to drag Carmen to the apartment yet. She was friendlier when they caught up with her, but as much a mystery as she had been before.

Regina started to put the ice tray away.

"Don't put that back empty, woman!" Jewell yanked Regina's belt off and handed it to her.

"Heifer." She looped the belt around her neck. "I have an idea for my birthday party."

Regina started organizing dorm parties last year. To cheer up her terminally homesick roommate she invited most of the seventh and eighth floors of Hewitt to celebrate Melanye's birthday. No one flinched at the dollar Regina asked them to cough up and she collected fifty-seven of them. She spent twenty-three dollars on chips, two jugs of Rhine wine which she stretched with Seven-Up, and a layer cake from Shopwell. Everybody was happy, including Melanye, at least for the moment—she didn't return sophomore year. Regina made thirty-four bucks and the party machine was up and running.

By second semester she'd thrown six birthday bashes and was ready to move off campus where there could be men, music, dancing and no rules to break. She found three brothers at Columbia who were willing to let her use their apartment on Morningside and 118th, for a share of the gate, and of course, the opportunity to talk to oodles of sisters. And since the apartment was much bigger than a dorm room, she increased her numbers and her profit. Now she was ready to grow again and decided her own birthday was the perfect opportunity.

"Your birthday's not until January. You should be having an idea for your Poli Sci paper."

"Yeah. Yeah. I'll get it done. But January will be here before you know it and this party requires planning 'cause this year I'm stepping out!"

"Me too," Jewell said as she headed for the door. "See ya."

Where's the stereo?! Carmen, still wearing her rumpled skirt and blouse from the day before, stopped short on her way to the shower and gawked at the empty space, outlined by dust. She never got as far as the living room when she came in from work last night. The late fall cold snap had caught her off guard and she dove under the covers, coat and all, to stop her teeth from chattering. Next thing she knew it was morning.

Great! We've been robbed. But that didn't make sense. All four locks had been in place. Even the super only had keys to two of them. Folding metal gates guarded the windows by the fire escape, which made it harder if somebody wanted to steal your stuff, but not impossible. *Probably one of Z's worthless friends. Serves him right.* The apartment was still freezing so Carmen wrapped her bathrobe around her shoulders like a stole and kicked a stray construction boot that languished in the doorway. It landed under the coffee table, near an envelope. She went in to get a closer look, absent-mindedly picked up the envelope, wondering if Z knew his precious stereo was gone, wondering what else was missing. *There's nothing left worth stealing.*

Carmen continued to the bathroom, turned on the hot water in the tub since it ran frigid the first few minutes. She flipped on the light, was about to toss the envelope in the trash. *What the...*It was addressed to Geraldine Webb. *From the marshal's office?* She yanked out the pages, began reading furiously. *Eight months non-payment of rent? I give Z my money every month!...your failure to appear at the hearing that was scheduled on...*Carmen sank to the side of the tub, the pages rattling in her shaking hands. *Eviction will proceed any time six days from the date of this notice.* "Z!" She charged from the room, hammered his door. No response. She shoved it open.

An icy rage flash-froze Carmen in place. Even in the pre-dawn darkness she saw the room was a shambles. Wire hangers, raggedy tube socks and trash littered the floor. Only lint was left in his drawers, but she knew there had been no burglary. The only thing her brother cared about besides getting paid, getting laid and getting high was the tri-corner folded American flag that had draped their father's casket. It was freezing at graveside the day of the funeral and Carmen had danced in place, wanting to get back in the warm car, not knowing that dead meant her dad would never ride her piggyback again. She thought it was some kind of game the way the soldiers folded the flag, but when they handed it to Geraldine she wouldn't play so the soldier gave it to Z. He clutched it the whole ride home, staring out the window. All these years he kept it, wrapped in dry cleaner's plastic, propped against the wall by his dresser. It had no value to anyone else, but it meant more to him than he would ever admit. And it was gone.

Carmen balled up the pages in her hand, hurled them against the wall. Z was her last link, the only one left she could call family, but he'd broken that chain without looking back. He'd been looking her in the face, taking her money for months, and now she was the chump left holding the bag. "I HATE YOU!" Her scream exploded in the tiny space, came crashing around her feet. The one-legged man upstairs rapped on the floor with his crutch, voicing his annoyance. "GO TO HELL!" She stormed from the room, marched up and down the hall, trying to unthaw her brain so she could think, because "eviction" was the only word she could hear and it looped around and around in her mind, faster and faster. Out of the corner of her eye she noticed steam rolling from the bathroom, ran to turn off the water. The soupy air enveloped her. She sat on the toilet seat lid, rested her head on the tiles, closed her eyes. Doing the math told her that eight months of rent was more dollars than she could come up with, which meant that she had to leave the apartment, not that she cared about the stuff. Not that the building or the block were more than a place to be from. Not that there was anybody there she'd miss.

Carmen sat up. The steam in the room left moist droplets on her face that hid her tears. *But where am I gonna go?*

4

"Everything costs something."

"Miss Webb."

Carmen heard her name and struggled out of her seat. Her body felt weighted down by a pressure ten times gravity, but using all her strength she managed to drag herself to the podium.

"Miss Carmen Webb." The voice grew more insistent, impatient.

She reached for her pocket to get her notes and was horrified to find she was buck naked. *I remember getting dressed!* She felt a finger stab at her shoulder. *That hurts*. Then she was being rocked to sleep. *Sleep?* Not rocked, shaken. *I can't be asleep*. She jerked straight up. "Damn."

"Damned would be the correct tense," Dr. Glenwood announced. "Past. Like the hour."

Carmen blinked, then zoomed in on her blue book and in one awful second she knew what had happened. "Why didn't you wake me up?" She didn't mean to screech. "I know this stuff."

"This is college, not kindergarten, but apparently your need for a nap was more urgent than your need to complete this exam." He reached down and confiscated her test folder. "Poor Mr. Hemphill had quite a coughing spell trying to wake you. It was very amusing."

"You can't do this!" The Twentieth-Century World was core curriculum and she had to pass it, pass everything. Her scholarship depended on it. Med school depended on it. *This is a nightmare*.

"You underestimate my powers." Dr. Glenwood dropped the papers into his briefcase. "Each semester I get dozens of you. Pre-med majors, poetry majors—doesn't matter—you think you're above having to take a lowly survey history course, and every class you make sure I know I'm wasting your time. The thing is, Miss Webb, you need me, and as a tenured professor, I can do pretty much what I want."

"You can't fail me for falling asleep." Carmen glared at him. "It was an accident."

"Perhaps, but I can fail you for not completing the exam. The course requirements were quite clear. Attend the lectures, pass the midterm and final. Modest, I think. And you've answered—let me see." He fished

Carmen's test booklet out of his bag. "My, five questions out of twenty-five?"

Carmen felt a fist in her chest, cutting off her air. "You don't know what it's like…"

"You're quite right. I don't. Nor am I likely to, Miss Webb." He put her paper back in his satchel, buckled the straps, sealed her fate. "We're quite done."

Carmen's eyes hardened. She hated his abrupt dismissal, hated being chewed up and spit out. She wanted to ask if he could hold down two jobs, go to class and study, without an address or a bed? If he could imagine having a father who was shot while working extra shifts, trying to save money so you could go to college? Or conceive how badly it hurt to pretend your mother was at home like everybody else's, instead of a crazy woman who walked out one day and never came back? How devastated would he be if his brother had cheated him, then took off, leaving him to fend for himself?

For half the semester Carmen had been a denizen of twenty-four-hour library study rooms, alternating so she didn't look conspicuous. She'd taken catnaps in out-of-the-way college parlors, showered in the gym, terrified that someone would figure out she had no place to live.

The day she got the eviction notice, Carmen was afraid to leave the house, scared the marshal would come and toss out what little she had. She strained to focus on the problem since there was no time for hysterics, or rage or sadness. She had to make a plan. There was nobody to call, no one responsible for rescuing her from her pathetic family drama. Carmen had no emergency fund; the money she made was spent before her check was cashed so renting another apartment was out. So was talking to somebody at school because as far as she knew there was no dean of dispossessed students. She already felt like a lab rat, her behavior observed to see how disadvantaged black youth would fare in an elite academic setting. She was determined that nobody would ever point her out and conclude there were too many problems to surmount to expect a positive outcome. The college was paying for her education. She could not get on her hands and knees and beg for any more because she was afraid she'd never get up.

So she hurried out to buy a shopping cart; Z had taken that too. She loaded her books and enough clothes to see her through. The only other thing she took was the photo she kept in her desk of her parents looking young and happy. She didn't know them like that, but she liked to imagine what they had been like. Then she left, no looking back or even locking the door. For what? She got a locker at the student center, and one in the gym. That would do until she figured out her next move. Campus security never bothered her.

She had a valid ID and nobody seemed to suspect an Ivy League student could be homeless. If she could hold it together until January she'd have the deposit for a room in a roach motel she'd found in Hell's Kitchen. She just hadn't figured out what to do while the libraries were closed for intersession.

Carmen didn't want any pity, certainly not from someone like Professor Glenwood who didn't care how hard it was to start each day feeling unequal to the task, worried that one day you'd lose your mind like your mother did. Or that by nightfall, you had no energy to hope or dream. She couldn't humiliate herself anymore, so head throbbing, heart pounding, Carmen got her jacket and books and left.

Milton Hemphill was pacing the hall, loose-limbed and awkward like a Great Dane puppy. "I tried to wake you up." He sounded as forlorn as she felt. Carmen had met Milton first semester, plowing through used biology textbooks at the campus bookstore. He let her have the one with the best cover and before they got to the cashier he had told her he was from Ohio by way of Indiana, but that living in New York was a dream come true. Carmen knew he wasn't from the city—he talked too much, had a kind of bright-eyed cheeriness, a wide open grin which, along with the bristle of hair dusting his round head, probably hadn't changed much since he was a boy and proud to be the hall monitor. Where she grew up, such enthusiasm would have been stomped out of him before he finished second grade. Milton told Carmen he was pre-med too, knew he wanted to be a doctor since the first time he listened to his own heartbeat at the pediatrician's office. Before he moved on to collect his economics text, he found out they were registered for the same bio lecture section and asked for her phone number. She told him she didn't have one; Z and his friends had taught her that guys were trouble sooner or later, so she wanted to steer clear. But that didn't stop Milton from coming by Butler Library when he knew she was on the desk, or asking if she wanted to study with him. He was just so different from anybody she'd met before, and eventually Carmen realized he was smart, he never hit on her, never dogged her or tried to make her look stupid, so she figured he was safe, at least to study with.

"I coughed my brains out—loud. Everybody kept looking at me, but you." Milton shoved his hands deep in his parka pockets, waiting for her to move or speak.

Carmen stared at him, but all she heard were Glenwood's acid words echoing in her head. She blinked back the tears, couldn't talk, not even to Milton. "I gotta go." Then she dashed down the corridor, out of the redbrick building and into the swirling bluster of an early December snow. The cold air shocked her lungs, made her realize that to hold her tongue, she'd been holding her breath too. She gulped the air, choking on humiliation and ferocious anger. Head down against the wind she trudged to the student center, jacket flapping in the wind, unaware of the snow that clung to her hair. Right now it was time to change into one of the outfits she saved for work and head downtown to salvage the rest of the day.

Once inside she passed through the afternoon hubbub like a zombie and headed for her locker. She dug out her gray skirt and grabbed the opaques she'd washed in the bathroom and hung over the hook to dry. The last thing she wanted to do was spend six hours dealing with jolly Christmas shoppers, filling their bags with holiday delights. Then she could look forward to another night in the library—studying not sleeping, because now she had to ace Organic Chem and Calculus if she was going to keep her scholarship.

"Hey, Carmen."

Carmen jumped, tried to slam the door shut, but it bounced open. She twirled around, hiding the clothes behind her back. "Don't scare me like that!"

"Sorry. I, uh—" Jewell was startled by how awful Carmen looked—smudgy circles underscored vacant eyes, and her parchment yellow skin was stretched over raw bone. "Regina and I just ran into Milton Hemphill. He said you were bummed out about a final—"

"Milton talks too much."

"Don't be mad. He was just worried. He thought you might want company."

"I don't have time. I have to go to work." Carmen spoke through clenched teeth, trying to hold back the bitterness.

"But what happened?"

"Didn't he tell you?" Carmen's voice was spiked, a hostile challenge.

"No."

Jewell's simple reply disarmed her and Carmen's angry momentum crashed at her feet. She slumped against the wall of lockers, let out a heavy sigh. "I fell asleep in the stupid final. Glenwood's gonna flunk me." She closed her eyes and the indignity of his pointy finger poking at her came flooding back. "I *hate* him!"

"Oh shit, you fell asleep? In the test?" Regina arrived, munching fries. She caught Jewell's warning glare. "I mean, sorry—I still have an incomplete from that tight ass. He failed half the class." Regina wasn't eager to talk about grades, or see *her* transcript. She noticed the open locker jammed with clothes and decided to lighten things up from the test fiasco. "What's with all the clothes? You living here?"

And there it was, out in the open. Hearing it aloud brought the horror of the past six weeks up into Carmen's mouth like bile and she was too wrung out to choke it back.

Jewell and Regina were stunned as Carmen's face contorted, etched with pain. She covered it with the skirt clutched in her hands, but her shoulders quaked with the silent cry. In a terrible instant they looked at each other and realized the truth of Regina's joke.

Jewell folded Carmen in her arms.

"I'm sorry—" Carmen's lower lip quivered with an involuntary gulp of air.

Regina couldn't believe it. "What the hell for?"

"You have nothing to be sorry about," Jewell said.

"This is not your problem." Carmen peeled away from Jewell. She had to pull herself together.

"Whatever you've been doing, you can't keep doing it," Jewell pleaded.

"Right now I have to get ready for work." Carmen stuffed the tear-soaked skirt back in her locker, rummaged around for another one. "I'm going to the bathroom. I'll be back."

As soon as Carmen was out of earshot, Jewell pounced. "She has to move in with us, at least for now. She can have the dining room." Jewell remembered how it felt when her world caved in at fifteen. Back then she needed a friend who would ask questions, but also accept that you might not want to answer. She hadn't found one so she managed without, but she didn't see why Carmen had to.

"I think she's your secret project, the inspiration for some part you'd like to play one day."

"Didn't you ever need a friend?"

"I thought I had one," Regina snapped.

"Of course we're friends you lunatic, but not everybody makes them as easily as you do."

Regina knew Jewell was right. She wasn't prepared for the new twosome to become a threesome, but she knew they had to take Carmen in, or at least offer. The idea that Carmen could really be living out of her locker wouldn't have crossed her mind in a thousand years. How could that happen?

When Carmen got back she had changed, but her eyes were puffy like a frog's.

"We have a spot in our apartment—"

"I'm gonna get my own place," Carmen quickly volunteered. "Right after the first of the year." Her feigned enthusiasm sounded hollow to all three of them.

This time Regina chimed in. "That's nice, but what about tonight? And winter break?"

"We had trouble renting a decent place together," Jewell added. "How are you going to do it by yourself?"

Carmen looked away, knowing the room she'd found was worse than the hellhole she'd left.

"You can leave when you want, but right now we're taking you hostage," Jewell announced.

And Carmen couldn't fight them anymore. They stuffed the contents of the locker in a big green garbage bag, then swung by the gym for the rest of her stuff. After a taxi to 5D to drop off the bags, she headed for work, feeling shaken and embarrassed at being caught, but relieved she could stop pretending.

Jewell and Regina got busy. By the time Carmen got home, Jewell had bought a futon which, thanks to a generous tip, would be delivered the next day. For tonight, they had fixed Carmen a spot on the red lounge and had a plate of Jewell's pepper chicken and wild rice waiting to be heated.

Carmen picked at her dinner and although Regina and Jewell hovered making small talk, Carmen nodded and smiled, but hung back from the conversation. She knew they were trying to make her feel comfortable, but there was so much going on in her head, like feeling she owed them some kind of explanation. She hadn't even known them that long, and she had no idea why, but they rescued her with no payoff in sight. Through the years Carmen had told so many half-truths that she was tired of keeping track of the odd bits of the story she'd meted out to people, tired of waiting to be found out. She was embarrassed to tell them that one by one, her family had abandoned her. Ashamed to admit that no one loved her enough to stay, but that was the only story she had to tell. "I used to live with my brother, until he took off owing eight months' rent and I had nowhere to go." And she told them all of it, her father, Geraldine, Z, her whole story except for Randy. That was too awful for anybody to know. In a way, it felt good to say those things. That way somebody else might understand her journey.

They stayed silent as Carmen talked. Jewell watched Carmen's eyes grow vacant sometimes, like she was crawling inside, leaving only an outer shell. She was sure there was even more to Carmen's story, but then there was more to her own than she was ready to give up. Funny how she never thought that about Regina who always seemed open, like the water in the

Caribbean, clear all the way to the bottom. Carmen was like an iceberg. You could see the tip but there was more below the surface.

When Carmen was done they were speechless. Regina couldn't imagine anybody's family treating them that way, but she believed Carmen. Nobody could make all that up.

"I don't know how you did it." Jewell had been through difficult times, but nothing like this.

Carmen shrugged. "Anyway, I appreciate what you guys did. I'll be out of your way by January."

"No rush," Regina said. "Dividing the rent by three is—"

"More than I can afford." Carmen got up. *I don't even know them.* But now they knew her, better than anyone else and she didn't know whether to hate Z for leaving or thank him for setting her free.

"Trust me, the rent's not that bad or my parents wouldn't be paying it," Regina chimed in. "And if two's company, three's a party!"

"Listen Carmen, everything costs something," Jewell added. "What you had to do cost you a whole semester's work, didn't it? How much will it be the next time?"

She looked from Regina to Jewell, searching for the trick. "Why are you doing this?"

"Because we're your friends," Jewell said matter-of-factly.

Carmen looked down at her lap to keep from welling up. Her notion of friendship was theoretical at best—like relativity and black holes. She had no concrete examples in her own world—there was always too much at her house to explain. But they hadn't gloated or made her feel worthless when she told them about her failure or when she dissolved into helpless tears. After the night they'd gotten stuck in the elevator, Jewell and Regina had never been anything but nice to her, despite Carmen's first impressions of them. Especially Jewell. *She always reaches out.* Carmen just needed practice reaching back. "Thanks," she said. And that night Carmen slept better than she had in months, maybe years.

The addition of Carmen to the household caused an immediate change in Jewell and Regina's holiday plans. Regina had been looking forward to her first Christmas in LaLaLand, planning her wardrobe and imagining the possibilities. Jewell warned her that Vivian's Yuletide wasn't exactly homey and warm, but Regina had had enough holiday cheeriness to last a lifetime. She was ready for palm trees and swimming pools in December. And who knew what New Year's Eve might bring? Jewell claimed not to be part of the Hollywood in-crowd, but whatever Jewell called regular was still a news flash in Regina's world. Her mouth watered, imagining the stars she could meet; maybe that super fine brother who got his start on *The Ted Hampton Show*, although she knew better than to bark up that tree. Jewell never mentioned her father, but Regina had known who he was from *Chocolate Teen Magazine*. Not long after they started hanging together, Regina asked if Ted Hampton was funny in real life. She hadn't seen Jewell get snippy often, but she went from sun to storm before Regina realized the clouds had rolled in. "I wouldn't know what his *real* life is like," she had said and by the time she finished Regina got the message that Ted was not a topic for discussion—ever. She couldn't imagine having a dad that hip and not wanting anything to do with him, but she never brought him up again.

Jewell had been looking forward to Regina's company for the holidays. Somebody to loosen up the atmosphere, because Christmas in the Prescott household was like an open wound—had been since December 24, 1970, her parents' last big fight. The hateful words they flung back and forth, and her father's final, window-rattling door slam echoed in six-year-old Jewell's head for years. She had crawled under her covers and instead of hoping Santa brought the Barbie she'd asked for, she promised she would always pick up her toys and be a good girl if only her dad would be there in the morning. He wasn't.

The mention of Ted's name, or a chance TV sighting would activate Vivian's venom in any season, and after years of exposure to her mother's poison, her father became the enemy in Jewell's mind too. But Vivian never let Jewell forget that he walked out on Christmas Eve. She'd start picking at that scab around Thanksgiving, and it would be a festering sore again just in time for eggnog and mistletoe. When Jewell was sixteen though, things suddenly changed. The house was trimmed in twinkling lights, a silvery fake tree towered in the living room, and she was braced for the annual tirade, but it never came. Then she saw the headline in *Variety*. "Comic Hampton Tapped for Summer Replacement," and she knew what had silenced her mother. It was okay to fume about the ne'er do well Chitlin' Circuit comedian who abandoned them. She saw his failed career as his just reward, but his impending television debut sucked the wind from Vivian's sails, left her adrift, but not for long. She bounced back, channeled her energy into finding Jewell's next big thing while convincing herself that her ex's lucky break would go bust before long.

So although Vivian now remained mute on the subject of Ted Hampton, the tension, like the artificial pine scent Vivian sprayed liberally around the house, still hung heavy in the air and Jewell figured this year would be worse since Vivian was now her ex-manager. In spite of the warning though, Regina had been a more than willing buffer. But with

Carmen in the house, Jewell decided it was better that they stay in New York, to cheer her up, keep her from doing something crazy, like moving out.

Regina grudgingly agreed, but she pouted for two days. Jewell was actually relieved by the change in plans and happily prepared for a fifth-dimension Christmas. She corralled Carmen and Regina and herded them to Broadway where they picked out an enormous Scotch pine and carried it home, Jewell at the bottom, Regina in the middle and Carmen bringing up the tip. They laughed trying to maneuver it in the elevator, but it wouldn't fit so they lugged it up five flights of stairs, continuing the hilarity and vowing that it was the last time Jewell got the last say on how big something was. Jewell and Regina gave each other the eye, glad to see Carmen laughing.

Next they raided Tip Top Bargains for a tree stand, lights and ornaments, the gaudier the better. After that, Carmen had to leave for work, but they waited until she got home to decorate. Regina led the carol singing. "I grew up in freakin' Santaland," she declared, settling the argument about what came after "nine ladies dancing." In keeping with the season Jewell wore an Icelandic sweater and made cocoa with marshmallows, because it seemed like the traditional beverage of tree trimming. Both Regina and Carmen threatened to put Jewell out if she said, "It smells like real pine, from the forest," one more time. Carmen was in charge of the low branches because she couldn't reach the high ones. She soaked up some of Regina and Jewell's holiday happiness because the season hadn't been merry in her house in a long time.

That first 5D Christmas tree was hardly a designer showcase, but when they darkened the apartment and turned on the lights they looked at it with wonder. It was their first tree, in their first apartment, which meant something different to each of them, but for Jewell, Regina and Carmen, it was also a special moment they shared.

The official Christmas celebration would be at the Fosters' house and at first Carmen was worried she'd be intruding. "Are you kidding?" Regina snorted. "The more the merrier, and if I have to go home and deck the freakin' halls with Mr. and Mrs. Claus, you guys are coming with me."

Carmen was hesitant, wary of such unfamiliar terrain as a family gathering, but she decided that if she wanted her life to be different, she needed to have different experiences. So as soon as she punched out on Christmas Eve the three of them took the train, crowded with last-minute shoppers and tipsy office-party revelers, to New Jersey. Al met them with the big square family-mobile.

As they traveled o'er the snowy fields, the scenery changed from town to country. Jewell sat behind Dr. Foster and wondered what it might be like to have a regular dad who picked you up from the train instead of a famous one you didn't know.

They turned onto a winding road, crossed a one-lane stone bridge. Carmen listened to snatches of catch-up conversation between Regina and her dad, tried to imagine what it was like to grow up with a mom and dad riding in the front seat, talking about everyday stuff. The crunch of gravel as the car eased up the driveway to the sprawling colonial brought her back from a place she didn't need to go.

As soon as the car stopped, Regina bounded out. If Jewell and Carmen wanted a full Foster winter holiday, she was going to give it to them. "Follow me! We always used to do this with the first snowfall. Remember, Daddy?" Regina winked at her father then led the way to the sloping lawn on the side of the house, which was covered in deep, powdery snow. "Perfect!"

"For what?" Jewell asked.

"Angels, California girl. Snow angels." Regina spread her arms, turned her back to the snow and let herself fall, then fanned her arms and opened and closed her legs. "Come on!"

"It does sort of look like an angel," Jewell said. "I saw it in an old movie once—"

"You're kidding, right?" Carmen was incredulous. "Who knows what's in that stuff."

"It's just snow." Regina propped on her elbows. "No dog pee or broken glass. Watch." She scooped up a handful and shoved it in her mouth. "Homemade snow cones."

"Now I know you're crazy," Carmen said just as Jewell threw herself into the snow next to Regina and started flailing.

"Come on in. The snow is fine." Jewell cracked up.

Carmen, arms folded across her chest, watched from the sidelines.

"It's really a lot of fun." Dr. Foster came and stood next to Carmen. "I'd join you ladies but I've got cakes to get in the oven." His inventive creations—mocha coconut, apple walnut spice, and lemon pineapple, were an eagerly anticipated gift to colleagues and friends.

"Dad thinks he's the Pillsbury Doughboy!" Regina scrambled to her feet and found a fresh spot.

It did look like fun to Carmen—fun and free. She wanted to let go, let herself fall, land in the soft snow. Regina and Jewell were giggling through the third set when Carmen finally gave in. At first she was awkward, worried she'd do it wrong, but then she relaxed, let herself play—in the snow—with her friends.

Half an hour later, silly and snow-caked, they tramped inside and quickly got settled in their rooms—Regina in her old one. Jewell in AJ's and Carmen in the room Keith and Michael had shared. They got dry and changed then it was off to candlelight and carols at Winthrop AME Community Church.

Carmen didn't mention that church made her nervous. The last time she'd been she was eight and her mother got the notion to go to the big church on Marcy Avenue. During the sermon, Geraldine marched up and down the aisle, making a ruckus nobody could understand. The ushers tried to calm her, but she got belligerent and stormed out. Carmen, bewildered and alone, stayed until the congregation stood to sing, then snuck out and found her way home. She convinced herself this time would be better.

Jewell's church exposure was limited too. Vivian took her on major holy days, but they never even attended the same one more than a few times. Her mother was skeptical of church folks. "—busybodies minding everybody's business but their own." But this was different. After the service she and Carmen were treated just like Regina by church members. They got big hugs and blessings and Jewell felt they were welcome because they were friends of the family, not because she was sort of famous.

But Regina had grown up in this small brick church, with these people, and was bored with the glad tidings and holiday hoopla. She expected the pride, praise and embraces that were heaped on her in generous servings. "You're in your second year at Barnard aren't you? Um um urn." "Smart just like those brothers of yours." "You all make us so proud, baby." But as Regina received another helping of compliments and encouragement, she felt like a fraud. Carmen and Jewell knew her grades weren't exactly dean's list, but even they didn't know she had dropped a class and now barely carried enough courses to qualify as a full-time student. They also didn't know Regina was counting on their presence to deflect some parental scrutiny so she could get through these two days without having to say anything specific about how school was going, because down the tubes wasn't the answer her parents were looking for.

"Christmas just won't be the same without any of the boys here, will it honey?" Lonnie said to Regina and hung her jacket on the hook by the back door. "They're all so busy and so far away." She tugged her Santa Claus sweater down over her red wool slacks. "Did I tell you we got a letter from Keith last week? His research is almost complete so he should be home by spring."

"That's so exciting," Jewell watched Regina toss her coat over a kitchen chair then folded her own over her arm. "It would be amazing to visit Zimbabwe, but to live and study there must be—"

"A trip," Regina snapped. "I couldn't do it." She opened the refrigerator, peered inside.

"Yeah. We know how much you like studying," Carmen commented.

Regina's head whipped around, and shielded by the refrigerator door she launched a death stare at Carmen. "Thanks a lot," she mouthed.

"What'd I say?" Carmen mouthed back.

"Speaking of studying, how were your exams, Queenie?" Lonnie lit the fire under the kettle.

"Fine," Regina lied, having no intention of mentioning the C, D and two more incompletes she had racked up. "Not up to the genius level of my brothers, but I'd never hope to compete with them." She pulled out a soda and closed the fridge, knowing she'd just gone on the offensive.

"Now Regina, you and your brothers are completely different people. Your father and I would never expect you to compete—"

"Come off it, Mom. You do it all the time. You've been holding them up to me since I went to kindergarten!" Regina popped the top of her cola. "Remember my fifth-grade science project? Of course not. Why would you? I made an Eskimo diorama. AJ built a working oil refinery or something."

Carmen and Jewell exchanged puzzled glances, suddenly uneasy in the shifting climate.

"AJ's was only a diorama too," Lonnie said. "And I do remember yours. You made the igloos from sugar cubes and—"

"Yeah, right," Regina scoffed. She turned to her friends. "Michael won some big-deal award as an Eagle Scout, and silly Queenie lost her Girl Scout cookies on the way home, before I delivered one stupid box of Thin Mints. And Keith? Keith's on the honor roll. Keith got a scholarship. Keith got a fellowship—"

"That's enough Regina." Lonnies's tone had a "case closed" finality. "We're proud of you the same as we were proud of your brothers." The wail of the boiling kettle punctuated Lonnie's statement.

Carmen and Jewell had been looking for an opportunity to escape. Whatever this was they didn't want to be in the middle of it. "I think I'll turn in now, Mrs. Foster," Jewell interjected.

"Me too," Carmen added. "Good night." They both headed out the door.

"Looking for the life rafts?" Before they got to the stairs, Regina was behind them. "See, it's not always smooth sailing on the Good Ship Foster."

On the landing Jewell whispered, "Why'd you give her such a hard time? She just asked a simple question."

"You don't know what it's like being an also-ran in your own family. They'd have been fine with their three sons. But oops! I showed up and spoiled everything." She felt the same pang she did at twelve when she stood outside her parents' door, overheard their conversation. It started with Lonnie's playful giggle. "*Stop Al. I know you think the playground's always open. Lord knows I shoulda had my tubes tied before Regina. I was too old to be somebody's mother—again.*"

Regina's sad expression shifted to defiance. "Screw 'em."

In spite of the skirmish, morning dawned uneventfully and from breakfast to presents to the houseful of folks who arrived laden with packages and casserole dishes, the day proceeded peacefully, Regina and Lonnie tiptoeing around any subject that might fan the flames.

Carmen, overwhelmed by Christmas à la Foster, was even quieter than usual. The huge feast, complete with china and silver was grander than anything she'd seen in her life. After dinner she sat by the fireplace, another first, keenly aware that two weeks ago she didn't know where she'd be sleeping tonight. When Lonnie asked if she was all right, Carmen blamed sitting too close to the smoke for the tears she wiped away. She'd heard you can't miss what you never had, but she'd just discovered that wasn't true.

Somewhere deep down, Jewell believed families like this weren't just movie magic and she found comfort in the lively chatter and laughter, underscored by Nat King Cole, the Mormon Tabernacle Choir and Mahalia Jackson. Jewell had spent too many silent, orderly Christmases trying to get through the day without her mother lashing out, mad at her father for his absence, ending up alone in her room with her shiny new games and dolls. But she refused to linger on those thoughts, just as she avoided looking too long at the baby pictures on the mantel and up the wall along the stairs. She tried hard not to get lost in the squeals of delight from children playing with noisy toys in the den, or wonder what made her daughter's eyes sparkle when she unwrapped it this morning. Her own holiday history was pretty dismal, but Jewell remained optimistic. This was the kind of family she dreamed about, and one day she would have it.

"LA wouldn't have been anything like this, Regina," Jewell said on the train home the next day.

"That's what I was counting on. If my father tells that joke about the reindeer stuck in the chimney one more year I'll kill myself." Regina put a finger gun to her head.

"I thought it was kind of funny," Carmen said. "And you look so much like your mother—"

Regina rolled her eyes, reached in her shopping bag of leftovers and pinched off another piece of the mocha coconut cake her father had sent home with her. "How can you say that? She's so—boring. Every year she drags out that stupid Santa sweater like nobody would know it was Christmas without it."

"Well, I meant it as a compliment." Sometimes Carmen took out that snapshot of her parents—her mother couldn't have been much older than Carmen was now—and searched Geraldine's face for a resemblance she couldn't find. "You've got the same nose and eyes. Your hair is the same color—"

"Yeah, dust-bunny brown. That's original."

"Anyway, I had a nice time at your house."

"I'm glad *you* had a good time, but that was not my idea of a party." Regina shimmied in her seat and sang, "Wait till you see how my birthday's gonna be."

5

"Born ready and tired of waitin'."

"Hey REGIN-A! Wait up!"

Not now! She recognized the husky voice and slowed because there was no avoiding Milton, but this had to be brief. Regina had worked up the nerve to put her birthday plan into action, and she didn't want any distractions now.

Heavy footsteps approached from behind. "Hey." Milton Hemphill trotted beside her.

She'd met him at a Barnard Organization of Black Women mixer. Lurking in the shadows like a ninja in a black Huckapoo shirt covered with Kabuki faces and fans, the moment Regina was alone, he swooped. Five minutes into his life story, when she couldn't get a word in edgewise, she patted his knee and got up. "We just got here. Don't bore me to death on day one." Milton wasn't exactly hip, but he was nice, and Regina could count on him like one of her brothers, so they got to be friends. Besides, she figured it was good to know at least one guy who wasn't potential date material.

"Hey Hemp. I'm in a hurry." Regina picked up the pace.

"Anything happening after the Fordham game?" he asked.

"Isn't there always?" Regina's party-hearty spirit had made her the talking drum for black student happenings. "*When is the Q party?*" "*Who's at the Garden?*" The answer was always, "*Ask Regina.*" "Call me Thursday." She checked her watch. "I gotta go. I have a meeting."

"With who?"

"That's confidential." She hadn't even run this by Jewell or Carmen yet because she didn't want to hear she should be putting her efforts into improving her grades which were definitely on the hump, so she certainly wasn't telling Milton. "But keep Sunday after next open. Six to ten."

"I love a woman of intrigue."

"Maybe I'll tell you tonight, unless you're *not* coming for dinner." She gave him a mock questioning look, knowing he'd be the first to arrive. Jewell's gourmet Tuesdays had become a 5D institution. Her attempts to bring fine dining to their college experience brought mixed results, but it was always fun. The guest list, a mixed bag of strays—fellow students, gypsies from Jewell's jazz dance class, or some yet-to-be-discovered artiste—rotated weekly, but no matter who else showed up, Milton would be there in circulation and he always helped clean up afterward.

"What should I bring?" Milton asked.

"The usual. Your appetite." Regina walked the last few blocks, giving herself a pep talk. *What's he got to lose?* Then she stepped into Le Professeur's Bistro. *Cool. It's empty*. She'd cut Spanish to beat the crowd. Prof's, as it was known, was a woody old joint that smelled like beer, full ashtrays and popcorn. The kind of place where students, grad assistants and professors nursed drafts and argued the merits of social anarchy, neo-modernism, Coltrane or Kierkegaard, whatever they were into.

"What's up, Red?" Regina spied the owner on his usual stool at the end of the bar. She assumed the nickname had once described his hair, but the rim he had left was a yellowed white.

"Jersey." Red barely looked up from the *Village Voice* splayed before him. "The usual?"

"Yep." Regina took the stool across the corner from him. She suspected she was one in a long line of Jerseys, but right now she was interested in his capitalist instincts not his lack of originality. Last year she had come to Prof's for the first time with her Spanish tutor who introduced her to the French onion soup and Bordeaux. She didn't like the dry red wine, but she developed an addiction to the soup and it became a staple in her supplemental meal plan.

Red shouted Regina's order toward the kitchen. "Don't you ever want anything else?"

"As a matter of fact, I do, but it's got nothing to do with food." She leaned an elbow on the bar. *It's now or never*. "It was like this when I was here Sunday, Red. Empty," Regina began.

"What else is new? Sunday's always slow, especially in winter. Thinking about putting a TV up there." He pointed to a spot above the bar. "Get the game crowd in here."

"Aren't you the one who said people who want to watch TV should stay home?"

"Times change. So do minds."

"What if I could triple, even quadruple your Sunday business?"

Red lifted his gaze over his reading glasses, and eyed her as the cook came out of the kitchen and set the soup in front of her. "Go on."

"Sunday is a miserable night on campus. Weekend's over, fun's over and we sit around moaning about Monday." The aroma of onions and beef stock called to her, but she had work to do. "And January is always dead, but my birthday is in two weeks and I want to party. I've got a lot of friends and if I tell them this is the spot, Sunday evening, they'll definitely be up for it."

Regina had learned from negotiating with her parents for an allowance increase or a pajama party, that presenting her case in an uninterrupted spiel netted the best results. She leaned in toward Red. "How many customers do you have on an average Sunday? Fifteen? Twenty? So you end up the day with what—one seventy-five in the register?" Red kept looking at his paper, but didn't turn the page. *You've got his attention. Just keep it straight and drive it home*. "This is the deal. I want the back room. No cover. Cash bar. I can guarantee at least fifty people, probably more. I'll get a DJ, but that's my expense." She didn't have one yet, but that would be the easy part. "You put out the usual happy hour spread." *Okay. Stay cool*. "Whatever you make, above two hundred bucks, we split fifty-fifty."

The idea came while she and Jewell ate in the deserted restaurant and she'd been running the numbers ever since, trying to contain her excitement. Regina knew her idea was good business. She was counting on Red to see it that way too.

"So, you want me to cut you in on my business, huh?" Red closed his newspaper.

"Only what I steer your way." Regina wasn't sure how to read him, but she was already hip deep so she just kept wading. "If nobody shows, it's a wash. But when they do—" She rubbed her hands, anticipating the gravy. Finally, she pushed her spoon through the gooey cheese toast and let the piquant aroma escape.

Red stared at his paper while Regina ate. She struggled to maintain her cool, but she couldn't taste the soup, only her disappointment. She stayed long enough to make a good showing, then put three dollars on the bar, already trying to decide who she would approach next.

"It's on the house." Red handed her the money back. "Music's off by ten. The house gets the first two seventy-five."

Regina felt a power surge so strong she thought she'd blow a fuse. She wanted to jump on it, but held back. *Keep dealing*. "Two twenty-five." She flipped him a "just say yes" glance.

"Two fifty." Red cracked a grin and it was a deal.

Regina floated home, fueled by her success. This was better than prom committee, or dorm parties. She knew it wasn't supposed to be, but this was the most exciting thing she'd done in college so far. This was her show. And by the time Jewell got home, with a bag of groceries, Regina had already designed the flyer.

"Sunday? Think people will come?" Jewell unpacked shrimp, clams and other seafood.

"Hell yeah. First of all, it's *my* birthday." Regina bowed, taking her curtain call. "Second, what else is there to do? You can't study all the time."

"You are demented." Then Jewell called to the other room, "Hey Carmen, you're not allergic to shellfish, are you?"

"No." Carmen joined them in the kitchen. She squinted at the shrimp. With the heads still on she thought they looked like bugs. In her world shrimp came take-out—battered and fried and then only once in a while—too expensive. "I was just gonna get a sandwich or something—so I don't get in the way of your company." She was still getting the hang of her new arrangement. Company on Tuesdays, parties on a Sunday; she thought only losers like Z did that, but it happened at 5D too. The crowd was a lot different though, and she'd met people she'd only seen in passing. But even with all the socializing they got their work done, at least Jewell did. She wasn't sure about Regina.

"'In the way'?" Jewell got spices from the rack. "You live here. You're included in the pot."

"That's right, you haven't been here for one of Bijoux's international extravaganzas. She dresses for the occasion too. Kimono for stir-fry, serape for Mexican. What goes with the fish? A net?" Regina glanced at Jewell, but kept talking before she could answer. "Depending on the week, you may still want that sandwich," Regina cracked. "I might want dibs."

"*You* go back for seconds. And thirds." Jewell filled a pot with water. "Ever had paella?"

"No," Regina said. "But here's the really important question. Do you know a good DJ?"

It was the hot question on Regina's lips for the next week. She knew the guys around campus who spun dance music, but she was bored with them. Regina wanted a new groove. She talked to several candidates. One guy said he could do it but she'd have to supply the equipment. Another told her he needed round-trip transportation from Yonkers. She still couldn't believe the guy who said he could do it all—for the grand sum of $500; way more than she hoped to clear. "This is a college party, not *Soul Train*," she told him, but with less than a week to go, she was getting panicky. Regina had been handing out flyers and talking up the event all over campus, making it sound like the only hip place to be that night. She had buttered up key people, the ones who always traveled with a crowd and she loved every minute of the plotting and maneuvering.

Regina had even let Jewell convince her to try on the dress she'd been eyeing in a boutique window. She had always been a junior shop kind of girl, opting for quantity over quality, but once she had the red silk dress on she loved the smooth feel on her skin, the way it made her look like the savvy New Yorker she'd dreamed of being. She plunked down her money, and every day she'd put it on, stand in front of the mirror and sway to tunes on her stereo until reality sank in. This was supposed to be her biggest party yet, but none of it would matter if the music wasn't together.

By Wednesday nothing had panned out, so as she minced down the spiral stairs of the student center, Regina decided to settle for one of the old reliable spin doctors. The new rhythm would have to wait till next time, because she was already sure there would be a next time.

Regina bought fries and a Coke, slipped into an empty seat at the back of the TV lounge and shrugged out of her coat. One of the regulars nodded. All other eyes were glued to the set. There would be no talking until the commercials when comments about Erica's latest marriage, divorce, or some other controversy, were exchanged by the die-hard soap fans who assembled for their daily drama fix despite the Ivy League setting. She opened her Labor Movement notes, scribbled a reminder to buy nail polish remover in the margin, then tried to decipher what she'd written about the Brotherhood of Sleeping Car Porters while keeping one ear on her story.

"Excuse me, I'm looking for Regina Foster." His voice was smooth, like a cool summer breeze.

Heads whipped around. A guy was a rarity in the room.

Regina lifted her gaze without moving her head. *What for?* Before identifying herself she examined the mysterious stranger. *Not a Columbia brother*. There wasn't a black guy on campus she hadn't checked out and cataloged for future reference. *Average height, kinda husky. Okay looking*. His boxy leather jacket was open, revealing a red sweater with a wide black stripe across the chest. *Nothing special*. Nothing to account for the disturbance in her force field. He surveyed the room from the doorway, then strolled in and stopped dead center, like he was comfortable standing out. Regina tried to ignore those who had abandoned *All My Kids* in favor of the scene unfolding before them. He looked around then focused on her, like he already knew she was it.

Aware she'd been tagged, Regina spoke up before his eyes rested on her too long. "You found her." She pushed back in her chair, awaiting his next move.

"Ty Washington." He extended his hand. "Heard you're lookin' for a DJ."

She took his hand. Firm, dry grip. *No soul brother, slap, clap, pump and bump.* Despite the winter chill, his hand was hot, too hot. She withdrew hers quickly.

"Where'd you hear that?" Regina crossed her legs and waggled her foot at the ankle. *You need to stop.* Her party was Sunday, she had no music and here she was acting like she could afford to blow him off, but she couldn't resist saying something smart. She always did with her brothers, although right now she wasn't feeling particularly sisterly.

"Oh, you're not?" Ty ran a hand over his close-cropped hair, then scruffed up imaginary bristles on his chin, sizing her up. With skin the sweet brown of maple syrup, his face was solid—broad and squared off at the hairline, but his small almond eyes teased you with a hint of mischief, like they held a secret you wanted to know. "My mistake." He turned to leave.

"I didn't say all that." Regina stood, arms folded across her chest. *Why am I acting like this?* "Let's find a table." She led Ty to the other side of the lounge, waved quickly at Milton who tried to flag her down, and slipped into an open booth. "First off, how'd you hear I need a DJ?"

"I'm up at City. Word gets around." Ty reached into his pocket and produced one of her yellow flyers. "There's not too many ladies promotin' parties so I had to check you out."

Promoting? Is that what I'm doing? That gave her a charge. Her flyers had made it all the way to City College. "So how'd you find me here?"

"A little investigatin', a little conversatin'." Ty drummed the table with his index fingers. "You don't seem like the type of young lady who flies below the radar, know what I'm sayin'?"

Regina had to laugh. "So who are *you?* Double O Soul?"

"No secret agent. Just a hard-workin' man with a plan." He produced a glossy black business card with silver print. "Since time is short a face to face seemed more direct."

Regina examined the card. *Nice touch. Guess he's legit.*

"What's happening, Regina?" Milton appeared at the end of the table.

"I'm having a meeting right now." Regina didn't want to encourage further discussion.

"You've been doing a lot of that lately." Milton gave Ty a twice over.

Ty introduced himself and Milton started an elaborate handshake, daring Ty to keep up, which he did, without hesitation. Then Ty handed him a card.

Milton examined it carefully. "You play music for parties, huh?"

"Congratulations, Hemp. You can read. Now if you'll excuse us..." Regina's look was a clear exit signal, and Milton reluctantly departed.

Regina went back to the business card. "'Tyrone "Ty" Washington. Let DJ Ty put the "TY" in your Par-TY.' Look good on paper, but can you do all that?"

"Don't mean to brag, but…hell yeah." Ty's easy gap-toothed grin revealed even, pearly white teeth. "I got references. Hollis, Queens Village, Cambria Heights, Jamaica. Ty Washington is the man of the hour. The DJ with the power. I do weddings, clubs, block parties, all social functions. I endeavor to please and always leave my customers satisfied."

Something about the way he said "satisfied" gave Regina a jolt, but she shrugged it off and before she got swept away by his momentum she countered, "No offense, but I'm looking for somebody with Manhattan credentials." *Choosy for somebody who should be begging. We haven't even talked about price.*

"I hear you, but you city folks think you're the only ones with somethin' goin' on. Even though I don't think you're *from* the city."

"What makes you say that?" Regina hated when her small town was showing.

"Just a vibe. Anyhow, here's an offer you can't refuse. I mean you can, but you'd be stupid and that, I know you're not." He leaned forward. "You need a DJ. I need to expand my horizons. One time only, no charge. I come fully loaded, turntables and mucho music. If you like my services, we'll talk money next time." He held her gaze, leaned back calmly.

A slow smile crossed Regina's lips. She wanted to jump for joy, but propped her elbows on the table instead. "You're right. I'm not stupid." And Regina felt that Ty, with his rhyming talk and confident swagger was the DJ for her. "You have to keep the crowd moving."

"Leave that to me. Soul. Funk. Disco. Oldies. Whatever the mood, I got the mix. Whatever the crowd, I got the fix." Ty shook the chrome-and-glass sugar dispenser like maracas. "I'm diggin' the Sunday concept. It opens up a new night to get down."

Ty didn't sound like anybody Regina had ever known. She liked that. "Since you got the flyer, you know the details. The owner's name is Red."

"I know. I checked the place out. Not exactly a club like Pippin's, but we'll make it work."

"Red let you back there?" Regina asked.

"Yeah." Ty winked. "Told him I was your DJ."

Regina slapped the table. "Are you always two steps ahead?"

"When I know the way."

"Okay Ty-Rone. We're on." This time Regina offered her hand. "I need you set up by six." She felt his meaty grip, skin a little rough and a warm current shot up her arm. When he let go she tucked her hand in her pocket. Ty wasn't super fine, which had always been high on her list. He was more like a Teddy bear, just not the kind she used to collect when she was a little girl. This bear had something going on she hadn't run into before.

"Sunday." Ty stood up. "I'll be there before you."

Regina was awake by 4 A.M. Sunday, impatient for the clock to strike party time. By ten the bathroom was a wreck, but she emerged to show off her new midnight black hair. "Definitely not like my mother's," she said as she modeled for Carmen. Jewell told her it looked dramatic, which was exactly the look she was aiming for.

By noon Jewell gave up answering the phone, because all the calls were for the birthday girl. Regina had to think fast when she answered the phone, "Party central," only to find her mother on the line. "Oh, we're just having a few friends over." Regina's parents entertained all the time, but she was sure they wouldn't understand her party for profit arrangement at a local watering hole.

Regina bounced off the walls, euphoric one minute: "This will be the coolest party in the history of parties!" Sure of failure the next: "I'm an idiot. Ty's not coming. What kind of name is Ty? And there's not even a jukebox." The festivities didn't start until six, but by quarter to five Jewell had completed Regina's curly upsweep and dramatic makeup and she headed out the door.

The first person she saw when she got to Prof's was Ty, talking to Red. *Yes!* Regina had never been so happy to see somebody she barely knew. *This is my night*. "You got here early."

Ty strolled over to meet her, a hint of a dip in his step. "Got to get up yesterday to be ahead of the T Man."

Regina had never known a guy who would wear a silvery Lurex shirt like Ty had on, but she decided it suited him. "Are you set up?"

"Born ready and tired of waitin'. And may I say, you are seriously wearin' that red dress."

Regina smiled. "You may." As she headed for the back room she caught a whiff of his cologne. He smelled like leather and lime. "Wow, you did all this?"

"My trademark colors. Festive, but classy." A constellation of black and silver balloons decorated the ceiling. Tables had been removed and clusters of seats lined the walls. "Over there is my command post. Where the sound goes down." A canopy of twinkling lights set off the area. Atop a silver-draped banquet table sat turntables, headphones and other meters and gadgets Regina couldn't identify. Megaspeakers faced the dance floor, and black milk crates filled with albums were at the DJ's fingertips. Front and center on the table were Ty's business cards.

"Looks like you've done this a few times before." Regina was psyched by what she saw.

"And a few times more if I have anything to do with it." Ty reached behind one of the crates. "This is for you, birthday lady." He handed her a slim cone of florist's paper.

Regina unwrapped the single pink rose surrounded by baby's breath. "Wow, it's ah…thanks." *Damn. What's your problem? Spit it out.*

"A little token of the beautiful night to come," Ty said.

What's that mean? She wasn't sure what she wanted it to mean. "I'll put this in water."

But before she left Jewell showed up, a vision from the Argentine pampas in sepia suede pants, matching vest, and a fitted white blouse tied at her waist.

Ty was on the case before Regina introduced them. "A sho' nuff star. I knew classy people hung together."

Jewell managed half a smile, wary of the Hollywood hello. After some chatter, the two friends left to await Regina's public. Ty stayed behind to "warm up the room," as he put it.

"Pretty slick isn't he?" Jewell whispered as they took seats at the bar.

Regina stuck up for him. "Give him some slack. He's got more on the ball than you think."

"And the posy?" Jewell was not about to let her off the hook. "Looks like he's—"

"He's just the music man." Right on cue the beat started bumping and Regina bopped nervously, aching to get the show on the road.

Carmen popped in just after six and they applauded. Jewell and Regina had had to twist her arm to come. First she had a lab report due, then she didn't have anything to wear, so after Regina left Jewell had played beauty shop with Carmen too, taming her fuzzy edges and crooked braid into a smooth French twist. Then Jewell dug in her closet and found a black cowl neck sweater that fit Carmen like a dress.

"Look at you, Miss It." Regina approved.

"I told her she looked hot," Jewell added.

Carmen was embarrassed. "It's not all that." But she couldn't help grinning a little.

Milton stormed in next, hands jammed in the pockets of his brown cords. "He doesn't matriculate at City." The news had been on his lips so long it spilled out before he could say hello.

Regina crinkled up her face. "What?"

"Ty, your DJ. He's not registered at City College. One of my friends…"

"Do you hear that music?" Regina asked him. "If he does that all night, I don't care if he finished kindergarten." She batted her eyes and flitted off.

The air seemed to seep slowly from Milton. "I thought she should know," Milton said to Jewell. "I only stopped by to be sociable. A late Sunday night will wreck my whole week." Jewell shrugged and excused herself. Then he turned to Carmen. "Wow, you look really nice. Want a drink or something?"

"Yeah. Sure." Carmen looked up at Milton. "Ginger ale I guess." She felt awkward standing in a bar with a guy buying her a drink, even if the guy was Milton. This was definitely a first and for a brief moment she tried to imagine if a date was like this, sort of.

Milton handed Carmen her soda. "Here's your sarsaparilla, ma'am."

Carmen shook her head. "You are the corniest man on the planet." They tried to talk about classes, but finally agreed the music was too loud for conversation. "I still have to finish a report. I'm outta here."

Milton tossed money on the bar. "I'll walk you."

"What for? I know my way." Carmen buttoned her coat.

"Company. Camaraderie. Conversation." Milton motioned toward the door with a flourish.

Carmen shrugged. "Suit yourself."

As soon as Carmen and Milton left, Regina hustled over to Jewell. "Did you see that?"

"I'm not buying any rice yet," Jewell said. "But they do look cute together."

A trickle of people began arriving at 6:30, and Regina was glad she could stop avoiding Red's "I knew this wouldn't work" look. She cracked jokes, made introductions and treated Prof's like her living room, cranked higher by each arrival. Wanting to spur commerce and take her adrenaline down a peg, she called to the bartender, "Make me a cute drink." She leaned over the bar, enjoying the flirty feel of her skirt on her thighs. "Cute and yummy." It was her night to celebrate.

"I got just the thing." Regina gabbed until he sat a tall glass on the bar filled with liquid streaked with colors that faded from crimson to orange to gold. "Try this. It's a tequila sunrise."

She took a cautious sip. "Oh yes." She saluted him with her glass, then a guy who had a late-night jazz spot on WKCR, the campus radio station, paid for her drink. By seven folks started arriving at a steady pace. There were veterans of her dorm parties and those who'd only heard about them. Most were from around campus, but there was a sprinkling from CCNY, FIT, NYU, friends of friends who spread the word. Regina herded guests to the back where Ty's music was cranking. She could feel him channel the energy in the room.

"It's not Monday, it's Sunday, and that's a Funday!" Ty chanted, hands waving in the air.

Whistles blowing, bodies undulating, the dancers answered in the rhythm, "FUN-day! SUN-day!"

And while Regina relished her spot at the center of the action, she kept an eye on the cash registers, a crowd count in her head and tequila sunrises became her drink of the night. Floating on a technicolor haze more seductive than a dream, she lost track of how many drinks she had.

Red stood by the door and watched, fascinated by the spectacle.

"Pretty good shindig for a Sunday—in January." Regina giggled. "How about next month?"

"Stop in for some soup. We'll talk," Red answered.

By nine Red opened the whole restaurant to Regina's bash. He dimmed the lights and Jewell presented a cake blazing with candles. It was her one foray from her spot at the crook of the bar, where she nursed a glass of Chianti and talked, mostly with people she knew. Jewell didn't much care for big parties. She'd found that the guys who usually approached her had big egos and were mostly in search of bragging rights. She had no intention of being the subject of some pumped-up locker-room narrative.

Regina led a "Happy birthday to ya" conga line around the dance floor and by ten Ty slowed the music, folks got coats, traded numbers, and told Regina they'd be at the next Funday. Red was cool about the time and the last guest left at eleven. Slightly tipsy, Regina skipped across the floor, plopped on the edge of Ty's table and held on until the room caught up. "Funday Sunday, where do you come up with that stuff?"

"It's the spirit in the room." Ty took a swig from his red plaid thermos.

"Home brew?" Regina asked.

"My speciality. Root beer and orange juice. Want some?"

"Sounds nasty." She screwed up her face.

"Keeps me goin'." He grinned. "Looked like about a hundred bodies swung through here."

Regina was impressed, but not surprised that Ty had been keeping track. "That's about what I figured. I'm waiting for the count."

"No offense, but where I come from, we do the countin' in the open. That way nobody's got a beef later. In a setup like this, other folks handle the bread before you do. You wanna make sure they leave you more than crumbs. Not that I have any stake in it tonight."

It never occurred to her that Red might not do an honest cut. "You ever been cheated?"

"Hell yeah. Never by the same dude—or chick—twice." He wiped his brow on his sleeve.

Regina crossed her legs. She didn't mean to flirt with him. Ty was business, but she couldn't help herself. "You were great tonight. Red is up for this again next month. We'll have to work out the money thing."

"I'm feelin' we can come to terms." Ty walked around and sat next to her.

There was no space between them. Regina felt the heat radiating off his body. *Ty is not my type.* But she got pulled up short by that same tug she felt when they first shook hands. *Must be the tequila.*

"You got a nice way about you. You can take that places, dependin' on where you wanna go." They sat there a moment. The silence seemed loud after so much music. "You wanna ride?"

Regina eased off the table, trying to stay cool. "Jewell and I can catch a gypsy cab." She wasn't ready to be closed up in a vehicle with him. After all, she still didn't know if Ty was really in school, how he'd found her in the first place, or why he set off a chain reaction in her central nervous system.

Ty took her hand. "I'm not sayin' anythin' bad's gonna happen, but you need to be careful when you leave spots like this. People might expect you to be carryin' lots of cash, you know what I'm sayin'?"

Regina had never considered the safety issue, but Ty seemed to have all the angles figured. "Guess I'll call that cab instead of waiting on the corner."

Ty squeezed her hand. "It's been real." And then he looked her straight in the eye.

She wanted to laugh it off, but he controlled the moment. As much as Regina had tried to avoid being trapped in his gaze, now she felt compelled to return it. His eyes kept her steady as he leaned in close, steady until she closed hers to savor the soft kiss he left on her lips.

"Call ya next week."

"Okay." Ty had added his tingle to the tequila's and Regina could barely walk straight.

Up front Red handed her an envelope. "Your birthday was happy for both of us, Jersey."

Inside was more than double what she'd made on any party so far. *This is just the beginning*. She wasn't sure of what, but she knew it would be good.

The envelope she got on Tuesday didn't bring such good news. It was from the dean, requesting she make an appointment to discuss the fulfillment of her four incompletes.

"I'll get it done—during Spring Break," she said, trying to convince Jewell—and herself. "It'll work out." *I'm just not sure how*.

6
"You've been where they want to go."

After five months as a trio, Carmen, Jewell and Regina found a rhythm for living together. They had arranged bathroom logistics, refrigerator protocol and clean-up schedules. Regina, the official slob of the bunch, was frequently in violation. Her room looked bomb-struck, and she left a trail of empty cups, abandoned shoes or wet towels in her wake. Jewell, the decorator, created harmony in the shared spaces and her own room—so despite its humble beginnings, 5D had style. Regina called Jewell's fussing and arranging her "housewifey shit" and could not be bothered, although she did like the citified air of the place, especially when Jewell brought home white roses. Carmen was too busy to worry about the niceties and was glad to help with the upkeep of her clean, tranquil home, but she did complain about Regina's messy ways. "The girl is spoiled. Does she think she has a maid?" But Carmen considered that minor because she never dreaded coming home the way she used to. Sometimes she still wondered what had happened to her mother, but she never, ever missed Z.

Mornings, Jewell and Carmen were up and out early in what became an easy duet, which pretty much described their friendship. The only time they argued was when Jewell wanted to pay Carmen's way to movies, restaurants and other extracurricular activities. Unlike Regina who had no problem with freebies, Carmen would get indignant. "I have a job. If I can't afford it, I'll stay home." That made Jewell feel bad, but she didn't want to hurt Carmen's feelings so she backed off.

Regina didn't have a class before eleven, so she got herself together after the other two had gone. Tuesday dinners were still on the menu and was the one night they all made an effort to be home.

Maintaining harmony still required fine tuning. When Carmen wasn't at work or in the library, she shut herself away, buried under sheaves of notes, textbooks and lab journals and worked her grades back from the brink, including an A in the Twentieth Century World. Regina was far less studious, and since her Funday Sundays had become a weekly event at Prof's, the phone sometimes rang for her late into the night. Jewell ignored the interruptions the way she tuned out noise on the set when she had lines to learn. But Regina and Carmen had almost come to blows over the disturbances. Finally Jewell suggested Regina get a separate line installed in her room, and that ended the discord for the moment. Like oil and water, Carmen and Regina probably wouldn't have mixed without Jewell to stir things up, but for each of them 5D had become part clubhouse, part support group, part laboratory. They had each come to Barnard to experiment, find out who they were and who they wanted to be, but a lot of those lessons were learned outside the classroom. So at the end of their first full semester together they all signed on for junior year and to celebrate Jewell got them each silver "5D" key rings.

"Hey." Carmen poked her head through the French doors to the living room. Windows open wide to the evening breeze, the sheer curtains billowed like sails. "What's all that stuff?"

"Homework." Jewell sat with her back against the chaise, a cigarette in one hand, two fat manila envelopes in her lap. In an arc around her were stacks of ragged-edged loose-leaf pages, cards with bunnies and lollipops, and pastel stationery, some covered in loopy script, others in jagged block letters. When she saw Carmen, Jewell snuffed out the cigarette and fanned smoke with the envelopes. She tried not to smoke when Carmen was around. "Maybe that'll make me stop," she had said.

"Finals are over." Carmen dropped her bag and sweater on her futon and perched on the chaise near Jewell. "I'm the one starting summer school. How come you have homework?"

"Fan mail. Homework from my other life." Jewell had hoped the time Carmen saved on commuting would allow her to relax, but she still seemed uneasy allowing herself more than the tiniest amount of free time. Instead of enjoying the summer break, Carmen had registered for two courses and was working full time at Alexander's. Jewell picked up a handful of letters. "*Daddy's Girl* is in syndication and these kids still write me like I'm ten years old. Vivian used to handle this stuff, but now Michael, my agent, gets them from the studio and sends them to me. He usually sneaks in a few scripts too." Jewell autographed an 8 × 10 glossy of her little-girl self. "Before the show was canceled, there were sacks of mail—you know like in *Miracle on Thirty-fourth Street* when all the kids write Kris Kringle. Anyway, now there's not as much, so I try to read them all. It reminds me what it was like to be ten."

Carmen got the feeling Jewell was a lot older at ten than other kids, like she had been, but for different reasons. She sat on the floor next to

Jewell. There was always some aspect of her career or the way she and Regina had arranged life in 5D that was new to Carmen. Some things took getting used to, like the weird sounds of Jewell's vocal exercises. Some things she embraced. She opened a checking account instead of buying money orders. Cussing was no longer a regular form of communication, although Regina could get a little raunchy sometimes, but mostly in fun. Carmen decided it was because she'd never heard a curse word at home or been called out of her name. Every day they ate on real plates instead of Melmac or paper, with the exception of Chinese takeout straight from the container. Friends popped in unannounced, especially Milton who was around so often it was almost like he lived there, but since they had the same career goal, Carmen liked having him around to bounce things off of.

Carmen picked up a Polaroid of a smiling ebony girl sporting two bushy ponytails. *I love you Tonya!* was scribbled across the bottom in blotchy blue marker and she wondered how people could love you when they didn't know you. She wasn't sure what it felt like to love the ones she knew. She put the picture back on the pile. "There are scripts here too?"

Jewell pointed to a stack of three-hole-punched booklets, secured with brass fasteners.

"Can I?" Carmen picked up the top one. Other than a newspaper, she hadn't read a word that wasn't required in over two years. "These don't look too long."

"Be my guest. I haven't read anything he's sent me in ages, but if it's bad, don't blame me."

Carmen flipped through the stack of screenplays and plucked one from the pile. "Don't you want to go back to Hollywood after you graduate?" Five D was a step up for Carmen, but it didn't make sense for Jewell to deprive herself when she didn't have to. Carmen knew that when she could afford to do better, she was never looking back. "Don't you ever miss it?"

"Sometimes I miss California, especially when it's two degrees here. And I miss getting in my car, putting the top down and taking off for the beach or up to Monterey." Jewell signed another letter, wiggled the Sharpie between her fingers like a cigarette. "But the business? I don't know if it's worth all the chasing again, not for the dumb stuff that's been coming my way." Jewell clipped the letter to an 8 × 10 photo and added it to the pile. "Besides, I don't even know what I'm doing this summer, much less after graduation." Jewell's major had hopscotched from English to philosophy to psych and there still wasn't a front-runner. She often felt pangs of guilt as she tiptoed past Carmen late at night, hunched over her books. Jewell hadn't worked that hard for anything, ever. It didn't seem fair that someone as dedicated as Carmen had to struggle, while she sailed along, without a destination, barely breaking a sweat. Jewell longed to find the thing she wanted so much it would keep her up until the wee hours.

But not like Regina's wee hours. She and Ty went clubbing a few nights a week, strictly business she said, investigating party venues beyond campus. Jewell was reluctant to admit it, but she envied the excitement and commitment that kept Regina moving toward a goal, if not toward a degree.

"I've got my bedtime story." Carmen got up, tucked the script under her arm.

Jewell went back to her mail, pondering her future and wondering if she'd spend another summer in the city taking voice and dance classes, maybe finally work with a drama coach. She'd been avoiding that. She didn't want to find out she'd lost the spark she once had, before she felt the pressure to light up so many lives. It was hard still feeling like a used-to-be before she hit twenty.

A phone call the next week from Marva Ducelle, one of her dance instructors, provided the answer, at least to her summer dilemma. "I need you to bail me out," she started. "I was trying to impress some students at the Harlem School of the Arts and I said I knew you. They said 'Then bring her up here.' So I'm asking you not to make me look bad."

Jewell was surprised. "First, there's no way you could look bad." Although in her sixties, Marva hadn't lost many steps from the days when she performed all over the world with the ground-breaking Kathryn Dunham. "Second, why do they want to listen to me? I haven't done much work in the last five years. I've never even taken an acting class!"

"Because you've been where they want to go, Jewell. They need to see someone younger than me who didn't just leave her dreams under the pillow."

So on the day of her visit Jewell was dressed and ready to go to HSA two hours early. She didn't smoke because she didn't want the kids to smell cigarettes on her breath or her clothes. *This is nuts. Why am I so nervous for seventh graders?* She'd spent hours making notes so she wouldn't forget what she wanted to say, but she needn't have worried. She might have been the star attraction, but the kids ran the show. They were bright, talented and hung on her every anecdote, then barraged her with good questions. For the first time in her life Jewell felt useful, like she had something of value to share, and her hour in the HSA library on a June afternoon turned into a summer project.

"You volunteered to spend the summer in a classroom?" Regina groaned. "Sounds like torture."

"I think it's great," Carmen said. "They'll hear what it's really like. When Milton and I went to a talk by these interns about what med school is like, they gave us the nitty-gritty blood and puke…"

"Spare us." Regina waved her off.

"I know it's Tuesday, but I'm too excited to cook. Let's go out!" Jewell turned to Carmen. "I know you're going to say you can't afford it, and you don't like it when I say it's my treat, so you can sign an IOU. In fact we can institute an IOU policy. You'll have to pay me back every dime I spend on you, Carmen Webb, but not until—when will you be a doctor?" Jewell counted on her fingers. "Okay that's in 'eighty-nine, then you need time for your internship. Let's say 1993. You can pay me back then."

"Deal." For once Carmen got caught up in Jewell's enthusiastic projections. "So since you've figured out when I can pay you back do I get to decide where we eat?" She grinned at Jewell and winked at Regina. "I hear Tavern on the Green is where the beautiful people go."

Jewell rolled up her HSA brochure and bopped Carmen on the butt. "Lunatic! We're going to Steak n' Brew. A steak and all you can eat salad bar for five ninety-nine."

"And a free glass of wine!" Regina added. "Ty's supposed to pick me up later, but we should be back by then."

Carmen and Jewell exchanged a look. They both thought she was driving the wrong way, down the wrong road, with the wrong guy, but Regina had her own ideas so they backed off.

"Still strictly business, or is there something you want to tell us?" Jewell elbowed Regina.

"To mind *your* business," Regina said coyly as they piled in the elevator. "Maybe we just found a way to mix our business with pleasure—for good measure."

Jewell squealed. "Business with pleasure, for good measure? You even sound like Ty." She and Carmen rapped the rhyme all the way downstairs with Regina holding her ears and humming so she couldn't hear. Giggling, they spilled into the lobby and ran smack into the Nosy Neighbor Patrol.

Right after they moved in, Jewell went to the mailboxes and was given the once-over by the five or six folks who alternated lobby watch-duty all day. Once she was recognized, word spread like a bad rash. They couldn't figure out why a TV star was living in their building, but eventually accepted that, like so many before her, and they could name names, Jewell had fallen on hard times. Some secretly gloated. Others shook their heads, whispered they were glad she was in school, trying to make something out of her life now, poor girl. Jewell knew they talked, but Vivian had taught her how to hover above the gossip, so their suppositions went unchallenged and Jewell had important mail sent to her agent's New York office.

"Have a nice night," Jewell called over her shoulder to their neighbors.

"Think we can make it out of here before Milton shows up?" Regina asked.

"Milton decided to go home for the summer after all," Carmen piped up.

"Ah ha!" Regina was on a roll. "Look who knows Hemp's last-minute plans. There's your love match, made in brainiac heaven! The nerdly, but true-blue Dr. Hemphill and the demure, but streetwise Dr. Webb! I can see it now. 'Dear, will you please pass the test tube?'"

Carmen tried to hide a flustered smile and Jewell pinched Regina before she could call her on it. Jewell had gotten to know Milton through her roommates, and unlike Ty and Regina, she thought Carmen and Milton were a perfect match. Same interests, same drive, Jewell had watched them study together, encourage each other, and she was sure they cared about each other for real, the way Jewell thought it should be, the way she had thought it was with Billy, but now she knew better.

By the time Regina got up for her third pass at the salad bar, Carmen put down her fork, full from her first trip. "You know that screenplay I read? I really liked it. Not that I know how they're supposed to be, but it's about this woman named Bessie Coleman…"

"Isn't she an old-timey singer?" Regina returned, plate piled high.

"That's Bessie Smith," Jewell answered.

"Bessie Coleman was a pilot in the twenties," Carmen said. "Jewell has a script about her."

"You read one of her scripts?" Regina sputtered. "How come you never showed me one?"

"You never asked." Jewell turned back to Carmen. "You liked it, huh?"

She didn't take Carmen's review lightly, but it still took Jewell three weeks to read *Fly Girl: The Bessie Coleman Story*, by William Christensen. She'd gotten so turned off by the material she'd been offered since *Daddy's Girl*—some of it silly, most of it just bad—that she hadn't given any project a chance to impress her. And she'd been wrestling with whether she wanted to be an actress or not for so long that her default answer had become simply no. But the next day, as soon as the hour would permit, she called her agent Michael in California to find out who she had to see to read for the role of Bessie. Nothing Vivian had shown her in years compared to the story of the daring aviatrix.

Jewell devoured all the information she could find. Even putting together her audition outfit helped her get in touch with the incomparable Bessie. For her casting call Jewell wore khakis, a thrift-shop work shirt and men's black, lace-up boots, because Bessie had entered a man's world. Sleeves rolled to the elbow, she pulled her hair back, twisted it into the smallest bun she could make and went without a hint of makeup. Sitting in a waiting room filled with other actresses pretending not to check each other out felt strange; she hadn't been to an audition in three years and her time as a child star didn't give her any points on the adult actress scale. Nobody seemed to recognize her and she vacillated about whether that was good or bad while she listened for her name.

"Where've you been, sweetheart?" He wore his trademark Greek fisherman's cap. His feet in well-worn Topsiders, sans socks, were propped on the table, crossed at the ankle. "Thought you retired, had seventeen babies, or became a nun." Oliver Oakes was one of the few successful Black actors in Hollywood who had refused to do the Blaxploitation thing in the early seventies, and when that bubble burst he managed to escape with a career. Now he was one of even fewer who had earned enough points to be allowed to sit in the big chair and call some shots.

"None of the above. I've been incognito, a Barnard student." Jewell sat in the chair across the table, reared back and propped her feet on the other side, cupped her hands behind her head and smiled, suddenly full of that old certainty that let her take charge of the situation.

"Ivy League, huh? I'd've figured you for a Spelman girl. I'm a Morehouse man myself. I can spot a Spelman girl at a thousand paces."

Before Jewell could question his eyesight, a voice came from the outer office.

"I've got the rewrites." He strode into the room, displaced the very molecules of air.

Jewell dropped her feet to the floor, and tried not to gasp, but the goose bumps traced her arms and her breath was sucked out of her, the same way it had been back then. *Billy.* Against the white polo shirt his skin seemed sun-burnished to an even warmer glow than she remembered. The years had only made him fuller, riper, more imposing.

He stopped, his mouth still open but the word lost. He stared at Jewell as though he was seeing someone fantastical, like Santa Claus or an angel—someone you long for, but don't know where to find.

"Jewell, this is William Christensen, our screenwriter," Oliver said.

She'd seen the name on the title page, but it didn't register, could have been John Doe or Joe Blow. *Breathe.* Jewell knew it was her turn to speak.

Four years should have been enough to slough him off, grow new skin. "Billy?" A tremble had started in her feet, but she knew it would rise.

"Billy? Aw shoot, you two know each other then." Oakes looked from one to the other. "Figures. You're both Hollywood brats."

Jewell forced herself to meet Billy's gaze, if just for a moment. *Breathe. An actor is nothing without breath.* But she couldn't put two words together, knew she could never audition for this part.

"Jewell—it's good to see you." His voice still held the music of different languages.

Billy, William or whatever he called himself was moving toward her, and Jewell had to leave—while her legs could still carry her.

Although a disappointment at the box office, *Hoochie Coo* had been a critical success. One of the reviews called her performance, "Dazzlingly poignant yet brilliantly comic," but Jewell didn't go to the premiere. She still had never seen the movie, because every frame of New Orleans would remind her of those exhilarating rides on the back of his motorcycle and of making the biggest mistake of her life. "I'm sorry. I have to go." She saw Oliver's perplexed expression. "My agent must have made a mistake." It didn't make any sense, but it was all she could think of and she was out the door, long strides carrying her through the waiting room and into the hall before Billy could catch up.

"Just read with me, Jewell." He stood in front of her, held up his hand to reach for her.

"Don't!" Jewell shrank back. She knew where running lines with him had gotten her before. He withdrew his arm and she caught the glint of a platinum band on his finger. It hit her like a backhand to the face. "What's with the William Christensen? You take your wife's name?"

"It's my mother's. I didn't want to trade on my father's—"

"I have to go." She tried to dodge past him.

But he wouldn't move. "Hear me out…"

"Get out of my way." She adjusted her shoulder bag to give herself something to hold onto.

"The whole time I was writing *Fly Girl*, I thought about you. I tried to get you out of my head but the more I wrote, the more you were right there with me so I stopped fighting and let you stay—"

"You *let* me stay! La de freakin' da," Jewell snarled, grabbing Regina's offhand expression. "What was I? Some kind of artistic experiment?"

"That's not what I mean." Billy jammed his hands into his pockets to keep from reaching for her again. "This part is perfect for you because I wrote it that way. Your lips spoke Bessie's words. You gave them life. I even called you when I finished the screenplay. Did your mother…"

"*Oh now you can find me?*" Jewell wanted to yell, let the words reverberate off the walls, but that would only incite her more and she didn't want to feel anything for him, not anymore. "You're a little late."

"Jewell I didn't forget—"

"Liar. I wrote you, and you never answered me. Not once. But you found my number when you wanted to. For your damn movie."

"I got your letters." He pulled his hands out of his pockets, paced a tight circle then stopped. "I couldn't write you back. When you left New Orleans I came to my senses. You didn't look it, you didn't act it, but you were fifteen, Jewell, and I should have backed off."

"You could have told me that." Jewell sensed the hurt and disappointment slipping from beneath her angry facade.

"If I wrote you, I'd want to talk to you. If I talked to you I'd want to be with you, so I had to leave you alone." He closed his eyes, rested a hand over his mouth for a moment, then looked at her. "I took a chance and sent you *Fly Girl*. It must have spoken to you. Your agent said you haven't been auditioning—" He twirled his wedding ring with his thumb. "Look Jewell, I hoped you wouldn't hate me, but even if you do, don't let that keep you from this role—"

"The only thing I want to be kept from, Billy, is you!" Jewell glared at him. She had to make a break because she wasn't about to let him suck her in again. She'd at least learned that much. "If you don't get out of my way, I'll scream."

Billy looked at her a long moment, but she borrowed Vivian's tactic and she wouldn't look back. Finally he stepped aside and Jewell brushed past without touching him, didn't wait for the elevator. She ducked into the stairwell, took the steps two at a time.

At home she blamed her bad mood on the audition because she knew she wasn't a good enough actress to hide her distress from Carmen and Regina. "It was some screw-up. I didn't even get to read." It wasn't exactly a lie, and she wasn't ready to live through it aloud, because to make them understand today she'd have to explain Billy and the baby and she wasn't ready to speak on that pain, that loss.

That night Jewell turned in early. Not to sleep, she needed to be soothed by the dark. Propped on a pile of pillows, she violated her rule about smoking in bed. She inhaled hard, spat out smoke in furious bursts until she felt dizzy and sick, but that didn't stop her from reliving, in tortured detail, the nine months that followed New Orleans and Billy.

February, 1979
Baldwin Hills, CA

"School's the other way," Jewell said as Vivian turned on LaCienega. "We'll be late."

"I'm well aware of where your school is." Vivian stared straight ahead, her voice unnaturally calm. "Just as I'm aware you've missed two periods. We're going to Dr. Markson."

The blood in Jewell's body shot to her head, pressed her brains against her eye sockets. She'd never been to a gynecologist, and she didn't know her mother kept count, but she was sure she was pregnant. She'd known for a month, since her nipples started hurting like she'd slammed them in a door, and the smell of any food besides graham crackers made her queasy. She also knew Billy didn't care.

Not about her. When she got home from New Orleans, Jewell wrote him every day, tried to convince him that in three years she'd be old enough to continue the dialogue they had begun. She'd drop her letters, carefully written on pale blue monogrammed stationery, in the box across from school, confident that his were on their way to her. But after two weeks, she was convinced the whole postal system had failed; they had not only lost her letters, but Billy's too. The third week her period didn't come and she started to fantasize—that Vivian would understand Jewell had adult responsibilities from an early age, and that she had earned a status beyond her years. That Billy would be surprised, but happy because in each other they had found a missing part, a companion piece they didn't know they needed until they matched up together. They would be a family—Billy, Jewell and the child of their hearts, because their love was real, not fleeting like their parents'. She was just waiting for one note from him, and then she would tell him their secret, but it never came. Jewell's rock-solid trust shattered into bits of sand. Now it had been two months, and she was on her way to the doctor who would confirm what she already knew and turn her private affair into a family crisis.

At Vivian's insistence the doctor made Jewell his first appointment so they could dodge the waiting room full of patients ready to speculate on the reason for Jewell's visit. They were silent as they entered the building, but Jewell felt her mother's anger and disappointment throbbing beside her.

In a hot hurry Jewell's happy fantasy met up with the cold reality of urine in cups, heels in stirrups and metal instruments clamped inside her. As she gripped the table, stared at the ceiling, and flinched at the doctor's probing, invading, hands, the achingly beautiful dreamscape of the love she and Billy had shared and the life they would live, turned into a swamp she'd have to navigate alone.

Afterward, in his office, Jewell sat across from the desk, her hands folded protectively across her belly. The doctor's voice was kind, but she could offer only one-syllable answers to his questions. When Vivian joined them, she and Dr. Markson discussed lab results and probabilities while Jewell tuned them out, floated in a bubble with her baby. She didn't know why, but Jewell felt certain it was a girl—she could just tell.

Jewell and Vivian didn't speak on the drive home, retreated to neutral corners once they got there. Two days passed in artificial silence and on the third day the drive to school took another detour.

"Where are we going?" Jewell sensed something was up.

"It's all taken care of. At a private facility." Eyes on the road, Vivian was silent a moment. "You'll have an abortion this morning—"

"No." Jewell wasn't sure if she'd said it aloud. The wind was knocked out of her and she could barely speak.

"Don't be ridiculous, darling. I know you're upset—"

"YOU DON'T KNOW ANYTHING!" Jewell yelled.

"Stop yelling, Jewell."

Jewell wedged herself against the car door. "I will not kill our baby." *Our daughter*.

"*Our* baby?!" Vivian spat a jagged laugh. "I gave you credit for more sense than that!" She struggled to keep the car between the lines. "And who is 'our'? One of those little bastards at school with pretty eyes and shit for talent?" Vivian shot Jewell two daggers then looked back at the road. "Don't be stupid, Jewell. He won't stand up for you. They never do, or are you so lost in your make-believe you haven't paid attention to the real world? Look at your father."

"Believe what you want to," Jewell answered. "You don't know what you're talking about!"

"And what does he say about *our* baby—or does he even know?"

Jewell looked away because she knew he didn't and that he never would. And she knew that whatever she felt was going on with Billy had turned out to be her own imagination. "Take me home, Vivian." But she knew she could not go through with this. "Take me home now, or I'll scream, and I'll keep screaming until somebody hears me and I know you don't want that!"

Vivian drove on for a few tense seconds, Jewell perched on the edge of her seat, then she hung a wicked U-turn and drove home.

The next week Vivian withdrew Jewell from the school for the rest of the year, claiming work on a film in France, but they headed for Leonard's Palm Springs bungalow. It was a stylish, modern ranch, with a pool and all the amenities, but for Jewell it became an air-conditioned internment camp in the desert where she was subject to her mother's brainwashing any time of the day.

Sometimes Vivian would wake her in the morning with fresh orange juice and croissants and they'd have "girl talk," about men. "They talk all sweet, make you think their world would stop turning if you weren't in it. And as soon as you believe it, and give them what they've been snooping around for, they pack up their show and take it on the road. Trust me. I was a woman before I was your mother. And I sure fell for your father. You see how that turned out."

Some days Jewell wanted to tell her mother about Billy, about riding on that bike and feeling so free, but she kept that to herself. This situation was complicated enough, but little by little Billy became a girlish mistake, a stunning trap she should have seen, and all their soul-baring conversations had been meant to lure her, slowly, carefully, so she wouldn't know she'd been caught until it was too late. She'd seen it a hundred times on the set, chastised herself for believing his sweet words and falling for such an elementary seduction.

Little by little the baby made her presence known, first as a small pooch in Jewell's belly, then she grew steadily. And every day, Jewell became more and more convinced it was a girl, but she refused to share her intuition with Vivian. In the evenings when it was cool enough to be outside, Jewell would float in the pool, letting the water soothe the itchy skin stretching over the roundness, trying not to feel so afraid and to remember she wasn't alone. She'd never be alone again. That's when her mother would bring her bologna and cheese sandwiches on pumpernickel with onions and mustard, the one food Jewell seemed to crave. And Vivian would tell her what to expect, reminisce about being pregnant with Jewell. They were stories her mother had never shared.

By the time the baby was kicking and Jewell started thinking about a name for her daughter, Vivian began her endgame, about how hard it would be for Jewell to look at this baby every day and be reminded of the man who had betrayed her. "It won't just look like you. Look at the two of us. I know you got something from me, but some days I can't see it."

"And did that make it hard for you to love me?" Jewell had asked.

"Of course not darling, but that was different. Your father and I were still happy when you came along. But where is your young man? He's already in the wind."

That's what brought the tears. She realized their whole relationship was based on the wind, on air, nothing solid, nothing that would last. Vivian held her, comforted her, like she hadn't since she became Vivian instead of Mommy. Jewell rested her head in Vivian's lap and she stroked her hair. "It's not fair, Jewell. Certainly not to this child. It deserves your love, free and clear. And you'll never be able to give it that."

Jewell tried to believe that wasn't true, that she would always love her daughter, take care of her. But the doubt shadowed Jewell, would not give light to her hopes, made her see how much a fantasy she had been living, and that now she had to be real, for her baby's sake.

"We can find a family who will provide the kind of home every child deserves."

So seven months along, Jewell gave in to the reality her mother had made so clear while they were together in the desert. Leonard arranged the details, making sure his client's anonymity would be protected. Her delivery would take place in a small private hospital where their exclusive clientele required discretion. He assured Jewell and Vivian that the child would be placed with an exceptional family, one who could provide the same level of financial security and care that Jewell could.

And Jewell spent the last two months saying good-bye. She talked to her belly every day, trying to make sure her baby knew that she was doing what was best for her. She wasn't giving her up because she didn't love her, but because she did.

The first sharp pains of Jewell's labor jarred her from sleep, but she didn't tell Vivian right away. She wanted the time alone, with her baby, her last time alone with her. They'd been together nine months—closer than Jewell had been to anyone. So all through the night, Jewell held her belly, handled her pain, kept telling the baby she would always love her, trying not to think that her daughter would never know her. The low heavy pain continued to expand, but Jewell didn't want it to end because that meant she and her child would have to part company and that would be worse. But in the morning, when the warm trail of her water traced down her legs, she knew it was time to go.

At the hospital, Vivian was too upset to stay with Jewell for long, but the nurse she hired was kind. She rubbed Jewell's back, fed her ice chips and didn't ask any inappropriate questions. Once Jewell got the epidural, things moved quickly. The doctor told her to push, and she did, but the whole time she wanted to hold on. Finally she felt a pressure too great to resist and she bore down. That's when Jewell felt her daughter slip away. A nurse whisked the baby off, out of Jewell's sight, but she heard the keening cry, wanted to reach out, but she held the bed railing instead and while the doctor took care of the afterbirth, Jewell cried heartbroken tears, because she already felt the void. Her nurse snuck back to her and whispered, "A perfect baby girl," near Jewell's ear.

Jewell had held onto that after she left Palm Springs and resumed her regularly scheduled life. Held onto it after she took a part in an after-school special and Vivian said, "You see darling, you would never have gotten this role if you'd been an unwed mother," and Jewell realized that Vivian wasn't concerned about her or the baby. She was protecting her client's career. And those words were all she had to hold onto since she was now sure that giving her daughter away had been a terrible mistake.

She hadn't seen or spoken to Billy until today. He never knew about the baby, didn't deserve to. Lying in the dark in her bedroom, Jewell pressed her hand against her belly, felt the thin wavy raised marks, her only tangible reminder that someone she had loved was lost to her forever.

Jewell didn't know how she'd have gotten through the summer without her drama class kids. They got her up in the morning and left her spent at the end of the day. She listened to their worries, encouraged their dreams, and helped polish their performances. She'd done well; the "real" teachers said so, and she was thrilled to have a full house for their final production—including Carmen and Regina—but not more thrilled than she was to see young brown faces performing Shakespeare.

While she milled around the lobby, signing programs and talking, a man Jewell had noticed from the wings approached her. "Councilman Dwight Dixon." In his navy blazer, blue-and-white striped shirt and foulard bow tie, he looked different from anyone in the place. "Great job, Miss Prescott. We need folks like you to get involved in the community."

"Well, they gave me a great summer." Jewell wouldn't have thought he was a politician. He didn't look like the gruff old men in smoky back rooms whom she imagined. *Too many old movies*. She figured him for around twenty-five. *Must be smart*. His face reminded her of a shield; broad and flat at the forehead, narrowed to a point at the chin, fashioned from tempered bronze.

"I enjoyed you on television too. You were always very clever." Dixon reached in his breast pocket and handed her a card. "I understand from Marva that you're in the district. If you ever need anything—anything at all. Don't hesitate to call."

Jewell thought his eyebrows seemed arched in permanent amazement above small, wide-set eyes. “Thanks. I won’t—hesitate.”

Regina and Carmen joined her as he walked away. “Somebody’s made a connection,” Regina announced.

“He’s the councilman from this district,” Jewell explained.

“I gotta tell you, he’s not just looking for your vote,” Regina quipped.

“Your head is screwed on too tight.” Jewell was glad she’d made it through the summer. She tucked the card and the program in her purse, smiled at the irony of the title. *All’s Well that Ends Well.*

7
"Yeah—maybe—I don't know."

"Did you see the way they dimmed the lights and let the spots hit his hands on the turntables?" Ty held open the elevator door and stood aside for Regina to enter. He always saw her to her floor when they went out. "Too many crazy fools out here," he always said.

"The whole place freaked." Regina's voice was hoarse from yelling over the music and her hearing was fuzzy from the wall of sound, but she still had a good club buzz pulsating through her body. On the ride home Ty had spun this whole tale about the halls he would fill, the music he would play, even badder than the DJ tonight. Regina understood, shared the fantasy, because she believed it could be real, that the coach didn't have to turn into a pumpkin at midnight.

When Regina and Ty went out they rarely danced. He didn't like to. They checked out the DJ's technique and equipment, and ended up in the office with the promoter where it was a man's world. Girlfriends, relegated to fetching drinks, wondered why Regina got to stand in the circle with the men, never far from Ty's wing. Tonight she overheard one of his boys say, "Man, you let that bitch run you?" Ty jumped in his face. "Ain't nobody runnin' me. And don't be disrespectin' my lady."

My lady. The words danced in Regina's head on the drive home. Sometimes he teased, called her his "college queen from *Ebony* magazine," which she didn't take too seriously. But Regina had been trying to dodge Ty's hints about the two of them for more than a year now. They had already celebrated the first anniversary of Funday Sundays and Regina knew Ty wanted more than a business deal, but he never pushed. He told her she was "quality," promised he'd always treat her like a lady. So she kept Ty hanging—weighing her options as she told Jewell and Carmen—but for all of Regina's flirting and man-a-minute talk, there hadn't been any action since Greg, her high school initiation to the basics of bodies in motion. With him it was skin deep. He was cute and he knew the mechanics well enough to get her going, but it was no trip to the moon. Ty was different. He could get her revved up with a casual touch, a brief kiss or even without it. She liked the way he knew what to say to people, how to make things happen, like tonight.

They arrived at Club 371 and the line was down the block. She wasn't happy about the wait; it was cold and this wasn't her favorite spot. Regina preferred downtown clubs like Justine's where the crowd was pressed and the drinks were classy. One of Ty's City College cronies was working the door, so they slapped five, talked about the old days in the CCNY lounge. Next thing she knew they were ushered inside past the poor slobs who'd been waiting, and she was sipping rum punch.

Until she met Ty Washington, Regina thought she knew how to handle people, how to get what she wanted using personality to smooth persuasion. Ty took it to another level. His grammar wasn't the best, the syncopated bop still lingered in his step, but Ty was the first guy to understand she wanted something different, to encourage her dreams, make her believe they'd come true, just like his. He got to Regina, more than she would admit and she'd been scared to strike that match because she didn't want to burn the house down.

"I heard you stick up for me tonight." In spite of cigarette smoke from the club that lingered in their clothes, Regina smelled the lime of his aftershave when he stood beside her.

"Wasn't nothin'." Ty turned to look at her and grinned.

"So you say." Regina leaned in, kissed his cheek. "Thanks for nothing then." He was a whisper away, his breath sweet, warm. Usually, when they got to her floor she only gave him time for a quick kiss and she was down the hall before she could get sucked into his orbit. Now she laid her hand lightly on his chest, looked through her lashes at his lips. Those plump, brown pillows always seemed so inviting. Without missing a beat he slipped his arm around her back and kissed her, soft as a tickle, but sure, not a competition of mouths and tongues like so many she'd had before. Regina felt herself drawn into him and this time her body had made up her mind about how far to go. The elevator door had opened and shut again before she could pull herself away long enough to say, "You wanna come in?" She hadn't discussed sleepovers with Jewell or Carmen—so far it hadn't come up, and she hadn't planned to set policy tonight; it just happened.

Regina held her finger to her lips as they tipped into 5D. She'd always thought the first time in her own place would feel free, like in the movies where they did it in the living room or on the kitchen table and broke lamps and dishes in fevered passion. At first this felt like sneaking Greg into her parents' house through the basement door, but that was the last time she was reminded of her old boyfriend.

"Sorry about the mess." Regina was embarrassed by the chaos of her room, but Ty just shoved aside the jumble of clothes on her bed and blanketed her neck, her ears, her mouth, with tender kisses. Regina lost track of the room and the mess, felt like she was floating. Clothes seemed to melt away as Ty's hands, strong, a little rough, moved deliberately over her smooth skin, made her hot and shivery. A warm syrup seemed to replace her bones as he nuzzled the hollow of her throat, her shoulders, her arms, worked his way down her body. Regina liked the heat of him, the bulk of him next to her, on top of her. And as their bodies came together, melted into each other, she understood what it was like to make love with a man, not a teenage boy. When it was over they snuggled under the covers and got lost in each other's hopes and dreams for the future. "We're a lot alike," Ty told her as they nestled like spoons. "I got buddies, all they want is a jive piece a job, so they can keep hangin' out like we did when we were kids. They ain't got nothin' and they won't get nothin'. Hell, my father's like that too, gettin' stinkin' drunk and bad-mouthin' anything I try to do. You and me, we want more than that." Resting in Ty's arms, Regina could feel how much that was true.

Ty snuck out before dawn, but Regina got snagged by an upturned toilet seat. Jewell couldn't believe she'd done "it" with Ty. "Have you ever seen the man in the daylight?"

Carmen couldn't believe she'd done "it" at all. "How do you know he's telling you the truth about anything? You don't know what he does when he's not with you."

And Regina stood up for him. "Why would he lie? He told me he earned half his credits toward a sociology degree then took a leave. College is not the only place to get an education. He lives in Hollis with his father who's a drunk. He works part time at a record store on Jamaica Avenue. And why do I care what he does on his own time? I know we understand each other."

"If you understand each other so well, why didn't you take him home for Christmas?"

"Because he's not my boyfriend," Regina said smugly.

The only thing the three of them agreed on that day was the out-by-dawn rule. Carmen and Jewell had no intention of trying to make small talk with Ty over orange juice and coffee.

Saturday morning Regina stumbled into the kitchen, still wearing a tiger-striped nightgown, sunglasses and remnants of red lipstick. She and Ty didn't get back to 5D until four-thirty and in order to comply with the newly established house rules, she shooed him out by five fifteen. It was only nine now, but Regina's head hurt so much she couldn't sleep. "Dr. Carmen, will I die if I take three aspirin? I've got to lay low on the rum punches. My head feels like there's an elephant in tap shoes up there."

"The aspirin won't get you, but if you keep eating my cheese slices, I will." Carmen, making her lunch to take to her MCAT review class, slapped a piece on top of her two circles of bologna, then closed her sandwich.

"How do you know it was me?" Regina shook two more pills from the bottle.

"'Cause Jewell hardly eats cheese, and when she does it has a French accent."

"What do you do, count "em?" Regina cupped her hand under the faucet and took a slurp to down her pills. "I only ate a little."

Carmen wrapped her lunch in foil. "I don't get an allowance like *some* people."

"I haven't spent one *dime* of their money since January, for your information," Regina shot back. "I've been strictly self-supporting."

"So, are you planning to tell that to your parents today, like you said?" Carmen snapped.

Regina leaned against the counter, massaging her temples. "Yeah—maybe—I don't know."

"Regina, it's March. They kicked you out in December."

"Kicked you out," sounded so much harsher to Regina than, "request that you withdraw," which is how the letter had been worded. It amounted to the same thing though. The notice was almost a relief, like "great, now we can all stop kidding each other." She had read the official proclamation at a Tuesday night dinner, after the overcooked chicken Florentine. "Go talk to the dean. You could promise to clean up your act next semester. Jewell and I will help you." Carmen had looked so worried, but Regina said, "Don't sweat it. I don't want to go back."

Deciding that the news would ruin everyone's Christmas, including her own, Regina kept the secret from her family. But then New Year's faded into President's Day and now it was almost Easter and she still hadn't let her parents know that she and Barnard had parted company.

Not that she had wasted her time. Freed from her academic cell, Regina was eager to treat her parties like a real business. One afternoon while Jewell was out, Regina had borrowed her student ID and spent hours researching different types of corporations after Ty told her it was what he'd done. "When you file taxes, you can deduct almost everything. It's the only way you keep your money."

Regina had been disappointed he didn't want to become partners, but decided it was better that way, and when she got back the certificate of incorporation for Good Tyme Productions, Inc., she finally felt like she was heading in the right direction.

But when she showed it off in 5D Jewell had said, "Good TY-me? Interesting spelling, isn't it?"

Regina hadn't noticed until then, but tried to play it off. "I just wanted to be different." Then she taped it in a prominent position on the wall above her desk, along with business cards, scraps of napkin with names, addresses, notes to herself and articles from newspapers and magazines about where the hottest events were happening. Her flyers, still on bright yellow paper, now screamed, "Good Tyme Productions Presents Funday Sundays, featuring DJ Ty." She posted them at bookstores near campuses, student union bulletin boards and at Ty's suggestion, record stores. "People that buy music are always lookin' for a good time." She'd also started circulating a legal pad she called "The Roster" at her parties, so she had a direct way to let people know what she was up to. On Mondays, when she dragged herself out of bed after her Funday night, she'd sit at her typewriter, drink coffee and add names to her list, trying to match them with faces because people liked it when she remembered their names. Then she'd hit the bank before closing. She'd opened a separate business account, and although she hadn't written any checks, she had envelopes full of cash to deposit once a week.

Now that Funday Sundays had become a weekly event at Profs, Regina had worked out a new deal with Red. They added a two-dollar cover, which they split, and a two-for-one drink special, usually some cute, sweet concoction, made with house booze, and not much of that. Music still started at six, but since the Funday Sundays had become a date night, the dinner crowd had picked up as well and Regina got a piece of that too. So her profits, which she now helped count, had grown nicely. Even after she paid Ty, she had a healthy chunk of change.

Regina had rehearsed all these selling points to pitch to her parents, including how financially self-sufficient she had become. She had geared up to take the train home and tell them this afternoon, except that after Ty left this morning and she was lounging under the covers, she had an idea. Campus would be deserted June through August and Fundays would be on hold until fall. Ty was already hustling in his neighborhood to DJ block parties, weddings and whatever else he could find, but Regina was anxious to come up with her own big summer event.

After Carmen left Regina picked up the phone and dialed the Circle Line. "I'm Carmen Webb from Good Tyme Productions." She figured Jewell's name was too recognizable "My boss, Regina Foster, would like to make an appointment to discuss chartering a boat."

Two hours later, dressed her executive part in a gray suit, black blouse, pumps, and the gold rope necklace she borrowed off Jewell's dresser because she knew she wouldn't complain—not too much—Regina hobbled across the cobblestones of the West Side Highway. She decided on red lipstick because it made her look older—at least twenty-two. The afternoon was warm and sunny, just like it had been the day her dad took her on her first sail around New York. Back then, Regina couldn't imagine the whole world being any bigger or better than Manhattan. She felt exactly the same way today.

"I'm Regina Foster," she said to the man behind the spotless desk. "My assistant called you earlier about a charter." It sounded just the way she practiced.

"Phil. Phil Bailey." He had mirror-slick black hair and snow white brows, bushy as caterpillars. "Like 'Won't you come home Bill Bailey,' but Phil." He offered her a seat and reached in his drawer for a price sheet. "For how many, twenty? Thirty?"

"How many does the boat hold?" Regina opened her notepad, ready to talk business. "I have July Fourth in mind." She whipped out her flyers, offered Red as a reference.

Phil examined the pages, tidied them on his desk. "Your scenic cruise lasts three hours."

A three-hour cruise around Manhattan with DJ Ty on the turntables sounded like a perfect way to spend a summer night to Regina. The holiday sail was way out of her price range, but the fifth was still open and within budget. She was convinced the boat ride would be a success because she knew folks liked to party all week if they could. Making a deal like this was scary. The math was different and she'd never had overhead before, but if she wanted to move beyond Prof's, she had to start somewhere.

"I need a one-third deposit to hold the date. Plus, you're required to have at least three security guards, you know, just to keep this—uh—organized."

She ticked off her questions one by one, which Phil Bailey answered patiently. Then Regina took a deep breath, made out her first business check and left the office ready to execute her plan. Bopping along the sidewalk headed for her next executive appointment, a hair salon rendezvous with Jewell, Regina felt confident she'd made the right choice, not that she actually chose to flunk out of school. She decided to tell Lonnie and Al about her ex-student status after the Good Tyme inaugural cruise, so they could see how well she had thought this through. And so she could use her untouched allowance to cover out-of-pocket expenses. *You were right, big brother. I can't live on the Circle Line, but it's gonna be mine for a day.*

"July Jam, huh? Good name for a boat ride." Jewell, hair wrapped in a towel, watched Regina examine hair-color swatches at the next station. "Did your boyfriend come up with that?"

"How many times do I have to tell you Ty is not my boyfriend." Regina held bright red fringe up to her forehead, like bangs. "I'm running a successful business enterprise. *He* works for *me*. And I don't have to answer to him or anybody else." She had recently joined Jewell on her visits to Chez Prince, the posh salon where Jewell had been going since she arrived in New York. It was a little pricey, but styles and services here were hipper than the tired press and curl shop where Regina had gone with her mother for years. And best of all, you never knew who would be at the next shampoo bowl. Last month she met Felicia Anderson, a disk jockey on her favorite station, the hippest trip in America. Regina didn't hesitate to introduce herself and exchange business cards. She'd learned from Ty that phone numbers were the key. And Felicia actually showed up with a bunch of people at the next Funday Sunday. Regina made sure they were well taken care of. Ty was surprised, and impressed.

"And no, Ty didn't name it. The plan came together kind of quickly. I haven't told him yet."

Regina wanted to tell him right away, but held on until Sunday when she saw him in person. She figured he'd be hyped. "You're the DJ. Ticket sales will go through the records stores that carry our flyers. You'll have this boat bumpin' down the Hudson by the light of the moon." Regina shimmied.

Ty sat on one of his speakers in the back room at Prof's. He took a swig from his thermos of root beer and orange juice. "How you know I can do it that day? I might be booked."

"Are you?" Hands on hips, Regina was unprepared for the sudden shift in the wind.

"That's not the point. You made all these plans that include me. I shoulda known."

"Then forget it." There were already diners in the restaurant, so Regina concentrated her voice in an angry whisper. "I thought of this the other night, right after you left. You *inspired* me, always talking about playing for big crowds in the city, and I *thought* having a boat full of dancin' fools at your disposal would make you happy, but obviously I was wrong."

Ty reached out, held one of her wrists. "That's not how you do business, Regina."

"Oh that's all this is? Business?" Regina took back her hand.

"This part of it is. And when we do business, you need to let me know."

Their stares collided. "Do you want to do this or not?" Regina's foot tapped the floor.

"Yeah." Ty closed his thermos. "But next time ask me first, you know what I'm sayin'?"

"Yeah. I know." Regina walked away, trying to dismiss the salty taste that lingered from what she thought would be a sweet surprise.

By April Regina had worked out a deal with Felicia to comp the station tickets for their June call-in contests in exchange for pumping the boat ride on air. Ty was psyched when he heard his name on the radio. So was Regina.

June was nerve-wracking because according to her ticket outlets, only half the boat was sold. Twice a day she'd do the math, figure how close she was to her break-even point. But she did a second wave mailing, worked the phones, kept talking it up at her Fundays. The day of the event Regina enlisted Carmen's help and they made rounds to pick up the remaining tickets. She was thrilled to find that more had been sold than she expected, but Carmen figured it out. "The stores kept your money until the last minute. Like a floating loan."

Good Tyme Productions' first July Jam was an official sellout, with people left on the dock, wanting to get on. They hit a snag when an unticketed partier tried to jump on board as they pulled away and landed in the water. People hollered and held their breath until he floated to the top and was fished out by security. The rest of the night was magic. Mostly.

"*Ain't no stoppin' us now. We're on the move.*" The boat bounced in the rhythm and Regina was in her glory in a white tube top and matching palazzo pants. Jewell looked cool in a sapphire blue jumpsuit, and thanks to another of Jewell's ambush makeovers and borrowed duds, Carmen looked like a firecracker in a red tank leotard and a matching wrap tap skirt.

"Red, white and blue. We are too cute," Regina declared as Milton posed them together for a picture. Arms around each other's waists, they kicked up their legs, à la Rockette. "Thanks Hemp. It's a good thing somebody thought to bring a camera." Regina brought Carmen and Jewell to the DJ booth to see Ty, meet his crew. They mixed like milk and mud and after a few minutes of attempted conversation, went their separate ways.

"The fat one in the red nylon track suit reminds me of this guy I know named Randy," Carmen said with a shiver.

"I felt like meat at feeding time," was Jewell's assessment.

Jewell and the radio station personalities formed an ad hoc VIP section at the bow of the boat along with the record store owners who had sold tickets. Carmen hung out there too, with Milton, who was even more gregarious than usual. He downed beers, one after another, and told her all about his parents, how proud they were of him. "I could never do anything to let them down."

"How could you let them down?!" Carmen asked, but Milton just shrugged.

When they ventured out for a stroll around the deck Milton draped a long arm around Carmen's shoulder. She didn't know exactly how to respond—it was Milton after all. It felt comfortable—*cozy* even, but strange with their bodies so close. After a while they stopped to look at the Manhattan skyline and she slipped a tentative arm around his waist. She was saying how pretty the city was at a distance, when she saw the strange expression on his face. Before she could ask if he was seasick, he swooped in, as if propelled by unstoppable momentum and their lips collided in a tense, hard kiss. He smelled like beer. Her top tooth nicked the inside of her lip. It was over before Carmen registered anything other than surprise. Then just as suddenly, his momentum swung in the opposite direction. Milton said he was going for more beer and ginger ale and disappeared, leaving her wondering what had happened.

Regina flitted about, taking it all in, toasting her success with white wine while Ty worked the crowd. The DJ booth was the hub of the action and Ty was in his glory. He took the music to the people and he took requests, especially from the ladies who flocked around him, giving him the onceover. His boys hung around, slapping backs, talking trash. "Regina thinks she's better than you, man. You can see it," they agreed. So Ty also had to take the crumpled papers and matchbooks the ladies slipped him with names and phone numbers, to show them that he was not under Regina's thumb, that he was the man.

At the end of the night Regina floated over to the booth while Ty broke down the setup. "How did it feel to have a boatful of people at your mercy, Mr. Par-TY?"

"Makes me wanna holler." Finally they hugged and kissed, celebrating their first off-campus success. But that night they went home to dream their future dreams in separate beds.

The man overboard incident got a two-inch mention in the *Daily News*. And the next day it was time for Regina to go home to New Jersey and face her own music.

"Are you on drugs?" Lonnie trembled as she paced in the kitchen. "And you're responsible for this?!" She shook the folded newspaper in her hand. "You call this a career? My god, a man fell overboard. He could have been killed. Then what would you do?"

"I don't use drugs, Mom." Not that Regina hadn't been offered. "I know you think—"

"You obviously have no idea what I think." Lonnie stopped pacing and glared at Regina. "Or you obviously don't care! You've been running these—these affairs for a year and this is the first we're hearing about it."

"I care." Regina looked at her father. "Ty and I—"

"Who?" Lonnie snapped.

"Tyrone Washington. He's my DJ, disc jockey. Kind of my partner."

"It's him, isn't it? That Tyrone—he dragged you into this," Lonnie shouted.

"Don't blame Ty. He thinks I should stay in school."

"I don't care what he thinks," Lonnie sputtered.

"Lonnie, calm down. You can't have a stroke over this." Al sat across from Regina.

"You won't have to take care of me anymore. I've been paying my own way." Regina dug a check out of her purse. "See? I'm paying you back my allowance from last semester. I never spent it."

Lonnie snatched the check from her daughter. "'Good Tyme Productions.' And this is supposed to make up for the lies you told us?!" Lonnie glared at her daughter.

Regina didn't have a good answer. The word "lies" burned as it settled over her.

Lonnie tore the check up, threw the pieces on the floor and stormed out.

Then Regina was left with her dad, which in some ways was worse. "I'm sorry, Daddy. I should have told you sooner." That, she knew, was the truth.

"I just wanted to get you through school. Get you prepared for life." Al took off his glasses, rubbed his eyes. "I wasn't done with you yet. I'm supposed to take care of you until…"

"Until I can take care of myself." *He's not crying, is he?* "I'll be okay, Daddy. You'll see." Regina couldn't bear to look at him anymore. "I gotta go." She went to the phone, scoured the bulletin board for the number of the cab company.

"I'll drive you to the station." Al got up.

"You don't have to," Regina protested.

"At least let me do that for you?"

"Okay." Her father's request nearly broke her heart, but she didn't crumble. As they left Lonnie scowled from the doorway. Regina turned to look at her mother. “If I’m not good enough, at least you have your boys,” she said.

8
"...back-when moments and what-if hopes."

Third, third, half, half. Carmen folded a pink bath towel, reciting the mantra her boss, Margaret Ann Caroll, better known as Mac, had taught her so the stacks were uniform. The mindless repetition kept Carmen from wearing out her new mantra—*Did I make it to med school?* Caps and gowns didn't matter. Seven weeks from graduation her real goal was in sight, but she wanted it in hand.

"You've been folding the same ones for an hour." Mac took off her glasses and let them fall the length of their gilded chain. "Give 'em a rest. The letters will come pouring in." Mac was all retail and all New York. She wore only black, had an encyclopedic knowledge of all things linen, and had put a son and a daughter through med school, apparently without help from a Mr. Caroll, so she recognized Carmen's anxiety even though she would never admit it.

"A guy I know got six already." Whatever else happened, Carmen knew Milton was set.

"I'm telling you, dear girl, it's going to be fine. Mac knows." She patted Carmen's arm.

Carmen wished she felt so certain. She didn't skip any steps, miss any deadlines. Her GPA and MCAT scores were more than respectable and her recommendations were stellar. Many of her classmates applied to twenty schools, but Carmen selected nine, all her budget would allow. Her choices were all within a day of New York by train or bus to make interviews feasible, and like a good do-bee, she followed each with a neatly typed thank you. But she had yet to hear a word. "I've been kinda jumpy. I think my roommates are ready to put me out." She patted the stack of towels like a favored pet.

"Hmm. Maybe that's why they're here now."

Carmen spun around and spied Regina and Jewell stepping off the escalator, each waving an envelope. "From where?" She almost bowled them over, then, braced between her two friends, she carefully opened the flaps, smiled. Both Cornell and the University of Medicine and Dentistry of New Jersey welcomed her aboard. "Now the real work begins," Carmen said.

"I don't believe you." Regina reached out, shook Carmen playfully by the shoulders. "Girl, can't you lighten up for once and just enjoy the moment?"

"She's right," Jewell said. "We're celebrating tonight. We're so proud of you."

"I'm not off until—"

"Get outta here," Mac interrupted. "I'll punch you out."

"But—" Mac had fired people for violating the sanctity of the time clock.

"Go! Have fun!" She shooed them away. "Have a glass of wine for me."

"Will do." Regina smiled and waved.

"You guys are so dressed up." Carmen noticed Regina's red wrap dress and Jewell's black suit. "Like you already knew—"

"Of course we knew, you lunatic," Regina said. "You're the only one surprised here."

"And it's time for a shopping drill," Jewell announced. "You get a discount here, right? So we won't add much to that IOU." She looked at her watch. "How are we on time, Reg?"

"Store closes in thirty minutes."

"That's plenty." Jewell dispatched Regina to the main floor for pantyhose, then grabbed Carmen's elbow. "Lead me to petites."

"We're never gonna make it." Carmen stood on the sideline enjoying the hubbub and the curious glances from other shoppers as tall Jewell sifted speedily through racks of short dresses.

"Trust me."

And Carmen knew she really did. Regina too, most of the time.

Jewell made selections and shooed Carmen to the dressing room, then appropriated the black patent pumps from a mannequin, knowing the displays were size six.

Regina appeared with hose and a beaded headband. "Thought this would come in handy."

Then Carmen came from behind the curtain, tentatively fingering the bow at the waist of the black faille sheath. The dress looked more expensive than it was, made her look classy.

"That's it!" Jewell clapped.

"Darling, you look *fab*-ulous," Regina concurred. "I wish I could get dressed that fast."

Carmen and Jewell looked at each other and shook their heads. "It'll never happen."

Jewell brandished her charge card, Carmen offered her employee ID, then they made a beeline for the ladies' room to pull it all together. Carmen balanced on one foot and gingerly put on the filmy hose. "They're gonna run." She was used to sturdy opaques, but these went on without a snag.

"Mascara—lipstick—brush—headband." Like a surgical nurse, Regina handed Jewell items from her makeup bag. Finally Jewell handed Carmen pearl studs and the extra evening purse she'd brought along and in five minutes Carmen had gone from mousy clerk to chic sophisticate, for once ready to hang.

"What now?" Carmen asked after they'd ditched her old clothes with Mac and stood on Lex.

"We're going where—what is it you said?—where all the beautiful people go, and doctors are definitely beautiful people," Jewell said as a taxi swerved to the curb.

She couldn't believe Jewell remembered her joke from two years before, but Carmen was still getting used to the kind of group memory that came with friendship. There was no one left in her life who remembered the things that happened before they came along.

From the moment she spied Regina and Jewell on the escalator Carmen had felt like she was dreaming. When their cab entered Central Park and let them out in front of Tavern on the Green the setting was pure magic. Arm, in arm, in arm they strolled beneath trees twinkling with white lights, then under the red canopy and into the restaurant.

And as Carmen fell asleep later that night she thought about the struggles she'd overcome, the sacrifice her father had made in his gypsy cab, and the glorious time she'd had tonight and she realized she'd entered a world she could barely dream, on her way to a life she couldn't fully imagine.

"The package is great, but the cost of an apartment could blow my budget." Carmen looked over her soda at Milton who picked onions out of his souvlaki. Five more admissions followed in the next week, but the medical school in New Jersey offered the best financial assistance so she was leaning in their direction.

"It's in Piscataway, not Beverly Hills. How much could a decent crib cost?" Milton still tried to sound hip. He was no better at it than he'd been when she first met him, which was one of the things Carmen liked. And his final med school choices had been between Harvard and Johns Hopkins, so hip was relative. "And Baltimore is right down the road, so I can pop up and see you sometimes on weekends."

"You know as well as I do there are no weekends in med school." Carmen still hadn't figured him out. Milton didn't bring up home or family much, but neither did she. The 5D crew seemed to be his tightest friends; he wasn't as at ease with others but she knew the same could be said about her. *Maybe that's why we're friends.* By unspoken mutual consent they'd dismissed their moonlit snuggle aboard the Circle Line. *Just friends*.

Milton piled lamb onto his pita bread. "Regina's from down there. Can't she help you look? That is if her folks are speaking to her again."

"Her dad took it better than her mom, but it's been almost a year. Even Mrs. Foster's head has stopped spinning."

"I knew that Ty guy was no good for her as soon as I heard he was a dropout."

"Regina says she's happy, and you know what, it's her life." Carmen picked up her burger, put it back down. "She has the right to mess it up if she wants to."

"But most of us don't, not if we can help it. Are you done with that burger?"

Carmen passed him her plate. "Look around you, Milton. I bet if you asked, half the people in here have messed up at some point or other."

"Some things you can't help." Milton gestured with a French fry. "Most people don't screw up on purpose, like a certain Ms. Foster. It's fate or—I don't know, but you'd do anything to change it, make it different. You just can't."

Carmen wasn't quite sure what he was talking about. She shrugged. "I guess I'll ask her to show me around, but I wish she wasn't acting so weird. Like last Tuesday, I was chopping onions, for Jewell's etouffee, you remember? Regina walks in while Jewell and I are talking about graduation, then all of a sudden, she left. Poof! Outta there."

"You two are graduating. She's not."

"Gimme a break, Milton. She's doing what she wants."

"Don't be surprised if she keeps acting funny," Milton said.

A week later, Carmen remembered Milton's words during her fact-finding sojourn with Regina. The day turned into a covert battle, Regina against her parents, with Carmen caught in the middle as decoy. Like when Al praised Carmen for getting into medical school, Regina added, "I thought *finishing* was the big deal."

The major affront came before Regina and Carmen ever left the Fosters' house. Regina had just backed her hand-me-down Honda out of the garage when Lonnie waved to stop them. "I don't know why I didn't think of this sooner. Maybe you won't even like it, Carmen, but we have this apartment over the garage. Nothing fancy, but we'd be happy to have you—free of charge. Come on up and I'll show you." Lonnie headed upstairs.

"The holding cell. That's just perfect—the Foster way. Nice and neat and tied with a bow." Regina pulled her keys out of the ignition. "Here ya go. You'll need these. And I'm never coming back here to live, so be my guest." She tossed them to Carmen.

They landed in her lap. "I don't drive," Carmen snapped.

"You're kidding. Something you can't do?" Regina pretended shock. "It's a requirement for life in the boonies."

"If you got a problem with this, just say so, all right?" Carmen turned to look squarely at Regina. "It's a place to live, and free means one less thing I gotta figure out how to pay for." *Not that you'd know anything about that.*

"No problem." Regina motioned toward the steps. "No problem at all. After you." *Gets me off the hook. Mom will have somebody else's life to run.*

Carmen dropped the keys on the seat and followed Lonnie, leaving Regina to stew in her own juices. The holding cell suited Carmen perfectly and Lonnie was happy for a reason to fix up the small apartment, telling her, "The boys never cared how it looked."

After lunch Regina and Carmen made up enough to go for a driving lesson. Once they got the seat adjusted so Carmen's feet touched the pedals, she took to the road like a pro. "Figures you'd be good at this too," Regina mumbled.

Jewell's plans for the future were the next to fall into place—at least the immediate future. "Aw, come on! Let's be vagabonds for the summer. My graduation present to us."

"Some of us haven't *earned* our degrees," Regina said.

"But we've all learned a lot in four years," Jewell countered. "Come on! We can start out in Paris, rent a convertible and drive the Grand Corniche." She traced her finger along the road from Nice to Monaco on the map she had spread across the kitchen table. "Who knows where we'll end up—Madrid, Rome…" Vivian's hopes to the contrary, Jewell hadn't reconsidered and rehired her as manager. She had also postponed her return to Tinseltown and was heading for Europe—post-graduate study, she called it. A chance to immerse herself in the art that had compelled her to minor in art history. And although she had majored in philosophy, all that critical thinking hadn't helped her keep the past from leaking into whatever she did, whatever she felt. She expected her trek to provide her with surprises, but none of them would involve *Fly Girl*, or Billy, or the empty place where her daughter had been, the place she worked so hard to fill. What she wanted most was to find a way to make peace with her mistakes. It had been four years and she could still hear Vivian's warning, "Running away won't change anything." And here she was leaving again.

Jewell looked eagerly from Regina to Carmen. "It'll be fun."

"What is this fun you keep talking about?" Carmen joked. "I think I'm allergic. And I have way too much to do to be ready, because the next four years *really* count."

"I love a gift as much as the next girl, but I'll pass this time." Regina drained her wine cooler, went to the fridge for another. "July Jam is coming up. Ty and I have strategizing to do for fall." She also had to prove to them, to her parents and to herself that she hadn't trashed her life.

"Be that way." Jewell folded her map, looked at Regina. "So what will you do about Five D? You'll be the only one here." Jewell hated to ask—she wasn't ready to hear that the home she'd grown accustomed to was about to dissolve.

For the first time Regina realized she'd be the only one left. "It'll do for now. I mean, I'm really only here to sleep, eat and…"

"We know what *and* is." Carmen looked at Jewell then Regina, then they all laughed.

Regina took a swig of her cooler. "At least somebody is getting some *and*."

"I'll leave you a check for my part of the rent for six months—"

"Six months? I thought you were going for the summer."

"But what happens if I meet a handsome prince who needs a consort or a tragic artist who can't paint without my patient inspiration?"

Carmen and Regina eyed each other. "Spare us."

Graduation morning, Regina was the first up. She knew Lonnie and Al were aware of the date and had sent their best wishes to Jewell and Carmen. *Screw 'em.* As usual, Vivian was at the Stanhope and Jewell didn't know what to do with her until she got back on her plane for LA. *Screw her too.* Carmen had given one of her tickets to the ceremony to Mac and one to Regina. Milton got one too because Columbia's commencement wasn't until the next day and it was only fitting he be there. Milton was still one of the gang, but Regina didn't know where she belonged, so for once she was the first one dressed. "I'll meet you. I'll be the one without the cap and gown."

Regina spent most of the morning wandering Thirty-fourth Street, looking at stuff she didn't want and buying stuff she didn't need, trying to keep any doubts about her own decisions in shadow. She almost blew off the ceremony—even came up with an excuse—but the longer she wandered, counting her successes, repeating her plans, the stronger she became in her conviction that leaving school had been the right choice—for her. So, too many shopping bags later, she stopped at Prof's to lighten her load until after the ceremony and to have a quick glass of wine. She was surprised to see Red behind the bar. "Glad you stopped in. I have something to tell you," he said. That's when the day that had gone from bad to better, went directly to worse.

The May afternoon was pristine and the sun shone high and bright over Lehman Lawn. Billowy clouds floated in a sky so blue it looked like a painted backdrop. Carmen found her place in line and fidgeted with the black-and-gold emblem below the collar of her dove gray gown until Jewell, in line on the opposite side, caught her eye.

"Where is she?" Jewell mouthed.

Carmen scanned the crowd in front of Barnard Hall and shrugged. Milton was easy to find, already snapping away with his camera, but Regina was nowhere to be seen.

When the processional began Carmen and Jewell found each other again and they each recalled a thousand back-when moments and what-if hopes given voice around their kitchen table in 5D. They were poised at the starting line of the rest of their lives, but where was Regina?

The ceremony was a blur of presentations, speeches, coronets and flourishes, culminating as they were instructed to flip their tassels from right to left. The Class of '85 was dismissed in a cacophony of squeals and shouts, leaving Carmen and Jewell to find each other. They stood hugging, a study in contrasts. Carmen, on tiptoes despite her black patent pumps, still looked tiny next to Jewell. Tall and short, light and dark, rich and poor. Parallel lives whose paths had crossed. Before the sentiment spilled over, they broke apart just as Vivian came up to join them.

"Have you seen Regina?" Jewell asked her mother.

"Right here." Regina popped through the crowd. "You did it!" She dove in for a three-way hug.

Both Jewell and Carmen noticed Regina's red-rimmed eyes and figured they knew why.

Milton appeared out of the crowd. "Now that's a picture! Stay right there!"

Regina broke from the group. "Just the graduates."

"Are you crazy?" Jewell said as Carmen dragged Regina back into the fold and Milton snapped away. "You belong right here!"

"I don't know where I belong." Regina took a deep breath and blurted, "Red sold Prof's." She didn't mean to dampen the day, but she had to say it out loud so she'd know it was real. "The building, the business. The new owners aren't interested in Fundays. I'm not even sure it's going to be a restaurant anymore."

"You've got other stuff. The boat ride, all your plans," Jewell said.

"Prof's was my steady. My cash cow. I counted on it to be there."

"I don't know if there's anything you can count on," Carmen said.

"We can count on each other," Jewell said. "Can't we?"

9

"...the wrong meat for this sandwich."

"Let's see, your spelling's good. Typing, fifty words a minute...with two errors." The woman flipped Regina's typing test over in her folder with one hand, took another bite of her sugar doughnut with the other. Lips smacking, she continued. "And you have two years at Barnard College. Hmm, I've heard of that. Where is it?" She looked at Regina over the application.

"New York. You know, part of Columbia University." *What hole did you climb out of?*

By October Regina had to face the fact she needed income to supplement her out-go. Jewell had called from Rome at the end of the summer to say she had stumbled on a gig as a semi-regular on an Italian TV variety show, singing, dancing, doing skits. "It's like *Ed Sullivan* meets *Saturday Night Live.* I'll hang out as long as I'm having fun." She sent rent for another six months, but Carmen was gone too, and unlike Jewell, Regina hadn't had any fortunate falls into a spot to replace Prof's, so it was time to take drastic measures.

She got hives thinking about a permanent J-O-B, but convinced that this was a temporary setback, Regina decided that applying at a temporary agency was the answer. That way she wouldn't owe anybody more than baseline competence in exchange for a check. She wouldn't be an actual employee—just a hired hand, on loan until Good Tyme Productions' next strategic move.

Regina scooched over on one hip, crossed her leg and tried not to snatch the application and rip it up. She was already losing her mind watching powdered sugar dust the front of H. Piedmont's cranberry boucle suit. *What does H stand for?* That was all the plaque on her desk said. *Helen? Hildegaard? Hortense? How can she stand this all day?* The flourescent light buzzed and blinked, casting the cubicle in shades of gray and grayer. Regina clasped her hands tightly, and pressed her lips over her teeth which was as close as she could come to a smile.

When Prof's first changed hands, Jewell said it was a sign that it was time to move on. Regina liked the sound of that. "Progress. A new challenge. Screw 'em." Her second annual July Jam went off as scheduled, but dreary weather meant that day-of-sail ticket buyers didn't materialize. Ty kept his customers satisfied, as usual, but he and Regina clashed over the new music he wanted to mix in. "They just rap 'cause they can't sing," Regina insisted. "Nobody wants to hear some fool talking over somebody else's record."

Ty argued otherwise. "The sound is fresh. You can keep listening to Lionel Ritchie and Michael Jackson if you want to, but I'm tellin' you there's a new sound goin' down."

Regina won that battle, but she just broke even. All summer she scouted for her new Funday Sunday headquarters, hoping she'd have a spot lined up by fall, but nobody was willing to cut her a deal that made her more than a paid hostess. "These are *my* people. I bring this crowd. What am I supposed to say, 'I'll just give you this money 'cause you seem like a nice guy'? Uh-uh. No way." Others turned her down, saying they didn't feel she would bring the "right element" to their establishment. She had a good idea what that meant. "Screw you and your elements too."

And the more she surveyed spots in Morningside Heights and near other campuses, the less she wanted to cultivate a new crop of college kids. "I am so past that," she told herself.

Last month, on the spur of the moment, while she was at Chez Prince trying out cinnamon hair color to spice up her life a little, Regina put out feelers with Felicia about a position at the station. Two days later, Felicia called about a special promotions job that was open. Regina decided the call was confirmation that continuing to go to the pricey salon was a smart business decision. She went on three interviews, was sure she had the job, even convinced herself it was a good career move. She could add another texture to her entrepreneurial résumé. But at the last minute they decided to hire from within—someone with a marketing degree. Ouch.

"I'm sure we can keep you busy," H. Piedmont finally said. "Do you do Dictaphone? Let's say you do Dictaphone. You're a smart girl. You'll catch on." She handed Regina a stack of vouchers. "Whatever we get by Friday, you'll have on Tuesday. We may call you, if not check in every day before eight A.M. and after five P.M. and we'll give you an assignment if we have one."

Regina felt sick in the pit of her stomach when she walked out. She hadn't had an office job since the summer before freshman year when she worked at her dad's company, supposedly typing and filing, but actually socializing with the other summer help. *Four years and I'm not past go*. She spun through the revolving doors and onto Madison Avenue, the dreary part below 42nd Street where grimy buildings blocked the sun. Waiting for the bus she watched pedestrians scurry like ants in a glass colony, hating the fact that she was about to join their ranks.

And the outlook at 5D was no brighter. Without Jewell or Carmen around, the apartment seemed depressing. Regina even found herself missing old Hemp. *Maybe I'll call Ty*. But the phone was ringing when Regina opened the door. She ran into her room, hopped over the pile of clothes that hadn't made it to the Soap-n-Suds. *Goodwin, Peale, Burris Associates*. She scribbled the name and address on the back of an envelope. "Eight forty-five? In the morning?"

Regina arrived at 8:40, which she considered a major hardship. She thought it might be a law firm, but the receptionist chortled. "They'd like to think so, but we do collections, dearie." She ushered Regina into the inner sanctum, rows and rows of putty green metal desks, all facing the rear wall, with one desk in the teacher's position up front. *This is a sick joke. I end up in an office that looks like a classroom*. At all but two of the desks, people sat reading newspapers, writing checks, eating bagels, using their last bit of personal time before the company day began.

"Teresa, here's your next victim." The receptionist delivered Regina to the woman at the head of the class who had ash blond bouffant hair and stumps of nails that she had chewed raw.

Before Regina could introduce herself she heard a rustle behind her as each worker put on a headset, settled a stack of printouts in front of them and started dialing their phones.

"You don't expect me to…"

"No, you won't have client contact. I have paperwork for you, but if you pay attention you could move up. We're short one collector. A few of these folks started as temps."

And they didn't have sense enough to escape?

Teresa settled Regina into one of the vacant desks, plopped an industrialsized box of envelopes and a ream of pre-printed letters in front of her. "These are first notices. You fold them so the address sticks out of the window, like this." Teresa creased her page with machine-like precision. "Once these are done, I'll show you how to use the quick licker and the postage meter."

I can hardly wait. By lunch Regina felt like she'd folded the prints off her fingertips and she'd overheard all manner of threats, tirades and reprimands. After her half-hour break she was treated to more. *Don't they ever lighten up?* There was little conversation, only the occasional, "You'll never believe the load of crap I just heard." By the end of the day she was punch drunk and couldn't get out of Camp Strong Arm fast enough.

Bursting to vent about her day, the moment Regina got home, she poured a glass of chardonnay and dialed Carmen's number. Regina had gotten into the habit of waiting for Carmen to call, otherwise when she came to the phone she always sounded like she'd been dragged out of surgery or something. But tonight Regina didn't care what she was interrupting. "It was so hideous. All they do for eight hours is yell at people."

"Welcome to the real world."

Thank you Dr. Superior. It wasn't exactly the response Regina was looking for. She rolled her eyes, took a drink.

"I used to take abuse at the store, but some of my professors now are way worse. They have no problem calling you an idiot in front of the entire class. I still study all night, and so far I'm on top of the work. Your mom is great. She leaves me care packages, keeps me fed—"

"Oops, doorbell. Must be Ty. Gotta go," Regina lied. She didn't want to hear another episode of *Gidget from the Ghetto Goes to Med School*. Part of her had enjoyed getting Carmen situated in New Jersey—teaching her how to drive, where to shop, the shortcuts and back ways, where the good stations were on the radio. She liked being the guide, the one in the know. But some days Carmen was too good of a student. She'd adapted a little too well to the life Regina worked so hard not to live, and Lonnie and Al were soaking it up. *Screw 'em all.* Regina hung up, flipped on the tube, sipped her wine and dreaded the sound of her alarm clock.

By Thursday she was really up for her outing with Ty, but when she reached him at the record store, he sounded mysterious. "Uh—something came up. I can't hang tonight." She asked why, but he didn't give up any details. "If it works out, I'll let you know," was all he said and she hung up, mad without knowing exactly at what. *Screw him. He's not my boyfriend.*

"Was that a personal call?" Teresa appeared at Regina's desk as soon as she put down the phone.

"Yeah. I needed to check with my…"

"Phones are for business use only. Any personal matters are to be taken care of outside on breaks. We can't tie up the lines."

Are you crazy? "I was just on a minute." Regina fed envelopes into the postage meter and sulked about Teresa's reprimand which gave her something to chew on besides how much she missed Ty and the way their weekly Funday Sundays had given shape to her week, to her life: designing the flyer, updating her mailing list, visiting her record stores and student lounges, strategizing with Ty. All that activity kept her busy, excited, in the mix. And all day Sunday she'd have the delicious feeling that something was coming and she couldn't wait to see what. Each week was a new performance and she was the director, setting the stage, moving the pieces, making it happen. But her show had been canceled and now all she felt was the windowless room shrinking around her. She wanted to bolt for the door.

Angela, one of the collectors, a munchkin-sized redhead with a pixie haircut stopped by Regina's desk with a stack of second notices for her to send out. Her back to Teresa's desk she whispered, "She's just pissed 'cause she wishes she had somebody to call." They shared a smirk. "Ladies' room. Five minutes," she said.

Regina left her desk first, got the key from the receptionist. Angela followed right behind and they marched down the hall together.

"I swear, sometimes I want to stand on my desk and do a strip tease just to see if anybody would notice." Angela examined her lips in the mirror.

"Maybe if you were making a personal call at the same time," Regina answered.

"Anyway, me and a couple of girls from the building are going to this networking thing at the Limelight tonight."

"What kind of networking?" It woke Regina right up.

"You know, who are you? Whatdya do? Wanna screw? Oops, did I say that? I meant to say, are there any opportunities at your firm?" Angela freshened her matte raisin lips. "They do 'em every week. If I make a connection to another company, great, 'cause I sure as hell don't plan to do this forever. Mainly I'm trying to meet somebody besides the stiffs who work here."

"I'm down for that," Regina said. *After work parties—right up my alley.*

Once Regina and the girls walked through the doors of the deconsecrated church, they joined the others looking for love and dressed for success. At first she stayed with the group, talking about dead-end jobs, idiot bosses, but after a while she strolled to the bar, ordered a glass of champagne because she saw someone else with one and it looked so elegant.

The formerly sacred setting gave Regina the creeps, but the more she roamed around, the more it reminded her of a Funday. Same early time slot; same bar mini-meat: chicken wings, Swedish meatballs, cocktail weenies. Music played, but not deafening so you could dance or talk. She fielded the occasional inquiry, was bought a drink by a guy who was way too impressed that he was a stockbroker trainee.

"I can make you a very rich woman one day," he said.

"I intend to do that for myself," Regina replied and sailed off across the room.

Regina counted heads, checked out the bar activity, felt that excited zip. *I can do this*. She just had to figure out where. She breezed home with her new idea, but the wind left her sails when she got to the empty apartment. *Man, it used to be fun living here*. And then there was one. She tried Ty on Friday but he wasn't home. *Where the hell is he?* She knew he had a gig on Saturday; a club in his neck of the boonies. The week before he had talked about picking her up so she could see it, see him, but he didn't call and she didn't either.

Mercifully, her Goodwin, Peale, Burris assignment was over because she couldn't stomach another week of envelope stuffing and debtor abuse. Regina fell asleep on the lounge that night—somehow it didn't feel as lonely there as it did back in the little bedroom. And she was surprised when Ty called early on Sunday—before noon.

"I gotta come over. You gotta hear this."

Ty didn't offer any explanation for Thursday or Saturday, and although she thought about it, Regina didn't ask for one. She dressed, practicing her blasé attitude, but the buzzer touched off that old Sunday anticipation.

"That's new." Regina checked out his boxy gray shearling as he came in the door. His black jeans were baggier than usual. *What's this, the urban ranger look?* He had two twelve-inch records in plain white jackets in his hand.

"Yeah." Ty gave Regina a quick smooch, then ducked into her room, tossed his jacket on the bed and headed for her turntable. "Check this out." He placed a record on the spindle. "It would sound even doper with mega speakers."

What-er? "Who is it?" Regina figured it was some new release.

"The next superstar." He rocked his body in the rhythm before the first note.

Regina jumped as a riot of sound filled the room. "Damn, turn it down."

Ty adjusted the volume, some.

Regina knew the riff from a dance track, but there was a vocal laid over it, rhyming and signifying. "*Strong like Hercules. Gonna bring you to your knees. 'Cause he's the king of the street. With a rhyme that can't be beat. Rap-zilla*."

"'Rap-zilla'?!" Regina was about to crack up, but Ty stood there, eyes closed, reciting every word, seriously into it. That's when she realized, "That's you?!"

"Yeah. I been writin' on it. Went into the studio Thursday. This dude Victor who's always in the record store started his own label. Bad Attitude. He's gonna release it." Ty spoke in an excited rush, then continued rapping along. "Wait, this part is the joint!"

That's the stupidest thing I ever heard. Regina couldn't figure out what to say because Ty was clearly savoring his masterpiece. It was nothing like the music he played that first Funday.

"I laid down the turntable track, then rapped over it. The place went wild on Saturday…"

"You did this? In front of people?!"

"Hell yeah! Call myself Boney T." Ty grinned.

"Why?" Regina had so many questions, but she wasn't sure she wanted the answers.

"I like the sound. I might have to come out from behind the turntables, have somebody spin for me. It'll be hard to find somebody good as me, but the guys out front, that's who people know. That's who makes the bucks."

Regina felt like he was talking more for himself than for her. "How come you didn't tell me about this?" She didn't mean to sound that hurt.

"Yeah, well, it happened kinda fast." He looked past her at the door when he said it. "But this is gonna be big. I can feel it." Ty reached and pulled her close, rubbed her back.

Regina wasn't feeling it, wasn't feeling much besides annoyed.

"I brought you one. And one to get to your friend Felicia, up at the station—"

"To play? On the radio?" Regina looked at him sideways.

"Hell yeah. I'm not plannin' to stack 'em in my basement for souvenirs. We got a few now. My store is already playin' it. We get more by the end of the week. Then we're gonna hit the record shops, clubs, radio stations. I figured you know the chick, so you could slide it to her."

Why would I do that? "Yeah. Okay." Suddenly the room seemed much too small.

"Don't act like you doin' me no favor," Ty said.

"It's not that, Ty." *How do I say this?* "Or is it Boney T? What am I supposed to call you?" Regina mustered a smile. She did not want to fight. She needed a taste of the old juice.

Ty started the record again. His eyes widened and he assumed the monster pose. "Call me—'Rap-zilla.'" Regina pretended to be the helpless maiden, let him catch her.

Ty never spent much time in 5D, other than for their nocturnal activities. He wasn't a chitchat kinda guy and he had had very little to say to

Jewell and Carmen; the feeling was mutual. So it felt strange being with him in the daytime. Her blackout shade kept the room dark, but not night dark. Not dream dark. So Regina went along for the ride, looking forward to afterward, the part where they talked, so she could tell him about her new after-work scheme and make it seem real.

"I want to see who else does them. Start looking for a place to set up. And I'll be needing a DJ." Regina peeped over at him as they lay under the covers.

Ty was as enthusiastic about her news as she had been about his. "Yeah, uh, let me know." Ty fished his briefs from under the covers. "You got any juice or soda or something?"

"I don't know." Regina was annoyed at the abrupt dismissal. "Look in the fridge."

Ty padded down the hall and Regina found a shirt and leggings in the pile on the chair.

"*How come the empty container's in here?*" Ty's voice echoed from the open refrigerator.

"What difference does it make? I guess I'm out of juice. I wasn't exactly expecting you." She pulled on clothes and passed a brush over her hair so it wasn't standing all over her head. When Ty had to be out by dawn, she never worried what she looked like after. He was just gone.

"You know, the place looks worse than when three a y'all lived here. Don't you ever clean up?" He appeared in the doorway drinking water from a mug.

"What difference does it make to you?" Regina snapped. "You don't live here."

"I heard that."

Ty was gone in minutes, and Regina poured a glass of wine to quiet the argument that was still raging in her head. *He never said two words about what it looked like in here when he was making his midnight stopovers*. And a second glass to dampen her disappointment. *Hope he's over this Boney T phase in a hot damn hurry*.

Two weeks later she still had both of Ty's records in her room. She had a chance to make the handoff, but how could she push it to Felicia if she wasn't convinced herself? Ty didn't seem to notice, but then she'd only spoken to him once since he came by. He called all excited to tell her "Rap-zilla" had been playing on Mr. Magic's Rap Attack, a show that aired on Saturdays in the middle of the night. *Where it belongs*. Regina promised to listen, but never did.

Weeks slid by in a blur of 9 to 5 boredom. Regina typed medical malpractice deposition transcripts, tracked orders for a manufacturer of no-name maxi pads, even returned for a repeat performance at Goodwin, Peale where Teresa offered to hire her. "You're kidding, right?" *I am not that hard up*. That made her twice as determined to find a home for her networking nights. She checked out as many others as she could find. Some were stuffy—aggressive handshaking, background sniffing, serious suits and ties—on the men and the women—and fierce competition to collect and pass out the most business cards. Most were more sociable, but she noticed a severe shortage of black attendees and knew this was opportunity's way of making temping worthwhile. She even phoned around to contacts she'd made when they were undergrads to test out her theory. Now these folks were in the workplace—professionals ready for a spot to congregate and make connections—business and social. Someplace adult, classy, with music to complement the conversation because nobody wanted to sweat up a $400 suit doing the hustle. So Regina's mission was to create the buppie place to be and see, but by November she'd approached club and restaurant owners from SoHo to Harlem, and Good Tyme still wasn't rolling.

So Regina's holidays were anything but merry. For the first time in her life she had no vacation during the festive season. She worked the days before and after Thanksgiving and Christmas which at least meant her visits home weren't long enough to disturb the fragile peace she'd reached with her mother. They did give her a glimpse of how well Carmen fit right in—chatting with neighbors about her first term in med school, discussing the side effects of some new drug with her father, complimenting her mother's new cranberry-pecan stuffing. Regina thought it was good too. *But not all that*. Regina and Carmen spoke in bite-sized generalities—about how things were at 5D, or whether it looked like snow. They left out the meat of their new situations, offering up nothing that was too hard to swallow.

Jewell sent them both lustrous Italian leather handbags for Christmas, with a note saying she'd gotten the lead in a whodunit and that she was still unsure of her return. *Great. Dr. Carmen, healer of the sick, living at my house as the daughter my parents always wanted and Signorina Jewell, international movie star. What does that make me?* Regina washed down her annoyance with mulled wine and rum-spiked eggnog. When Carmen drove her to the train, the silences were filled mostly by the radio—Carmen had found a new station.

And to turn up the heat under Regina's simmering cauldron of doubt, Boney T had a bonafide hit. Ty had hinted he wanted to accompany Regina home for the holidays and for a moment she got a kick imagining her family sitting 'round the hearth, listening to "Rap-zilla," but she put him off. "I'm only going 'cause I have to."

"Well New Year's I'm on the bill at the Diplomat. You comin' to that?"

Regina wanted to say no, but she could hear it was a command performance. "As long as I can stay backstage with you." And just so she couldn't forget, she was reminded of the upcoming event every time she passed the streetlight on the corner, with the SLAMMIN' HIP HOP NEW YEAR'S poster, FEATURING "BONEY T" stapled around it.

New Year's Eve, Ty was ready for liftoff. "We gon' knock it out tonight! You hear me!" Dressed in his signature silver and black, with two thick silver chains around his neck, Ty sat in the passenger seat, his arm wrapped around Regina's shoulder; his record store coworker and sometime assistant, Nut, at the wheel. "Now this is the kind of thing you should be promotin'. One night. A couple thousand people. We could make a killin'."

We? "It's not my thing." Regina, wedged in the middle, felt like the wrong meat for this sandwich, and it didn't get better when they got to the hotel. There were six acts, and not nearly enough space backstage for everybody's equipment and entourage. Regina sized up the girls with multicolor metallic marcels or butt-dusting braids, wearing gold door-knockers and baggy clothes or very skimpy ones. They checked out Regina's blown-straight bob, red sequined tank and black chiffon skirt and sent out, "who does she think she is?" attitude. Men in droopy pants, side-turned caps and tongue-flapping sneakers sans laces, "yo-yo'ed" and slapped five in greeting.

She stuck close to Ty as they mingled in the crowd of people passing forty ounces of malt, and paper cups of gin, vodka and Courvoisier. In shady corners, you could find whatever else you had the head, or nose, for. And it was loud—sound checking, music blaring, bass pounding so hard Regina thought the building would come down. Ty was like a kid with an open pass to Disney World. After a while Regina got bored with tagging along so she got a split of champagne and a straw, found a spot on a beat-up couch, crossed her legs and put on a "do not disturb" face.

Ty went on as midnight approached. By then the crowd was rowdy, hopped up on hard-edged sound. "Rap-zilla" went over big. Regina peeked from the wings and saw the crush of people at the foot of the stage, spotlit faces bobbing in time, rapping along, gazing up at Boney T. Ty looked different onstage—bigger, rougher, rawer. And when he came off he was pumped full of their frenzy, swollen with it, sweat dripping, body twitching. "You see that?" He lifted Regina, bounced her like a baby which was as close as she came to joining him in orbit this night, but he seemed too far out there to notice. "This is gonna be the year, Regina, you watch. This is it."

She felt it too. She just wasn't sure they meant the same thing. When he put her down, Ty's wet heat clung to her, marked her. For Regina, the best part of the night was counting out the old year because she was too through with it. She answered Ty's root beer and orange tinged midnight kiss with tight lips.

"Somethin' the matter?" he asked.

Everything. "Nothing. I got a headache," she said.

"Oh." Ty was stoked for the night to continue. "'Cause I was thinkin' we could drive my stuff back to the house. There's this after-hours spot…"

"I need to go home," Regina announced.

"Come on, baby, it's New Year's, and it's a big night for me." Ty draped his arm around her, massaged her shoulder. "I wanna celebrate…"

"I'm not stopping you." She pulled out of his reach.

"You ain't exactly soundin' happy for me neither—" Ty stepped back "—actin' all funny."

"You're doing what you gotta do, so I'm happy for you, see." She turned up the corners of her lips with her fingers. "You want me to jump up and down?"

"Not unless you're feelin' it. Though you might feel a little somethin' 'cause this is important to me, but that's okay." Ty caught Nut's eye from across the room, remembered what he and the boys had said, about Regina thinking she was too good. "Guess all this is not up to your standards and I don't wanna be the one to drag you down." The look that passed between them was cold as the dark side of the moon. "Yeah. I hear that."

Ty walked away, leaving Regina suspended between regret and relief. Before long he returned to say he had arranged for a car to take her home. And there was nothing more to say, so she turned and left.

New Year's Day, when the doorbell buzzed at noon she didn't answer. She knew it was him, but she wanted to be alone in the bed with her coffee and a whole 'nother 365 days to make her move. In a minute there was pounding on the door. She stomped down the hall and snatched it open. "Are you crazy? Making all that noise—"

"You mind tellin' me why all of a sudden you actin' all high and mighty?" Ty stormed in.

Regina rolled her eyes. "I don't know the words to 'Rap-zilla' so I'm high and mighty?"

"I thought we were partners. I help you, you help me—"

"*You* didn't want to be my partner if I'm not mistaken, so I got my own freakin' company. Now I'm glad since you're into this rap crap. It's not my thing." Regina could tell that hurt Ty. She meant it to. She folded her arms, tapped her foot impatiently trying to look blasé while her heart pumped like a jackhammer.

"Whoa, hold up." Ty leaned forward, like he hadn't heard her correctly. "You mean it's okay when we're doin' your thing, but mine's not good enough? Is that what you tellin' me?"

"Take it however you want Ty-rone." The look in his eyes made Regina want to cave but she was not about to back down.

"Yeah. I heard that." Ty grinned, but it wasn't a smile. "I thought we were goin' all the way, but it looks like I'ma have to get there without you." He walked past her and slammed the door so hard the walls shook.

Like I freakin' want to get where he's going? Regina switched from coffee to wine, sat on the lounge and looked out at her city. *I got places of my own to go. And this year I'll be traveling light.*

But winter melted into spring and Regina's only travels were to her temp assignments. Jewell, on the other hand, was getting around. "Why don't you come to Rome this summer? I'm renting a villa and I've got lots of room."

Because I have to pay the rent on this dump and find a way to afford my own damn villa. Regina had been sitting on the chaise, convincing herself she was right to turn down the latest job she'd been offered when the phone rang.

"I've got a little Fiat and we can bum around, get on the autostrade and go to Tuscany, stop in Venice on the way. There are a million gorgeous little towns on the drive north! We'd have so much fun!"

"The auto whata?" Regina asked, feeling like the country cousin too slow to keep up with her globe-trotting friend.

"Autostrade, the Italian freeway, except it's not free of course, and some of the drivers are crazy since there's no real speed limit, but I've learned how to stay out of their way! I'll call to set it up when we get back from Villefranche and—"

"Whoa, whoa, whoa. We?!"

Jewell lowered her voice. "Yes, *we*. His name is Gianni. He's getting dressed for dinner."

"Oh, so you like the foreign ones," Regina needled.

"No. I like the grown ones. Men, not students. I'll write you all about it. *Ciao bella*."

Carmen called to say she was working at a hospital for the summer. "Your mother told me you were born there."

Deliver me. Regina had toyed with resurrecting the July Jam, but it seemed like a step backward, especially after she saw Boney T on *Soul Train* with his new single "I Heard That." He also introduced a singer named Misha who had on a coppery red wig with bangs so long she could barely open her eyes, and a gold jumpsuit that fit like spray paint. He had produced her new single from Bad Attitude. Regina turned off the set while Misha was saying how grateful she was for the opportunity. *Bet she shows it too.*

By mid-summer Regina had become proficient at typing correspondence and benefits claims in the human resources department of an insurance company, her latest short-term trick. She had also gotten acquainted with a spot called DeVille which was down the block on 39th Street. She'd gone there for lunch with some of the staff on their payday and liked the decor-sleek, with an ebony-stained circular bar, buttered-rum banquettes and mirrors galore. From every seat you could watch the goings on across the room, down the bar—perfect for networking. She liked the location too. It was accessible from points east, west, north and south. DeVille served a crowd at lunch, mostly garmentos from nearby showrooms, but she made it her business to stop after work on Thursday, and a few mimosas later found there wasn't much going on. She also learned the owner's name was Reuben Kelso and that the best time to talk to him was after lunch.

The next day Regina arranged to take a late lunch and, uncharacteristically, she was too nervous to eat all morning. At a quarter to three when she walked in DeVille a few tables still picked at plates, lingered over coffee.

"Sorry angel, lunch is over."

Regina had seen the host before. She'd decided he must have been a jockey who'd hung up his silks, although he still wore a swirl of color tucked in the pocket of his black blazer. *That jacket would fit Carmen.* "I'm looking for Reuben Kelso."

"Does he know you're coming?"

"No. I was hoping to catch him. I have a business proposition I'd like to discuss," she said.

"Hmm. A proposition from a pretty girl. Today must be my day." With one small hand on his waist, he made slight bow. "You're looking at him, at least what there is."

Regina was surprised, but she went with the flow and bowed back. "Regina Foster."

"Let me see, have you got some new, exotic liqueur that will be the next wave in after-dinner drinks, or maybe a praline cheesecake that will make me think I've died and gone to dessert heaven?" A chuckle bubbled just beneath the surface of Reuben's voice. His head was shaved clean, and Regina figured he was somewhere between fifty and a hundred and two.

"You look like an intellectual man. What I have is a concept." Regina played along.

"Then let's go put our heads together." Reuben showed her to a table in the back. Busboys cleared the last dishes, and servers hurried out after their shift while Regina explained her idea.

Reuben listened intently. "So you take the three martini lunch, add women's lib and take it after hours. I get it."

"And I know lots of people who get it. I've been collecting them for years." Regina realized she felt hungry which meant this was going well.

"'For years' she says. What are you, twelve?" Reuben quipped.

"A little older, but that's about when I figured out I like people and parties."

"You and me both. And speaking of people—what kind of crowd are we talking? I don't want headaches. My head is too soft and old for headaches."

"People like me. Smart, funny, charming. And even a few men to keep us company."

"Ugh. Men. You had to go and spoil it." They laughed. "Okay angel, I'm with you so far. What song are you singing about the do re mi?"

This was always the hard part, but Reuben didn't blink when she laid out their splits. They talked about the numbers of people she brought in the past, his overhead for the evening.

"If you can get people here on a Thursday night—that's a miracle."

Regina floated out feeling ravenous, and making mental notes about DJs to call.

There was so much to do to get ready for her DeVille debut that Regina stayed in perpetual motion. She moved her desk into Carmen's old room and got a hundred-foot phone cord so her hotline could move too. She went to every party she could get herself invited to and some she wasn't, anything to get the word out that a new, sophisticated kind of gathering was coming to Thursdays. She stopped by all the businesses she had worked for, left flyers with them as well as in any other office where the receptionist was accommodating. Fortunately, the insurance company had a liberal policy on personal calls. As long as she got her work done, nobody cared how much time she spent on the phone. Regina sent postcards for her Thursday Network

Hook-up, made sure everybody at the radio station was invited, because this had to work.

On the first Thursday in September Regina booked herself out with the agency; she was only working for Good Tyme Productions that day. She touched bases with Reuben. "I'm ready for you, angel. You and maybe a couple hundred of your closest friends."

It was a long day in 5D with no one to model her wardrobe choices for so they could take a vote. No one to tell her the night would be a success. She started dressing early, so she'd have time to do her makeup and put on false lashes the way Jewell used to do it for her. After three attempts she nixed the lashes, decided on the red jacket with the nipped-in waist, short black skirt and killer pumps—red on the arch side of both shoes, black on the outside. She added big, golden disk earrings with jet centers to complete the look, gave herself the thumbs-up, then tucked business cards, flyers and her new Roster, a Lucite clipboard with attached pen into her portfolio.

"If they all look like you I may do this every night." Reuben greeted her in his usual dapper uniform. Together he and Regina supervised rearranging the tables to provide more flow space. They sat at the bar, drinking wine. "It's a calmative, I always say. Good for the digestion and the disposition," Reuben advised.

The white roses Regina had ordered to sit up front next to The Roster, arrived at four. And her DJ arrived shortly after that, set up in the back, asked if there was anything in particular she wanted him to play. *That's how it's supposed to be.*

The first guests arrived a little after five—Angela and some of the girls from her first Limelight night. Regina ushered them in, asked the bartender to make her a drink. "Something cute." *And quick.* Because starting over made her more nervous than starting from scratch. Once she heard the DJ she settled down. He played good grooves, with a mellow edge. The way Ty *used* to. *No time for that now.* As people came in they tuned right in to the sound. Regina stayed busy meeting, greeting, directing traffic, keeping the atmosphere loose. Busy enough not to hear the music, because it used to be so much more than background.

Some people who showed up were from her college days, even a few from high school who had moved to the city. Some were told by friends of friends, others she had never met at all. They just saw the flyer and thought it was a good idea. Reuben had been telling his regular customers as well, and some of them stopped by to give the night a try, so there was a stew, a gumbo of New Yorkers, looking to spice up their lives.

Regina missed running over to Jewell or Carmen for moral support, or to tell a funny story. Missed seeing Ty, feeding off his energy. But she'd check in with Reuben, who was doing plenty of mingling on his own.

"Now, you really are my angel. Look at this place."

Regina glowed, the mirrors magnifying her success. If she did this right, she could retire from her temp career, but for once she wanted to go slow, make sure her next Network Hook-up was even bigger and that required work—and planning time. She sipped her daiquiri. "Same time next month?" And this time, her success would be even sweeter.

10

"I don't need nobody rockin' my boat."

March 4, 1988
Franklin Park, NJ

"Somehow I never imagined you in the driver's seat." Milton folded himself into the car beside Carmen, leaned over and kissed her cheek. "I mean of a car. Your feet touch the pedals?"

Unlike their lip collision aboard the Circle Line, this time the kiss was gentle, careful, like she imagined a brother's kiss would be—if Z had been a kissing kind of brother. "Are you kidding? If this doctor thing doesn't work out, I'm gonna be an Indy driver." Carmen gunned the engine and they laughed at the anemic sputter of the old car. One of the things she liked most about the burbs was relaxing in her own private capsule on the drive to the hospital instead of fighting for space and air on an overpacked subway. She had even browsed car showrooms, sat behind the wheel and talked to salespeople about the options. The new models sat different, smelled different, came off the assembly line shiny and in the color of your choice, and although she knew she was a few years' worth of paychecks from a new ride, it would be a symbol she'd made a clean getaway from her old life and was on the road to a new one.

"What's with the lip?" Carmen asked. Milton had grown a thick, shiny mustache since Carmen had last seen him. And for once he didn't look like he got dressed in the closet. His pants were still brown corduroy, but they were tailored with cuffs and pleats and under his buttery brown leather bomber she could see that his tan ribbed sweater hugged his chest. He looked slimmer than before so she figured his metabolism was still working overtime because she was certain he still ate whatever was in his path. This was the first time she'd noticed the angles in his face, the squareness of his jaw, that he was actually—cute. *It's just Milton.*

"I think facial hair makes me look older, more commanding." He buckled his seat belt.

"Just fuzzier, Milton. Just fuzzier." Johns Hopkins wasn't that far away, but in the last three years Carmen and Milton had only snatched conversations whenever they could get their timing synched up. First year during Gross Anatomy they shared survival tactics, like remedies for getting the formaldehyde funk off your clothes, and out of your hair. Since then they had compared professors, complaints, procedures they'd gotten to perform and bad doctor jokes—but it was hard to believe this was the first time they'd seen each other in the flesh since college graduation. Carmen hadn't realized how regular and familiar he'd become until he wasn't around. Milton was the bridge between her personal and professional lives and she missed him—and the craziness of 5D. Competition was too stiff to get up close and personal so med school had only netted Carmen colleagues with whom she studied or practiced splints and sutures.

She caught up with Regina once a month or so but the calls were usually exasperating. Carmen couldn't understand why Regina didn't grow up, realize that life wasn't a nonstop party and finish school or at least get a real job. Regina swore her Network Hook-ups had been going great but Carmen knew Regina would cut off her own nose and somebody else's to prove a point if she had to, and she seemed determined to make partying her life's work. Jewell wrote regularly and Carmen looked forward to her letters. Her exploits were better than fairy tales because they were real.

Milton's visit was unexpected, especially mid-semester. Even though she'd just be coming off her second week of back-to-back twelve-hour-plus shifts, when he said he'd be in New York for a couple days and asked if she could squeeze him in, she found the time.

"You look great. This medical school thing obviously agrees with you," Milton said. Carmen wore no makeup, but she looked bright eyed, with no raccoon rings. Lonnie had cajoled her into a beauty shop visit every other month so Carmen's hair was longer and thicker than ever. "Feel like a doctor yet?" he asked as they merged into traffic.

"There are moments when my lab coat is fresh, and I make a call my resident missed, or on grand rounds when I know the symptoms and progress of some obscure disease you see once in your career, that I feel like Carmen Webb, M.D. The other seventy-five percent of the time I could be the janitor. I've cleaned up enough puke to last a lifetime."

"As long as I keep from wearing it, I'm having a good day." He shifted in his seat, trying to find room for his long legs.

Before long Carmen pulled into the driveway. "I love it here, Milton, have from the first day, the trees, the birds, the quiet." The studio was just her size, her first private oasis, and Lonnie had helped her make it cozy. All of her things were exactly where she left them when she came home. She didn't have Regina's mess and unauthorized "borrowing" to contend with. Or even the swooping trills of Jewell's vocal exercises. For once she was in control. "Living out here made me realize the pace in New York is brutal. Here it's like a thirty-three rpm album and all I ever knew were forty-five's. Nobody ever told me there *was* another speed." She slammed the car door. "The good news is that for once I don't feel like I have to kill myself to keep up. And just between you and me, sometimes I feel a step or two ahead."

"That's the spirit." Milton crunched across the gravel behind her.

"Regina thinks I'm nuts, but I'm planning to turn in my subway tokens."

"Don't miss the old hustle bustle?"

"Puh-leez! The best thing I did was get out alive and I'm not going back—not to live, not to practice, not if I can help it." Carmen dusted her hands. "I am through." She trotted upstairs.

"Wow, lace curtains?" Milton tossed his jacket over a kitchen chair. "And flowers?"

"Picked 'em up on the way home. Sometimes I need a pretty booster." And white roses reminded her of the good times in 5D. At eight bucks a dozen they were still a splurge, but they gave Carmen hope that one day it would only be pocket change.

"Classy bachelorette pad." Milton made himself at home on the loveseat by the windows.

"Bachelorette pad? What is this, *The Dating Game*?" As soon as she said it Carmen felt flustered—she didn't mean it the way it sounded. "I mean, you're still terminally corny." She made a beeline for the kitchenette and got the casserole Lonnie had prepared into the oven. Until this moment, she'd never been alone with a man in a room with a bed in it. Studying didn't count. They had both been too focused on work to venture into extracurricular activities, but all of a sudden thinking of Milton as a man made her fidgety. "Anyway, what's up with you?" *Should I sit next to him, or does that mean more than sitting?* Randy, Z and his crew were the men she'd known and she wanted no part of that. Al and her dad were men too, but they were fathers—different species. And since she and Milton never spoke about their smooch on the boat, she didn't know where that fit or even if he remembered. He drank more beer that night than she'd seen him consume before or since. "What brought you to the city?" She walked to the window, straightened the curtains.

"I've made a few trips up before—quick ones so I didn't call or anything." He picked up her copy of *Grant's Atlas of Anatomy* from the coffee table, flipped through the extensively annotated pages. "I've got a couple of days this time and I wanted to see you while I—uh, while I have—I just wanted to make the time."

Carmen turned in his direction briefly, but decided to keep moving. "You want some coffee, ginger ale, orange juice—"

"You need to sit down. You're making me dizzy." He tapped the cushion beside him.

Carmen sidled up to the seat and slid back, hands folded in her lap. "Have you looked at cardiac surgery programs yet?" Career tactics seemed like a safe subject. "You Johns Hopkins people always get the match you want." She sat still when he draped his arm over the back of the sofa, his hand brushing her arm. *What the…? This is how it started on the boat.* And this felt just as confusing, although this time he was high-noon sober.

"Not always." He smiled and squeezed her shoulder. "At any rate, I've changed my mind."

His hand is still on my shoulder. "About what?" Carmen forgot her question. *Am I supposed to do something?* She had an urge she couldn't explain, an urge to be close, lean into his arm, to be touched. Other than the lathering and combing that went with her hairdresser visit every other month, Carmen went untouched, which hadn't meant anything until right now, but the ache was unmistakable. She let her hand slip from her lap, rest on the cushion, next to him.

"Becoming a surgeon."

"Oh." She felt light-headed with his hand on her arm, her pinkie touching his thigh.

"I'm looking at research fellowships." He crossed his leg in the opposite direction.

Carmen withdrew her hand as if she'd been burned then scratched her ear like she had a sudden, urgent itch. *Stupid move, Carmen.*

Milton didn't seem to notice. He released her shoulder, looked down at his lap and rubbed his palms against his pants legs like he was drying them.

She struggled to form an intelligible response out of the gibberish in her head. "Research? Why?"*—can't you get it through your head he just wants to be your friend?* "For as long as I've known you—"

"I'm tired of studying *to* be something." Milton stood. "I just want to *be* it and the surgery residency is endless." He jammed his hands in his pockets.

"It's not like you'd be twiddling your thumbs." She looked up at him, trying to figure out where this was coming from because her thoughts were too far in left field for her to handle right now. She needed to concentrate on something real to keep from crawling under the sofa. "Right now we're all sick of being students, but the end is near."

A slow smile spread over his lips. "Yep, it is, but plans change, priorities change." He walked to the bookcase by Carmen's desk. "There's important work being done with lesser-known cancers, in immunology. I can make a difference now instead of waiting around." He picked up a copy of *The Lancet*, fanned the pages. "Carmen—there's something I want to—"

"Smells like dinner's ready." *Don't spell it out so I feel like a total imbecile.* She headed for the oven.

Milton followed. "Did you ever want something to be one way, except it's the other, and no matter how much you want to change it, how hard you try, you can't?" His voice trailed off.

"Yeah. That's called life." Carmen lifted the dish out of the oven. "At least my life."

He shrugged. "Not just yours." He stood awkwardly, watching her set the table, get a bowl of salad out of the refrigerator.

She flitted busily in the small space, avoiding Milton's explanation and her embarrassment.

And then, like he'd flipped a switch to redirect the current, Milton changed the subject. "Hey, looks good. Jewell's Tuesday cooking rubbed off on you."

"Hardly. Regina's mom to the rescue." Carmen followed his lead and retreated to the safety of doctor talk and current events as they pushed Lonnie's turkey tetrazzini around their plates. *He must really be upset. He never leaves food.* Claiming fatigue and an early morning, Milton declined dessert and coffee and Carmen drove him to the station. They were saved from a clumsy good-bye when they heard the hoarse train whistle.

"I'll call you soon," and Milton ran for it.

Carmen saw him wave, mouth something else, but his words were swallowed by the rumble.

Like the rest of the crap I don't understand. At home Carmen cozied up with her confusion, squirming and twitching, unable to name or quiet her gnawing frustration. She replayed their conversations, berated herself for not recognizing the mirage before she dove in. And then she bundled up her jumbled emotions and dropped them overboard. *Later for this. My job is to figure out how to be a doctor. Anything else can wait.* And that included figuring out men. *Like I actually have time for a stupid social life.* After her shipwreck of a childhood, Carmen had managed to pilot her life raft into smooth water alone. *I don't need nobody rockin' my boat.*

After snatches of sleep Carmen woke to the sun slanting through the lace curtains, casting florets on the floor. Instead of bounding up, brewing coffee and heading to campus, the usual routine on her day off from the hospital, she burrowed deeper into the covers, unable to shake the weariness that came from a night spent dodging other pieces of personal debris that washed ashore with the unexpected storm. She shivered against the raw wind of her memories and pulled the crazy quilt up to her neck. Lonnie told her the patchwork riot of fabrics and shapes joined by delicate but sturdy stitches, had been made in Mississippi by her grandmother, Regina's great-grand, and passed down lovingly through the years. Carmen clutched the family heirloom, marveled at the hand-to-hand connection, one generation to the next. *You'll never have it so get over it.* And the tears came, mad, hurt tears that she fought to stop because they made her feel weak and vulnerable. Whatever she'd achieved in her life had come from her strength. Even at the hospital, the best compliment was, "Strong work," so there was no point going to pieces over something she never had. *I've got enough. Nobody gets it all.*

She spent the rest of the day in bed staring at old movies on the thirteen-inch black-and-white TV and nibbling last night's dinner out of the pan. The first Christmas she'd spent with the Fosters, she found out that you could miss something you never had, but where did that get you?

By the next morning she was back to speed, attacking her work with single-minded drive. Carmen felt almost at ease in the hospital. She pulled into her favorite parking space, all the way in the back, but right in line with the door to the doctor's entrance. She locked up, glanced at the sticker that granted her parking privileges in the doctor's lot, and smiled, then made her way through the rows of cars, sizing up the fancy and expensive ones, weighing which one she might choose when the day came. When she got an excellent evaluation at the end of her rotation she even called Milton, just so she knew she could speak to him again—as a friend.

My career, my reputation and the ability to take care of me. That is all I need.

11
"...time makes you more of who you are..."

January, 1990
New York, NY

"One-hundred-tenth Street between Adam Clayton Powell and Frederick Douglass." Jewell settled in the back of the taxi, remembering the first day she and Regina trudged down that street. *Wonder if the deli still has a red and yellow awning?* She held up a pack of Gitanes. "You mind?"

"Go right ahead." The driver held up his own pack in solidarity.

Jewell lit up, opened the window a crack and leaned back, anxious for the jagged skyline to come into view, excited to see Regina and Carmen because when she left New York she never intended to be gone four years. She never dreamed her European holiday would resurrect her career, not that she'd exactly call the work she'd done overseas acting. Vivian certainly didn't, but Jewell enjoyed her stint on *Settimana Divertente*, literally "Funny Week," the Italian TV show she'd done, as well as all the other projects that came her way.

Rome had been Jewell's first stop and she had planned to use the city as a base then hop around to explore Florence, and Venice. After all the togetherness in 5D it felt strange to be totally on her own, but Jewell had taught herself enough Italian to get by and she was enjoying her next solo flight. At first she thought the whispers and pointing when she strolled the strade were because they didn't see many blacks, but other black tourists didn't cause such commotion. Finally, one afternoon while sipping Limonata on the Piazza di Spagna the producer of *Settimana Divertente* introduced himself and asked if she was Jewell Prescott, star of "*Il Cuore di Papa*" which was what they called *Daddy's Girl* in Italy. Jewell didn't realize the show was still in syndication there, or that she looked enough like her preteen self to be recognized, but it explained the stares. The producer asked her to appear on his show, just like that. No audition, no urgent phone calls and negotiations, no meetings, no pressure, just an invitation. She could just hear what Vivian would say, about them taking advantage of her, about it being a giant step backward, but Vivian wasn't in charge anymore, and it was what Jewell wanted to do. She had seen the show in her hotel room and decided it would be a hoot. She knew they'd frown on it in LA, but who would know?

For her first appearance, Jewell sang "Last Dance" and did a zany skit involving a hapless waiter, a girl named Penny and too many orders of penne vodka. Apparently the audience enjoyed it and when she returned from Venice she had an offer to join the cast. Jewell was elated, like she used to be at the beginning of her career, when each job she booked felt like a victory to enjoy, not a booby trap that would explode if you didn't handle it just so. The show was performed live, but they promised she could have as flexible a schedule as she wanted and there were no marathon days or endless weeks. It was a great incentive to improve her Italian and she couldn't say no. So Claudio and Alberto, the producer and director, as well as the cast welcomed her with *apra i bracci*—open arms. They became her new family and for the second time in her life Jewell became a TV star, just on a much smaller, more manageable scale.

Not long after that, she began to get offered parts in the detective equivalents of Spaghetti Westerns. Jewell called them "tortellini thrillers." Vivian had been apoplectic when Jewell told her what she was doing—and when she figured out what lira converted to in dollars, she was through. "If I gave you a screenplay like that you wouldn't condescend to read it, but you're obviously hell-bent on trashing your career and your life. So be my guest."

Jewell was always the exotic actress/singer/dancer girlfriend of the male star, who got in trouble, either by accident or at the hands of a terrible villain. At the end of the movie, her character was either rescued safely or her savage death was avenged. They took about three weeks to make, the locations were inviting, and while they didn't stretch her as an actress, they showed her that she still had the chops, and without Vivian's carping and badgering, she had a good time. And this time her off-screen dalliance turned out just the way she wanted—light and sweet, with no bitter aftertaste.

"That it on the corner?" the driver asked.

"*Sí*—I mean yes." *Why does she still live here?* The old building looked grimy against the sky's January pallor. Sooty remnants of an old snowfall laced with wads of paper, chicken bones and other garbage clung stubbornly to the curb. *Maybe it's just the weather*. Her cheeks tingled in the crisp air and she pulled the fur of her collar up around her face. Mediterranean winters had been mild, and the blustery months had always been her least favorite in New York, but weather or not, it was time to come home and somehow Manhattan still felt more like home than LA did.

Although Jewell stopped sending rent two years ago, she thought 5D would feel like home too. So when Regina said she hadn't found a new roommate and her old room was just as she left it, Jewell decided living together again might be fun. At least for a while. She clutched the keys in her pocket, fingered the silver 5D, wondered if they still worked after so long.

"That's about a nice coat." The scrawny man appeared as suddenly and quietly as breath vapor in cold air and Jewell jumped. Bouncing on the balls of his feet, he blew into his cupped hands. "Lemme help you with them bags." He moved to grab her luggage.

"No!" Jewell yelled, now warmed by the fright.

The man darted forward but stopped short when he saw the cabby clutching a tire iron. "Bet. Somebody gon' take that shit offa your skinny ass anyway." He shuffled around the corner.

"You oughta be careful, Miss." The cabby lifted her bags. "People are crazy these days."

Welcome home. Jewell had to steady her hands, but the lock hadn't changed and in the lobby she was greeted by the aromas of cabbage and chlorine bleach, and by the afternoon shift of the Nosy Neighbor Patrol. She nodded as she walked by, ignoring the unmistakable buzz of conjecture in her wake. At the elevator she paid the driver, and tipped him generously for his help and protection. She was glad she'd arranged to have the rest of her things shipped later. Jewell was surprised at the graffiti now striping the walls—dirty rhymes, crude sketches of body parts, and a tag that read DIZZY D in letters that seemed to vibrate had been scrawled directly over the sign that read 924 PARKVIEW REAL ESTATE, INC. *That's new.* The inside of the car was decorated to match. Standing in front of 5D she decided against her key and drummed on the door.

"Who is it?"

"Bi-joux," Jewell sang.

The door flew open. "I can't believe you're really back!" Regina threw her arms around Jewell's neck in a hug worthy of an Olympic wrestler. When they unlocked she stroked the arm of Jewell's mink coat. "Look at you, glamour girl!"

"Look at you, Reg! Your hair is so—red." Auburn really. Jewell thought it was a little brassy. So was the hot pink sweater and leggings she wore. Regina had been naturally Kewpie Doll cute, but her look now was more contoured and tweezed, too much blush replacing her natural glow. But still, up until now Jewell didn't realize how much she'd missed her.

"A girl's gotta stay up to date." Regina patted the spiky top of her 'do. "Come on, come on. The party's not out here." She helped drag the suitcases inside, then grabbed Jewell's hand and led her toward the living room.

"What's up with the graffiti out there?" Jewell asked.

"New owners, new super, new attitude." Regina shrugged. "I stay so busy I don't pay it any attention. I make my phone calls, do my thing, then I'm in the wind."

"And this scary-looking guy tried to rip off my luggage, right by the cab." People had always looked at her a little differently in the neighborhood, but she hadn't felt threatened until now.

"That happens when you're a sta-aar, dah-ling." Regina's teasing had the hint of a bite.

On her trip down the hall Jewell noticed Regina's attempt at cleaning which meant the dishes were soaking in the sink, not piled all over the counter. She saw that Carmen's old bedroom had become Regina's office, but it was as messy as her room probably was—the door had been closed when they passed. Stacks of flyers, rolls of tickets, manila folders and legal pads surrounded an electric typewriter sitting on the bistro table that used to be in the kitchen; now it served as an extension of Regina's desk. Towers of magazines and newspapers stood halfway up the walls. The top half, covered with taped-on notes, invitations and ragged-edged articles, had become her bulletin board. The futon obviously served for sorting and collating, or at least those piles looked more organized than the others. *Reggie is still a mess.*

"The decor is pretty much the same," Regina said as they got to the living room. "Nobody here to do the housewifey shit anymore."

The furniture sat exactly as Jewell had placed it during her last redecorating frenzy. She was glad to see the red chaise still in front of the window. "Not any better at cleaning I see." She lifted a vase from the mantel, blew the dust away. "When was the last time they painted in here?" The once-white walls were stippled with the grime of the city.

"Heifer, please." Regina stuck her tongue out. "You may as well put your white glove away 'cause I'm gonna fail the inspection. For your information I still don't cook either. I'm sure Doc Webb will cite me for some health code violation when she gets here."

"It'll be a shame to have you carted off to dust detention just when the three of us finally get back together." Jewell flung her coat on the end of the lounge. She hadn't even made it back for Carmen's medical school graduation because she'd been on location in Sardinia. She sent a dozen white roses and they talked on the phone for an hour, about Carmen moving out of the holding cell and into her own apartment, about finishing what she started, about being scared, but not letting it stop you.

"Whoa, this is "luxe." Regina picked up the mink and put it on. What was full length on Jewell, puddled on the floor at Regina's feet. "Niiiiiice! I like."

"It was from Gianni. *Un dono*. A gift."

"My my. A gift huh? What else do you have new words for?" Regina piled the coat back on the chaise.

"Almost everything!"

"And is this the same man-o you were with in France?"

Jewell nodded. "Wait till Carmen gets here. I don't want to tell all this twice." Jewell caught Regina's look, realized she had already written an end for the story. "And before you get carried away, there is no ring involved, see." She wiggled her fingers.

"Too bad. You'd make a beautiful bride and I could plan the wedding of the decade for you. Something small and tasteful. I see a castle—"

"I guess time makes you more of who you are, and in your case that would be crazy." Jewell sat down.

"Get back up so I can look at you!" Regina put her hands on her hips, stood back and inspected Jewell from head to toe. Black cashmere turtleneck, slim black pants, taupe suede boots, a white silk-fringed scarf that covered her shoulders. Knotted at the nape of her neck in a low chignon, a few wisps of hair tickled Jewell's jawline and popped through the large gold hoops that dangled from her ears. Suddenly Regina's new hot pink tunic and leggings didn't feel as snazzy as they did yesterday in Bloomingdale's. She had learned a lot from Jewell about clothes and style and buying good things, but in the time she'd been gone, Jewell had moved to another level and Regina felt left behind. She plopped down on the edge of the chaise. "You look good, Jewell. Different." At first Regina couldn't put her finger on it, but then she knew. "You look so grown," she blurted. "Like a certified woman."

Jewell laughed. She felt more grown, she just didn't think it showed. "You telling me I'm no longer an ingenue?"

"Don't they give you shots for that when you come back in the country?"

Before they got any further, the buzzer rang and Carmen arrived to complete the trio. She saw Regina at the door, shook her head. "Your hair is never the same color twice." Carmen rarely got to the city since she had started her residency and Regina visited home even less often. But when Carmen had seen her six weeks ago, her hair had been almost burgundy.

"One day it's all gonna fall out." She breezed past and headed straight for the living room.

"Most people say hello when they come in somebody's house," Regina fussed.

"Are you two at it already?" Jewell grinned as Carmen entered the room. What her stride lacked in length, she made up for in velocity and she seemed to be thriving on the long, erratic hours of a first-year resident. With her hair smoothed into an orderly ponytail and wearing a white blouse, blazer and trousers she looked more authoritative than stylish. The strong, steely look in her eyes hadn't been there when Jewell left for Italy, but she liked it—thought it inspired confidence, like you really could trust her with your life.

"We wouldn't want you to think anything had changed while you were away." Carmen winked, gave Jewell a quick hug and sat next to her on the lounge. "Still smoking, huh?"

"Guilty," Jewell added. "Everyone smokes in Europe, so I've been thoroughly corrupted."

Carmen patted Jewell's knee. "It's great to see you. It's been too long."

"You didn't say that to me," Regina quipped as she came into the room. "I've been trying to get you here forever, but you act like you forgot the way."

"Well see me good today, because I don't know when I'll be in again. Man, the streets are nasty. I hated to leave my car outside—"

"Your car?"

"*The* car. *Your* car, okay, but my day is coming." Carmen looked through the French doors at the papers littering Regina's desk. "That place is a hazard. How can you find anything?"

"See? I told you she'd bust me," Regina said to Jewell. "But while Doc decides if the joint should be condemned you can fill me in on your adventures with Count Gianni."

"He's not a count."

"You said his family owns olive groves, right?" Carmen asked.

"He's a farmer? How come she knows that and I don't?" Regina spouted.

"Maybe I wrote her more often because she actually wrote me back." It was Jewell's turn to stick her tongue out at Regina. "And Gianni is definitely *not* a farmer. I met him at a dinner at Alberto's villa."

"Let me see. When was the last time I met a farmer, or whatever, at the villa of my close and personal friend?" Regina scratched her head, winked at Carmen. "Oh, I remember. Never." Her smile was laced with saccharine.

Jewell rolled her eyes. "As I was saying, Alberto, the director of my show, told me Gianni was like his brother, and he was such a good dinner companion I agreed to go out with him."

"Must have been the wine, or a full moon. I've seen guys try to talk to you and you never cut any slack." Regina smirked.

"He was charming, funny, forty, smart—"

"Hold up." Regina waved for a halt. "You didn't say the man was a senior citizen!"

"Believe me, Gianni didn't look—" She grinned. "Or act old. He kept me laughing. He knows so much about the world. Dresses great. And he's a great—" She smiled, enjoying the unexpected replay of a memorable caress. "Sometimes age means you know what you're doing."

"And exactly what did he know how to do? Hmmm?" Regina asked semi-sweetly.

"Treat me. He wasn't macho or insecure and he wasn't trying to score points by showing his pals he could pull an actress." *Or make me fall in love with him then conveniently forget I'm on the planet.*

"Yeah, but do you ever really feel you can trust them?" Carmen's experience was still secondhand, but so far she hadn't seen much reason to believe otherwise. She had decided she couldn't count Milton. That didn't get more than two steps from where it started. Nowhere. "Didn't you worry that he was running some kind of scam? Then bam! Soon as he gets what he wants, he's outta there." Not that she had any examples of that either, just lots of hospital hearsay and patient confessions to bolster her position.

"Gianni? Never. No games. Nothing to prove. He had too much fun just being himself. I mean, one day he pinched fruit from the market and gave it to children in the piazza because it made them laugh. He went back and paid for it, but he did crazy things like that. Then we'd be in a church and he'd practically weep over the frescoes. Being with him was definitely an event, sometimes too much. Once he told me, 'I work so that I can enjoy my life. I am very lucky. I don't have to work so hard, so it is my duty to enjoy even harder.'"

"And when are we going to have the Gianni experience?" Regina asked.

"Probably never. Unless you go back with me one day. I'm sure we'll stay friends, but it wasn't a forever thing. He likes variety too much to settle down—"

"Sounds to me like he can't make up his mind," Carmen said. "Like he wants to have his cake—"

"And torte and biscotti, but it was cool. He never pretended otherwise and I wasn't expecting forever." *I just needed to prove Billy doesn't own me.* "Gianni's not a settle-down kind of guy. He comes from a big family, tons of nieces and nephews. That's enough for him."

"Hmm, but not enough for you? Sounds like somebody's itching to enter the diaper zone," Regina observed.

"No rush. I'll be ready when it happens. If it happens." *Again.* After a day in the country playing pretend games and dress-up with Gianni's nieces, she'd feel hollow and so alone. "When the time is right I'll find somebody who looks like they'll be around for the duration. And before you start wording the personal ad, Regina, I'm not actively looking to fill the position."

"Suit yourself, but I'll tell you one thing. He sure as hell gives good parting gifts." Regina modeled the coat for Carmen.

Jewell decided not to tell Regina that she declined Gianni's gift of the Fiat he'd lent her while she was in Italy—that coming back, starting fresh, meant getting her own wheels.

"And he's the first man you've seen more than once since I've known you. But not to worry. You'll meet plenty of fine, interesting, eligible men when you come to my weekly soiree at DeVille. Okay, some of them only *act* like they're eligible."

Jewell wanted out of the hot seat. "So Reggie, what about Ty?"

"Ty who? That's been over so long he's barely a memory. I know you both tried to tell me it was a mistake. Maybe next time I'll listen."

"No you won't," Carmen said.

Regina had to laugh. "You're right. Anyway, I've made it a policy to never get involved with the hired help."

"Ouch," Jewell said.

"Yeah, but Ty was Mr. Big Stuff for a while—had some hits." Carmen crossed her legs.

"His real talent was getting people to buy that crap he was singing. Excuse me, rapping, 'cause the man cannot sing." Regina's rendition of "Rap-zilla" cracked them all up. "Right now I'm not interested in anybody full time. I like my variety pack. You know, like the cereal. You get bored with Cap'n Crunch, you got your Count Chocula so nobody gets stale. And since Dr. Milton seems to have fallen by the wayside, maybe we can ship Doc over to Gianni for a while, so she can get some of that experience."

"Nobody told you to mind my business. I am getting all the experience I want at Mid-Jersey Hospital, thank you very much. Some experience I can do fine without."

"You haven't had the right one yet," Regina remarked and licked her lips lasciviously.

Carmen pretended to ignore her. "Moving to the next subject—" Carmen dug in her purse and pulled out a small black box, tied with a pink ribbon. "—I have a presentation to make." She handed the box to Jewell.

Jewell looked at her quizzically, slipped off the bow and the lid and started to laugh. Inside were receipts from the speed-run through Alexander's, along with a check.

"It's the first of my IOU installments—more to follow. I don't know what I would have done without my resident loan shark."

Jewell looked at the check. "You didn't have to do this, you know."

"Yes I did. I'm just glad that I finally can."

They exchanged a look that said thank you and you're welcome. Before Jewell got choked up she said, "I have an announcement too. I didn't want to say this on the phone because I don't want to jinx it. I'm only going to whisper now." Jewell dropped her voice and the others leaned in, eager to be part of the conspiracy. "I've been talking to my agent for the last couple of months—about getting me work here." She had him double-check to make sure Billy Roland or William Christensen was not involved with whatever he found. "I have an audition next week—"

"That's great," Carmen said.

"I don't know what took you so long. You should have been here from the beginning," Regina said excitedly. "Are you shooting at a studio or on location—"

"I'm not shooting anywhere yet. I'm auditioning—"

"For?" Regina squeezed in on the other side of Jewell on the lounge, so they sat in a row, three birds on the back fence again.

Jewell looked back and forth between her friends. "*Through It All.*"

Regina screamed. "*Through It All*!. No way! You?! A soap? You used to give me grief about going to Macintosh to watch my stories."

"You'll give me grief about this, so we're even," Jewell announced. "And it was my idea." Thinking soaps would be great exercise for her acting muscle and a good way to introduce the new adult Jewell to American viewers, she suggested her agent try to drum up some interest.

"My mother used to watch that show when I was little. She used to talk about the characters like they were people she knew." Carmen shifted in her seat. She didn't say Geraldine got upset when they didn't answer her back.

"That is like, the best, the coolest." Regina prattled on. "Wow. My friend Jewell a citizen of Clearfield."

"Where?" Jewell asked.

"Clearfield. Where everybody in *TIA* lives. I figured out it's somewhere between here and Chicago because that's where people on the story go."

"So what's the role?" Carmen asked.

"The character's name is Adrienne Berrard. She's rich, new in town—been living in Europe—there's a stretch. Secretly she's the illegitimate daughter of one of the main characters and I think she has a half-brother—don't ask me, Regina. I don't know who any of these people are."

"I bet her father is J.C. Billings! Or is it her mother she's looking for?"

"I just know she's supposed to be like hell on the Concorde. Part of my appeal for the role is a gimmick. You know, little Tonya explores her inner bitch."

"That shouldn't be too difficult for you." Regina grinned. "Anyway, this calls for a celebration." Regina got up. "I may not have milk or eggs, but I keep a bottle of champagne chilled for just such occasions."

"Make mine small," Jewell said. "I'm going to be jet-lagged as it is and I don't want to fall asleep and leave you two to your own devices."

"Make mine ginger ale," Carmen added. "I have to drive home and I've got an early call—"

"Damn, I remember when you two were fun," Regina groused. She returned with the bottle, two flutes Jewell had bought before she left, and tossed a can of ginger ale to Carmen. "I think this has been here since you left."

The champagne bubbled and so did the stories, one on the heels of the other, catching each other up on the characters who had peopled their lives since their day-to-day had moved so far away. They spent as much time covering new territory as they did trying to bridge the gap that had grown between them and it was nearly one in the morning when Carmen caved. "I'm due at the hospital by seven."

"I haven't watched *TIA* in ages, but I'll start again tomorrow," Regina said as she and Jewell walked Carmen to the car.

"Don't go overboard. It's only for twenty-two episodes. Then they'll probably kill me off, but I've had a lot of practice. Dying in English should be like dying in Italian."

"In soaps they can bring you back, without the marvels of medicine. It wasn't you in the plane crash. It was the twin you never knew had been separated from you at birth," Regina said.

"You're kidding, right?" Carmen said as she slid into the driver's seat.

"What am I getting myself into?" Jewell moaned.

"Don't knock it." Regina closed the door and they waved as Carmen pulled away. "If the fans like you—you can live forever!"

12
Through It All

"Let's read through it again. I won't ad-lib today. Promise." Regina sat a saucepan of leftover coffee on the stove. "I got up early especially for a last run-through."

"Early? It's almost noon." Jewell used to think it was Ty's fault Regina kept such late hours, but he was history and she still stayed out past the middle of the night. "Besides, I'm through rehearsing. Either I've got it, or I don't." She looked in the refrigerator trying to decide what she wanted, but the real answer was for this audition to be over, so she closed the door.

Jewell's Italian career had fallen in her lap, so she hadn't read for a part since *Fly Girl* and the Billy debacle, but she'd convinced herself that was a once-in-a-lifetime jinx. The *Through It All* scene they had sent was a tricky one, taking her character from sly conversation which unleashed simmering anger, followed by long-held regret. She knew they needed to test her, to see if Daddy's Girl had matured into today's woman. Jewell had her lines down and had created a more detailed background for the mysterious, scheming Adrienne Berrard than the thumbnail history she'd been given. Rounding out her characters had become Jewell's practice in preparing for her thinly written parts in the tortellini thrillers. She knew that if this daytime-drama queen had any chance at survival, the viewers needed to feel her weight, identify with her contradictions.

"I *know* you've got it. That's why I want to start planning Adrienne's coming-out party at the Network Hook-up. I can make it coincide with your first week on the show and—"

"I told you I can't think about that now, Reg." Jewell's potential role on *Through It All* had become Regina's obsession. Jewell knew her cheerleading was well meant, but containing Regina's enthusiasm without hurting her feelings became an annoying job, one Jewell didn't need. "They have to offer me the role first."

"Be that way. Oops—" Regina lunged to turn off the coffee which had bubbled over onto the stove. She poured some in a mug, added milk and sugar.

Jewell was about to say, "Aren't you going to clean that up?" but she knew the answer was "no" and it was easier to sponge it up herself than to argue. In the week she'd been back, Jewell had busied herself unpacking, tidying the apartment, prepping for her audition and struggling with the realization that 5D didn't remind her of Paris anymore; the view was still amazing, but it was a run-down tenement flat and she couldn't figure out why Regina still lived there if her business was doing so well. They were getting along okay, mostly, but during the years Jewell was abroad she'd always lived alone, and had come to enjoy home as a sanctuary. Regina, on the other hand, used the place as the launch pad for her weekly events and the crash pad where she landed, so there was nothing tranquil about it. "Don't you have a hair appointment?" Jewell hoped for a few quiet hours to get ready. Landing this part, her first as an adult in the States, without Vivian's guidance, meant more than she wanted to admit and she worked to keep her nerves in check.

"Yeah. I'm getting in the shower. But you have to promise you'll come to DeVille as soon as you leave the studio. You wouldn't come out with me before, but tonight we celebrate—"

"Reg." Jewell gave her the "can it" look.

"Okay. Okay. Just come." Regina left with her coffee.

Once Regina was out of the way, Jewell took a long hot shower and let Gianni's words wash over her. "*Cara*, we do our best. Tell me how does it help to worry?" She could see him shrug his shoulders, feel him massage the knots out of hers. It was one of many lessons she'd learned from him. In addition to being her lover, Gianni had been her brother, her teacher, her sounding board. He had been good to her, good for her, encouraged her to become herself. *But it was time to move on. He was great, but I want something real.*

So, hours later, wearing a pinstriped Valentino suit Adrienne might have purchased at the designer's Piazza Mignanelli boutique, as she herself did, Jewell was ready. With her hair draped over her shoulders, both seductive and confident, she took her place on the set, seated on the mahogany desk of a posh office. She took a deep breath, the one that escaped her for *Fly Girl* and waited for her cue.

And by the time she arrived at DeVille, Jewell's head was still spinning.

"What can I get you?" The bartender slid a napkin in front of her before she chose a stool.

"Sparkling water." It wasn't until the audition was over that she realized how thirsty she was, like she'd run a long, sweaty race. She spied

Regina in the far room deep in conversation with an elfin man in a black blazer. When the bartender put a tall glass in front of her, she removed the straw and took a long drink, then smiled to herself.

"What are you grinning about?" Regina hopped on the next stool, flipped her freshly reddened hair. "Sooo, do we have a reason to toast?" As if on cue the bartender appeared with a glass of champagne for her. "Thanks, Eric." She moved in close, looked Jewell eyeball to eyeball.

Jewell sipped her water, watched the anticipation bloom on Regina's face and enjoyed dragging out the news a moment longer. Her mile spread slowly. "I start taping in two weeks."

"See, I told you! I knew you'd get it!" Regina bounced up and down, hugging Jewell.

"Hold up, you're about to take my head off." Jewell pried Regina's arms loose.

Regina lifted her glass. "*Through It All*, Bijoux."

"And through much, much more." Jewell clinked and they both took a sip.

"This is fantastic!" Regina was off and running. "Now I can plan the party for you and—"

"Slow down," Jewell insisted. "Let's take this one step at a time."

"I'd like to thank our guest today, Jewell Prescott. And I'm sure I speak for all of our viewers who knew you as the adorable Tonya Gifford when I say, you've come a long way baby." Thelma Simmons, host of *New York Now*, smiled at Jewell.

Even after the cheesy line Jewell broke out her media grin. "I hope your viewers stay tuned to *Through It All*. There's lots more to come."

Thelma turned to the camera. "And thank you for stopping at our spot on the dial. Tune in next week when our guests will be the dynamic duo who prove that sometimes it is all in the family, Harlem real estate tycoon King Dixon and his outspoken son, Councilman Dwight Dixon." She held her smile until the lights dimmed. "Great interview. Come back any time."

Jewell stood up, unhooked her mike. "Thanks. I had fun." It wasn't exactly a lie, but this cable program wasn't the *Tonight Show* either. Still, it was press which was the point. In addition to a week spent in wardrobe consultations, light tests with makeup, and a dozen meetings with the directors and writers, Jewell had done five print and seven television interviews in the past four days. She was both glad and surprised by the media interest.

"Bravo." The voice came from the wings. Then he stepped into view.

That's why the name was familiar. She couldn't place it, but in his navy blazer, blue-and-white striped shirt and foulard bow tie, Dwight looked just like he had that night after her kids' performance at the Harlem School of the Arts. He wasn't in the green room when she started taping so this was a surprise. Jewell's face lit up to full meet-and-greet brightness. "Thank you, Councilman. It's good to see you again."

"Glad to see you remember me." He chortled as he shook her hand.

"Of course." Another semi-truth. She hadn't thought about Dwight Dixon since that night, but she recalled his inquisitive, arching eyebrows and the way he seemed so sure of himself.

"And apparently we'll be seeing quite a bit of you—not that I have time for television, especially during the day—my constituents wouldn't approve, but I'm sure a lot of them watch."

"I'm counting on that." Jewell smiled. "And so are the producers!" She noticed the heavyset older man, sprawled on the low-slung sofa and assumed it was Dwight's real estate tycoon father. He watched intently, but made no move to join them.

"You're sure to be a hit." Dwight slipped a hand in his trouser pocket. His open blazer revealed red-and-navy suspenders. "We need positive representation in the popular media."

"Calling Adrienne Berrard positive is a bit of a stretch." Jewell tilted her head, unconsciously raked her hair behind her ear.

"But you're there, on the screen every day. That's what counts. We need as many role models as we can get—our kids need them—"

"Jewell, your car's waiting." The *TIA* publicist interrupted Dwight's speech.

"That's my cue. I've got a table read back at the studio," Jewell said.

"Really wonderful seeing you, Jewell." Dwight touched her upper arm, briefly, lightly. "I hope to have another opportunity."

"Every day, two to three—that is if you find yourself with spare time." She tossed a wave over her shoulder as she walked away, wondering if she would see him again.

Three weeks later, Jewell sat in her dressing room, swathed in gold velour. She puffed the latest in a string of cigarettes she'd smoked since she got off the set half an hour ago and tried to will the phone to ring. The haze curled lazily around the limp heads of the two dozen white roses that sat on her dressing table. *I need to toss those*. They had been waiting when she arrived at the studio last week on Valentine's Day. Jewell knew she wasn't anybody's sweetheart, and made a joke about having a secret admirer. That's when Carin, her makeup artist, told her the production company usually sent the whole cast roses on Valentine's Day, birthdays and show anniversaries. "Nobody expected them this year since our ratings were in the crapper—till you showed up."

What a week. Jewell tossed the dead flowers in the wastebasket. Her character, like so many in soapland, was created as a transient and had been slated for an untimely death in a tragic fall from Clearfield's only skyscraper, but three days ago Adrienne and Jewell's fortunes got an unexpected boost when her agent called. "Fans love you and your story line. The show's had its first ratings bounce in ages and they know it's you. They're talking a year. If you want to consider it, I know I can get 'em to do better." Consider it was all she'd done for the past seventy-two hours. She hadn't told Regina because she needed to make this decision on her own. Yesterday she told Michael to start the ball rolling. Since then they'd been attached by phone cord and she awaited his next communiqué. A knock on the door interrupted her vigil.

Molly, from wardrobe, entered with the emerald strapless gown Jewell would wear in tomorrow's party scene. She held the dress high overhead to keep it from dragging on the floor.

"Think it's right this time?" Jewell had already sent the gown back twice for alterations. "How do they expect Adrienne to be the crowned witch of Clearfield in a dress that doesn't fit?" Jewell got up, squashed out her cigarette and took off her robe.

"What a body." Molly unzipped the gown. "I don't know why you wear that all-in-one."

"Habit." A habit Vivian started to head off speculation about Jewell's stretch marks. Her mother had them custom dyed because no one carried a color that was even close to Jewell's nude skin. During her days in 5D she had freed herself from elasticized bondage, but she still kept the stretch marks hidden, even from Carmen and Regina, although at times it had been tricky—no mad dashes from the shower in a towel or answering the phone in bra and panties. But when she started wardrobe fittings in Italy, she dug out the old supply, and ordered some new.

Jewell wished she could think of them as a badge of honor. That, along with the joyous call of "Mommy" from a nine-year-old, would show she had done something wonderful—grown a baby, raised a child. Instead the ridges on her belly were the scars of shame that Vivian told her she deserved. They were the reason she ultimately turned down the lead in a movie called *Bordo Duro*. She told the director of *Hard Edge*, as it was called in English, that she had moral issues with the nudity, which was partially true. There wasn't really a good reason for the scene except as a chance to show some flesh, but her rippling skin, tan stripes on the velvet black, was the overriding reason she avoided revealing her body. Every bath or shower reminded her of the hole in her heart and she didn't want to talk about it. No one but Vivian had seen them, except Gianni.

From the moment she met him, Jewell knew he was trouble, knew she couldn't brush him off the way she did most men. It wasn't just physical. Gianni was shorter than she was, and stocky. He wore his longish salt-and-pepper hair in a ponytail and clothes that skimmed his body. Nobody would have thought of him as her type. Neither did she, but although their mother tongues were different, he read her like a primer and she had no choice but to respond.

They'd kept company for weeks, talking, teasing. For Jewell it was like an old-fashioned courtship, slow and very romantic, but he never spoke about forever. Strangely, that made it easier for her to get involved. Jewell loved his energy, his enthusiasm, his sensitivity and when she agreed to go with him to Villefranche, she knew she would make love with him. Finally she was ready to take that risk, but there was something she had to tell him, before hearts were racing and clothes were shed, because she wasn't in the mood for surprises. Billy had been her first, and since the baby, since her body changed forever there had been no one else. So, sitting in the front seat of his Lancia, before they drove off she told him the story. She shared her shame and told him why she was so reluctant to share her body. "There is no shame in that. Why would you think you can hide from your past? Why would you want to? It is your life, you take it with you wherever you go." He smoothed a hand across her cheek. "A man loves a woman. Her body is part of her experience—whatever that is. If he does not love that too, he is a pig, he is not a man."

Jewell shook off the memory. "I just like a smooth silhouette," she said to Molly.

"Too bad some of the others don't see it that way. You wouldn't believe the lumps they expect me to hide."

Before Jewell stepped into the dress the phone rang. "Sorry. I have to take this. I'll call you when I'm done." She gave Molly an apologetic smile as she left the dressing room.

And this time the call gave her exactly the news she was waiting for.

"We got two years! That's nearly unheard of for a new character. Time off for films or whatever else comes along." Jewell skipped around the room like a boxer in the ring as she listened to Michael outline the deal. "It's exactly what you need to erase little Tonya."

Jewell hung up feeling giddy. Acting in Italy had been like baby steps. Now she was really walking, on her own, and soon she'd be ready to run. *Now I'll tell Regina.* They had planned to rendezvous for an early dinner before Jewell knew she'd have good news to share. With Jewell's early call times and Regina's late nights they spent a lot of time passing each other in the apartment, which was the real reason Jewell had suggested they meet. She'd decided it was time to move to her own place.

After Molly returned and they made certain that Adrienne's dress would cause a stir at Clearfield's charity ball, Jewell gathered her stuff, picked up her pages for tomorrow. "See ya," she said to the receptionist on her way out.

"Wait a sec. These are for you." She handed Jewell an envelope and a small package, but before she could look at them she felt an arm loop through hers.

"Yea for you!" Although she was twenty-eight, Marta played an unwed, pregnant teenager suffering from amnesia on *TIA*. With blond pigtails and no makeup it was easy to see why that worked. "I know it's not official yet, but we all know! We're glad you're staying!"

"Me too!" Jewell shoved her mail in her tote as they headed outside. Her arm was barely raised before a cab cut across three lanes of traffic to pick them up. "Which way you heading?"

"East Sixtieth," Marta answered.

"Want to share? I'm going to Murray Hill. You can drop me off and keep going."

"Sure thing."

During the twenty block ride Marta filled Jewell in on some of the behind-the-scenes intrigue on *TIA*. At Thirty-third and Third Jewell reached for her wallet to give Marta her fare.

"Keep it. Your turn next time, cast mate," Marta said.

Regina was sitting at the bar when Jewell came in. "I can't believe I beat you, for once." The dark, cozy restaurant was Regina's choice. It was a few short blocks to DeVille so she liked to stop in to eat before the battalions of buppies and yuppies became her sole focus. And they had "portions" as she called them, plenty of food for your buck.

They settled at a table in the window. Regina ordered a burger with extra fries and a glass of white wine. Jewell decided on the spinach salad. "And I'll have red please."

"You? Wine? On a school night?" Regina sputtered. "Damn! Rough day?"

"The usual." Jewell lit a cigarette. "Got to the set, run-through, makeup, wardrobe, taping, a two-year contract with *TIA*." She grinned at Regina.

"See! The very first day I told you they wouldn't kill you off!" Regina drummed the table. "Do you know how much time you'd save by listening to me? I'm in touch. I know what's happening, what people like. And I knew they'd like you. Now I can plan the party!"

"Now there's a new idea," Jewell said as the waiter brought their wine.

"Hey, it's my job. Speaking of—" She grabbed the waiter's arm. "I've got to be out before four. Where's our food?"

"It'll be right up." The young man snuck a peek at Jewell. "Aren't you on *Through It All*?" Jewell smiled and nodded and he continued. "I watch that show all the time. You need to watch out for that old evil J.C. Billings. He's got it in for you."

"Nice to meet you—" she paused, read his name tag. "Tom." Jewell gave him her megawatt smile, even though being interrupted during meals was a part of the fame game she hadn't missed. "I know you're busy and my friend and I are—"

"Oh yeah, right. Sorry." He backed away from the table. "You look way better in person."

"You see? The fans are looking out for you already." Regina sipped her wine.

"Oh yeah. I almost forgot." Jewell reached in her tote. "I got fan mail at the studio today." She took the package out first and was surprised by the return address. "What is he sending me?"

"He who? I bet it's nasty underwear or diamonds from your Italian mystery man."

"Noooo. It's from Councilman Dwight Dixon."

"Who's he?"

Tom returned with their plates so Jewell waited for him to leave. "Remember that summer in college when I taught acting?" While Regina ate Jewell reminded her about the night after the play at HSA, and recounted their recent meeting after she taped *New York Now*.

"Him?! Ah ha! The plot thickens. After a hard-fought campaign to retain his seat, the victorious councilman reconnects with the jet-setting actress who's recently returned to—"

"You sound like my script for tomorrow," Jewell said.

"Open it!"

Jewell used her knife to loosen the paper. Inside a white box she found a gilt-edged, leather-bound copy of *All's Well that Ends Well*, a business card and a note tucked inside the cover. "Welcome back. Yours, Dwight," she read. *I can't believe he remembered the play*. He'd given her his card after that performance, but this time his home phone number was on the back.

"'Yours,' huh?"

"It's just form, like sincerely."

Regina licked ketchup off her fingers and grinned. "Sounds like he's interested in more than form, unless of course, it's yours."

"He didn't say all that. You always jump to the nastiest conclusions." But Jewell was happy to hear from him. It wasn't exactly his looks, although she definitely found Dwight attractive. He was so self-assured, so solid, so different.

Regina teased her about calling him, and made observations about men who wear bow ties. "They want you to see them as a giant present, waiting to be unwrapped."

"You're not well." Jewell laughed, but Regina was almost done eating and it was time to bring the conversation around to serious matters. Jewell thought it would be easier to talk about leaving 5D when she wasn't actually there. "Regina—I've been thinking—"

"Didn't I just tell you to leave the thinking to me? Don't worry your pretty—"

"Shut up, Reggie."

"I missed that! With you and Carmen both gone no one says such sweet things to me."

"As I started to say—" *I don't want her to take this the wrong way*. Jewell took a deep breath. "I've been thinking about moving." She waited. No response. "You know the studio is pretty far downtown. It would be easier if I was closer. I'm going to have some pretty long days and I'll have about twenty-five or thirty pages of dialogue to learn every night for the next day's taping and the phone and stuff didn't used to bother me, but I don't know, something changed while I was in Italy. I think I got used to more quiet—but it's not just the noise thing though. That door downstairs in unlocked most of the time and I should probably have a doorman—fans can get a little looney sometimes. You should have a doorman. I mean anybody could—"

"Are you going to take a breath or just keep talking till you pass out?" Regina wiped her hands on her napkin.

"Huh?" Jewell had over-prepared to champion her decision, but she just didn't want to hurt Regina's feelings.

"It's cool. You're right. If I were you, I'd move too. I mean I'd be a famous television actress and I don't know how I could possibly stay in a building like that. Let's not even talk about the neighborhood." Regina smiled at Jewell but her sarcasm was unmistakable. "Except if I remember it was you who was hot to live there in the first place—your 'Left Bank hideaway' I believe you called it."

"Regina, that was almost eight years ago." Jewell had convinced herself she had no reason to feel guilty, but right now it wasn't working.

"I guess time flies when you're having fun." Regina looked at her watch. "I gotta go."

Jewell didn't want it to end this way. "We'll talk about it later or over the weekend."

Regina reached for her coat, got her wallet out of her purse. "Won't you be out looking at real estate?" She stood up.

"Please don't be like this." Jewell shook her head. "I've got this."

"Later." Regina was gone before Jewell could say another word.

She sat for a while, had another glass of wine and a smoke, wondering how she could make this right with Regina. To give herself something to do she reached for her other piece of mail, pulled the heavy vellum notecard from its envelope. "Congratulations! Keep knocking 'em dead. Billy." There was a postscript. "*Fly Girl* is still waiting."

She dropped the note on top of her half-eaten salad, ground her cigarette out in the whole mess and watched as the busboy cleared it all away.

13
"Kiss? Cheek? Lips? Too much to consider."

"So I said, 'I'll leave the chaise. When you move or get something you want to replace it, let me know and I'll come get it.'" Jewell knelt on the floor of her new living room next to Carmen and ripped open a carton of books. "She never looked up from her Rolodex. She just said 'Whatever,' in that tone she gets when she acts like she's bored." Outside the window, in the distance, a yellow and orange variegated sun was being swallowed by Hoboken, but Jewell was too riled to notice. "I mean, it just seems like that lounge belongs in front of that window. I knew it when we first found it." Jewell got lost for a moment in the memory of that early shopping expedition. "Anyway, she pretended like she didn't care, but I know she does." Jewell was still stinging from that slight and all the others before the move.

They'd had plenty of disagreements in the past, over dumb stuff, like borrowed clothes and undelivered messages, but none had lasted this long. For the weeks after Jewell made her announcement, she and Regina didn't say more than ten words a day to each other. Only their opposite-end-of-the-clock schedules made the time bearable. When she left, Jewell only took the contents of her bedroom, despite the fact she'd furnished the living room and kitchen. Her new apartment was still virtually empty and she kept telling herself she was looking forward to decorating, but so far she hadn't done much beyond kitchen basics and bed linen. She hadn't even finished unpacking. Her heart wasn't in it. She'd found a lamp at an antique store on Greenwich Street, and a wrought iron tri-fold screen which stood in the living room dividing nothing from nothing, but Jewell had been in her new place a week with no word from Regina.

Carmen took the armload of books Jewell handed her and put them on the built-in shelves along one side of the room. She stood up, looked out the window. "Was the sunset a surprise or did you see it before you took this place?"

"See it?! I made them put it in the lease!" Jewell sat on a battered steamer trunk she found on the curb on Bethune Street and dragged home in a taxi. "I'm glad you're here, but I am feeling a little guilty that I put you to work."

"No guilt. You've helped me plenty." Not wanting to get too sentimental, Carmen added, "Next time you can come to my town house. I've got plenty for you to do." She grabbed the next load of books. "It's small, but how much room do I need? I'm hardly there. The upside is that I have an option to buy it. I'm not far from Al and Lonnie's, so my commute to the hospital is the same and I already know where the dry cleaner and supermarket are!" She laughed. "It's not as fancy as this, but there's a pond out back and I might even plant a garden this spring. You'll probably think it's boring. I know the fabulous Ms. Foster does, but *I* love it." Carmen arranged the books on the shelves, picked up a leather-bound one with gilt edges. "Don't worry about Regina. Remember how weird she acted senior year? Like she was mad at us for graduating? She'll have some juicy news she's dying to share—and since I'm not that easy to reach these days, you'll be the lucky one." Carmen leaned against the wall and grinned. "Speaking of juicy news, tell me about you and Councilman Dixon." She waved Dwight's present.

"How do you know that?" Jewell worked to untie the string around a bundle of papers.

"She may not be talking *to* you, but she still talks *about* you."

"He sent the book, I called to say thanks and invited him to dinner on Tuesday—"

"*You* asked *him?*"

"I need to know somebody who's not an actor."

"So it's table for two on Tuesday, huh?" Carmen teased.

"Now you sound like Regina."

"She's not here. Somebody has to do her job."

"It's just dinner. No big deal." Jewell continued to wrestle with the knot, which was a good way to avoid looking at Carmen, because it was at least a little deal. She wanted to see Dwight when they weren't running in opposite directions. "What about you? Anybody special?"

Carmen snorted. "I do not have time to be bothered."

"What about Milton?" Jewell asked as she finally unraveled the string. "I always thought you two might get together. I know Reg teased you, but you guys had so much in common."

"Why, 'cause he's a geek too?"

"Hemp wasn't exactly a geek, just a little too earnest for his own good."

"I don't know—I kinda liked him, he kinda liked me and that's kinda all, folks." She shrugged. "We're still in touch—he's doing a research fellowship in Chicago. Now if you ask me, I think he really had the hots for Regina, but who knows? Maybe he's found somebody and he's not telling." Carmen reached for the batch of papers Jewell handed her. "Regina's parents are always trying to fix me up. They know an endless supply of 'suitable young men,' as they call them, but it's just not a priority." She was about to place the papers on another shelf when she noticed the one on top. "You still have this?" She held up the script.

Jewell pretended to read the title. "Didn't know I did." But Jewell was well aware she still had *Fly Girl*. "I should probably toss all those old screenplays." She had tried, but somehow Billy's story always ended up out of the trash and back on her shelf. "And even if men aren't a priority, they might be the prescription for a little fun, Dr. Webb."

Carmen put her hands on her hips. "Like you can pass out medicine. How many boyfriends did you have in school? That would be zer-o. Then you left for four years and there was what, a fling with Gianni? Unless you didn't write me about the others—and now you're back and who are you going to dinner with? A bow-tie-wearing politician you met seven years ago after a school play. You can hardly talk!"

"Fine. You win." Jewell flounced across the room, pretending to pout.

"Save it for the camera," Carmen said. "But I do expect a full dinner report next week."

Tuesday's weather was textbook March, dreary with intermittent sleet. Jewell hunched her shoulders against the wind as she rounded the corner onto Bleecker heading for the restaurant. She hadn't eaten there before, but she chose it because it looked rustic and cozy and the smells that wafted onto the street had made her mouth water. Dwight had offered to pick her up, but she suggested they meet instead. Her apartment still wasn't visitor friendly and she wanted the evening to be relaxed, a getting-to-know-you dinner, like the first time she hung out with Marta when they left the *TIA* studio. Just because he was a man, didn't make this a date, she told herself.

Jewell taped late on Tuesdays, so she had hurried home and spent an hour agonizing over what to wear. She'd left her bed buried under an uncharacteristic explosion of reject outfits that reminded her of Regina and made her sad that her buddy wasn't around to give her grief about it. In the end she settled on a winter-white cashmere skirt and sweater, casual but chic, quiet but not mousy, and she liked the way ivory looked against her dark skin. She wore brown low-heeled boots—Dwight was her height or a hair shorter, and she didn't want him to feel uncomfortable. She also wore the mink Gianni gave her, a reminder that this was just a moment, just dinner, period. She dodged a couple trotting toward her, laughing at some shared joke, and Jewell could tell they didn't care if nobody got it but them. She snuggled into her coat. *Just dinner*.

Jewell was two doors down when she saw him get out of the taxi. She liked the dashing figure he cut, the collar of his trench turned up, walking with purpose toward the door. "Dwight!" She called and waved, her smile broader than she meant it to be.

"Great to see you." He kissed her cheek, held the door and guided her inside. Coats hung, they were shown to a table by the fireplace. "Nasty night, but this is definitely an improvement." He adjusted his bow tie. "I'm glad you called. I wasn't sure you would, busy lady like yourself."

"After such a thoughtful gift?" Jewell wanted a cigarette, but Dwight had the look of a devout non-smoker so she resisted the urge. "It's prominently displayed on a bookshelf, which is about the only part of my apartment that's organized. I haven't quite settled in."

"I was sorry to hear you left the district. And before you got to vote for me," he teased.

Jewell smiled. "The good news is, I won't get to vote for your opponent either."

His robust laughter rolled through the narrow restaurant. "You've got a point there."

They paused long enough to look at the menu, listen to the waiter recite the specials and order. "Something to drink?" the waiter asked.

"None for me. I have work when I get home and a breakfast meeting with local clergy tomorrow. I need all my wits about me later—not that I don't need them now."

"I'll pass." Jewell wanted to be sharp enough to keep up.

"Now where have you been hiding yourself since I saw you all those years ago?" Dwight leaned in, captured Jewell in the spotlight of his gaze.

"I lived and worked in Europe for four years." Jewell liked the warmth of Dwight's attention. "Rome was home, but I got to see a lot of the continent—Paris, Madrid, London, Amsterdam, you know, the big cities, but lots of tiny out-of-the-way places too. There's a beautiful little town called Reno. Nothing like our Reno. No casinos, no desert. This one sits lakeside, right on Lago Maggiore—what a breathtaking view of the Alps." She felt odd recounting tales that involved Gianni, but this was just dinner with a friend.

"Sounds quaint. I've never been to Italy, but I did go to Paris and London with my mother when I was young, eight I think. I didn't like the food and I haven't been since." He leaned back in his seat. "The world comes to my city—some for a visit, some forever. Those who don't come, want to, so I figure why go anywhere else? There's no finer place on the planet. It's my home and I've chosen to make it my work too because I love this crazy place."

"I can tell," Jewell said, settling in to listen.

"This city is about neighborhoods, like this one, unique in character and in what it contributes to the picture of the city as a whole. In the early eighties I realized there were huge areas of the city being neglected." He leaned toward Jewell to make his point. "I decided to do something about it, so I ran for city council, and won. I will admit I had an advantage. Everyone knew my father and they knew my name, but to them, I was King Dixon's son, Junior. A lot of the old-timers still call me that even though I'm not now, nor have I ever been, King Junior."

"Your father must be fascinating. That was him with you at the cable station, wasn't it?" Jewell asked, recalling the heavyset man, lounging in the green room.

"Uh, yes, that was King." For the first time since they sat down Dwight seemed hesitant. "And he's definitely a—character." He hurriedly steered the conversation in another direction.

After their food came, Jewell continued to listen, fascinated by Dwight and what he had to say, the way he combined his political point of view with personal anecdotes and bits of history, history that was his foundation. He was someone with roots, deep ties to the people and to the place where he lived. Something she hadn't been exposed to in the circles she was a part of in LA. It was different in Rome too, and while Gianni was wonderful, her time with him had been like living on dessert—tantalizing, deliriously sweet, but lacking in the essentials. Dwight was a solid meal, filling and good for you.

"It's the neighborhoods that make the face of the city. Without Chinatown or Chelsea, Hell's Kitchen or Harlem—it would be like losing teeth one by one. At first you might not notice—if they were in back. You might have difficulty chewing, but you'd switch to the other side until they rot too. Then the front ones start to go and before you know it, the once-bright smile is just a sad snaggletoothed version of its former self. And New York's face would be a pretty sad one."

"I never thought of the city like that." To Jewell he sounded fresh, like an original thinker. Dwight had drawn her in and she never even felt the pull.

She felt his passion for his work. It wasn't until she glanced down at her empty bowl of bouillabaisse, that she realized she had eaten. *I don't even know how it tasted.* Feeling silly, she put her spoon down.

"My job is to do what I can to keep the city smiling. And my commitment is to keep Harlem an up-front part of that smile."

"Very impressive, Councilman. I can see how you stay in office." From the moment she met Dwight, she'd like his confidence. His work wasn't frivolous like worrying about head shots or whether your character has the most lines. He made decisions that affected thousands of lives. Dwight Dixon wasn't like any man she'd ever known; what he did made a difference, and Jewell found his conviction extremely attractive.

Dwight continued to regale her with tidbits from his high school days at Horace Mann, and college at Brown. Jewell was glad not to be talking about herself. She was tired of that saga and it was a pleasure to listen to someone with so much to say. He seasoned his stories with dashes of spice from his current political and social agenda and even a little sugar with memories of his mother who died when he was twelve. The firelight warmed his already golden brown complexion and once in a while Jewell found her mind drifting, wondering what he was like with that tie loosened. She was sorry when he signaled for the check.

"I could talk to you all night." Dwight smiled at her. "But duty calls. If I don't read those reports for tomorrow's Budget Committee meeting, I'll be a dead duck." He left a hundred-dollar bill on the table and got up for their coats. "You wouldn't let me pick you up, but I know you're going to let me drop you home. How would I look letting you fend for yourself in this weather?"

Jewell slipped her arms in the sleeves as he held her coat. "All right." She had wanted to avoid the awkward farewell. *Do we stop in front, the lobby, at my door? Kiss? Cheek? Lips?* Too much to consider, but she couldn't turn down his thoughtful offer.

"Wait here."

Jewell watched through the window as he searched the horizon for a taxi, wondering for the first time how Dwight thought dinner had gone. When she saw the yellow cab stop at the curb she hurried outside and he helped her into the car. His hands felt cool, but strong, sure hands you could depend on.

They gave directions and settled in the backseat. "I had a wonderful time," Dwight said. "You're a great audience. I should practice my speeches on you."

Jewell was flattered that he'd even tease about including her in such an important part of his life. "I'm a good rehearsal partner." Billy jumped into her head as soon as she said it, but she dismissed the thought of him immediately.

Dwight gripped her hand in both of his. "Listen Jewell, I have a dinner to attend next Thursday, it's not a big deal, but I'd like to take you, if you're free, that is."

"Sounds like fun. I don't have my calendar, but call me tomorrow and I'll let you know."

"I'll make sure my secretary gets to you in the morning." He let her hand go, fingers playing a bit with hers as he did.

The taxi stopped in front of Jewell's building and Dwight got out to open her door. He relieved her good-night protocol worries by giving her a gentlemanly kiss on the cheek. "So long for now."

For now. Jewell hurried inside. For some reason having him watch as she walked away made her nervous. Once safely out of sight she did a two-step jig, already looking forward to the next "just dinner."

14
"The better to sleep with, my dear."

"You are a bottomless font of ideas, my angel." Reuben stretched out on a banquette, his usual spot after a long night. The Manhattan phone book lay open, a pillow under his head.

"That's my specialty. It's what I'm good at." Regina sat on a bar stool, her legs propped on the neighboring one. The slit of her red skirt had fallen open, revealing a thigh. The Thursday Network Hook-up still started after work, but now it went late; sometimes things didn't get good before midnight. Regina and Reuben always stayed until the bitter end to dish about who wore what or who was with whom this week, and of course, to count the proceeds.

Regina had shaped Thursdays at DeVille into the place to be for people who had connections and wanted to make more. Bankers, ball players, models, entrepreneurs, people with style who were not looking to settle for less, swung by for a dose of social interaction and exploration with their refreshments. Always dressed in her signature red, usually with a champagne glass in her hand, Regina worked her room better than anyone. If you were new to the mix, she would seek you out before the night was through, get your story and make some perfect introduction for you, make you feel welcome, at home. It was a lesson she learned at Prof's and it was still her key, making her guests feel like they were visiting a private club with a lot of class.

"Tonight was brilliant. Everybody loves to be the 'It' girl. Perhaps party hats next time. They're so—festive." He rolled on his side, a hand propped under his head.

"Skip the head gear. Champagne makes every day a holiday." Regina poured the dregs of a bottle into her glass. She didn't know how many she'd had in the course of the evening, but she was nearing meltdown, the point where she'd take a cab home, fall into bed, and not remember much about the end of the night come morning.

Tonight was the first of what she planned to be monthly evenings featuring a prominent guest of honor. When Jewell got the part on *Through It All*, Regina intended to make her the first. That changed after Jewell abandoned ship, so Regina went with the sultry sound of New York radio, Felicia Anderson. It was also a personal thank you from Regina for the support Felicia had shown her from that very first July Jam. So Regina had spent the last week on the horn to her roster of personalities from other stations, journalists, record execs, and friends of Felicia. It made for a jumping night, with guest DJs who roasted the honoree. And at the height of the evening Regina took the spotlight and presented Felicia with a magnum of champagne.

Then there was Glen Parker, the artist development guy from Big Bang Entertainment. A smooth cup of cocoa with dark curly hair, and thick, shiny brows framing eyes that posed a question Regina wanted to answer. She tuned in to him as soon as he walked in and guided him to her section of the bar—midway around the side so she could use the mirrors to keep an eye on both rooms. She got him settled with a Remy on the rocks and they exchanged the basic personal data: born in Newark, status—single. Then they slid into the business portion of the proceedings.

Regina asked about Big Bang while she checked out his suit and phonograph cuff links.

Glen explained that Big Bang was a new record label. "We produce urban contemporary music. Hip hop to neo-soul. Down the line we're looking to move into movies."

Even though Regina was focused on his eyes and the cute crease he got between them when he talked serious, she heard her business cue. "We should talk. My company, Regina Foster Productions—" because she'd decided Good Tyme sounded juvenile—"can produce a variety of events, on-site and on-location. Launch parties, holiday celebrations, always with panache."

Party planning was Regina's next frontier. She had been researching locations, equipment rentals, caterers, florists, some recommended by Reuben, others she had scouted on her own. There were parties in the city every night of the week and she wanted some of that action.

"You music people do a lot of entertaining." Regina placed her business card, cream with curly script, in his hand. "I'd be happy to give you a call."

"I'd be happy to answer it." Glen traded her a card. It was black and silver. "But you need to speak with Tyrone Washington."

Regina almost swallowed her tongue. "Tyrone Washington? Alias Boney T?"

"He's president of Big Bang."

Regina curbed a laugh attack so Glen wouldn't think she was nuts. "New York isn't so big if you know the right people." It was one of the first things Ty had said to her. "Tell you what, give Ty-rone my card. Tell him Regina says to give a call if he wants to talk business." She patted his hand and put herself back in the mix, since his association with Ty took Glen off her personal interest list.

Now Reuben swung his feet to the floor. "Shall we retire to the counting house, my dear?"

"If I can drag myself off this seat." Regina stood slowly, wiggled her body.

"I'm the old man here." He led the way to his office, a narrow niche just big enough for a desk and shelves lined with binders, phone books and photos of his three children and their kids.

"I told some people I'd meet them for a nightcap, but I'll never make it." Regina plopped on the edge of his desk. "I'm toast."

"No need to cut the night short. You know I can fix that for you." He cupped his thumb under his chin, patted his nose with his index finger.

Regina knew that from time to time Reuben indulged in a hit of cocaine. She had always turned him down when he offered. "I'm naturally high," she would tell him. "Coke doesn't make you high, angel. It just helps you go from flat to fluffy," is what he said. She had to admit he never looked high. Neither did any of the other folks she knew who added extra octane to their fuel.

"You'd hate to miss something juicy." Reuben twinkled with mischief.

"Well—there is this PR guy I want to make my close personal friend. I mean that in a business sense." Regina peeked over at Reuben. "Okay, Mr. Wizard. Just this once."

"Welcome to Oz, Dorothy." Reuben pulled a green enameled box from the back of his drawer. "Take a dip." He scooped some of the white powder with his pinkie nail, inhaled up each nostril, tweaked his nose closed with his fingers and sniffed. Then he ran his finger along his gums. "Think of it as gaining a little extra time."

Regina dipped a red nail into the box. "I always thought it looked like crushed-up aspirin."

"Much more effective on the head," Reuben said.

Regina felt nerves nudging her ribs. *That's never stopped me from flying solo*. She took a tentative sniff. A cool, wet sensation shot straight from her nose, up behind her eyes and into her head, like she'd inhaled pool water. "This feels weird."

"A temporary inconvenience. Come on, do the other side. You want this in stereo."

Regina completed her initiation. The feeling traced down her arms, quickened her, like she'd downed a double espresso. Then she rubbed a powdered finger over her gums, waited a moment. "That made my numbs gum—" She giggled. "I mean my gums numb."

"Wait till you're in full bloom." Reuben produced a mirror, held it up to her face. "Very important—always check for telltale dust."

Regina did as instructed, realizing her party light was on again. "See you, Wiz. I got biz to do." On her way out she reached behind the bar and retrieved the metal box where she had Eric deposit the business cards she collected. The silver-and-black Big Bang Entertainment card migrated to the top. *President Boney T.* Feeling on top of the world, she stuffed the cards in her purse. *I'd love to see his face when Glen gives him my card.*

Regina made her next play date downtown at the Odeon feeling sharper and funnier than ever. She scheduled lunch with her PR agent, schmoozed the restaurant manager, and got home a little after four, still full of energy. *Reuben's right, that was no biggie.* She showered, made herself a sandwich from some leftover chicken, then left it uneaten when she decided to arrange all of her shoes by color and heel height. The sun had been up two hours when she finally conked out.

The next afternoon over cola and phone calls, the memory of the day in Macintosh when Ty handed her that first black-and-silver card kept pushing its way to the front of Regina's mind, giving her shivers. She tried to dilute it with snippets from his Boney T days but before long Regina had a running slide show of the two of them and so many Fundays. *Screw him.* It wasn't like she'd been alone in her room wasting away in the almost five years since they'd been together. *Not really together.* Regina knew women who complained about a shortage of men, but there had been no clog in her pipeline. At any given moment she could call up the three or four regular starters, or try out somebody new from the farm team. *No strings required.*

Regina wanted to share the Ty update, but these days there wasn't anyone who would get it. Carmen would end up making her feel bad because her parties didn't contribute to the fight against cancer. *Always sucking up to my parents. Bet she got a stupid Santa sweater to match my mother's now that she's bought a town house practically in their backyard.* And Regina still wasn't speaking to Jewell. *I don't have to stay in this dump. I can move too.* Regina looked at her watch. *Six o'clock. Cocktail time.* She poured herself a glass of wine. *Screw 'em.*

On her way home early Sunday morning, Regina picked up the *Times* and spent the afternoon sitting on the chaise studying the real estate ads, circling items for further investigation. It landed on the floor with the other discards and went out on Monday with the trash.

On Tuesday while Regina was watching Jewell's Adrienne connive her way into the office of her alleged father, the phone rang. She hit the mute. "Regina Foster Productions."

"What happened to the Good Tymes?"

Regina knew the smooth voice from the first word and her heart hiccuped before she could will it back into its regular rhythm. "Nothing stays the same, Tyrone." It sounded funny, calling him by name. She'd only called him that once. When they first met.

"I hear that."

On the silent screen Adrienne rifled papers and desk drawers in the empty office, while Regina fought for words. "And I hear you're the president." She walked around the room, the phone in one hand, the receiver in the other, wishing she felt as sharp as she did after her cocaine hit last Thursday night. "Big Bang Entertainment. I could go off on that."

Ty chuckled. Regina could see the gap in his front teeth. This was the kind of conversation she'd normally breeze through while doing six other things, but now she had to concentrate.

"Hey, I'm kickin' it. Makin' some moves. Glen told me your moves are pretty smooth."

What does that mean?

"And I do wanna talk some business," Ty said.

By the time she hung up, Adrienne had secreted several pages in her handbag, and Regina had a meeting with Ty at two o'clock on Thursday. He said he wanted a launch party for Misha's second CD. When the messenger arrived with it she realized it was his protégée, the one she'd seen with him on *Soul Train*. She looked very different. The long coppery wig had given way to a sheet of blond, parted down the middle and she wore a gold lamé tube of a dress that outlined everything but her short and curlies. The record was called, *More than Money Can Buy*. Ty said he wanted to do a party, something with class. "I been hearin' about DeVille, so I know you got the class. But nobody had to tell me that."

Regina spent the next day and a half preparing for her first party proposal—working out a theme, consulting with vendors and trying to forget this proposal was for Ty.

She arrived too early for her meeting so she sat at a lunch counter across Fifth Avenue with a piece of gummy apple pie and some acidy coffee.

To keep Ty off her mind she talked to the waitress, a dowdy woman in a baggy pink-and-white uniform, who had strong opinions about the weather. After checking her watch ninety-seven times, Regina paid up, walked across the street.

The elevator in the grimy brick building on 20th Street creaked and groaned, but she could tell when it reached Big Bang Entertainment—she could feel the thumping music. The doors opened onto the reception area, a wall to wall graffiti canvas, with Big Bang written in rubbery silver letters, surrounded by an explosion of stars and planets. A black lacquered desk centered the reception area, surrounded by a constellation of slouchy leather sofas. There were people everywhere, conferring in the halls, lounging on the couches, rushing from one wing of the office to the other, dressed in everything from baggy jeans to double-breasted suits. The scent of a recent pizza delivery lingered in the air.

"Regina. You see, I'm a man of my word." Glen raced by with videotapes in one hand and the *Wall Street Journal* in the other.

All the activity made Regina dizzy, or was it because her breath came in short snatches? "Regina Foster to see Tyrone Washington." The whisper barely made it out of her throat.

The receptionist's inch-long orange nails clicked on the phone as she punched in the extension. "Down the hall. Last door on the left."

Before Regina could put her hand on the knob the door opened. Their eyes met and the tingle radiated from her neck to her knees. "I guess you *are* the president—windowed office, the works." Regina hurried past him, into the room before they could touch. She headed directly to inspect the framed grouping on the side wall. There were gold records for "Rap-zilla" and "What You Need to Know." Ty's photo in a *Billboard* article hung between.

"I hardly look. Not much to see." Ty closed the door and sat in his big leather chair, his back to the staggered landscape of rooftops, water towers, peeling billboards and fire escapes. He propped his feet on his orderly black desk, popped a button on the stereo shelved at his fingertips. An achy tenor crooned softly in the background. "You plannin' to sit down?"

Regina had gotten herself together by now. She slid into the chair in front of his desk. "I was surprised you called." He wore a pale gray suede shirt jacket over a black silk T and pants. Regina sensed there was something different about him. Something more sure, in control.

"I'm full of surprises." Ty scruffed up his chin. "When Glen came in here with that card, I decided you must be the right answer to a question I'd been askin', so I picked up the phone."

"That simple?" Regina sat back in the chair, crossed her legs.

"I like things simple. I want this party to be something different, a little loud, but classy. You know how to do it." He shrugged. "Simple."

Then they took care of business. Regina laid out her concept, showed him samples, talked budget and scheduling. She called the location, made sure it was available and booked the date. Ty gave her the names of the Big Bang people she'd be working with to coordinate PR and transportation. All the while she made sure she didn't graze his hands, still wary of the heat.

"I don't need to know every detail. You know your job. I'ma let you do it."

I know he's talking about that boat ride. He thinks he's slick. "What happened to Boney T? The man out front?"

"Retired. I found out the man behind the curtain's got the power. DJ booth wasn't back far enough. Boney T got my name out there, made some connections, made some money. I produced some records with Bad Attitude, learned about the business, about publishin'. Now, I run my own show." Ty cupped his hands behind his head. "Develop talent, like my girl Misha. I produce, deal with the sound. And I put the whole package together, get it out there in front of the people. I still produce rap. I dig it 'cause it's raw, uncut, from the gut. But that's not how I like all my life to be. Sometimes I need it to be sweet and mellow." He cocked his head toward her, and Regina knew it was time to go, before the conversation moved in a more personal direction.

Ty started to get up to see her to the door.

"Don't bother. You look all comfortable where you are."

"Can't get too comfortable. Don't want to lose my edge."

Regina paused, hand on the knob. "Why are you doing this?"

"We used to work good together," Ty said. "I think we still can."

Regina made notes on her way home, and tried to sort out how she felt about Ty being the one to pass out the pay envelope this time. *That makes me the hired help.*

Limos started pulling up in front of the ornate bank building on 42nd Street after dusk, after photographers had taken their places outside the velvet ropes. Inside, the towering cathedral of the dollar bill had been transformed into a lush garden, with "More than Money Can Buy" pumping from hidden speakers. The huge central teller cage was tented in gauzy blue fabric, painted with clouds. A carpet of sod covered the elaborate mosaic floor; lacy trees and gazebos dotted the landscape, and there were jonquils, peonies, daisies, all kinds of flowers, perfuming the room. Misha arrived in a white carriage, wearing a column of sheer, skin-toned fabric, covered in silk flowers so she looked like part of the garden.

Regina had hired two freelance assistants for this project, and along with her Big Bang liaisons, she coordinated entrances and interviews, kept Reuben after the kitchen and wait staff, made sure a waiter found Ty and offered him root beer and orange juice, in case he still drank his strange concoction. Regina had helped rally an A-List crowd, including Jewell whom she broke down and called at the last minute because she was, after all, a celebrity, and because she couldn't imagine doing such a big event without her there. She even left Carmen a message about the party, but didn't expect her to be interested in anything to do with Ty. True to form, Carmen left Regina a message saying she was on call and couldn't attend.

"This is genius." Jewell swept in and gave Regina a huge hug, as glad to be there with her friend as Regina was to have her. "It's a long way from Prof's." They were two of the three people in the room who knew what that meant. "Guess Carmen and I were wrong about Ty. Too bad she couldn't be here."

"People are having fun. Why would she want to come?" Regina leaned in close to Jewell and whispered, "Where's Dwight?"

"Community Board meeting, but we're wonderful." Then Jewell introduced the *Through It All* producer she'd brought along as a stand-in.

"How's your place?" It was the first time Regina could bring herself to mention Jewell's new living arrangement without getting pissed off.

"I love it. You have to come." They hadn't said it in so many words, but Jewell knew they'd reached a truce. "And I bought a car so we can drive down to see Carmen when she has a free weekend."

"Bijoux on wheels. Will the streets of New York ever be safe again?" Regina teased.

"Ha ha, very funny," Jewell cracked. "So, where's Ty, hmm?"

"Oh, he's around," Regina said casually. "Gotta go. The hors d'oeuvres are great. Enjoy." She returned to her official duties, all the while keeping an eye on Ty as he squired Misha through the scene, making introductions, letting her shine. And even though he was technically not the guest of honor, Regina noticed the parade of women who clearly thought Ty was the main event, wondered which one would go home with him for a few extra rounds—not that it mattered to her. *Can't they do any better than throwing it in his face?*

With the party winding down, Ty found Regina standing by one of the trees. "I'm gonna put Misha in her limo. I'll be back, don't leave," he said.

Guess she's not the lucky contestant. Regina did her end of the evening rounds then took a seat in the grass, her back against the gauzy sky. Shoes off, she sipped champagne while the clean-up crew scurried to turn the paradise back into a money palace before morning. It was a huge leap from promoting a party to planning an event. *How the hell did I pull this off?* Regina always felt sad when her parties were over—empty. She spent so much time and energy looking forward to them, that there was a hole when there was nothing left to anticipate.

"Do I need to tell you this was off the hook?" Ty sat down on the grass beside Regina.

Even though they weren't touching, she could feel the heat of him beside her. She held up her glass for a toast, but realized he didn't have one. "There's more in the back—"

"Nah. And I had enough root beer and OJ." He cocked his head. "Glad you remembered."

"You really still drink that nasty stuff?" She thought it would be a joke. *I didn't mean for it to mean all that.*

"Told you. Keeps me goin'. When all the folks around me are actin' crazy, I still got my head on." Ty held up his fist like he was holding a beer mug. "To one hellified night."

Regina raised her glass to his fist and her eyes closed as they met knuckle to knuckle. *Keep it neutral.* "I don't guess you still drive that old car with no heat."

Ty chuckled that deep, hoarse laugh of his. "Nah. Finally broke down and got me a classic. That's high-class for old. Anyway, it's a sweet little Benz two-seater. But my house won't have any heat this winter if I don't lay on my contractor." Ty explained he had bought a brownstone on 124th Street. "Got it at auction and I'm restoring it."

"So where do you live now?" Regina asked.

"There. The bottom floor has the basics, plumbing, electricity. I got a long way to go, but I got time. Come on, I'll show it to you, then drop you home. You still live on—"

"Yep." She rested her head against the wall, turned to look at Ty. He was so close. And the familiar warm vibration started, slow, but sure. *You need to stop.* She was not supposed to be the one he tagged as "it." Not again. "There are some things I need to check on before I—"

"I'll wait. I'll get my car. Meet me outside."

Regina got up, trying to convince herself this was just a ride home because she wasn't ready to admit how glad she had been to cross Ty's path again.

"Looks like angel's hit the jackpot." Reuben popped a leftover crab cake in his mouth.

"He's an old friend, Reuben."

"The better to sleep with, my dear." His eyes twinkled.

Regina plucked a yellow snapdragon out of an arrangement and flung it at him. "Are you guys almost packed up?"

He snapped to attention. "Yes, sir. Sergeant sir." He sidled up next to her. "And are we feeling a little flat?"

Regina waved him off. "I'm flying high on all this. Besides, the man doesn't even drink."

"What does that have to do with you?" Reuben posed with the snapdragon in his teeth.

"I'm leaving." Regina walked away, checked with her assistants. They would supervise the breakdown, call her by 6 A.M. to confirm that all evidence of the night was gone. *I love assistants*. She swung past a mirror, tucked hairs into place, swiped on some lipstick and started to feel how little sleep she'd had in the last week. *This is not the time to run out of gas*. She had to keep her wits about her, keep her feelings in check because there was no point getting worked up over Ty. They tried that before and it didn't take. She started toward the door, doubled back to find Reuben. "I could use a little Oz," she said.

The top was down on Ty's roadster—black with glistening chrome. He sat on the fender, waiting. "You'll look good in that seat." He opened the door.

"How fast does this baby go?" Thanks to her pick-me-up, Regina was already flying. As they drove, the balmy air felt refreshing blowing over her skin, teasing the tingle that came from within. She gazed up at the sky as they zipped along the streets, feeling like she owned the night.

"This is it." Ty stopped the car, grinned. "The castle."

"You're kidding right?" Regina scanned the block. "Half the buildings look bombed out. The rest look like they just missed a direct hit."

"But what I see is the potential. I mean it's just like in the studio. I start with something rough, bring it up to a shine. Nothing feels better." Ty looked up at his house. "Now this place here, it's a hundred years old. They don't build stuff like this no more."

"But you have to rebuild something that's already been built once," Regina said.

"Yeah, but it was strong to start with, it just needs time and attention." Ty draped his arm over Regina's seat back, rubbed her neck. "You'll see."

What is he talking about? "I need to get home, Ty."

On the ride to her place, Regina's head raced a thousand miles an hour, trying to figure out what he wanted, what she wanted, what to do. If she went up to 5D alone she'd explode. This was Ty, and tonight felt like magic—like the old magic.

He double-parked in front of her building, turned to look at her.

"My place looks the same as it did the last time you were here, so if you can't deal with—"

"Peace." He kissed his two fingers, held them to her lips. "I don't care about the place. I care about you."

"Okay." It was all she could manage. Ty took her hand as he saw her upstairs, but they didn't talk. She couldn't tell if the quiver was from his touch or the drugs, but "*I care about you*," screamed in her head like a broken record on maximum volume. When he left to find a parking space, Regina had two quick glasses of wine to come down and rinsed out her mouth before Ty got back. And as soon as she opened the door and they looked at each other, the years they'd been apart dissolved. Tonight they had triumphed again. And there was not another soul who knew how much that meant because they had dug the foundation together.

"Baby, I miss you." Ty folded her in his arms.

Relaxing against his broad chest, Regina spoke in the soft, honeyed voice only Ty ever heard. "I miss you too." The truth slipped out and then their lips met in a reunion that spoke more than words. They stayed that way a long time, pressed together, eyes closed, kissing foreheads, eyelids, noses, hands touching faces, squeezing backs. After what could have been forever or the blink of an eye, he scooped her up, carried her to the bed. Ty's hands, strong and rough on Regina's skin, felt so familiar, but new again. Sure of his route Ty led the way, and Regina followed. She was surprised when they stopped at new places, tickled when they visited old ones—until, finally, they both reached their destination.

After Regina's 6 A.M. "all's-clear" from her crew, she snuggled back into Ty's arms, nuzzled the hair on his chest, for once took a deep, slow breath. She had maintained the "out by first light" rule with the men in her variety pack. It saved her from idle chitchat in the morning. But when he said he had to go, it felt too soon.

"You free for dinner tonight?" he asked just before he left.

"Uh, sure."

Ty looked at her a long moment, like he used to. "I really been missin' you."

And Regina went back to bed to figure out what it all meant.

15
"...everything is business, especially family."

"Come on, Jewell. It's three lines, and we can all get the hell out of here," Liz Cantor called from the other side of the pool. "Take it from 'I can't do it.'"

"Sorry Liz." Jewell went back to the patio door to start the walk to her mark across the terrace. Looking up into the lights to blink frustrated tears back into place, she adjusted her black-and-gold caftan, Adrienne's afternoon poolside attire, took a breath and nodded at Liz. This was her seventh take, and she just couldn't keep her mind on the scene.

"Action."

Crossing to the edge of the pool, Jewell turned to face Eden, the pregnant teenager played by Marta. "How many times have I told you Eden, I won't do it your..."

"Not again! Cut," Liz yelled. "Jewell, the line is *can't*. I *can't* do it your way."

"I know. I know." Jewell twisted her hair around her neck, pretended to hang herself. "I swear I'll get it next time." *Because I have to get out of here.*

"Ten minutes everybody." Liz stormed off to confer with the lighting director.

"What's bugging you?" Marta patted her padded stomach and picked up a bottle of water secreted in the poolside foliage. "You always know your lines and everybody else's."

"Sorry. I can't get it together today." They had been shooting for three days at the Long Island soundstage where they did *Through It All's* exterior shots. The building, large enough to service a fleet of 747s, was where the front doors, backyards and streets of Clearfield existed in a two-dimensional reality, ready for flowers to be tended, doorbells to be rung or cars to come to a screeching halt, on cue. Jewell knew this was their last scheduled day here. They had to finish.

"Is 'he' the reason you're screwing up?" Marta asked. In the last few months, if Jewell was moody or unpredictable, Dwight Dixon was somehow at the root of it.

"I'm meeting his father tonight." That was part of it. Jewell was definitely on edge about her introduction to the senior Dixon, but all week she'd struggled to stay in character and remember her lines while she did her scenes with the pseudo-pregnant, pseudo-teenage Marta, who was unfortunately a very good actress. Eden was waiting for her boyfriend, Clearfield's smooth-talking bad boy from a good family, to come back and marry her, like he said he would. Eden was so earnest and Jewell wanted to scream, "He's not coming," which she knew was true. The actor had been written out to film a movie, but it was more than that. *TIA*'s storylines were generally so outrageous that Jewell didn't take them seriously, but this one hit too close to home.

The trusting fifteen-year-old Jewell had been right under her skin this week, still aching for her own baby, wondering what her name was, what she looked like now that she was nine and a half. Jewell would remember how important the half was at that age, remember herself in pigtails, and then she'd forget what Adrienne was supposed to say.

"Ah. An audience with the King," Marta said.

"Yep. Himself." Jewell had spent an afternoon at the Jefferson Market Library reading magazine and newspaper articles about the Harlem Dixons. Colorful was the word most often used to describe King, so she figured he'd be a real character.

"And you stopped smoking too. I'm amazed you remember your name."

"Day's not over yet." Jewell grabbed a tin of breath mints from the bushes where Marta had hidden her water. What she really craved was a cigarette, but for the first time since she was fifteen she was a nonsmoker. The habit had started after Billy, flourished with Gianni, but she had been right that first night at dinner. Dwight didn't care for it. A couple of days after her last smoke, he had kissed her. "You don't taste like ashes. I like," he had said, and she was determined never to start again. Jewell popped two peppermints in her mouth.

"You had dinner with the mayor last week. Why sweat this?" Marta asked.

"I know, I know. Dinkins was great and King should be too, but I can't shake the jitters." Jewell remembered seeing him that day on the set of *New York Now*, wondering why he hadn't spoken. He just looked at her, but then she'd barely had time to speak to Dwight. So tonight would be their first official meeting and she wanted to make a good impression.

Jewell had called both Carmen and Regina for pep talks and they both had the same advice. "Just be you," Carmen said. "Screw 'em," was how Regina put it, but Jewell was still nervous. From her reading she'd learned the Dixons were venerable, black New York. They'd been at the head of the receiving line for a hundred years. After attending a variety of "boneless breast of chicken or beef tips" banquets and fund-raisers with Dwight, Jewell also came to realize this wasn't like Hollywood where your latest success opened any door you knocked on. You didn't crash this level of black society. You were invited by someone who belonged, but she didn't want to explain that to Marta. Nor could she explain to herself why it was so important for her to get this right, except that she wanted to fit into Dwight's world.

"Well think of it this way, first parents' meeting isn't as weird as first sex."

Jewell laughed knowingly, but she and Dwight hadn't had sex yet either. They'd had eleven dates in the last three and a half months, but she hadn't even cooked for him. There had been some kissing, but no undressing or hands in intimate places, which had so far spared Jewell the stretch-mark saga, but she had rehearsed that scene, playing both parts. Dwight was always understanding. Why wouldn't he be? And Jewell was in no rush. Billy had been like some crazy stunt, a tightrope walk with no net and she'd come crashing down. Gianni was like an amusement-park ride with great spins and swoops, but she had to come down to earth sometime. Dwight's slow, deliberate progress felt real, no tricks, no games. It was romantic, from another time, like his ties. Dwight's parents had been married until his mother's untimely death, so he knew about lasting relationships, although sometimes she wondered if they'd ever get beyond this genteel courtship.

"Okay." Liz clapped her hands. "Think you're ready to do the scene as written, Jewell?" Liz was not only the director of this episode. She was *TIA*'s head writer. Liz knew every syllable cold.

"Ready." *I have to get this right.* Because she had to go. It would be dicey heading to the city at rush hour, even though *TIA* provided a car and driver when they shot on the Island. On Liz's signal, Jewell crossed to the pool. "How many times have I told you Eden? I *can't* do it your way." She took Eden by the shoulders. "It will never work. Never. I won't allow Jason to get away with it." Adrienne gripped Eden tighter, almost shook her. "And you shouldn't either!"

"Cut! That's a wrap, folks."

"Hallelujah!" Jewell made a mad dash for her dressing room. It only took thirty minutes for her to shower, tone down her on-camera makeup, slip on her dress and run a brush through her hair. She gave Marta her tote to take back to the city, then headed for her car.

Cocktails at five thirty. Dwight had said it at least three times, adding that he held this party at his house every June before the Children's Literacy Benefit at Aaron Davis Hall. She knew that meant "please be on time." Although she hadn't adopted the more casual Italian attitude toward time, her schedule on the show was unpredictable and she had been late on a couple of occasions. At this point she knew it would take a miracle to get her to 139th Street before six, so she settled back in the limo, trying to erase the stress of her day sans cigarettes, and quizzing herself on King trivia until the driver turned onto the street.

The first time Jewell had come to Dwight's house was for a brunch he hosted to woo a businessman to open several coin laundries in his district. She had marveled at the simple grandeur of the block, like Notting Hill or Knightsbridge in London. Striver's Row had been the vision of well-to-do blacks who decided they wanted more for themselves than whites would allow them. So they hired the best architects of the day, and built two blocks of spectacular town houses.

This one had been Dwight's family home since King bought it in 1949, one of four he'd purchased on the Row. The others he renovated and sold, but he kept the grandest for himself. "They brought me here straight from the hospital, and except for college I've never lived anyplace else," Dwight had said. Some years ago King moved to a Fifth Avenue duplex across from the Metropolitan Museum. Dwight told her he had said, "I own enough of Harlem not to have to live there," but that hadn't stopped him from acquiring as much uptown real estate as he could get.

Through a minor miracle, Jewell rang Dwight's doorbell at five fifty-five. The door swung open almost immediately.

"Come on in!" The woman in a seashell pink dress and matching beaded jacket held the door wide. "I'm Forestina Braithwaite and you must be Jewell! We've been waiting for you!"

So this is Aunt Tina. Dwight mentioned her often. She was his favorite. "Sorry I'm late." Jewell heard the party mix of voices, laughter and tinkling ice coming from the upstairs parlor.

"Oh my dear, you're not late. We've been waiting because we're anxious to meet you!" Forestina was tall, though not as tall as Jewell. Her skin was the color of churned butter and her freshly coiffed hair only slightly darker. "Has he been harping on that CP time thing of his?" Forestina's lyric laugh accompanied the click clack of her dyed-to-match pumps across the marble foyer. "Don't let him get to you. His mother was a stickler about time. Lord, I can hear my sister Willie now. 'Common people keep CP time. It has nothing to do with being Colored.'" Forestina's smile was bright and her blond head bobbed as she spoke. "I used to be late just to annoy her. King did it too." She paused a second. "Or maybe it's just his nature. Anyway, Dwight can't abide tardiness. Prides himself on being the opposite of his father, but you know what they say about the apple." She winked at Jewell and led the way upstairs.

Jewell spied Dwight on the wide landing, handsome in his tux. For once his bow tie didn't look like a quaint throwback. Not that she didn't like them. In a world of four-in-hands, his bow ties showed he was confident enough to be an individual and she liked the statement they made.

"At last." Dwight came down two steps to meet her. "I was beginning to worry." He kissed her cheek. "I hope Aunt Tina didn't tell you too many things I'd rather you not know yet!"

"I've been on my best behavior." Forestina sailed off in the direction of the bar.

"Sorry I'm late. We went a little long." Every other word out of Jewell's mouth today seemed to be "sorry" and each one made her feel more off-balance.

"I won't put it on your permanent record card," Dwight said.

He is teasing? "Promise?" She couldn't always distinguish between jest and jab. A burst of wheezy laughter exploded above the chatter and music. Jewell looked toward the front parlor to see King holding court and she got a nervous rush. *Just be you*. She heard Carmen in her ear.

"Let's dive in. We've got catching up to do." Dwight took her hand and their first stop was a couple by the rear windows. "Jewell, this is my buddy P. J.—Peter Jackson, and his fiancée Edwina Lewis. We went to Camp Atwater together—how long?"

"Campers from eight to fifteen, counselors the next two summers. You do the math. I'm a lawyer," P. J. said.

"Or *will* be when he passes that bar exam," Edwina piped up.

P. J. shot her an annoyed look then turned to Jewell. "So you're Dwight's actress. I dabbled in acting, but decided on a career where you could earn a living."

"I've been earning quite a nice living at it since before I was eight—instead of going to camp." She could hear Regina cheering her zinger. Jewell smiled guilelessly and took a glass of champagne from a passing tray.

"Lovely to meet you." She slipped her arm through Dwight's and he back-patted his way to the next introduction.

Jewell had shaken her share of hands in her life; fans liked a touch and a smile, and she'd met more than her share of strangers, but tonight it seemed each greeting signaled the beginning of a qualifying round with questions to be answered, lineage and credentials to be checked. She got points for having gone to a Seven Sisters school, and from a few people for having lived in Baldwin Hills although others had never heard of the place. When Dwight brought up *Daddy's Girl* there were nods of recognition, but in this crowd the statute of limitations to award credit for that had run out. Her European work and her soap opera role didn't give her much play either. Nobody had seen them so they didn't count and among the assorted bankers, lawyers, dentists and other professionals, she felt like her career had been reduced to the level of a hobby, like macrame or bowling. An older woman with perfectly arranged, steely gray hair and an ivory-handled cane asked if she knew John Roland, as if that would prove she was a serious actress, but Jewell declined to connect that dot to Billy. And one young woman, a CPA wearing pale pink chiffon, with a tousle of chestnut curls piled high on her head, gave Jewell a particularly hard time until she caught Dwight giving her a warning glance. Jewell figured she was either an ex or a would-be contender, and it gave her a little boost to be the one he had chosen.

After they had made their way through the back room, Dwight paused by the entrance to the front parlor. "You look wonderful." He brushed her hair off her shoulder.

"Thank you." Jewell felt at least she'd gotten something right. She had chosen the slim black strapless dress because it was classic and with the double strand of pearls she felt tasteful, elegant, the things Dwight always admired. But so far tonight she felt more like she'd crashed a party than the time Gianni had boldly waltzed her into a private celebration in Monte Carlo.

"King's free. Come." Dwight took her hand and led her across the room.

"I'd like you to meet Jewell Prescott." Dwight put his arm around Jewell's bare shoulders, looked in his father's eyes defiantly.

"So you're this Jewell I've been hearing about." King eyed her from beneath the oil portrait of his late wife Wilhelmina, a pale beauty who resembled Forestina, but with sadder eyes.

Jewell was pleased to hear Dwight had been talking to his father about her. "Delighted to meet you, Mr. Dixon." Jewell held out her hand.

"King. Nobody would know who you were talking about if you called me Mr. Dixon." He gripped her hand tightly in his pudgy one, shook twice, then let go.

"King it is." The handshake was just shy of painful, but Jewell managed not to wince. From the painting she could see where Dwight got his looks. His bronze complexion was an amalgam of his father's rusty brown and his mother's pearly shade. But where Dwight's face was a study in angles, like his mother's, King's was mostly curves, with a wide triangle of nose, and black circles under hound-dog eyes. His wavy black hair had a hint of white roots, and he wore it much longer than Dwight's, parted on the side. He reminded Jewell of big band leaders from old movies she'd seen, imagined him waving his baton. Jewell guessed King was about five foot six and weighed one person more than she and Dwight together. She wondered what he had looked like when he was young, when Dwight was young.

"You're one of those tall ones," King said. "Like that tribe in Africa. Real tall, real—"

"Watusis, King." Dwight arched an eyebrow.

"*That's* what I'm talkin' about." King poked his son's arm merrily, turned his attention to Jewell. "Now, Dwight tells me you're on some kind of television show."

"Yes, off and on since I was a child, but now I'm on a—"

"Not much on TV worth watching except the news." The buttonholes of King's pleated-front formal shirt strained against his onyx studs, looking like a row of shiny black fish eyes.

"Jewell, I'll be right back. I need to check on a few things downstairs." Dwight rubbed her shoulder, then he was off.

Jewell was startled at Dwight's sudden departure. *But I'm a big girl.* "I don't watch much TV either," she said. "But I have to keep up. Otherwise it would be like—you're in real estate right? It would be like you saying you buy and sell houses, but you don't live in one."

"Hmmm." King downed his scotch, looking slightly indignant. "Interesting way to put it."

Jewell sipped her champagne, wondered why she felt uneasy. *I'm just being paranoid.* She decided to turn the conversation to King's strong suit. "I've read about how you expanded your real estate acquisitions through the years. I've been afraid to spread myself too thin. Of course I haven't been at this as long as you have."

King banged his empty glass on the mantel. "You're in real estate?"

Jewell warmed to the subject. "Commercial and residential properties in—"

"Everybody with two sheds and an outhouse thinks he's a mogul."

"Excuse me?" Jewell was stunned by this outburst, but King looked past her and flagged down a slender woman who looked half his age, with peachy skin and a face full of freckles.

"Barbara! Come over here, and get me another scotch on your way." He leaned in close to Jewell. "You know I saw Ted Hampton once. At Peg Leg Bates' Place in the Catskills. It was all a little too nig-rafied for me, if you get my drift." He grinned like the Cheshire Cat.

"No. I don't." The floor under Jewell's feet seemed to wobble and she struggled to keep her balance. She didn't know about Peg Leg Bates or why her father was being thrown in her face, but like lye, the words continued to burn.

"Here you go, King." Barbara scurried over, old-fashioned glass in hand, and planted a kiss on King's meaty jowl. He finished his drink in one slug.

And Jewell walked away, clutching her glass so tightly she was afraid she'd snap the stem.

"Let me tell you about King." Forestina appeared at Jewell's side and spirited her across the room. "I don't know what he said, but he is not a jolly fat man. He's not even a nice fat man."

"So I see." Jewell was still reeling.

"King is a cobra," Forestina said. "Without warning he'll rise up, look you straight in the eye, and strike before you blink. Then he'll wait for the venom to paralyze you and while you're trying to catch your breath, he'll swallow you whole. I guess it works for him in business, but to him, everything is business, especially family. If you and Dwight stay together, you'll have to do like the rest of us—develop your own anti-venom and keep it handy." She smiled. "Consider this chat your first dose. It's only temporary, but it might get you through the rest of the evening."

"Telling tales again, Aunt Tina?" Dwight joined them.

"Just a little girl talk," Forestina responded. "Lovely girl. I like her." She kissed her nephew on the cheek and was gone. That's when Jewell looked around and realized most of the guests had already made their exits.

"You all right?" Dwight took Jewell by the arm.

"Uh, sure. Yes." She didn't know what had just happened, much less how to explain it.

"Okay. Let's go. We don't want to miss the curtain."

They proceeded down the stairs. Dwight opened the door, and that's when she heard the raspy whisper from behind her.

"If I say white he says black, but that girl is black as my shoe. And do you know what he had the balls to tell me? 'Black is Beautiful'! That's some leftover horse shit from the sixties. I didn't buy it then either."

Jewell whipped around and looked directly at King as he lumbered down the stairs. He was talking to Barbara, but he looked right at Jewell, and she knew he meant for her to hear.

Dwight squeezed her hand. "Let's go," he said and closed the door.

Jewell put one foot in front of the other as they walked to the car, but she burned so hot she was numb. Her school, her childhood, her neighborhood had been an isolated pocket, removed from the rest of the world, so she'd avoided schoolyard taunts about her color. She'd escaped not being invited to birthday parties because she was too dark. Then she was a TV star, warned by her mother that her celebrity was the reason people would like her, not cautioned that her dark skin was the reason some wouldn't, especially not one of her own.

"My father is an ass sometimes." Dwight took both of Jewell's hands. "He's got some backward, destructive ideas, and I apologize for his ignorance."

Jewell looked into Dwight's eyes, nodded because she couldn't speak.

The theater was less than ten minutes away, so she had no time to recover. Dwight drove through the City College gates, dropped her at the Aaron Davis entrance and went to park, but as soon as Jewell walked into the rotunda, she was in the middle of a new scene in the day's drama.

"I can't believe it's you!" Instead of taking Jewell's ticket, the usherette grabbed her hand. "I go to school here and we watch you every day in the student lounge."

Jewell wasn't prepared to switch to her public persona, but it was show time so she managed a smile, signed a ticket stub for the girl. Then Jewell was welcomed by a circle of women who were tickled to meet her, asked if they could have their pictures taken with her. "You should make more movies," one said. "I loved you in *Hoochie Coo*." And just that quickly the sand under Jewell's feet shifted again, but she pasted on a smile for the camera.

After a few more minutes of answering questions, meeting and greeting, she saw Dwight watching her from a distance and waved him over.

"Oooh Councilman Dixon, you're with Jewell?" The woman in the sequined butterfly top stepped back to look at them. "Well now you *know* you got my vote!"

Jewell slipped into her seat, pretending not to see King and Barbara in the next row, just as the emcee for the evening, Felicia Anderson, took the mike. Felicia did her plugs for the radio station and other sponsors, her audience warm-up spiel about the stellar treat they had in store. Then she introduced dignitaries from the audience, which to Jewell's surprise included her. "Once our favorite pigtailed, wise-cracking tyke, she's now the baddest babe on daytime television. Jewell Prescott, stand up so we can give you an uptown soul welcome!"

The spotlight found her and she stood and waved to the house.

"That was worthy of a presidential convention," Dwight whispered as she took her seat. "Obviously there are a lot of folks home in the middle of the day." He winked.

"How'd they even know I was here?" she asked.

"A little birdie might have told them." Dwight grinned.

The singers, dancers and children's choir were received with great ovation, but the performances were lost on Jewell. She just wanted to go home, open her windows to the summer night, pour a cognac and try to clear King and the rest of this day from her head, but then there was the reception afterward. "We'll only stay a little while," Dwight said. He worked the crowd and Jewell tried to hang back, but she was soon drawn into his swirl. It took an hour to make a getaway.

On the walk back to the car, Dwight was practically buoyant. "What a night! And you are the best part of it. You make me proud to have you by my side."

Jewell was surprised by his words and by the arm he wrapped around her waist to pull her close. "Dwight, what a nice thing to say."

"Pure truth. Firstly, you look like, I don't know, some dream I don't ever want to wake up from. And that bunch at my house is tough. I know how they are, but you were perfect, Jewells."

Jewells? He's never called me that. And she certainly felt less than perfect. The ground under her feet was shifting again, but she'd never seen such bright light in his eyes and it was shining on her. She smiled. "Thank you."

Once settled in the car he took her hand. "And as for my father, I'll have words with him tomorrow. King likes to shock people, thinks it gives him the upper hand. I should have warned you, but at least you know what you're getting into." Dwight reached out, fingered the pearls around her throat. "And I hope you want to get into it with me because I fell for you the first day we met. I know I'm a little slow, but I've always felt that something precious is worth the wait."

Dwight's words made Jewell dizzy. Her reply was a jumble in her mind and her mouth. "I am—I feel—yes."

Dwight's kiss felt different to Jewell, like he was free to give what he'd been holding back.

When they moved apart, Dwight adjusted his tie. "There's plenty of champagne left. Will you stop for a nightcap?"

Jewell nodded and they headed to his house, her brain tripping over itself. *I should tell him.* All her rehearsing didn't help her now. She couldn't find words that fit.

As soon as Dwight closed the door, he embraced her, kissed her neck, followed the smooth line of her shoulder. With her body she matched his moves, responded to his caresses, but her head was engaged in a debate about what she should say, how she should say it. Then he tugged her zipper down to the small of her back and she knew the time for talking had passed.

Jewell's dress was left on the bannister, but she didn't undo his tie until they stood beside his four-poster bed. For weeks she had imagined how their bodies would fit together, had flashes of their limbs intertwined, skin to skin with nothing but heat between them. Dwight's skin was cooler than she expected, smooth to touch. He explored her back and hips with his hands and Jewell closed her eyes, tried to will herself to relax. *Can he tell? What will he* say? Too anxious to succumb to her own sensations, she focused on enhancing his. By the time he reached in his night stand, pulled out the foil packet, he was almost in a frenzy. She coaxed him with her body until he squeezed her so tight her breath caught in her chest, until he shuddered and went slack.

They were a tangle of legs and sheets, Jewell's head resting in the crook of his arm, his fingers playing in her hair until his deep, slow breathing let her know he was asleep.

Jewell was still too wired to fall asleep in this new bed, so she lay awake, adjusting to the sounds of his sleep, wondering what he liked for breakfast, wanting a cigarette.

At first light she saw it, the sepia family portrait above the mantel. Dwight looked like he was five in his velvet-collared jacket, short pants and knee socks. Wilhelmina looked dignified in her brocade dress, a double strand of pearls tucked just below the neckline. And King's unrelenting stare followed Jewell wherever she looked.

"So you're awake." Dwight pulled her back toward his chest. "That was the best sleep I've had in my life."

Jewell felt snug, secure, until his hand began a lazy stroll down her body, familiarizing itself with new hills and valleys. She lay still, knowing he would discover the interruption in the smooth, satiny landscape when he reached her belly. She thought about pretending to be cold, clutching the covers and curling up, or rolling over claiming to be ticklish. But then he was there. She felt the hesitation, the tentative re-exploration, and knew she had to say something.

"Stretch marks. I hate them," she offered quietly. "I gained a ton of weight after *Daddy's Girl* got canceled. It was a pretty rotten year. I got rid of it, but those are my lovely parting gifts." She rested her hand on her belly, wondering why she lied.

16
"...no training wheels..."

Stethoscope in the pocket of her white coat, Carmen popped the swinging doors of the ER and got the adrenaline boost she'd come to expect when she walked into the unpredictable chaos. This was the final rotation of her first year as a resident and she thrived on the whirlwind. Emergency was like a tornado that picked up whatever random assortment of people and ailments were in its path, then dropped them at Admitting.

"Webb. Just in time." Sandrine Hawley, the ER attending, handed her a chart. "We're up to our butts and it's rising fast. Make sure a parent or guardian is coming for the boy in curtain three, then take a history from the woman in one—chest pain. When you're done find me." Her curly head disappeared into an examining room.

Then Carmen was sucked into the storm, transported to the hyper-state where her nerves pulsed with every word spoken or task undertaken, yet she was possessed of a calm that dropped the maelstrom to slow motion. Carmen revved at full alert, with no time to feel, only to do.

Five hours and twenty-two cases later, desperate for a cup of mud from the coffee machine, Carmen was heading to the cafeteria when she was intercepted. "Got a bike accident in six." Sandrine handed Carmen the chart. "X-rays are negative, but he's got a forearm laceration that needs stitching up."

Carmen's caffeine dreams swirled down the drain. It was early summer—school wasn't even out yet, but still prime season for bike and skateboard mishaps. Usually the patient was a kid or a sullen teenager, so she was caught off guard by the man stretched out on the exam table in a hospital gown, tube socks and dreadlocks that grazed his shoulders, except for the one that flopped over one eye.

"I'm Dr. Webb." She still got a jolt whenever she said that. "I'll be taking care of your cut."

"Dr. Webb?" He folded his good arm behind his head. "You must be a prodigy. I mean, no offense, you look like you'd still be reading *Charlotte's Web* or something." His skin was the glossy brown of a caramel apple and his smile was like sunshine.

One of those—thinks he's cute. This had been a busy day, Carmen was a pint low on coffee, and in no mood to have her authority questioned. She looked back at him, attentive, but deadpan and tried to ignore the high-beam grin. "I assure you Mr. uh—" She glanced at his chart. "Mr. Wyatt, I have all the necessary credentials to stitch up your arm." Carmen pulled up a stool and sat down to examine his injury. A couple of times a day some man—patient, doctor, X-ray technician—would make the mistake of talking to her like she was a little tootsie he could intimidate, or who would be grateful that he winked in her direction. She always straightened them out quick, fast and in a hurry.

"Now I didn't mean that as an insult. I think more doctors should read *Charlotte's Web*. It would teach them kindness and compassion. We patients appreciate that." He cocked his head to check out her reaction.

Carmen raised her eyes without moving her head, but looked away as soon as she saw him peering at her. She got up, grabbed a suture kit from the cabinet and went to the sink to scrub, feeling strangely flustered and trying to shake it off. Except that when she sat back down and covered his arm with a sterile drape, she could feel him looking at her and his scrutiny made her stomach flip-flop. *Usual procedure jitters.* She directed her full attention to prepping her patient.

"Now, I know you wouldn't hurt a brother," he teased.

Carmen raised a brow, shot him a look. "You wouldn't say that if you knew my brother." Then she went back to his cut.

"I hope you won't hold that against me." He shook his head to coax the hair out of his face. "I'm Malcolm, by the way. I'd offer my hand, but you got it already."

"You're a regular comedian, Malcolm-by-the-way, but I'd be still if I were you. The needle is the worst part." Carmen held his arm steady, felt his muscles stiffen as she injected lidocaine down the length of the wound, but he never made a sound.

Malcolm relaxed his arm and Carmen wished there was something to do besides sit next to him waiting for the anesthesia to take effect.

"Are you gonna tell me your first name?"

"Thought you decided on Charlotte." She gently fingered the skin near the cut. "Feel that?"

"Feel what?" He grinned again.

Carmen ignored him and the flutter she felt when he smiled. She irrigated and cleaned the now numb wound then stole a quick peek at Malcolm Wyatt who stared at the ceiling.

Carmen proceeded to stitch the cut closed. She preferred doing procedures like sutures by rote, distracted by chatter, letting her hands take over. But for the first time since she walked in the room her patient had gone mute, and for some reason she couldn't think of two words to say, so she worked silently on the neat row of sutures, carefully guiding the curved needle. "There you go. That's likely to smart when the shot wears off. An over-the-counter analgesic should do you." She dropped the needle in the red disposal container.

"How's it going in here?" Dr. Hawley came in just as Carmen finished.

"I'm still alive. That's a good sign huh?" Malcolm teased.

"I left you in very capable hands. I knew you'd survive. What did you do here, Webb?"

Malcolm listened intently as Carmen explained. "—simple interrupted sutures…excellent wound edge…no complications. There should be vigorous healing and negligible scarring."

"Good." Dr. Hawley nodded and left.

"Vigorous healing. I like your prognosis, Dr. Webb."

Carmen bandaged Malcolm's arm, had a fleeting awareness of his smooth, firm skin. "You don't want to move that around too much. Keep it dry. Should I put it in a sling?"

"No, I'll remember not to use it as a battering ram." He swung his legs over the edge.

"Good. Get dressed and stop by the desk to pick up your script for an antibiotic—take all of it—instructions for caring for your wound, and a referral for an outpatient appointment to have the stitches removed." Carmen peeled off her gloves, tossed them in the appropriate container.

"I am dressed." He pulled off his gown revealing Lycra bike shorts. "Mostly."

Carmen was on her way out, but something kept her glued to the spot like she was hypnotized, watching him slip a yellow T-shirt over his head, gingerly insert his bandaged arm.

"You're really not going to tell me your name?" He hopped off the table, tugged the shirt the rest of the way down over his smooth lean torso then sat on the metal chair. "That'll make it pretty hard for me to ask you to dinner."

Carmen snapped out of her trance, headed for the door. "Did you hit your head when you fell off the bike?"

"As a matter of fact I did, but I'd still like to take you out."

She turned to look at him. "Why?"

"I like you. I think you're interesting. Don't you eat?" He slid his feet into his sneakers.

"Of course I eat." Carmen would have blamed the racy feeling on caffeine, but she hadn't had coffee yet. "And you don't know me well enough to like me or find me interesting."

"So go out with me and let me find out if I'm right."

"Listen Mr. Wyatt—"

"Malcolm. I'm thirty-one years old. I teach algebra and geometry to kids who'd rather practice hands-on biology with their classmates than formulas and theorems." He gingerly tied his shoes as he spoke. "I'm straightforward, easygoing, an only child, and no I'm not spoiled. My parents retired back to Georgia—outside Atlanta—five years ago. I realize I've missed my chance at the Tour de France, but I ride my bike as often as I can, just for kicks, play some tennis, shoot some hoops. I like to keep moving." His voice was warm and crackled with the hint of fun. "On the quiet tip, I've been collecting stamps since I was eight and started as a Boy Scout project. I like Beethoven, Bach and the blues, red wine and red meat." Malcolm stood up. "And I'm a dynamite cook."

"Thank you for the résumé, Mr. Wyatt. You only left out vaccinations and dental records." Carmen grabbed the knob. "But I don't date patients." *Like I actually date anybody.*

"When I walk out that door, I'm not a patient anymore, at least not yours." His eyes cajoled a yes.

"Good-bye Mr. Wyatt." Carmen opened the door.

"I'll take back the dinner invitation, if you tell me your name." He followed her out.

She stopped, turned around. "Carmen." *What difference does it make?* "Carmen Webb." She headed off before he could say another word and got back in the mix so she'd have no time to think about Malcolm Wyatt, math teacher, and his warm smile, his candid confidence, his smooth skin.

At the end of her shift Carmen ran into Sandrine in the parking lot. "You ever date a patient?" she asked.

"Are you nuts?" Sandrine called as she ducked into her hatchback.

But for the rest of the week Malcolm would pop into Carmen's mind at odd moments—while driving to work, notating a chart, lying in bed. Then she'd get annoyed with herself and push him away by reciting diseases of the central nervous system or the steps of an orotracheal intubation. Eventually the memory faded, like a mirage.

After her stint in the ER, Carmen started her second year of residency with pediatrics where her ability to remain detached was severely tested. So many children, sick or injured, and they weren't all going to get better. At the end of each shift there seemed to be one little face she couldn't erase, one story she couldn't forget no matter how many others had happy endings. That's when she'd remind herself this was just a job, she was not responsible for the world's problems.

So on a rainy Thursday, Carmen had just finished twenty-four hours on and was about to head home, glad that Lonnie hadn't listened when she told her to stop leaving casseroles by her front door. Lasagna and real sleep to supplement the catnaps she'd grabbed in the doctors' lounge would make her a new woman. She had signed off on her last chart when she heard her name over the PA. She picked up a phone at the nurses' station, wondering what "T" she'd forgotten to cross, and hung up heading for the first-floor clinic, trying to figure out what they wanted.

He was sitting across from the reception desk.

"What the—" Carmen stared at the eye patch, so surprised she forgot to be mad.

Malcolm looked up from a stack of looseleaf homework papers. "I know it looks like I'm trying out my pirate costume and we're a long way from Halloween." He smiled. "It seems that vision problems can crop up after, what is it he called it—?"

"Closed head injuries. No, don't get up." He had moved to stand but she waved him down. At least this way they were eye to eye. And she'd have a head start if she needed to escape.

"Two days after you sewed me up I started seeing double." Malcolm's hair was secured in back with a rubber band. "Freaked me out, especially when my twenty-five summer school kids turned into fifty. That's too much challenge, even for me. In the summer they act like prisoners of war."

Carmen laughed before she could take it back. She blamed her inability to keep a straight face on lack of sleep.

"She laughs! After last time I wasn't sure." Even in school clothes—blue oxford cloth shirt, two buttons open, tie pulled away from his neck, khakis, tassel loafers, Malcolm didn't look like he stayed between the lines. "You were pretty serious."

"I'm always serious when there's blood involved." Carmen tried to ignore the tiny bubbles sputtering in her belly. "How's your arm?"

"Vigorously healed." He laughed. "Wanna see?" He unbuttoned his cuff.

"No thanks." Carmen held up her hand. "But your vision—"

"It's improving. I'm down to maybe one and a quarter instead of double. By my next visit I should be back to one on one."

Carmen shoved her inexplicably sweaty hands in her lab coat pockets. "So why exactly did you have me paged? I assume it was you."

Malcolm moved his briefcase and papers to the next seat and slid forward. "I thought as long as I was here, I'd try to get you to go out with me again—not exactly a sympathy date, but this eye patch should be good for something."

Carmen didn't know how he managed to look earnest and mischievous at the same time—out of one eye. He had tricked her into an unnecessary stop when she was already tired, sleepy and hungry, but instead of anger she felt—flattered. *Why would he go through all this?* But underneath the tickle and tingle she was trying mightily to suppress, lurked the nagging feeling that if she said yes, the joke would be on her again. "It's really not a good idea for me to see patients outside of the hospital." She gave him a tired smile. "I've got to go Mr.—Malcolm."

"Listen, I understand. I don't want to come off like some crazy stalker. Honestly, I just liked you, thought maybe we could connect." Malcolm stood and gathered his papers and the black bike messenger bag he carried them in. "Hey, thanks for coming down here." This time he was the one to walk away. After a few steps he turned, glanced over his shoulder. "Take care, Doc." He waved and kept going.

Malcolm's stride was smooth and long, and watching him walk away gave Carmen a sinking feeling. "Wait!" The word exploded from her lips. *Now what do I do?*

It took a month to come up with a date they were both free. When Malcolm suggested an outing to Lambertville, she thought it was a great idea. She'd been meaning to explore the town on the Delaware River, and New Hope right over the bridge, since Lonnie told her about its antique shops and flea markets, but for years she had been too busy for sightseeing.

Until a week ago Carmen had successfully kept their appointment, which is what she called it instead of a date, out of mind. Then she started stressing about what to wear and panicked. Jewell was away on a publicity junket so she broke down and called Regina. "Go shopping. I know your closet. You don't own any cute clothes," Regina had said. "You can't show up looking like an insurance adjuster." Carmen kicked herself for calling in the first place, knowing Regina's idea of cute meant something red with a slit. Besides, shopping wasn't in the budget, and if he didn't like what she had on—tough.

So when she answered the door, Carmen felt fine in jeans, sneakers and a blue sleeveless T, a UMDNJ sweatshirt tied around her waist

Malcolm seemed to approve too. "Hey lady, you're looking good." He kissed her cheek. His lips left a hot spot. She floated down the stairs behind him, watching his slightly bow-legged trot, trying not to stare at the sculpted muscles of his calves, his thick thighs, wondering what had come over her. After all, Regina was the one who checked out every man who crossed her path, and some who didn't. Carmen saw bodies every day, carefully keeping her observations strictly clinical. She made herself release the eye-lock.

"You said a picnic." Two mountain bikes were secured on the rack in back of Malcolm's old Jeep, a cooler and a sack of equipment were stowed behind the seats. "You never mentioned bike riding." Carmen climbed into the front seat, wondering what she'd gotten herself into.

Malcolm, sans eye patch, clutched, shifted and roared off. "We've gotta work up an appetite. I guesstimated the size of your bike at the rental place, so I hope I'm close. Got you a helmet too. Don't want any closed head injuries."

"Haven't you had enough? You just got your eyes straight." Carmen had to talk loud to be heard above the engine and the rush of late summer air through the open windows. She tried to hold her hair in place, but it escaped around her fingers and fluttered in the wind.

"You kidding? That was nothing. I've broken bones, torn ligaments. Injury is the cost of staying in the game. Besides, if I hadn't gone airborne, I wouldn't have met you." He winked.

And Carmen felt that sunny smile again. "Yeah. Right. Does meeting people usually leave you needing a tetanus shot?"

"Only if they bite."

A warm flush spread from her cheeks to her shoulders and she rode in silence for a while, recovering her composure. Soon she relaxed against the headrest and let the lazy feel of the Sunday afternoon wash over her. She glanced over at Malcolm, noticed a small scar on his forehead right above his left eyebrow, probably from some other sports mishap, but in a split second she realized that all she knew about him was what he'd told her. Suppose he lied? Suppose he was like Z or Randy? She was on a lonely two-lane road, beneath a canopy of trees, with a man who could easily overpower her—if that's what he wanted. *Lighten up. This is not the city.* She shook the thought from her head. "Who said I even like bikes?"

"Oh? I didn't take you for one of those prissy types who don't sweat."

"That's not what I said." Carmen mustered her bravado. "Everybody doesn't know how to ride, you know."

"Serious? No trikes, no training wheels, no nada?" He gripped the wheel in mock horror.

"Where I come from, you either got ripped off or run over." With anybody else she would have taken offense, but Malcolm's easy manner had already cracked her rough and ready shell.

"Is that right, pard'ner?" Malcolm hitched a thumb in imaginary suspenders. "Well, I reckon we can fix that, unless you think it's too hard, in which case we can just go get us a sarsaparilla."

"Did you hear me say it was too hard?" Carmen leaned toward him.

"Well then, let's get it on." He turned off at a place called Opossum Lane. Cows grazed on one side of the road, corn grew on the other. "This looks like a good test track, no other riders to get in our way." He unlashed one of the bikes, handed Carmen a helmet. "Just a precaution."

"It's plastic lined with Styrofoam. How's that supposed to protect you?" Carmen asked as she gave the secluded surroundings a quick once-over.

"Works for car bumpers. Besides, I predict your head won't come within two feet of the ground." Malcolm held the bike steady, motioned to her. "Ma'am."

"Thanks for the vote of confidence, cowboy." Carmen put on her head gear, swung her leg over the bar and Malcolm adjusted the seat, declared it a good fit. She listened intently as he explained how to shift gears, use the brakes.

"How am I supposed to balance on this thing?"

"Don't think about it. Your body will find the balance if you let it." He positioned her hands on the handlebars. "Put one foot on a pedal and push off with the other. The most important rule is to have a good time. I mean, I'm not the doctor here, but I believe that acute seriousness is the leading cause of warts, wrinkles and bad attitudes."

Carmen laughed. "I wouldn't want any of those." She rolled back and forth, working up her nerve. Finally she lifted her foot. The front wheel wobbled as she strained at the pedals.

"Keep going! You got it." Malcolm jogged beside her, his locks swinging side to side.

It was work, but Carmen rode in a mostly straight line, hands tense, eyes focused directly ahead. She wanted to look at Malcolm but was afraid she'd topple over. "Now what do I do?!"

"Shift gears. I showed you where the levers are."

Hesitantly Carmen unclenched her fingers and the bike began to waver, but Malcolm urged her on. She moved the levers but the grinding and clanking of the chains on the derailleurs stopped her. "I'm gonna break it!"

"It's supposed to sound like that. Make small adjustments. When it slips in you'll feel it."

Sure enough the chain landed in the grooves, the wheels turned easier, faster, and Carmen let out a triumphant whoop. Malcolm ran alongside until fourth gear, then he said she needed to try the brakes. "Squeeze 'em slow, so you don't go flying."

Carmen followed directions and eased to a halt, tickled at her first solo ride. Malcolm teased her that she'd known how to ride all along, then raced her back to the car. He swore he let her win, to be nice. She noticed the thin sheen of sweat that coated his skin, made him glow.

When they got to the river they headed directly for the dirt path along the canal. Biking at a leisurely pace, side by side, they passed old stone houses and barns turned into artists' lofts on the shore side, kayakers, jet skiers, ducks and geese enjoying the water. And they laughed all afternoon, like Carmen hadn't done since 5D days. She couldn't remember the last time she'd worked up a sweat, from playing of all things. Not since mandatory PE in college and that wasn't fun; she just needed the credits. Even though she was tired and hungry as they walked the bikes back through the crowd on Main Street, she vibrated with energy.

"Have I earned lunch yet?" At the car she took off her helmet, looked in the side mirror to rein in her hair.

"Pretty good for a first effort. Definitely sandwich worthy." He sat in the driver's seat, pulled off his sweaty shirt and yanked on a fresh one. "I have an extra if you want to change."

"I'll pass." Her damp shirt stuck to her body, but taking his felt too—well, intimate, although she got a charge when he asked. She accepted a towel, dabbed perspiration from her face and arms. Then Malcolm gave her the blanket, hoisted the cooler and they hiked to a spot under a maple tree overlooking the water.

Malcolm handed her a hero stuffed with the works. He'd also brought celery and carrot sticks and chips—"Whatever you like to crunch,"—grapes and brownies, and a half gallon bottle of lemonade. "Squeezed it myself."

"Uh-huh." Carmen dug in the cooler. "Cups?"

"Hmm. Knew I forgot something. We can chug-a-lug. I swear I don't have cooties." He offered her the bottle. "I did just have a tetanus shot."

Carmen eyed the container, then him. She was even thirstier than she was hungry. "I'll chance it." She took a swig, then he did. It went back and forth between them as they ate and talked. "I like being with my kids. Showing them numbers won't bite. Some of them—if they learn enough to balance a checkbook, maybe make a budget, I'll be satisfied. But then there are the ones who get it as fast as I can throw it at 'em. Not just the numbers—the concepts. Their minds are nimble but they don't think it's cool. I want to make it cool. I have a master's in applied mathematics which makes me a certified geek. And I'm trying to decide whether to go for a Ph.D. which would make me Dr. Geek or a second master's in Education." He unwrapped a brownie. "And I want to complete a triathalon."

Another Dr. Geek? Milton popped into her head. How could he not? He was the last, the first and only time she'd gotten this close and she didn't need a reminder of how that turned out. And to top it off, Carmen hadn't spoken to him in almost a year. Last time she called, she got a recording saying his number had been disconnected, so he had become the latest missing person in her life. "I've decided on family practice." She talked about her future instead of lingering on the past. "It's a new specialty, kind of a general practitioner for the new age. I can treat day-to-day illnesses, recommend specialists when I need to and mostly have time to live my life, buy a car, a real house, plant a garden."

"Have a family?" Malcolm asked.

"Maybe. Maybe not. Haven't gotten that far yet." Carmen gave him her standard revised childhood story—the one without the runaway mother and the hoodlum brother. She felt uncomfortable with the fuzzy version of her life but it would do for now.

After a while they lay side by side on the blanket, making bets on which kayaks would tip. Carmen relaxed, for once not worrying about tomorrow or patients or if she had gas in the car. She did have a fleeting thought about when they'd go out again.

When Malcolm took her hand on the walk back to the car, she could hardly see straight. The summer sun still shone bright; their hands swung between them, and Carmen tried to act like this was normal. On the drive home she debated with herself about whether to invite him in. She imagined sitting on the sofa next to him but he wouldn't move away like Milton had. Malcolm might kiss her the way Regina and Jewell talked about and she'd finally know what it felt like. By the time they got back she'd decided it would be okay for him to come in. If he wanted to.

"Carmen, there's something I need to tell you." Malcolm preempted her invitation.

Here we go. Carmen squared her shoulders, expecting the "let's be friends" speech.

He swung around to face her. "Well, two things. First, I was right. I said I liked you, and I do. Not only are you interesting, you've got the makings of a fine biker—with a little coaching."

"This was the trial lesson? Do I have to sign up for the rest of the course?" She teased, relieved. *He likes me.*

"I'll leave that up to you, after you hear the second thing." Malcolm looked away, then back at her. "Okay, the short story. My girlfriend and I broke up three months before I met you at the hospital—"

Girlfriend?

"She had moved out—"

Moved out? Carmen felt sick—and stupid. *I should have known better.*

"Went back home to DC. When I asked you out, she was still gone. We were over." Malcolm sighed. "Two weeks ago she called and said she wants to try again."

"Thanks for a lovely day." Carmen opened the car door. She had to get out while she could still put up a good front. "Have a nice life."

"Carmen, wait." He grabbed her arm. "I need to find out if there's anything there, so I know for sure. Honestly I don't know. But Terry—we were together since grad school. Guess I figured we always would be." Malcolm let go of her arm. "I'd like to stay in touch."

"Why did you wait till now to say this?" *It's not fair.*

"Truth? I wasn't sure I was going to tell you at all, but you deserve to know."

"So now I know." *Didn't I always?* "Bye Malcolm."

17

"...I'll sleep when I'm old."

"You plannin' to get up this morning?" Ty stood in the doorway, stepping into his pants. "You got a business to run."

Say something original. Regina rolled over enough to see him. "That's why I have assistants—so nobody needs me before eleven, preferably twelve." She closed her eyes again.

Misha's party last spring had been the booster rocket Regina needed to send her into a higher orbit. Based on that night, she'd received lots of inquiries to do other events, including one from the *Through It All* producer who had accompanied Jewell. He hired her to handle the company's holiday party. In December she'd pulled off a lavish affair for them at an intimate private club tucked away at the Metropolitan Opera House. Regina tickled herself when she came up with the theme. "An operatic ovation for the divas of daytime."

Nineteen ninety-three dawned with Regina on the short list of bright lights in town and she scrambled to capitalize before her bulb burned out. She finally took the leap and moved Regina Foster Productions out of 5D and into an office two blocks south of Big Bang. Nothing elaborate—same kind of soot-caked, nondescript building, creaky elevators, washroom down the hall, but that wasn't where she saw clients. That happened at their places or over lunch or drinks. The office was a quarter floor with high white walls, perfect for displaying swatches and other samples, charts, permits anything she needed at her fingertips. Jewell helped Regina turn it into an airy, modern studio with the tall windows sheathed in scads of shear white fabric to mask the ho-hum view, but let in the light. Glass-topped desks on rolling black-gloss file cabinets meant the layout could change to meet the needs of a particular project, or a whim. Potted ficus trees and palms added life and there was a seating area with a plump sofa upholstered in Regina's signature red. Mainly, the office provided desk, phone and work space for her two employees—Glenda, who had become Regina's right arm and appointment book, and Sydney, an experienced event planner who approached Regina at a benefit she was working and pitched herself. Both were excellent at details, the nitty gritty Regina hated. And the extra hands meant she could take on additional, overlapping projects. "Can you believe I have real employees and a payroll? Maybe it'll make Mom see I'm not a total screwup," Regina told Jewell on the phone. "It's like I can be in two places at once. Plus, I get to look fab and do the fun stuff. That's my forte. People skills."

Now, cotton-mouthed and still groggy, Regina struggled to talk with Ty, and resented having to do it. "You know Tuesday mornings are always late for me." *He should have gone to his own damn house last night.* In addition to the Network Hook-up, Regina had initiated Funday Mondays at Afrique, a club right off the West Side Highway in the '50s, in what used to be an auto parts warehouse. Thanks to her connections, and some of Ty's, the VIP section always drew music people as well as others who were notable or notorious, looking for a night out when the amateurs were home in bed. Regina took excellent care of them in the Savanna lounge, a balcony away from prying eyes and overzealous fans. A celebrity could come to the railing and wave at people on the dance floor if they wanted to be noticed, or disappear into the plush interior, featuring a zebra-striped playpit, and duck out the back door if they didn't.

"I was there as late as you, remember?" Ty sat on the corner of the bed.

Regina could feel him there, looking at her. Sometimes she'd wake up and catch him, just staring at her with this dreamy look on his face and she'd wonder what he saw in her, worry it was something she couldn't be or maybe never was.

Ty pinched a lock of her hair, tickled her nose and forehead with it.

Regina shooed his hand away. "What time is it anyway? It's still dark out." She had peeked at her windows. There wasn't a trace of light at the edges of her shades.

"Seven thirty, and you know I have a flight to Miami this morning, except you don't seem to remember much after the fourth vodka tonic."

Not that again. "Ty, woman does not live by root beer and orange juice alone." Regina whacked his leg, then reached toward the foot of the bed and grabbed her robe. "I can't keep up with my own damn schedule, much less yours. That's what Glenda's for." She also knew four vodkas wasn't the half of it. The bartender took care of her. He never let her glass stay empty. She tried not to let Ty see how much she drank because he always had something to say. She couldn't make him understand she was just being social. That was her job. Usually she had a rough idea of how much she'd consumed, but she'd lost count last night and had to resort to a personal pick-me-up—the cocaine she now kept in an aspirin bottle in her purse for emergencies. For some people it was a social drug—shared lines on glass tables snorted through crisp new hundreds rolled into straws. But for Regina it was private.

No one needed to know how she stayed so on. In Oz the Wizard always stayed behind the curtain. Reuben was right. There was no need to miss the action. For what? To sleep? She could do that after a nightcap and the last laugh.

Regina poked her arms in her sleeves. "So, when did you tell me you're coming back?"

"Saturday. We're going to your parents' for dinner on Sunday."

Don't remind me. Regina had tried to get out of it, like she had a hundred times before, but Ty wasn't having it. In all the years they had known each other, she had never taken him home. He got all huffy, accusing her of being ashamed of him so she gave in to shut him up.

Ty ran a brush over his close-cropped hair and checked his shaved-in part in the mirror. "I got a couple of groups to check out, and I been puttin' out some feelers for a movie project. There's this director who wants to take me deep-sea fishin'. He's got a script he wants to pitch."

"You? Deep-sea fishing?! Bring me back a shark." Regina poked her lips out for a kiss.

Ty gave her a peck. "Girl, you cute, but your breath stanks." He stood up.

"And you are just what I need to start my day. Lock the door behind you." As soon as he left, Regina flopped back in the bed. She and Ty didn't exactly live together, but they lived back and forth between his place and hers. He kept hinting that she should move into his brownstone which had come a long way since he first showed it to her. Two of the four floors had been redone in a kind of nouveau-retro mix of sleek contemporary and classic grandeur. His master suite had a king-sized leather sleigh bed sitting in the middle of the floor, and a Jacuzzi in the bathroom big enough to swim in. But that was his place. Ty was neat, maybe even neater than Jewell, particular about where things went and how they looked. They had already gotten into it about her carelessness—once over how she hung her washcloth on the brass towel rack.

"But you need to move out of this dump," he kept telling her. "They don't keep the building up right anymore." Which was true. Since 924 Parkview Real Estate Management took over, the hallways didn't get mopped as often, lightbulbs took longer to be replaced. Regina had all of her mail sent to the office since the mailboxes had been vandalized. She was planning to move. The realtor who found her the office space still called to see if she was ready to look at apartments, but Regina kept putting her off. "I'm concentrating on the business first. I only sleep there anyway." Which was true. In 5D, she was either leaving, arriving or asleep. The Regina Foster of

Regina Foster Productions, who made deals, talked fast, and dressed in red, existed outside of that apartment so she didn't pay attention to how things looked inside. And no matter how big a dive she let it become, she could still sit on the red chaise, look out the window on the park and wonder if she could juggle fast enough to keep all the balls in the air. As long as she could still see Oz, she convinced herself she was all right.

Regina slept until Glenda called at eleven thirty to remind her that she and Sydney had a one o'clock appointment to pitch their services as the new producer for the annual fund-raiser, Brother's Baking, at the Harlem Y. The event showcased high-profile men in the community and their sweet treats. For the price of admission, ticket buyers—mostly female—got to sample their wares. *Good thing it's only 135th Street.* Regina dragged herself into the shower. Then she took a hit from her stash, swallowed three Excedrin with her coffee. She would even have been on time if the dress she planned to wear had fit, but when she looked in the mirror she found it was too baggy—*Did I eat last night?* She found a plan B, in the pile on the floor, gave it a quick press and vowed to take the rest of the clothes she'd been stepping over for two weeks to the cleaners.

Fortunately Sydney was punctual. She blamed Regina's delay on a meeting that ran long, and bad traffic, then started the presentation. Sydney relinquished the floor when Regina arrived and took over seamlessly, adding flourishes to the groundwork that had already been laid.

"Whipping up media interest will be a piece of cake." She cracked herself up and everyone else laughed too. Regina rattled on, brimming with excitement. "Remind me to call Felicia. She'll definitely want to be in on this," Regina instructed Sydney. Then off the top of her head she added, "What about an auction? We'll have the women bid to spend an evening with a brother who'll bake his specialty just for her. I *know* the ladies will go deep in their piggy banks for that!"

Regina left the meeting confident she had added another event to her schedule. "Thanks for saving my butt in there," Regina said to Sydney as they waited in the lobby for their car.

"No problem." Sydney Mayfield was the gray to Regina's red. Soft-spoken where Regina was brash, her understated pantsuits, simple pageboy and minimal makeup seemed designed to make her fade into the background. When they met, Regina assumed they were contemporaries, but when she decided to bring Sydney on, she was surprised to find she was ten years older, a single mom with two young sons. Regina was sure that's what had kept her from progressing further in her career. "The auction was a good idea."

"It was, wasn't it?" Regina said.

By Friday they got the official word that Brother's Baking was in their hands. It was scheduled for the second Saturday in June, which gave RF Productions another pot to put on the back burner, while the ones up front came to a boil.

"He had this screenplay called *Fly Girl*, about this chick who was an aviatrix. I love that word." Ty headed down the narrow road toward the Fosters' house, chirping happily. "The story's been around a while, but his money people backed out. I read it on the plane, but it's not my thing. I'm looking for somethin' contemporary, a story from here and now, know what I'm sayin'?"

"Turn right at the gas station." Regina tuned him out miles ago, trying to prepare herself for the afternoon.

"I picked you up something." Ty reached in his coat pocket and tossed a ring box in her lap. "Maybe this will put you in a better mood."

"What the—?" She looked at it suspiciously, then over at him.

"It won't bite. Open it." Ty shifted his eyes between the road and Regina.

She flipped the lid, stared at the square-cut ruby surrounded by diamonds.

"I saw it and I knew it belonged on your finger." Ty smiled, looked satisfied. "Put it on."

Regina removed it from the velvet pillow, feeling caught between shock and dread. *What's this supposed to mean?* She slipped it on her right hand, looked over at him. "It's beautiful. Definitely my color." She was so busy looking at her hand that she almost missed her house. "It's right there," she said at the last minute and he made a sharp turn into the driveway. Normally she used the back door, but when Ty parked behind Carmen's brand-new Saturn, she took him around the front so he wouldn't think that meant something she didn't intend. Her comment about him looking like a funeral director in his black suit and silver-and-black tie had already caused friction, but unfortunately, not enough to make him want to cancel.

Regina had been irritable the whole morning, pouting like a child out playing who's been made to come in to study. She hadn't brought a man home since Greg in high school, which meant he was only a boy back then, she was a girl, and it all felt like somebody else's life.

Ty carried the four bottles of champagne she'd picked up because she knew it was the only way she'd get through the afternoon. The huge bouquet of exotic tropical flowers he brought her mother was in his other hand. Regina took a deep breath, then went in the door talking.

"Damn Keith, you're starting to look like a professor." Her brother was watching football in the living room with their father. Keith had been appointed full professor at Rutgers, his alma mater. "Do you wear those sweaters with the suede elbow patches like in the old movies?"

"I'm just glad you recognize me at all. We don't see you much these days." Keith got up to hug his sister. "And it looks like there's a lot less of you to see."

Regina ignored his comment about her weight, made introductions all around and the men fell right into talk about the game. *How cozy, like they do this every Sunday.* She knew those two were easy. Her mother was the one with the long memory and the short fuse. Regina wondered if she still blamed Ty for her dropout status. *Serves him right if she does. He's the one who wanted to come.* Before the men got too involved discussing the last play, Regina ushered Ty into the kitchen where she expected to find her mother. Instead, there was Carmen standing at the stove.

"When did you learn to cook?" Seeing Carmen in an apron, clutching a wooden spoon, sent Regina into domestic shock.

"I didn't. But I can stir a pot of greens as well as the next person."

"Spare me." Regina put three champagne bottles in the refrigerator, and one in the freezer for quick drinking.

"Nice to see you, Doctor." Ty pecked Carmen's cheek.

"A kiss? You two barely got close enough to snarl at each other in 5D," Regina said.

"We've all mellowed with age, isn't that right?" Ty said to Carmen.

"Most of us." Carmen looked over at Regina who screwed up her face in comment.

"What is that on your finger?" Before Regina could answer, Carmen lifted her hand to investigate. "That's the prettiest ring I've ever seen." She looked at Ty. "You have something to do with this?"

He just grinned. Regina wanted to puke.

"What's so pretty?" Lonnie swished through the swinging doors. Regina watched her face, waiting for Mr. Hyde to appear, but all that came over her was a smile.

"Tyrone, welcome."

"Mrs. Foster, I'm glad to finally meet you." Ty handed her the flowers.

"Now come look at this," Carmen said, pointing at Regina's hand.

"Oh my! That is magnificent." Lonnie looked back and forth between Regina and Ty with a gleam in her eye.

"Don't get any ideas. It's just jewelry. Okay. See? It's on my right hand." *Like anybody these days falls in love and lives happily ever after like you and Dad. What a freakin' fairy tale.*

"Whatever you say, dear." She winked at Ty and he just grinned.

And Regina wondered who this woman was and where they had stashed her real mother. It was all too weird, so as soon as she could arrange it Regina called the family together to toast Keith's new position because she needed to suck down a glass of champagne, fast. She needed another one when her mother scolded her for not mentioning that Ty was such a root beer lover.

"There's a wonderful stand right up the road where they sell their own brand. It's really delicious. Their vanilla creme soda is my favorite," Lonnie confided conspiratorially.

I'm gonna kill myself. It was all so regular and civilized. At dinner Al presided over one end of the table, passed the au gratin potatoes and asked Ty a hundred questions about Big Bang.

"I know Motown and RCA Victor, but how exactly do you start your own record label?"

RCA Victor?! Like he's freakin' Thomas Edison. Regina moved food around her plate.

"Are you on some kind of diet? You've hardly eaten," Lonnie asked her daughter.

"I've been asking her the same thing," Ty added. There's nothing wrong with a little meat, if you know what I'm sayin'." After he said it, he looked sheepish.

Spare me. "Fat and happy is for the suburbs. I stay light and travel fast." She pretended not to see her mother's wounded look. Regina wanted to skip dinner and sit on the back stoop with a champagne bottle and a straw until the baloney course was over. Carmen flitting around the kitchen was bad enough. Ty had been Regina's partner in crime, her walk on the wild side, her rebel in silver chains and here he was with her family treating him like a courtly gentleman and a suitable spouse. And he—the originator of "Rapzilla," which brought adoration from hordes of break-dancing, rhyme-spouting fans—was loving it.

"You're rather quiet tonight, Queenie," Al said.

Carmen smirked. "I think somebody's nervous about bringing somebody home." She raised an eyebrow at Ty, who sat across the table from her.

Ty laughed. "I was a little nervous too, you know what I'm sayin'?"

Regina shot Carmen a look, while everybody else laughed. "Excuse me." She pushed back from the table. She had surreptitiously finished the second bottle of champagne by herself, and no one else seemed ready for a third, so she headed upstairs to the bathroom for an attitude adjustment from her aspirin bottle.

Carmen and Keith were clearing the table when Regina came back fully charged, ready to light things up. "So you two, since I'm sure neither of you is dating anybody, how about it?"

Carmen glared at Regina over a stack of plates.

"It's perfect if you think about it. 'She found true love with her college roommate's brother.' Hey! I can give you hints about how to sneak him in the basement like I used to do with Greg. Oh that's right, you finally moved out."

"Let's change the subject?" Lonnie suggested, trying to remain pleasant.

"What? Okay, everybody's all embarrassed now." Regina put her hand on her hips. "It's true though. You two kinda remind me of Mom and Dad, except they started earlier, quite advanced for their day, Ty. They had my two older brothers before they graduated from college. In fact they had a nice little family plan going—till I showed up and blew it."

"Regina that's enough." Al bristled this time.

"I'm just filling Ty in on a little family history—"

"Come help me in the kitchen." Carmen grabbed Regina by the shoulders and pulled her into the next room. "How much have you had to drink?"

"It's only champagne and it's none of your business. Damn, you're all so phony. A few years ago Mom would have hired a hitman for Ty if she knew how. Now he's the golden child."

"You should be happy they like him," Carmen said. "And for your information, your brother and I are just friends."

"Probably for the best. Since you've become my parents' replacement daughter, you and Keith together would be a little too freaky, don't you think?" Regina batted her lashes.

"Listen Regina," Carmen hissed, "I've told you before, I'm not trying to take your place, not that you seem to appreciate your family anyway."

"And when did you become the expert on families?" Regina swilled the dregs from someone's champagne glass. "Was that in one of your med school courses?"

Carmen looked like she'd been punched in the face. "You know what, you're a spoiled, selfish bitch Regina, and you can kiss my ass." She plowed out of the room.

The evening didn't last much longer. Two sips of coffee, a bite of cake and Regina was ready to go.

Ty had a few things to say on the drive back. "How could you disrespect them like that? They're your parents. And you don't hold your liquor that good."

"Don't lecture me Ty-rone. What I said had nothing to do with liquor." Suddenly hot, Regina cracked her window and held her face to the cold air. "You go in there acting like you grew up in a damn palace. The people who buy your records would laugh in your face."

"You don't know what you got." Ty gripped the wheel. "You know why I never took you to *my* house? 'Cause my father's a sad, mean man who lives with a chip on his shoulder that he used to whip my ass with. He never wanted anything he couldn't find in the bottom of a bottle. I'd be embarrassed for you to see that. Your folks are quality people. Like I thought you were."

"Am I supposed to feel bad?" Regina drummed her fingers on her knee. She didn't want to feel anything. "I have to go to the bathroom. There's a rest stop at exit eleven." Another hit would take care of that.

Ty and Regina stayed on the outs that week and she was miserable. She partied hardier and slept later so she wouldn't have to admit that to herself. On Friday when she left the office Ty was parked in front of her building and she felt like running to get in but she made herself stroll. For a while they drove in silence, staring straight ahead, then she reached over for his hand. "Sometimes my mouth works faster than my head," she said.

They had soul food takeout at Ty's place. Regina had extra helpings of sweet potatoes and black-eyed peas and she didn't drink or make any extra trips to the bathroom the whole night. After all, she only did it for fun. She could stop when she wanted to, if she wanted to. Ty played old records, back from when they first met. They laughed a lot and she fell asleep in his arms.

Winter turned into spring in a blur of proposals and deadlines. By the end of May Regina and her staff were ragged, but still had a few more events on the calendar including Brother's Baking, before they were home free. Regina and Jewell hadn't been able to squeeze in a face-to-face for ages, so after plans to get together had been sabotaged too often by last-minute emergencies or opportunities, they decided to try to coordinate at least one hair appointment a month. Jewell tried to include Carmen in the get-together, but she still wasn't too keen on seeing Regina although she didn't tell Jewell why. All Regina would say was, "Some people can't take a joke." So Jewell and Regina were on their own the week after the Daytime Emmy awards.

"You should have been nominated, not just a presenter!" Regina raised her still-dripping head out of the bowl to look at Jewell.

"You're gonna get wet," Simee, the shampoo girl, warned.

"That's what towels are for." Regina put her head back down and let Simee finish rinsing.

"I've only been on the show a year. I wasn't expecting a nomination." Jewell sat across from Regina, waiting for her blow-out.

"Save it for the interviews Bijoux. You should've been up there." Her now-auburn hair turban wrapped, Regina plopped next to Jewell. "And I would have done such a party for you—"

"You are relentless." Jewell laid the *Architectural Digest* on her lap. "How do you keep it all going? Between the show, my appearances and Dwight's schedule, I can barely keep up. You have twenty things happening at once. I'd lose track or lose my mind."

"That reminds me." Regina grabbed her tote bag, pulled out a small folio. "I need to tell Glenda to reschedule a flower delivery." She jotted down the note. "I love it, love it, love it. Business is great. I'll sleep when I'm old." Regina grabbed Simee as she walked by. "Tell His Royal Hairness I need to be out of here by one, will you?" Then she turned back to Jewell. "And what time does your mother get in?"

"Plane arrives at three, she'll go to the hotel first, so she'll be at my door by five. Dinner reservations at seven." Jewell practiced her super-sweet smile, then resumed flipping pages. She was glad she wasn't taping today. Dealing with Vivian would require enough of a performance.

"I can't believe she hasn't visited since you got back."

Jewell let the magazine fall closed. "It's just as well. When I was in LA in February I went to the house. I told her about Dwight. She told me I was ruining my career. I told her I had to go. She never even asked if I was happy. I'm not convinced today will be any different, but she's only in town one night and at least I'll have Dwight."

"Wasn't he supposed to go on that trip with you?" Regina hopped up and headed for the Plexiglas periodical rack on the wall.

"Emergency budget meeting, and you know how he hates to travel."

"Yeah, and you love it, so how does that work?" Regina waved a copy of *Soap Digest* at Jewell, pointed to a blurb about *TIA*'s Emmy wins on the cover. "Should be you." She put it back, picked up a copy of *Details* and sat back down.

"I'm managing just fine."

"You're always the one managing. What does he do?" Regina drummed her fingers on the magazine cover.

Jewell looked down at the *AD* again. “He’s a busy man. I can’t expect him to drop what he’s doing and fly all over with me—hang around South Bend or Tuscaloosa while I sign autographs and answer the same questions about how I like playing Adrienne Berrard.”

“You do it for him.”

“It’s different Regina.”

“So are you.”

“And you’re not?” Jewell looked at her. “Aren’t we all different when we’re with them?”

“Nope. I don’t go changing myself or what I want to do for Ty. Not this chickie.” Regina twirled the ring on her finger. “I like this ruby, but it doesn’t mean Ty owns me.”

“This works for us. It’s almost been a year.” *And I still haven’t told him the truth*. Jewell tossed the magazine on an empty chair. She’d started to tell Dwight about the baby dozens of times, but always came up with a reason to put it off. “Anyway we’re planning a weekend getaway to DC in a couple of weeks. It’s been impossible to get our schedules coordinated.”

“Big whoop. Washington is hardly Rome.” Regina looked unimpressed.

“You bring your romance with you. Anyway, I think the only reason Vivian is stopping here is to put Dwight through the Prescott hoop jump. She could have flown directly to Paris. Of course, it can’t be any worse than when I met King.”

“Karla’s ready for you Miss Prescott.” Simee came to get Jewell. “And Himself will be with you in five minutes,” she said to Regina.

An hour later, Regina blew Jewell a kiss and ran to catch a taxi discharging a fare at the corner. Jewell meandered home, using the time to prepare for Vivian’s guest appearance.

Jewell’s buzzer sounded at five of five.

“Being announced by the doorman! This is infinitely better than your old building.” Vivian swooped in, stopping a moment for Jewell to bend down and kiss the cheek she offered. “Lovely.” She moved into the living room. It had taken Jewell months to decorate the apartment and her whimsical decor from 5D had been supplanted by a breezy Mediterranean blend that combined comfort and style, reminiscent of her Roman *casa*. “Just lovely.”

“Thanks.” *The empress gives thumbs-up*.

“I was afraid you were still in your gypsy period.” Vivian walked to the window. “And a view—of—exactly what is that?”

“The Hudson River and New Jersey.”

"Wouldn't the New York skyline have been nicer? Oh well, you can't have everything."

"No, I guess you can't." *Vivian giveth and she taketh away.*

"You look good, Jewell. I may be forced to admit this town agrees with you."

Jewell nodded, but didn't rise to the bait. "Can I get you anything?"

"Perrier if you have it."

"Coming right up. Make yourself at home." Jewell disappeared into the kitchen. When she returned, Vivian examined a framed snapshot.

"He doesn't look at all like I pictured. I wouldn't have thought he was your type." Vivian perched on the edge of a deeply cushioned club chair that looked like it would swallow her whole if she slid back.

Jewell exchanged the glass of water for the picture and put it back in place on the sofa table. *And what would you know about my type?* "How's our legal eagle?"

Vivian whipped around. "Uh—Leonard's fine. He sends his best." She collected herself. "I may see him in Paris. He's got business there, so we'll try to meet for dinner or something."

Or something. Jewell and Vivian still hadn't discussed Vivian's extra-legal relationship with their lawyer. "He mentioned the trip when I spoke to him. Tell him I said *bonjour*." Jewell smiled at her mother and sat down on the arm of the couch. "*If* you get to see him that is."

Vivian took a sip. "I've watched your program. I couldn't bear one more person telling me how terrific you were without having seen you. I even got sidelined by Oliver Oakes at a party for Bill and Camille. Why didn't you tell me you auditioned for him? He said the project, whatever it was, never materialized, but he remembered you." Vivian didn't notice the involuntary shiver that passed over Jewell. "So anyway I made myself sit down and watch. Of course you weren't on the first three shows, but then finally! There you were!"

"And?" *Did you hate it? Do I care?*

"You were very good. I was surprised. Of course, I think it's a waste of your talent playing an overwrought daytime troublemaker."

Jewell smiled and didn't bother to mention that Vivian had been the inspiration for much of Adrienne's single-minded driving ambition.

They made small talk on the taxi ride to the Russian Tea Room, each avoiding subjects that might upset the delicate balance they'd reached. Although its star had faded from the red hot glow of the eighties, Jewell thought Vivian would enjoy dinner at "Hollywood East" as the restaurant had been known. Dwight was waiting at the bar when they arrived.

Jewell enjoyed his simple kiss, the casual familiarity of his hand claiming hers. He proudly announced he had snagged the first banquette by the bar. He didn't reveal that his own clout hadn't been enough to get one of the most coveted tables in the restaurant, but Jewell's was. So under the glimmering gold leaf ceiling, crystal chandeliers, etched mirrors and soaring firebirds Vivian and Dwight played getting to know you.

Jewell quickly found herself the observer in a duel between two apt opponents. She was glad to see Dwight could hold his own against Vivian's deceptively pointed jabs. He led Vivian over the same biographical ground that Jewell had come to know so well. Jewell still laughed in the right places, occasionally beaming an "Isn't he wonderful" smile Vivian's way. At discreet intervals between caviar, blinis and borscht, other celeb diners stopped by with a double-miss-kiss for Jewell and a little gossip or genial banter. Vivian enjoyed the recognition Jewell received. Dwight tolerated the interruption of his momentum.

Jewell maneuvered in and out of the conversation as her supporting role required. Dwight finished his "New York is a magnificent quilt and Harlem is a patch that's wearing thin" soliloquy, and Jewell was proud of the sentiment and his artful rhetoric, not bothered by it's similarity to the "face of New York" speech she'd heard so many times before. *That wasn't too awful.* Jewell and Vivian strolled to the ladies' room while Dwight took care of the bill.

"He certainly thinks highly of himself, doesn't he?" Vivian washed her hands.

"Why shouldn't he?" *Leave it to her to find something wrong when everything is right.*

Vivian's eyes shifted up to catch Jewell's in the mirror. "Be careful you don't get lost."

"What is that supposed to mean?" Jewell eyed her mother with annoyance.

"Just that I know a thing or two about men who are so obsessed with what they do that there's no room for you."

"You're comparing Dwight to my father? A man who walked out on his family and tells jokes for a living? You can't be serious!"

"The message doesn't matter. Only that nothing stand in its way. Including you." Vivian grabbed a cloth from the basket on the counter and dried her hands.

"Dwight isn't like that." Jewell got a breath mint from her purse.

"That's all I'll say. You'll probably do the opposite just to prove me wrong."

"After all this time, you still don't get it, do you? This is my life. I'll do what's right for me," Jewell said and headed out the door.

18

"...you've probably been looking for my horns."

The Honorable Harold L. Beechum, Supreme Court justice, peach cobbler crunch. With two weeks to go before the Brother's Baking event, Regina sat in the office reviewing the alphabetized list of participants and making notes. *Perry Donaldson, network news producer, apricot spring rolls—that's easy coverage, even if it's his own station. Ted Hampton, comic, carrot cake?* "A-freakin'-mazing." She tossed the pages on her desk.

"Something wrong?" Sydney looked up from a stack of sample invitations.

"No. I uh, was just surprised to see Ted Hampton on the Brother's Baking list."

"He is so-ooo funny." Glenda, a round-faced cherub with a bouncy personality, leaned over her typewriter. "I mean, for an older dude, he's still pretty hip."

"Yeah. Well, I guess I need to check with him. See if he's available for press." *See what the hell he's like and figure out what to tell Jewell.* Regina always thought he was hip and funny too, but those qualities left his daughter unmoved. *She just dates guys old enough to be her father, or ones who act like her father. She won't have anything to do with her actual father.*

Sydney made most of the calls to check for availability, but Regina saved Ted for herself. "It's a Las Vegas area code. You know, entertainers, late nights. I'll give him time to be awake."

Regina took the number home, paced the apartment dragging her red phone. It wasn't that he was famous. Anybody else, she would have been talking them up, inviting them to Mondays at Afrique. But they weren't Jewell's father. Regina always felt like she was supposed to hate him to be loyal, but she also thought there might be more to the story than Vivian's angle. *She could drive anybody crazy.* Regina poured herself a glass of wine, cleared a spot on the futon, sat down. *What the hell.* And dialed. *This is probably his agent's—*

"What's up?" That familiar craggy voice was in her ear.

"Yes, uh, Mr. Hampton, this is Regina Foster..." She explained who she was and what she wanted, not the questions she would have preferred, but the ones she had to start with.

"I'm up for whatever's on the plate. I get in that Monday, do a couple of nights at Caroline's, then after the event, shoot down to Harrah's in AC. I can plug that too, along with these damn cakes. Incidentally, I'm baking a couple now. Can you smell 'em?"

"Wish I could." She tried to imagine the man who prowled the stage, skewering the high, the mighty and the masses, sifting flour and creaming butter. It never occurred to Regina that Ted Hampton and her father shared a hobby. Ted was hip, cool, a Brother Baking. Albert Foster was a Dull Dad who baked cakes in the basement.

"I bake in my spare time, freeze 'em, and I'll ship the whole magilla before I cut out. Now why I don't just send a check and forget this foolishness is beyond me."

"Uh, Mr. Hampton—" *Your daughter is one of my best friends. She's great and she needs to meet you, but she's too stubborn.* "—I do these parties on Monday nights and I'd love it if you stopped by." Regina wanted to check him out first, before she figured out what to say to Jewell.

"Thank you darling, but I'm not much of a clubgoer. Those late nights'll tear ya up."

Ted was booked on *Live* the day before the event, which didn't leave much time for Regina to do an assessment and tackle Jewell, but that's all she had to work with. When Regina phoned to let him know when the limo would pick him up, he said he didn't want any fuss and that he and his cake would meet her at the studio. *Jewell never wants a fuss either. Maybe she gets that from him because it's sure not from Vivian.* Regina toyed with whether to call Jewell and let her know Ted was in town. That she was working with him. *I'll wait till there's more to tell.*

Two days in DC wasn't a cozy weekend at the beach or in a mountain chalet, but Jewell had been looking forward to the trip since Dwight first mentioned it. Aside from the night they stayed at Forestina's Sag Harbor house after a party, they hadn't been away together and they spent that night in separate rooms. Even if it wasn't a weekend, Jewell decided there was something illicit and delicious about stealing away during the week. She had first suggested they drive to Washington, have some quiet time in the car just the two of them. She'd had her BMW for a couple of months and hadn't taken a real road trip yet, but Dwight said he didn't care much for traveling by car.

"If it's longer than a taxi ride I get itchy. Besides, driving is a waste of four perfectly good hours." So Jewell revised her fantasy. Cruising along the highway with the top down and the wind in her hair was out, replaced by holding hands on the shuttle, gazing at the clouds, relaxing into each other.

But as soon as he was buckled in Dwight retrieved papers from his briefcase. "A few things I want to get out of the way," he told her.

Jewell flipped the pages of the airline magazine to chill her frustration. When she looked over at Dwight she was surprised to see a letter on 924 Parkview Real Estate Management stationery among his papers. "That's my old building."

"Oh? It's one of King's." He shifted the page to the back of his stack.

"He's not taking good care of it these days. The halls are a mess…"

"I steer clear of King and his holdings."

"But the building is in your district," Jewell said.

"I have to walk a fine line between the interests of tenants and landlords. All renters are not as responsible as you were, Jewells." He leaned over and kissed her—end of conversation.

Dwight had taken care of booking the hotel and Jewell was pleasantly surprised to find an elegant old one where she imagined long-ago ladies in hoop skirts, sauntering through the stained-glass arch in the lobby, past the same oil portraits, delicate settees and tea tables as she did now. "This is lovely," Jewell said when the bellman left them alone in their suite. The yellow-and-white striped wallpaper looked prim and proper, a delightful contrast to the rich tones of the elaborate drapes and the lush damask sofa. On the mahogany bar, a bud vase held a single, sensuous orchid. "Hmmm, our love nest." She sauntered to him, folded her arms around his neck, let their foreheads meet. Jewell closed her eyes, released a sigh she wasn't aware of carrying.

Dwight put his arms around her waist and they rubbed noses, nibbled lips. His voice husky, he said, "This old place has been a hub for power brokers since the turn of the century."

Not exactly the sweet nothing Jewell was expecting, but she gently redirected. "That's downstairs. I suspect some very different negotiations went on up here." She guided his hand to her thigh where the garter met the lacy top of her stocking. She'd had a delicious time picking out lingerie to surprise him and spice things up.

"You have a point." Dwight's hand traveled back up to her hip. "But further explorations are going to have to wait. I made dinner reservations downstairs, and there are some folks we're likely to run into at the bar that I want you to meet."

Jewell hadn't been aware of the agenda, but she put her seduction on hold and went along with the program after a change of wardrobe from the body-skimming coral dress to a more appropriate salmon pink collarless suit and her pearls.

"How do you always know what's perfect?" Dwight came out of the bathroom after a quick shave, a fresh shirt and tie.

"And there's still a surprise for you later, when you take off the wrapper," Jewell purred.

The bar was a dark, clubby hive, filled mostly with men in serious suits and very white shirts, who drank bourbon or scotch to oil the conversation. Some people she recognized, like the diminutive former secretary of state and the journalist whose toupee looked worse close up than it did on TV. Dwight was in his glory, back-slapping, belly-laughing, introducing her to a bipartisan parade of legislators, lobbyists and think tank policy wonks. Having found a place where she felt anonymous, although not unnoticed, Jewell smiled on her bar stool, sipped her wine. "What's a beautiful woman like her doing with the likes of you?" was the standard comment. Dwight never failed to work her claim to fame into the discussion. "Nice catch. Don't blow it, Dixon," said a Southern senator from Dwight's party. "Ninety-four is around the corner." But Dwight got a chilly reception from the portly congressman from New York's fifteenth district, the one that mostly closely corresponded to Dwight's city council precinct.

This must be what he feels like when we're with entertainment people. In between meeting and greeting Dwight told her about each person's role in the DC power grid, the components of which would be scrambled come election year.

"How do you know all of them?" Jewell asked when they finally went to dinner.

"Let's just say King and his cronies have been around. He has friends in high and low places. I used his connections, made a few of my own. Nobody succeeds in politics alone."

Once away from the hurly-burly, Dwight seemed edgy, anxious to get through dinner. Before Jewell could order coffee he said, "I've got something I want to show you." Hand in hand they left the hotel and strolled into the heart of picture-postcard Washington, DC.

"I've never been here." They arrived at one end of the mall and Jewell gazed at the Lincoln Memorial and the Washington Monument, bathed in white light. This nighttime tour was a lovely surprise and the perfect way for her to take in the sights without having to give autographs or pose for snapshots. *How did he know that?*

"Never? If I'd known that we'd have come here sooner." Dwight gestured toward the grand buildings laid out before them. "This is a magnificent place. I almost think of it as holy. The home of democracy practiced with a forthrightness and determination that has never existed in the history of the world."

Jewell liked the animation in his face when he talked about things he loved. The way the arch in his brows heightened, an affirmation of what he believed in.

He pointed out museums, galleries, monuments on the tour until they arrived at the foot of Capitol Hill. "Isn't it magnificent?" Dwight looked at the Capitol dome. "This is where the real decisions are made, the seat of true power." He took Jewell's hand, led her partway up the steps.

"Sounds like you've spent a lot of time here." She looked up at the building and at Dwight in silhouette against it.

"I'd like to spend even more." Dwight had a curious twinkle in his eye. He mounted the next step, took both her hands. "Jewell, you know how committed I am to what I do. Nothing is more important to me than serving my city—except the chance to be part of a broader forum."

Where is this going? Jewell's brain was yelling "spit it out," ready for the resolution to the cliffhanger.

"As you know, I'm not the most spontaneous guy, but I'm dedicated and hard-working. Always looking down the road, trying to see what's ahead." He paused, took a breath. "So, I'm sure it won't be a surprise to you that I'm building a coalition to mount a congressional primary challenge in '94. It's time for some new ideas."

"That's fantastic," Jewell gushed.

Dwight stepped back, held her at arm's length. "There's one more thing." He locked her in his sights. "I don't want to do this without you."

"Don't be silly. You'll have all the support I can drum up. I'll be your biggest cheerleader." Jewell smiled. "I never got to be one in high school!"

"That's not what I mean." He lifted her face in his hand. "I want you by my side." He cleared his throat. "I want you to marry me Jewell. Will you?"

Jewell was stunned. *Of course I have to say yes.* She believed in Dwight. He was everything a man was supposed to be. *I can count on him.* "I'd be honored." She heard herself say it, but half expected a director to say, "Cut. Can you try it again, and this time make me feel it?"

Dwight reached in his pocket, untied the knot from an embroidered handkerchief. "My mother wasn't with me very long, but she's been the most important woman in my life, until now." He lifted Jewell's hand. "This ring was hers. I'd be honored if you accept it from me." He tried to slip the cluster of diamonds on Jewell's ring finger, but it didn't fit. "I guess we'll need a little adjustment." He slid the ring on her pinkie, then brought her hand to his lips.

Their walk back to the hotel was quiet and for Jewell, the grandiose architecture was now merely a backdrop. *I'm getting married. Dwight will be my husband.* She searched for how she felt, looked for her motivation, but this was a scene she wasn't expecting to play quite yet. There were no thunderclaps or fireworks when they were together. *Not like with Billy.* No aching emptiness when they were apart. *And that got me exactly what?* And her frolic with Gianni had been fun, but nothing to build forever on. Jewell suppressed a chill and wrapped herself in a calm resolve. *I'm so used to drama I don't know what real life feels like.* And this, she determined, was as real as it gets.

"Now, where were we this afternoon." As soon as he closed the door to their room Dwight was all over her, squeezing, rubbing, reaching under Jewell's skirt for her garters. He covered her face in a frenzy of kisses, almost till she couldn't breathe.

"Come on now, let's slow down. We've got all night." Dwight's love-making was a lot like he was: direct, determined, single-minded. He generally took the expressway to satisfaction, and as he'd gotten to know the route, he traveled with increased speed. Jewell had hoped to encourage him to take a leisurely ramble through her unexplored pathways. She pulled away a little, tugged playfully at the end of his bow tie with her teeth.

"Let me." Dwight yanked off his tie, quickly got out of his clothes, barely noticing the lacy enticements she had carefully chosen to please him.

Jewell sensed he was in overdrive and there was no throttling back so she held him tight and led him to the place that only she gave him, a place where her talking man needed no words.

Afterward, once he'd caught his breath, Dwight rested his head in the crook of her arm. "I'm the luckiest man on the planet, Jewells."

And that was her fulfillment, especially tonight. Sex was a fleeting, overrated pleasure, but tonight they had made a commitment to become each other's family. That's what was important. Jewell checked to make sure his mother's ring was still on her finger, waited for his breath to slow and his head to weigh heavy on her arm. She eased him over onto the pillow, then lay in the darkness, imagining how her life was about to change and how she'd tell Regina and Carmen the news. *As soon as I get back to New York.*

Regina's Thursday Hook-up lasted until Friday morning, leaving her just enough time to regroup and meet Ted at the studio. She showered, letting the warm water run over her face to help clear the congestion that was a side effect of her self-prescribed pick-me-ups. Wrapped in a towel, she squeezed a couple of extra shots of nasal spray up her nose, doused her eyes in Visine and stopped in the kitchen to reheat yesterday's takeout coffee and get an eye-opener hit from the cream of tartar jar—left in the back of the cabinet from some long-ago Jewell recipe—where she kept her fresh stash of cocaine. This week she had Reuben dispense her cut of the proceeds in white powder, since she was tired of running out midweek and having to stop by DeVille for a refill. What used to feel like a lightning bolt to the brain, was now more like a jumpstart from a spare battery, but she needed it because this was no time for sleep.

Regina found Ted in the green room, newspaper spread out on the table, reading. *Jewell looks so much like him.* Regina had never realized it because in his act he was always in motion, loud mouth roaring, putty face contorted to capture the essence of his subject. Regina never imagined he could be so still.

"Mr. Hampton—"

He looked up, back from where the news had led him. "Ted'll do." He folded the paper, crossed his legs.

Regina's morning picker-upper had her pumped, ready to keep up with the rapid-fire conversation she expected from Ted, but now she found herself throwing the emergency brake on while the car was doing eighty. They talked quietly about the city, about the event and his Atlantic City gig. He seemed genuine, warm, like someone Jewell should get to know. *Either he's changed a lot or Vivian got it wrong.*

A producer came to get Ted and Regina followed him to the set. She stood in the wings and watched him enter his zone. Right at his intro he popped into gear and Ted Hampton, irreverent comic, was on turbo. The segment was only four minutes, but he commandeered the show, and did a two-minute riff on black men baking. "It's not to get in touch with my feminine side. It's pure survival. You ever read the ingredients on a pack of snack cakes? Half that stuff makes you crazy, the other half makes you too stupid to notice."

Regina wasn't really listening. She was trying to figure out how to tell him about Jewell.

As soon as Ted had shaken hands, waved to the studio audience and ducked backstage he had returned to neutral and coasted over to Regina. "So I'll catch you tomorrow."

"Yes, okay. And—uh—Mr. Hampton—Ted—" The time was speeding by so fast she hadn't figured out a graceful transition, so she just plowed ahead. "I know your daughter, Jewell. We went to school together. She's really a good friend. We even shared an apartment."

Knuckles planted on narrow hips, he nodded. "So you've probably been looking for my horns."

"No. I've been looking for a way to convince her to talk to you. I—I think she'd like you."

"You like big challenges, huh?" When he smiled, his face came alive the same way Jewell's did. "My door is open, my phone is on. You know where to find me. She was a great kid." Some memory passed before his eyes, then he put it away. "You can tell her I'll meet her anywhere, just let me know, but don't get your hopes up. Past experience tells me this is a hard sell." They headed out to the street. "Thanks for wanting to plead my case."

Regina headed to the office and tried to reach Jewell off and on for the rest of the day, but got no answer and this was not a message she wanted to leave on a machine. After midnight, she gave in. "Bijoux, it's me. Call as soon as you get this."

They had only been away two days, but so much had happened that Jewell felt like she'd been gone longer. She'd awakened Saturday after a fitful night, with a throbbing headache which only intensified on the plane ride home. Instead of the peaceful sleep of a bride to be, her wakeful dreams bounced from bridal gowns to what she knew would be Regina's glee at being asked to coordinate the wedding, to incorporating her furniture into Dwight's house. And while she was sailing along on that happily-ever-after fantasy, she'd bump into which room to make a nursery. Then she'd careen smack into the wall of truth she'd been bypassing. *I have to tell him*. So sleep had been elusive and the last thing she wanted right now was another meet and greet, but her first official, soon-to-be-Mrs.-Dwight-Dixon duty called.

"This won't take long." Dwight squeezed her hand. "It's part of the big picture."

Jewell smiled, rubbed her thumb on the underside of her newly adorned pinkie finger. "It'll be fun." *The show must go on*. At nine she had performed like a trooper on the *Daddy's Girl* set even with a painful earache. She danced on a network special with a sprained ankle when she was twelve and auditioned a week after she'd given birth. Public appearances as the star were second nature, but she was still figuring out her new supporting role with Dwight.

On either side of the entrance to the Harlem Y stood ten-foot balloons shaped like gingerbread men. Once Jewell and Dwight passed the sugary sentries, the aromas of cinnamon, butter and cocoa guided them to the gym which was a sea of tables draped in red-and-white checkered cloths. Behind each was posted a Baking Brother. Some were garbed in chef toques, others in kente cloth aprons and kofis, but all laughed, jived, and talked up his special confection.

"What's up Mr. Dixon?" said a boy in shorts and a baggy Y T-shirt. "You gotta taste Mr. Nichol's brownies. They're the bomb!"

Jewell smiled as Dwight gave him a high five. *He's good with kids. He'll be a great father.* They hadn't talked about a family, but Jewell assumed—*Congressman and Mrs. Dixon and their two lovely children—a boy for you, another girl for me.*

Dwight took a handkerchief from the hip pocket of his khakis, wiped the brownie goo off his hands, and dove into the crowd, Jewell at his side.

"Ms. Prescott—" Sydney appeared next to Jewell. "Regina Foster sent me to get you. She's running this event."

"I didn't know she appeared before dark." Dwight patted Jewell's arm. "You go on. I'll be right back." He headed for the table manned by the *Eyewitness News* reporter.

"She just went to the ladies' room, but she'll be—oh there she is. Wait here. I'll get her." Sydney melted into the throng and in seconds returned with Regina in tow.

"What are you doing here?" Regina asked excitedly.

"That's some hello. You know this is Dwight's turf. We just got back from DC and I—"

"Come here." Regina pulled Jewell by the hand.

"I have something to tell you!" Jewell sang.

"It can wait. This can't." Regina reached the hall and dragged Jewell to a quiet corner. "I called you fifty times since Thursday. Don't you check your machine? It could be something important, not that this isn't. But I mean something like work or something."

"What are you babbling about?"

Regina shifted her weight from foot to foot, kept watching the door. "This isn't the way I wanted to tell you—I don't even know how to say this, but I didn't know what to say on the phone either." She took a deep breath, like she was about to go off the high board. "Your father's here." Regina watched, waited. "He's one of our Baking Brothers."

"What are you talking about?" Jewell hadn't been in the same room with her father since she was six years old and suddenly the eleven-story building was reduced to the size of her bedroom in their house in Culver City. "He can't be here." *I don't need this today*.

Regina nodded. "He's doing a radio remote with Felicia now. And Jewell, he seems like a great guy, I mean I've talked to him on the phone, I met him yesterday. I know you haven't gotten along—"

"I don't know the man! How could you let me walk in here without telling me?"

"I wasn't expecting you. Someone on Dwight's staff said he might stop by, but why would I think I'd see you? Anyway, I wanted to talk to you after I met Ted—because I like him."

"*You* like him? Isn't that great?!" Jewell didn't want to deal with this. It had become pretty easy for her to pretend Ted didn't exist. Years ago, he would catch her in a sneak attack as she channel surfed. Or she'd hear a promo announcing him as a guest on *The Tonight Show* and she'd avoid the program that night. But he'd been replaced by younger, raunchier comedians and rarely surfaced on TV now, so how could he show up, in the middle of her Saturday, the day after she got engaged? She didn't want a scene or a confrontation. She simply did not want to see him.

"There you are," Sydney called from the doorway. "They're ready to announce the winners of the silent auction." She joined Jewell and Regina. "The councilman has consented to do the honors." Sydney turned to Jewell. "He asked me to find you. He'd like you to join him."

"It'll be okay." Regina looked at her, hoping to see a sign she might be willing to at least speak to Ted, but all she saw was a frosty stare worthy of Adrienne Berrard—or Vivian Prescott.

Sydney waited for them to follow her and Jewell realized she had no choice. They reached the front of the room just as Dwight took the mike.

"I'm sure you're anxious to find out which of you has won a night with a Bakin' Brother. Talk about being able to stand the heat!" Dwight chuckled at his joke. "But before I get to the business at hand—I'd like to introduce you all to somebody. You've probably seen her around here today and I know you all have been talking—some of you behind my back and some right up in my face—" Dwight waited for the laughter to die down. "But today, I'd like to officially introduce you to my fiancée. Come on up here Jewell—Miss Jewell Prescott!" He started to clap.

"Fiancée?!" Regina screeched.

Jewell nodded slowly to Regina as Dwight pulled her on the stage and kissed her full on the lips. The sugar-high crowd roared. Jewell held tight to Dwight's hand and smiled even though she couldn't feel her face. She forced herself to let go and wave to the person who shouted "Yo Adrienne!" But as

Dwight announced the winners and joked about their evenings of home-baked fun, Jewell was in a vacuum. Then Dwight was steering her off stage, oblivious to her discomfort.

"There's a photographer here from the *Amsterdam News*. I told him he could take a few shots." And he led the way to the backstage area.

"Councilman, could we get a couple with you and the winners first? Out front. You know with them holding their cake or something," the equipment-laden photographer asked.

"Sure." He pecked Jewell's cheek. "Duty calls."

"Seems like a decent guy. I wish you every happiness, but that's all I ever wanted for you, Jewlee."

Jewlee. Only one person ever called her that. She turned and looked into a face that was as familiar as her own. Ted was as long, lean and bittersweet as she remembered. His slim slacks were the same gray as the Italian silk sweater he wore over a white T-shirt. *He looks like me.* She knew it was the other way around, but that was an acknowledgment she couldn't give. "It would make me happy if you just leave me alone."

"Come on Jewlee, it's been a long time." Ted's hands hung at his sides, like he didn't know what to do with them.

"Stop calling me that!" She growled at him, low and angry. "You have no right!"

"That's what I always call you," Ted said softly. "I've never stopped talking to you. Or thinking about you."

"I've had enough." Jewell stepped over cables, tried to find an opening in the curtain. "Where's the damn way out of here?!"

He took a step toward her. "I tried, Jewell. I did. I tried to see you. I tried to call. And I guess Viv called herself doing what was best for you, but—"

"You have no right—"

"Maybe I don't. Maybe I didn't try hard enough. Things weren't like they are now. Mothers always won." He sounded sad. "But you can't carry this kind of bitterness. Not into your marriage. Not into your future. It's too heavy. It'll drag you down." Ted took a step forward, stopped when Jewell stepped back. "Okay. You don't want anything to do with me. I wasn't there when I should have been. I can't change that or what that did to you, but don't let this live in your heart, Jewlee."

Stop calling me that. The voice screamed in her head.

"You might find love. But it can't grow if the place you plant it is hard. You have to turn up the ground, get it ready to grow something."

"Listen Farmer Hampton, I don't want your fatherly advice on planting season. I don't want explanations or excuses. I don't want anything from you!"

Ted slipped a hand in his hip pocket, flipped open his billfold and held it out to her.

"I don't need your money!" She spat.

Ted continued to hold the wallet in front of her. "Look."

Jewell let her eyes drop and under a cloudy plastic window was a picture of Ted holding the hand of a little girl as they played in the surf.

"I don't know how many wallets I've been through, but the picture's always there." Gingerly he slipped it from its place and handed it to her.

The snapshot had been folded to fit the small window and the creases were brittle. Jewell held the photo like it might crumble into a thousand pieces which is how she felt looking at it. *I remember that day. I wanted another hot dog and you said I would spoil my dinner and Mommy would be mad.* Before any more memories surfaced, she shoved it back at him.

"I'd like for you to have it." His voice was soft. This wasn't an excuse. It was a gift.

And she couldn't accept. In five short minutes, he'd shaken her foundation, made her question things she thought she knew, for real and for true. She shook her head, watched him put the picture back in its place, then brushed past him and went in search of her future.

19
"...truth hurts less than all the lies..."

"I'm visiting a clinic in New York, and there's somebody I want you to meet," he had said. Carmen showered, dressed, and tried not to keep wondering about Milton's cryptic phone call. "You left me hanging for over a year? You could have been dead for all I know," she told him, but he swore he would explain. At that point she was just relieved to hear from him and now she looked forward to meeting the woman who, as Regina would say, had finally captured the heart of the elusive Dr. Hemphill. Carmen wasn't even sure what that meant. Admittedly, she was a poor judge in matters of romance, but the examples set by Jewell and Dwight, and Regina and Ty didn't exactly make her want to get on board the love train.

Carmen gave Ty credit. The fast-talking, always hustling guy she used to distrust seemed to truly love Regina. Why else would he put up with the outrageous things she said and did? Especially since Regina's mission seemed more about testing the limits of love than giving it back.

Carmen had a harder time putting a finger on what bothered her about Jewell and Dwight. Jewell swore she adored him and his commitment to saving the world, or at least his council seat while pursuing his next political conquest. But every time Carmen saw him he said exactly the same thing. "Good to see you. How are things at the hospital?" It made her feel like she wasn't worth another question. On the surface they seemed a good match, but whenever Carmen was around them, Jewell seemed stiff and unsure, certainly not the Jewell Carmen knew. Carmen's misgivings were reinforced last month when she met Jewell, Vivian and Regina to select gowns for the Valentine's Day nuptials. Carmen had only made peace with Regina to keep from spoiling Jewell's wedding plans, and then a little of Regina went a long way, but that afternoon they were united to keep Vivian in check. The three of them reminisced about 5D days because the past was on more solid ground than the present, and they oohed and aahed over dozens of gowns until Jewell chose the one. Or more accurately, the one she thought Dwight would think was perfect. She preferred an ivory satin sheath with long sheer sleeves, but picked an elaborate traditional number with lace, pearls, crinoline and a cathedral train. “After all, I’m dressing for him that day.” As far as Carmen could see, the whole event was for him. Jewell said she would have preferred a barefoot sunset ceremony on a secluded beach. It was Dwight who wanted the pomp and circus.

Carmen heard the kettle whistle. She dashed downstairs, poured boiling water over the coffee in the French press. She’d learned to love brewed coffee in 5D and making it in the kitchen of her own home was a daily treat. After renting for a year, she had exercised her option to buy the modest two-bedroom town house, proud of herself for finding the faith to take that leap.

Borrowing a page from Jewell’s notebook she had made the place her own, furnishing it with comfy sofas, chairs and curtains in soothing pastels and florals. On every vacant wall and shelf she displayed mementos of the life she had built, like talismans against the one she had escaped. There were ceramic doctor statuettes, a hand-painted banner that read HAPPY BIRTHDAY WEBB from a surprise breakfast party her fellow med students had thrown her. And there were loads of pictures: Al and Lonnie, Milton clowning with a pot on his head at one of Jewell’s Tuesday dinners, med-school graduation. On an end table was the picture Milton had taken of her with Jewell and Regina, dressed in red, white and blue at the first July Jam. And in her bedroom, in a small silver frame on her nightstand, was the snapshot she had kept of her mother and father on the Coney Island boardwalk. Geraldine holding a fluff of pink cotton candy, Z Sr. carrying a big brown Teddy bear, they were frozen forever in a happy time Carmen never knew. And there was nothing in her house to remind her she’d ever had a brother.

Ready for her morning caffeine jolt, Carmen fixed light, sweet coffee in her thermal car mug. She had suggested Milton bring his girlfriend out to the house and she’d ask Jewell and Regina to come too, like the old days. “Not this trip,” he had said so she checked the train schedule and headed out the back door to the garage. She hadn’t bought the car of her dreams yet, but this one was new, affordable, shiny black and not Regina’s. She got in, pressed the garage door opener. Her life was good, full, rewarding. Simple—until she backed out.

He sat on the fender of his old Jeep, blocking her driveway. One foot on the bumper, he wore a T-shirt that read Tour de Franklin, and the same lock flopped over his eye. It had been a year since she’d seen him, almost to the day. He’d left a few messages soon after their outing, but she’d hit the erase button the moment she heard his voice. *I’m not getting out of this car.*

Malcolm hopped down like he'd heard her, came and stood by her window. "I was hoping I'd catch you today. I tried this before, but you never came in or out." Malcolm beamed at her.

Carmen stared straight ahead at the garden tools hanging on the wall. "I'm in a hurry—"

"I'll be out of your way in sixty seconds—"

"I have nothing to say." She shifted into reverse, held onto the wheel.

"Hold up," he gripped the door. "I was straight with you. At least let me finish." She kept her eyes fixed, but did shift to neutral. "Terry came back and it took me exactly two weeks to realize we'd spent seven years fixing something that never worked in the first place. All I really had to do was look at my parents, how they're still crazy about each other after thirty-some years. That's what I want, and that I did not have with Terry."

"And you're telling me this *because?*" Carmen asked.

"I would have told you last year, but when you didn't call back, I decided it was for the best. If I took my time, and took the chance you'd still be around in a year, then we'd both know I wasn't just lonely." He leaned down to her window again. "I may have blown this completely. Hope you're not on your way to meet your boyfriend." For the first time Malcolm looked at her left hand. "Good. No ring." He smiled.

"Touching story." She tried to glare at him. "I've got a train to catch."

"All right. My minute's up." He patted the door and stood up. "I'll back off, but just in case you want to give me another go." He handed her a piece of notebook paper with his phone number on it, walked to his car and drove away.

Carmen shoved the paper in the door pocket, and took off. She barely made her train, plopped in a window seat, sweating, still catching her breath, and still fuming. In two minutes Malcolm had disrupted the day she had carefully laid out. She was prepared to meet Milton's girlfriend and have such a good time at brunch she'd have no time to wonder why the two of them never clicked. They'd part on the sidewalk, promise to see each other sooner next time. Simple. Except now Malcolm would be there too. *Screw 'em.* Carmen had plenty to keep her life full. So what if she'd never know what Jewell and Regina did about men and sex? They'd never know what it was like to save a life or deliver a baby. She had everything she needed and more.

Carmen stood on the stoop of the West 10th Street building, putting a smile on her disappointment. As long as Milton was happy, she'd be fine. When she was buzzed in, she saw a well-muscled man in a black tank with a flat-top haircut waiting in one of the doorways.

"You must be Carmen. I'm Bernard."

"Oh. Hi." *Guess it's four for breakfast. I hope this isn't some kind of fix up.*

Bernard moved into the hall, closed the door to a crack behind him and lowered his voice. "I wanted to warn you, he doesn't look like you remember." He saw the concern in her eyes. "But he's still Milton. You'll see."

"Warn me?" A phantom hand squeezed Carmen's heart.

"I tried to get him to tell you before now." Bernard ushered her into the small apartment.

"Hey Carmen."

Tell me what? "Milton?" The voice was weak, but familiar, and she followed it toward the thin figure sitting on a daybed in front of the bay window, until they were face to face. "What happened?" The calm, flat tone she used to mask distress from her patients failed and her voice spiked with alarm. Milton was a rail, draped in baggy clothes and wrapped in a tartan throw despite the sauna-like heat in the room. His wide eyes and his teeth seemed too big for his gaunt face, and his skin, which hung slack like it didn't fit him anymore, had a matte gray pallor. *He looks ancient.* She sank down beside him. Carmen had seen young men with this look before, especially at the free clinic where she did a rotation—the emaciated appearance like the body was slowly collapsing inward, consuming itself until there was nothing left. *It can't be that.* Carmen overruled her instant diagnosis. *Maybe it's cancer—like that's better.*

"I guess it's an understatement to say I'm having a bad day." Milton found a brittle smile. "Truth is there have been a lot of those, especially in the past year." He raised his hand like he was going to reach for hers, then let it fall back on his lap. "I practiced how to say this, but I guess direct is the best. Carmen, I have AIDS." He looked at her like he was waiting to see if she'd run.

"Milton, no." She shook her head in disbelief. *It's not fair.* She could feel the tears pooling behind her eyes. *The last thing he needs is to see me cry.* "At the hospital?" She'd heard about medical personnel being accidentally infected. It was the newest risk of the health-care professions.

"No." Milton smiled wanly. "But I toyed with telling my parents that until I decided the truth hurts less than all the lies I've lived already." He took her hand. "I'm gay, Carmen."

Carmen held onto his hand, rubbed it with her free one, trying to warm his cold, bony fingers and let this last statement sink in. It came so quickly on the heels of the other word she hadn't absorbed. *This isn't real.* This was

Milton, her friend, the first guy she ever trusted. She had a flash of that first day they met in the bookstore when he let her have the best biology text and she didn't know what to make of him. Now they had gotten each other through the grind and it was time for the gravy and she didn't want to believe Milton wouldn't get to savor it. "How sick are you?" Before he could answer, she noticed the prune-colored lesions under his collar, behind his ear and knew there were more she couldn't see.

"Pretty far along." Milton sighed. "I'll spare you the pesky details. Suffice it to say it started with a lot of opportunistic infections. I was getting sick all the time. At first I figured I was run down because of all the long hours. Then I came to my senses and took an HIV test." Milton closed his eyes a moment, shook his head. "Thus officially began the nightmare. The hospital wasn't too happy. They frown on their doctors looking sick—even those of us who spend our days locked in the lab—said it causes poor morale. So I quit. The long hours were too much anyway. If I've got limited time I'm certainly not going to spend it where I'm not wanted." He looked at her. "There are a lot of people who don't need to know I'm sick. As far as they're concerned I just rode off into the sunset, but I had to tell you."

"What meds are you on?"

"I didn't want to see you so we could discuss my case, Carmen. I'm being treated, for what it's worth. Let's leave it at that. Okay?"

Carmen knew he was right. Talking about his T-cell count, analyzing his treatment, second-guessing his doctors, was pointless. All that mattered now was time and how much of it he had.

"Look at us. *Now* we're holding hands." He gave Carmen's a squeeze, coaxed a grin from her. "I needed to let you know because I really did love you, still do, but like my sister or a best friend. I tried to make it different, but I think I just confused both of us and I'm sorry."

"It's okay Milton." Carmen worked up a shaky smile. "I love you *way* more than I ever loved my brother." The words felt funny coming from her lips. She hadn't said "I love you," since the last day she saw Geraldine, hadn't heard it in longer than that. Suddenly Carmen's long-ago turmoil about Milton's intentions seemed inconsequential. The kiss on the boat? Her pinkie on his thigh? It never once occurred to her that he could be gay, but what did it matter now? "Why didn't you tell me sooner?"

"I planned to—the time I came to your place and you cooked dinner. But I was so glad to see you and everything was so nice and I didn't want to spoil it so I chickened out. And this isn't exactly a long-distance conversation. I needed to look at you when I said it."

"What about your parents?"

Milton dropped his head, shook it slowly.

They held hands for a while, their silence more potent than whatever they could think of to say, but finally Milton spoke up. "We're here so I could see some doctors. Bernard—" Milton called and Bernard emerged from the shadows. "Carmen, Bernard is my partner." He reached out his other hand and Bernard took it. "We met after this happened, at the post office of all places." He smiled at Bernard. "I don't know how I'd get through this without him."

Carmen could feel the warmth and strength between them. She reached out a hand to Bernard, completing the circle.

"This place belongs to a friend of Bernie's who's away. Tuesday, we leave for Miami. I'm going to work at an AIDS clinic there a few days a week. I wanna live where there's blue water, sunshine and palm trees. Maybe get a bungalow and a hammock, like on *Gilligan's Island*."

"*Gilligan's Island?* I swear, sometimes you're so corny, Milton," Bernie said.

"Yeah, yeah. You tell me all the time I'm an embarrassment to gay men. I don't like musicals and I can't dance."

Carmen had to laugh and Bernard went to make brunch while Carmen caught Milton up.

"So Ty turned out all right. I didn't see that one coming." Unlike the old days when he scavenged everyone's plate, Milton just picked at his waffles. "Our Jewell, the next Jackie O—the power behind the throne? Who'd a thunk it?"

Carmen dreaded good-bye. Milton tried to keep it light, but she knew this was more than "see ya next time." They hugged and he gave her two extra squeezes, "For the girls." Just before she left, he added, "Work is good for you Carmen, but it's not everything. You need a whole life to be a whole person." His face clouded over. "I spent years hiding from mine, in a book, in my work, pretending it was enough, but it's not. I'm not sure what you're hiding from, but it looks like you're doing the same thing." He rested a hand on her shoulder. "It took me a while, but I found a life. Don't spend yours acting like you don't need that, like I did. Go out and get yourself one."

Carmen walked out the door in a daze. She couldn't call Jewell or Regina yet. She needed to think. About Milton. About how unbearably real this was. She needed to dig around in her heart and mind, replay the last ten years. She needed to remember Milton, healthy and strong, but it was the image of him waving like a skeleton in a haunted-house ride as she passed that front window that she carried with her. She held herself together until she got home, but the moment she dropped her keys in the basket by the door, her hands began to shake. She started to make coffee then realized caffeine might not be what the doctor ordered this time. So she dug around in the fridge, found a bottle of wine she'd bought months ago just to have one on hand, and took it out to the patio. She didn't think about a glass until she was already curled up on the wicker settee, so she shrugged, took a swig, then another.

She lay there, gripping the bottle by the neck, gazing at the bee bumbling around her zinnias. The scent of charcoal and hickory floated over from a neighboring yard and a chorus of cicadas chirped from the nearby woods, but the weight of her sadness kept her from the usual pleasure she found in these little things.

Carmen turned the bottle up for another swallow. Life and death were an everyday part of her gig. She had a sixteen-year-old car-accident victim who coded yesterday. It was tragic, but not personal. There was her father of course. Carmen's memories of him were nice, but sketchy, faded—the smoky smell and taste of the warm peanuts he used to shell for the two of them, his bushy mustache tickling her cheek when he kissed her good night. But she had been so young when he was killed he'd almost become like a character from a favorite story, no more real that the *Cat in the Hat.* Geraldine remained a puzzle with missing pieces. Carmen didn't know if her mother was dead or alive so she never got that whole picture. She'd learned in med school that her mother was probably bipolar, manic-depressive they used to call it, with moods that swung wildly between high and low, but that clinical diagnosis didn't let her fill in the blanks. Her hazy connections made those early losses easier to take. And Z? She didn't know him, she didn't miss him, and her life was definitely better without him.

But Milton—Milton was different. And she already felt the ache in her heart. She had chosen to bring him into her life, chosen to care, and he cared back. They'd been through a lot together and today she'd found out how much she didn't know about him, but even that couldn't break their bond. Unlike her parents, unlike Z, she and Milton had built and shared memories and although he wasn't gone yet, it was inevitable and that felt like the most profound loss of all. "It's not fair," she said to no one. She let the tears stream down her face as she stopped holding on.

The next afternoon she called Jewell, and Regina too because this was too important not to tell her. They shared stunned conversations, bits of recollection, each wondering how they hadn't seen it. They knew gays, they knew people with AIDS, some of whom had already died, but none of them was Hemp.

In mid September, Carmen received a huge box, postmarked Miami Beach Station. It contained Milton's medical books, his framed Johns Hopkins diploma, his employee badge from his last research job, with Dr. Milton Hemphill looking wide-eyed and eager for the camera. Then there was a picture of Milton and Bernard smiling with the ocean and an orange sun as the backdrop. The note on the back read, "Work is good, but not enough. Go and get yourself a life."

After a fitful night, Carmen got up the next morning and retrieved the piece of paper she had shoved in the pocket of her car door a month ago. She knew it was early, but school started early, and if she didn't make the call at that moment she would talk herself out of it. She hesitated before pushing the last digit, then closed her eyes and pressed. One thing she learned from Milton is that time is not promised and regret is a waste of it. Malcolm answered on the first ring.

"This is Carmen—Webb. I uh—" *I need some help here because this is kinda new to me*. "It's early and I know you're on your way to work, but—"

"Nope. Teacher's conference. Kids are off. We spend the day in boring seminars, but my first one doesn't start till eleven. Otherwise I'd be at school already. Enough. You called me and I'm doing all the talking."

Which is perfectly all right with me. "I thought about what you said. I've been thinking about a lot of things in the past few weeks. And I—I would like to—see you again. I mean sometime, you know. Maybe we could uh—"

"How about breakfast?"

"Okay. My schedule is kind of funky, but sure, breakfast sounds fine. When?"

"Now."

"*Now?* Now?" Carmen asked.

"The very same. What time are you due at the hospital?"

"Ten."

"See you in fifteen minutes."

Fifteen minutes? Carmen caught a glimpse of her green scrubs in the smoked-glass door of the wall oven. *Where are we going? Probably the diner. Should I change? Then I'll have to change back again. I sound like Regina*. Which made her decide to stay exactly as she was. She checked her hair, put in the tiny gold studs that had been sitting on the coffee table for a week, and swiped on some lip balm before she grabbed a sweater and went outside to wait on the steps. Technically it was still summer, and in a couple of hours the day would heat up, but the cool September morning felt like autumn. *Teacher conference, huh?* But she did notice the absence of lumbering yellow buses at the corner and parents prodding foot-dragging kids.

Twelve minutes later Malcolm pulled up and Carmen started down the walk, but he met her halfway. "Thought I'd make this easy." He held up a grocery bag. "Brought everything I'll need." Today he was dressed in school clothes again, his tie still undone.

"Here?" Carmen was surprised for the second time in less than thirty minutes. "You're Mr. Spontaneity, aren't you?"

"Good for the soul. Makes you feel alive, not like another brick in the wall. At least that's my theory. Now if you don't have a kitchen—"

"Like new." Carmen unlocked the door. She wasn't sure if the nervous flutter was because of him in general or because *him* was in *her* house, but she brushed it off. *Work is not enough.* "Only used on the occasional Sunday by a little old resident from Somerset who spends too many hours slaving over patients to slave over a stove." She led him to the kitchen. "I've become the queen of takeout. Pizza? Chinese? Subs? Thai?" She tapped her forehead. "The phone numbers are right here."

"If you show me where the pans and utensils are, breakfast will be on quicker than corn flakes wilt." Malcolm started taking ingredients out of the bag.

Carmen directed him to the appropriate cabinets and drawers, watched him assemble what he needed, feeling more than a little in the way. *But I can do this*. "Coffee?" She held up her French press.

"*Mais oui mam'selle docteur*," he teased in a bad French accent as he laid strips of bacon in the skillet. Then he spoke to her over his shoulder. "I should probably leave well enough alone but since I'm not that smart, what made you call?"

Carmen reached for her coffee canister. "I don't know you very well, but for some reason I have yet to diagnose, I like you."

"I hope you don't think of it as a disease. 'She liked him until she found the cure.'"

"I think the telethon is next month." Carmen set the table and watched him move deftly from pot to pan, stirring, turning, buttering, serving.

It looked to Carmen like there was enough food for the neighbors too, but she smiled as he slid two sunny-faced eggs on her plate then spooned grits next to them. He put a generous helping on his own plate then sat across from her.

"Not bad huh?" He grinned—another sunny face in front of her.

"I'll tell you in a second." She picked up her fork, saw Malcolm lower his head. She paused an awkward moment, then put her fork back and waited for him to say grace, which was eloquent, short and sweet. Carmen expected to feel self-conscious with a man who just prayed over a breakfast he brought *and* cooked. But she didn't.

They chatted about easy stuff, hope for a warm fall and a short winter, his students this year, his decision to delay the second master's or Ph.D. choice another year, her job prospects—work at a clinic or health center for a while, start her own practice, join an established one. He cracked up when she asked if leftover grits could be microwaved. "You'll have to tell me. I've never had any left."

With his plate clean and her belly full, Carmen folded her hands at the edge of the table. "I didn't tell you the whole reason I called you."

"Uh-oh. That's got a foreboding we have to talk sound."

"No, no. Not foreboding, it's—I just want you to know." She pushed her plate away. "A friend told me to—well not exactly to call you, but he told me to go out and get myself a life."

Malcolm leaned back in his chair, listened as Carmen told him about Milton, about their friendship, about his illness, about the years of confusion over mixed signals. She didn't know if Malcolm understood what that meant—that there had been no boyfriends, no lovers. She wasn't even sure why she brought it up, but it felt right so she went with it. He didn't interrupt or hurry her. He allowed her the space to find the right words, to say what she really meant. She explained how much control it took not to fall apart when she first saw Milton's condition.

"The ultimate control is deciding you don't always have to have it."

"Sounds like psychobabble."

"Maybe. But it's true. This is going to be a rough ride and you'll need to know when to hold on and when to let go. Milton is lucky to have Bernard. Close to the end it gets real hard—not that all of it isn't hard as hell. But it helps to have somebody there. At least I hope it helped." Malcolm opened the sliding glass door, went out on the tiny deck off the kitchen. Carmen followed. "My cousin Mark. Three years ago. He was twenty-two." Malcolm sat on the railing, looking back in the house.

"I'm sorry." Carmen sat next to him.

"Me too. About your friend." Side by side on the railing their hands touched and neither moved. The sun had started to warm the day and they stayed that way for a few minutes. "Can we do this again?" He shoved up his sleeve, then held up his open palms. "No tricks. No surprise announcements. We could even do dinner and a movie—you know, a real date."

Carmen tilted her head to look at him. "Yeah. My new schedule comes out day after tomorrow. I'll call when I know how it looks."

"Promise?"

Carmen nodded. "Yep."

Malcolm looked at his watch and stood up. "I'd better get going. 'Increasing Class Participation' and 'Homework: How Much Is Too Much?' await my presence, but I feel like a jerk leaving you with the dishes."

"No KP for the cook. That was the house rule in 5D—my old apartment." She stood on the top step, and with him at the bottom of the three redwood planks they were almost eye to eye. She wanted to reach out and move his hair from in front of his eye.

"I'll roll with that," he said.

The kiss followed so matter-of-factly Carmen had no time to panic. It was short, his lips were smooth, and her whole body tingled.

"Talk to you soon." And he was gone.

She went inside, fingering her lips, feeling dizzy—not sick, but silly, happy, indescribable.

By the end of October, Carmen and Malcolm had gone on two official dates, dinner and a movie, and a Sunday hike in the Poconos. They met for coffee when they could, spoke on the phone when they couldn't. Malcolm came over on Halloween, dressed like a pirate, complete with his old eye patch and helped her pass out trick-or-treat candy. Afterward they ordered a pizza but she fell asleep on the couch before it arrived. She awoke the next morning, still in her scrubs, but snug in her bed, and found his note on the pillow next to her. "Pizza's in the fridge, makes a pretty good breakfast (don't ever tell my mom I said that). You're cute when you're asleep." *Cute?* She felt warm and tingly. *Maybe it's time to tell Jewell.*

20
"She'd have to juggle like a champ to keep all her balls in the air."

"It must have been excruciating for Milton to keep that secret so long." Jewell twisted her hair into a loose braid and watched Dwight fiddle with his bow tie in her bathroom mirror. "He knew we cared about him." Jewell conveniently ignored her own failure to share her secret with the man she planned to love, honor and cherish till death do them part. That chapter was closed and everyone involved, including her, had moved on with their lives. Wasn't that the point?

"Will this person be coming to the wedding?" Dwight concentrated on his reflection and his knot-tying. "I mean, does he look sick?"

"What are you saying, Dwight? Gays aren't part of your magnificent quilt?" They had been so busy with work, wedding plans and official obligations that she hadn't told him about Milton until now. Carmen's bubbly phone call about Hemp's Miami photo and the man she'd brought into her life as a result, made it easier to talk about, but Dwight's reaction wasn't what she expected.

"That's not what I meant."

But by then she'd walked away, desperate for a cigarette. She'd officially quit more than a year ago, but right now she felt like she could blow smoke without one and with the fund-raiser tonight the urge would only get stronger.

"Don't be mad. I'm just distracted. Of course he's welcome." Dwight joined her on the sofa. "I've got something for you." He put a black jeweler's box in her hand. "The minute I saw this I knew it belonged on your finger. I even think I got the size right this time."

The wide, filigreed band looked medieval to Jewell. "It's nice—but I had a more modern style in mind. I thought we were going shopping for wedding bands together."

"But this one is outstanding—like you. Trust me, like I trusted you to let your wild-card friend Regina run our wedding." Dwight stood up, kissed her forehead. "I've got to go."

And Jewell held her peace. She had too much to get done to start the day arguing.

The wedding, or as Regina called it, "The Greatest Show in Harlem," had driven Jewell's activities since June. The first challenge she gave Ringmaster Regina was to find a spot uptown for the reception since Dwight wanted it in the district. Regina toured countless banquet spaces, trying to find one grand enough. Finally she called Jewell, all excited. "I've got it and it's perfect. Faculty House at Columbia. It's the right neighborhood and I can bug you about returning to the scene of your past academic glory, not to mention where you had the good fortune to meet me."

Jewell's work on *TIA* remained challenging—Adrienne was currently involved in a hostile takeover of the bank run by the man who still had not admitted she was his illegitimate daughter—and Jewell was still having fun. The writers had worked her ten-day wedding absence into the story line and she got a chill when she asked the producer to change her credit to Jewell Prescott-Dixon after the ceremony. Regina had teased her. "You gonna get his name tattooed somewhere unmentionable too?" But the *TIA* crew was as excited as when they had a wedding on the show. They even considered having Adrienne marry the same week—Valentine's weddings were a huge ratings draw—but in the end they decided to keep Adrienne on her ball-busting mission.

Jewell and her agent had been focused on getting her a prime-time series, but she asked Michael to scale back his efforts. "I'm crazy right now. I need to see how much I can handle and after we're married I know there'll be more. And if Dwight runs for congress, he'll need me."

The low-key fall she had hoped for was turning out to be anything but. Dwight had asked her to host tonight's fund-raiser for him at her apartment. "I need a place where I can talk to the kind of businesspeople who don't normally take an active interest in uptown. I want to show them how we can form a partnership that will strengthen the Harlem community *and* promote their interests in an area ripe for development," he had said. So in spite of Jewell's hectic schedule they settled on a November date after the elections, when the next cycle of politicking would begin.

Carmen called a week before the party to say she and Malcolm would be in town that same afternoon and asked if Jewell had time to meet before they left the city. She had been anxious to meet Carmen's first—first whatever, so Jewell invited them to stop by the party. "Come early, before all the bigwigs arrive. That way we can talk. And Reg will be here too—she helped me plan this shindig. That way Malcolm won't have to go through the onceover twice." Since Carmen and Regina had become warring factions, Jewell struggled to maintain detente between them.

Jewell spent the day receiving deliveries, supervising the wait staff and peeking at her wedding band, trying to imagine it on her finger every day for the rest of her life. By late afternoon she was glad for the distraction of getting dressed, and when the doorman buzzed a little before five to announce Dr. Webb and Mr. Wyatt, Jewell could hardly wait.

"I'm so happy to meet you, Malcolm." Carmen hadn't given any description. All Jewell knew was that he taught high school math, so the shoulder-length dreadlocks were a surprise.

"My pleasure." He smiled and Carmen smiled at him smiling.

Jewell had never seen that look on Carmen's face. "I wish this party business wasn't in the way. This is not going to be my favorite part of being a political wife, but I'll get used to it."

"I've been to a few of those deals. Sometimes there are too many important people in too small a space—they don't leave much air for anybody else." Malcolm laughed.

"We won't stay long," Carmen said. "But I had my first fitting today, and I must say I look pretty good in my maid of honor getup." She strutted in a circle as if she had it on.

"And you're willing to admit it?" Jewell looked at Malcolm. "It must look amazing."

Malcolm grinned at Carmen. "She couldn't help but look good."

Jewell was tickled, watching the two of them together. They seemed like a good fit. "Come on, let's get a drink." She ushered them toward the living room.

"If you don't mind I want to check out the menu. Maybe get some ideas from the pros."

"Be my guest." Jewell saw Malcolm's fingers lightly brush Carmen's, a personal "be right back" before he wandered over to the dining room.

"He fancies himself quite a cook," Carmen whispered.

"Looks like you two got something cooking. I saw the finger thing." Jewell wiggled hers.

"Good friends. We hang out together when we can. That's it."

"Regina used to call Ty her good friend," Jewell sang.

Carmen felt the heat rise from her neck and spread over her cheeks. "We haven't gotten that far." Carmen's stumbling explanation was interrupted by the door.

"Everything on schedule here?" Dwight called as he came in the apartment. "Oh. Hello Carmen." He pecked Jewell on the cheek. "Good to see you. How are things at the hospital?"

Jewell made a note to tell him he asked the same question every time he saw Carmen.

Malcolm materialized at Carmen's side. "Hey man. You must be Dwight." He held out his hand. "Malcolm Wyatt."

"Good to see you. Friend of Jewell's?" Dwight in his chalk-stripe suit and shiny black wing tips gave Malcolm a quick evaluation.

"Hope so." Malcolm caught the appraisal. "I'm with Carmen."

"Ah." Dwight rubbed his hands together. "Are you related to Justice Eugene Wyatt? U.S. Court of Appeals, second circuit I believe?"

"Not that I know of." Malcolm folded his arms across his chest. "I'm the son of Conductor William Wyatt, New Jersey Transit."

Jewell felt the edge, wanted to smooth it over. "Malcolm teaches math, in high school."

"High school eh? That's terrific. Our young people need more black male—uh—positive male role models."

"Indeed they do." Malcolm passed a hand over his locks.

"We gotta go, Jewell," Carmen interjected.

"So soon?" Dwight protested, but his relief was visible.

"Yep. It's a school night." Carmen looped her arm through Malcolm's. "I'll call you."

Before the door clicked shut Dwight offered his assessment. "She's a doctor for chrissakes? What does she want with a nappy-headed schoolteacher?"

Jewell was caught off guard. "That's a little judgmental."

"We all make judgments. The trick is to make good ones," Dwight said.

Regina was a no-show. Sydney came to make sure everything was running smoothly, and made apologies for Regina who was home with a sinus infection.

As expected the party was well attended by Dwight's well-heeled, wheeler dealers. Jewell was surprised by how different this downtown gathering was from his uptown events. His message sounded different too, but she got so involved with her own entertaining—it seemed everyone liked meeting a TV personality—she didn't pay much attention to his rhetoric.

November rolled into the holidays and Christmas à la King had more than one trying moment, but Forestina helped Jewell get through the day. When she opened her gift from Dwight—a three-strand pearl bracelet that had been his mother's—King accidentally on purpose let it slip that he had been rooting for Dwight to marry the CPA he dated before he, "shacked up with this one." Auntie Forestina kept her hands firmly on Jewell's shoulders, patting calmly.

New Year's marked the official start of the Prescott-Dixon wedding countdown, putting the ball squarely in Regina's court. The beginning of the year was usually slow for parties but she had all she could handle. Jewell's wedding was a capital B, Big Deal, and on top of that, two of Ty's artists, Misha and an edgy R&B fivesome called Word Up, had given Big Bang their first Grammy nominations. Ty had called her, whooping like a kid, like he did way in the beginning. "You know you got to do it up!" So she was planning the mother, father and grandpappy of all parties, a week after the nuptials. She'd have to juggle like a champ to keep all her balls in the air.

"That car costs money, Regina." Ty had a Town Car waiting to take him to his lunch with a music magazine reporter.

"I'll be ready in five. You know it's better to keep them waiting." Regina pulled on yesterday's bra and panties. She wanted to hitch a ride on his company's dime, not hers. She had to make an office appearance today to take care of a few fiscal details she couldn't trust to Sydney or Glenda. While Ty played Super Mario Brothers in the living room on the Nintendo he had gotten her for Christmas, she stared in her closet for something that fit, trying to tune out the tinny arcade bleeps and bloops that danced on her nerves. *Stupid freakin' game.* She wanted to throw it out the window, but at least he was occupied. Realizing she wasn't going to make any progress until she got her head together, Regina padded to the bathroom, feeling like she'd been run over by the D train. She soaked her washcloth in hot water, perched on the side of the tub and draped it over her face to soothe the pressure. The inside of her nose felt like it had been raked with the coarse side of a cheese grater, but a little blow was all that would get her out the door this morning. She hated doing it while Ty was around, but this morning it couldn't be helped.

She tipped to her bedroom to take a discreet dip from her aspirin bottle instead of hitting the kitchen-cabinet stash. Then she'd head back to the closet. She scooped some with her pinkie nail, unaware the game noises from down the hall had stopped. She dipped again, felt her heart start pumping and her brain light up.

"What the…" Ty snatched the bottle, dumped powder in his hand. "Uh-uh Regina. Not you. Not this."

"It's no biggie." She hated the disappointment in his face, knew there was no explaining, but had to try. "I do a little now and then. I needed a jump-start this morning. What's the harm?"

"A jump-start?! Spoken like a true junkie. No wonder you so damn skinny." Ty flung the powder at her and walked out.

Regina wiped at the dusting on her face and hair, but that did nothing to rid her of the hot swell of embarrassment. She followed him to the front room, found him sitting on the chaise, his head in his hands, tears streaming through his fingers.

Ty looked up at her. "Please let me help you. I love you Regina. You gotta stop, you hear me? You don't know, this shit will fuck up your life."

I love you? Ty had never said that before, not that he didn't act like it. Not that she didn't know, but the words made it official and that made her panic. "I'll stop." She knelt in front of him, wrapped herself around him. "Baby, it's over." She'd promise anything to make him stop crying.

Regina stayed on her best behavior with Ty, made an effort to eat, even put on a few pounds. She was not a junkie. She could quit anytime she wanted. She just didn't want to, not with so much on her plate. She felt the coke gave her the boost she needed to stand out and get to the top in the city and she was almost there.

Timing was critical when she planned to see Ty; she knew he watched for signs, even suspected he checked her purse for the aspirin bottle, so she switched to an empty lipstick tube. Fortunately he stayed busy and traveled so much now that curtailing her activities while he was around was manageable. The rest of her juggling act wasn't so simple.

"Just in time." Glenda put her call on hold. "It's the liquor guy again. Says he'll lose the twenty cases of Billecart if he can't send them the total amount due today."

I know. Welcome to my world. "He'll have his money this afternoon." Regina sat at her desk, wrote the check, dropped the binder on top of the stack of bills and locked her drawer. She couldn't put this off any longer. The champagne, one Jewell fell in love with in France, was a special order and the wedding was less than a week away. "Call the car service and Quick Run."

Glenda dialed the messenger service. "Didn't Dwight send a check for that a while back?"

"No. That was for—I don't remember now—but it wasn't for champagne." Regina drummed her pen on the edge of the desk. "The invitations maybe?" She wasn't about to say that instead of paying for the wine, she used Dwight's check to make payroll. That the sixty to ninety days after an event it took most clients to pay were killing her and money was going out faster than they were collecting it. That snow on the past two Funday Mondays had put a major crimp in her cash flow. That she didn't pick up the mail at the post office because their early-bird carrier left it in front of the door before they opened. It was so no one would see second- and third-notice stamped in red on the envelopes—exactly like the ones she used to stuff at Goodwin, Peale, Burris. Or the increasingly regular letters from the IRS. Regina was depending on the Big Bang Grammy party to get her caught up, but she knew the check to City Wine & Spirits would bounce unless the check she was on her way to pick up from the Bountiful Bed for their April launch party was ready and she could make it to the bank before two.

Regina grabbed her purse and the ladies' room key. "I better go to the little girls'." In the dingy bathroom she went in the last stall, took a double dip. *I'll stop after the wedding. Can't slow down now.* Regina flushed the toilet, just in case, washed her hand, checked her face for fallout.

"Your car's downstairs," Glenda said when she got back. "Number one fifty-one."

"I won't be back today, but I'll call you later for messages." Regina put on her coat. Just as she was about to grab the two boxes sitting on the floor by her desk, Eddie, their favorite messenger from Quick Run came in the door. "Perfect timing. Give me a hand with these."

"No problem." Eddie stuffed the envelope for City Wine in his bag and hefted the boxes.

Regina didn't know how Jewell would react to the gifts from her father, but her day couldn't get much worse. Ted had sounded so sincere on the phone, Regina couldn't turn him down. He heard about Jewell's wedding on *Inside Info*, a celebrity news show. Afraid she would never open a gift from him, he enlisted Regina as a go-between. Two boxes arrived from Las Vegas three days later. She'd been stalling for weeks, figuring out how to present them to Jewell.

"Glad I'm not takin' these on my bike." Eddie chuckled as he loaded the packages in the car trunk. "There you are, R."

Eddie prided himself on being clever but his hokey humor reminded Regina of Milton. She didn't need that on top of everything else today so she just smirked and got in the car.

On Groundhog Day she had gotten the call she'd been dreading since August. It had been a bright blue Saturday afternoon and Regina had just stepped out of the shower. She had missed the news that morning—that on his hundredth anniversary, Punxsutawney Phil had seen his shadow, so she didn't know there would be six more weeks of winter. Didn't know Carmen's call would bring the winter right inside and chill her bones. She and Jewell drove to Carmen's on Sunday morning. They sat around the kitchen table over a box of glazed doughnuts and talked about Hemp.

"'He's free.' When I answered the phone, that's what Bernard said." Carmen repeated her conversation. "No funeral. He's been cremated. Bernard will spread his ashes off Key West." She paused. "His parents never came around." Jewell and Carmen had cried, talked and remembered, but Regina hadn't shed a tear. Still hadn't. Her friends didn't die. And even though she hadn't seen him since graduation, she found it impossible to think of Milton gone. *I can't be thinkin' about Hemp now.* His death was a bizarre counterpoint to Jewell's wedding and Regina hadn't found a place to put it so she just kept moving so it wouldn't catch up.

Despite the clogged Midtown streets, Regina managed to complete her banking mission, and she arrived at Jewell's door feeling safe for a little while longer.

"Been shopping?" Jewell helped Regina inside with the boxes.

"Wedding presents. Came to my office." Regina shoved her packages down the hall.

"Why'd you get them?"

Regina shrugged and headed for the bathroom—she hadn't had a boost in nearly three hours. "I'll give you a status report in a sec. But no snags so far. Everything's on schedule."

"I had a message about the champagne—"

I don't believe the store called her. "Done. Taken care of. Not to worry," Regina answered and closed the door. Hoping the contents might cushion the impact, she decided not to tell Jewell who the gifts were from until after she opened them. But when she got back, Jewell was sitting on the floor, a black lacquered box the size of a loaf of bread open in her lap. She stared at an envelope. "I didn't know what to do, Jewell. Don't be mad." Regina sat beside her. "It's too close to the wedding to fire me," she teased, her loose screws feeling tight again.

"Look at this!" Jewell shoved the envelope at Regina. "Look at the postmark!"

It was addressed to Miss Jewell Hampton, but "Return to Sender" was scrawled across the front. "March 3, 1970?" Regina looked puzzled. "Why did he send you this stuff?"

Jewell pulled out a stack of envelopes. "They're all from the seventies! Vivian told me he didn't care, that he never wrote or called or tried to see me, but he did!" She threw the letters into the box, knowing how painful it was to miss the child she never knew. What was it like for her father to miss a daughter with whom he already shared years of love and memories? "I'm getting married in five days! Vivian gets in Thursday. I can't deal with this now."

"I'm so sorry. I thought it was gonna be a tea set or a punch bowl, I didn't know." She knelt next to Jewell. "I guess the seating charts are off tonight's agenda. You want me to stay?"

Jewell cradled the box in her lap. "Go. I need some time."

When Regina closed the door, Jewell looked at the note Ted had enclosed with the letters. His handwriting was small, neat and round—youthful—like a child's script. "I don't need you to forgive me, Jewlee Dew. I just want you to know love really does grow if you keep your heart soft. I know. Have a happy life." His phone number was there too—so small he might have added it as an afterthought, so small that if she didn't call, it might be because she didn't see it.

21
"...storm clouds brewing, with no hint of the sun."

"You gained weight after the show went off?!" Dwight loomed at the foot of Jewell's bed, brandishing a manila envelope and bellowing like a wild boar. "What kind of half-assed truth is that?! And I was stupid enough to believe you."

Jewell shot straight up out of a dead sleep and into Dwight's ambush, squinting against the harsh light of the ceiling fixture that blinded her like searchlights. Instinctively she pulled the covers around her but felt no less exposed. She didn't know how he found out, but she knew what, and she knew she had been charged, tried and convicted before he unlocked her door. "I thought it was better…."

"For who Jewell?! Better for who?" He glared at her with eyes like bullets.

Up until then it had been a good day in what was shaping up to be a great week, to be capped by the Valentine's wedding. She had one more day of taping and all was running smoothly, despite Dwight's worries about Regina's ability to pull off the event.

The ceremony was slated for the historic Harlem church where his family had belonged for decades. That would be a full house, including long-known members, political supporters, and community leaders, as well as a host of Jewell's show business associates, followed by a cake and punch reception at the church hall. In the evening they would host a sit-down dinner for two hundred. Dwight had been thrilled when she offered to cover the bulk of the cost—her considerable net worth outdistanced his politician's salary by miles. But that was what partnership was all about and she was proud that Dwight thought of her as an asset to his future in many ways. They were both happy King had not been asked to contribute a nickel to the proceedings. Jewell had drifted to sleep envisioning their Hawaiian honeymoon.

"And I have to hear your dirty little secret from King?! Do you have any idea what it was like to stand there like a jackass in my own house—no, excuse me, in *his* house—which he informed me he was glad he'd never signed over since I'm too *stupid* to handle my personal affairs—I had to listen to him drag the woman I'm supposed to marry in four days through the mud, and I can't say two words to defend myself because I don't know a damn thing about it?" Dwight rolled the pages into a tight tube, smacked it against his leg. "God, I can still hear him cackling. 'You can call her a star if you want to. In my book, a knocked-up fifteen-year-old is common as flies on shit. Now you wanna marry that, be my guest.' You can imagine how much he enjoyed that."

Jewell could hear King's sneer, see him sprawled on one of the parlor chairs, hands clasped over his belly looking oh so satisfied and she hated making him feel like he had won. "How did he find out?" Jewell could not believe this grenade had exploded in the middle of her life, before she'd had time to recover from yesterday's sneak attack from her father.

"You can find anything if you pay the right person. The real question is why didn't you tell me?! Huh? And what else don't I know?" Dwight flung the envelope on the bed and stormed out of the room.

Jewell trembled in the silence, collecting the pieces of herself that had been blown about the room. *I should have told him*. But she hadn't given Dwight a chance to know or understand. *I should have trusted him*. She pulled on a robe, reached for the envelope. Inside she found pages of medical records from 1975 for Jewell Anne Prescott. She leafed through the grainy copies, documents she'd never seen before, feeling like they described someone else's life, but she knew it was hers. Hers and Billy's and their baby's. Jewell had erected a wall around what had happened, and right now she couldn't tell if she'd been inside of it or out, but it was rubble around her feet.

Jewell let the pages slip through her fingers, flutter to the floor. She wanted to close the door, get back in bed and pull the covers over her head, but she knew hiding wasn't the answer. Summoning the strength for whatever came next, she left her room and found Dwight, eyes closed, head thrown against the back of a living room chair. "I was fifteen, I was shooting a film—I thought I was in love." It was still hard to put "thought" in front of that. "There's nothing else, Dwight. No lurid movies, no string of lovers. I'm not like that."

"Do you realize the position you put me in?" Eyes still shut, Dwight spoke deliberately. "Suppose this comes out during a campaign or while I'm in office. It's all the distraction an opponent needs to slip past me, or make me look like an idiot. If King could find out, somebody else can."

Jewell had been prepared for him to still be angry or hurt, something personal. She wasn't expecting the cold logic of the bigger political picture.

"If it ever comes out we'll say you were raped, that's all." He opened his eyes and sat up.

"But I wasn't raped. I was in love."

"You were fifteen. You didn't know what it was, and I don't care. How old was he, huh? Old enough so that I bet we could make his life hell, even now." Dwight stood up, satisfied with his impromptu strategy.

Jewell eyed him quietly, suddenly full of outrage to add to her shame.

"We'll deal with that if the need arises," Dwight said, and walked past her to the door—leaving Jewell wondering who she was marrying and why.

"You have to have a big fight right before your wedding. Otherwise you're an alien or something," Marta said the next morning.

Jewell never went back to sleep. Her thoughts ricocheted across decades and between people who seemed to be joined in some kind of pact, forcing her to throw out whatever she had known or felt, whatever was comfortable and familiar and discover a new truth. She was jumpy and distracted on the set. Cast and crew winked and whispered about wedding jitters, but she confided in Marta that they'd had a fight although she didn't say about what.

"Two days before we got married I told Jeff to get the hell out of my house, that he was a squirelly-eyed, worthless sack of shit and I never wanted to see him again. After a day and a half, I missed him so much you couldn't pry me off him."

Dwight's call to the studio confused Jewell even more. He sounded perfectly normal, confirming seating and limo pickup times like last night never happened. She hung up, unsure how he felt—did he still trust her, respect her, need her, love her? It was a word they didn't use, like it was too obvious or easy. *Billy told me he loved me*. Jewell had told him too and felt the dizzy exhilaration she was so proud of herself for avoiding. This time she relied on reason, not romance.

When Jewell got home she sat in front of the shiny black box from Ted. A ballerina en pointe decorated the center. She decided he must have bought it not long after he left. She loved ballerinas then and had even wanted to be one until she grew "too hopelessly tall to ever partner with anyone," her teacher had said. The box had dings and scratches, like it had traveled miles with him. Some letters were on hotel stationery, others on crinkly onion skin. Jewell wasn't ready to read them yet, but she touched them, dared to open a few. One was from New Year's and confetti fell out of the envelope onto the floor. They all ended "I love you, Jewlee Dew."

Regina called Thursday afternoon, fast-talked through the pre-wedding tasks she'd checked off on today's to-do list, and kept calling her Mrs. Dixon. "So you can start getting used to it." The name made her think of Dwight's mother and her sad-eyed portrait. Carmen called twenty minutes later. "Are you excited yet? I can't believe you're really getting married."

Jewell wasn't sure she could believe it either. She almost broke down and told Carmen about her late-night raid, but she didn't know what to say, where to begin and she wasn't ready to say anything aloud that she couldn't take back.

But Jewell had plenty to say to Vivian. The more she had looked at her father's letters, the more upset Jewell got at her mother for sending them back, so by the time Vivian arrived later that afternoon, Jewell had a full pot of anger at a rolling boil.

"Look at these!" Jewell shook a fistful of letters. "How could you keep them from me?"

Rather than shaping her defense, Vivian slumped on the couch and listened. She dropped her face in her hand a moment. "I'm sorry, Jewell," she said quietly. "It was our fight—him and me, and this isn't an excuse, but I was so hurt and scared and so mad at him that I wanted to make him pay every way I could." Vivian looked up at Jewell. It was an expression Jewell had never seen before. No belligerence, so unsure it was disarming.

"Every time I saw those in the mail, they reminded me he still loved you, but he didn't love me anymore. I couldn't take that. And I couldn't take it if you loved him and you stopped loving me." Vivian looked up with tears in her eyes. "I could have just thrown them away, but I wanted him to know you hadn't read them and that you never would."

Jewell had never seen her mother cry—not through all of their arguing, not even when she got pregnant. Jewell sat beside her, put a hand on her knee. "I loved you Viv—Mom. I was a little girl—I loved you both. It wasn't supposed to be a competition." Jewell felt surrounded, crowded into a corner by her anger, her sadness, her empathy, her love. *What am I supposed to do?* She couldn't seem to find a way out of the swirl of emotions that hung over her like storm clouds brewing, with no hint of the sun.

"I know now it doesn't make sense." Vivian looked over at her. "And I know it's hard for you to imagine, but I was young and I thought I was supposed to have all the answers, and I didn't, but I had to act like I did. Then you blossomed into this amazing, talented little person and I knew how to handle that—or I thought I did." Vivian lifted one of the envelopes from the box, ran her hand across the surface.

"Did you love him?" Jewell wasn't sure why she asked, or what the answer would mean.

"Hell yeah. Like crazy. When we were first together I just wanted him to swallow me up so I could get closer." She smirked, embarrassed. "I still remember that feeling—wouldn't trade it for anything." She patted Jewell's knee. "But you should know a little something about that."

"I don't know what I know—about anything," Jewell replied.

Vivian only stayed long enough to get her marching orders for Friday. Just before she left for her hotel she stopped, looked up at Jewell. "I haven't said this for a long time, too long." She cupped her daughter's cheek. "I love you Jewell, very very much." One of Jewell's tears slid across Vivian's hand.

"I love you too." They met in an awkward hug, one stooping down, the other stretching up. They had lost the habit and the feel of each other's embraces, but this was a start.

And that evening Jewell sat in the dark, waiting for Carmen and Regina. She had insisted they spend the night so they'd all be together one more time, like in the 5D days except it was different. She knew they had both been reluctant. They did it for her, but right now she needed them, not just for laughs, the way she had envisioned. Jewell's world had been turned upside down. Her father had tried. Her mother had lied. And then there was Dwight. She had lied to him. His father spied on her. Where was the love? *Does Dwight love me? I hope so. Do I love him? I think so.* But Jewell knew she loved Regina and Carmen and she had lied to them both by leaving out a big chunk of who she was and why.

"There's something I need to tell you." The three of them sat cross-legged in the middle of Jewell's bed and she looked into the puzzled faces of her two best friends.

"A pre-wedding confession! I love it!" Regina exclaimed. "You were secretly married before, to Gianni. No. You have to tell Carmen that her new boyfriend is your long-lost brother."

"Give it a rest, Regina. This is not a TV show," Carmen said.

Jewell stared at her hands, spun her engagement ring on her finger looking for the "once upon a time" to start this story. "When I was fifteen I fell in love." The story seeped out, a trickling stream meandering over a rocky, but familiar bed, except this time she told it the way it repeated over and over in her head—the unedited version, but with an addendum, King's disclosure to Dwight.

Carmen looked stricken, both for her big-hearted friend still longing for the child she was never allowed to know, and for the daughter, who had no explanation for why she wasn't worth keeping. "Why didn't you say something sooner?" Carmen remembered how relieved she felt after she told Jewell and Regina why she was living out of her locker. And through all this time, her secret had stayed safe with them.

"I was ashamed and embarrassed. Everybody thought I was such a good girl—"

"Like we'd care?" Regina poked Jewell's leg with her big toe.

"I cared. I care. I didn't want to give her away, but Vivian convinced me it was the best thing I could do."

"What about Billy?" Carmen asked.

"Typical. You got knocked up. He got in the wind." Regina humphed.

Jewell shook her head. "He never knew. Still doesn't." She told them about the *Fly Girl* audition, how he said he'd written it for her.

"You still have that script," Carmen said.

"I can't bring myself to throw it away."

"Are you still in love with him?" Regina asked.

"Of course not," Jewell answered quickly. "I'm marrying Dwight day after tomorrow. I'm just sorry this happened to him. He shouldn't have found out like this." There was usually a light in Jewell's face, but today it seemed burned out.

"You're kidding, right?!" Regina was fired up. "He spied on you!"

"His father did it." Jewell twisted her hair in a knot, then let it fall. "But I wasn't fair to Dwight. We were about to start our marriage with a big lie." Jewell's eyes brimmed. "And it wasn't fair to my daughter. That lie invalidated her existence." Jewell drew her knees up to her chin. "But two days from now Dwight and I will start our life together." She stopped short of telling them Dwight's plan if the story ever went public. That was husband and wife talk. That was between them. "I want a cigarette." She'd been craving one for two days.

"No you don't. You'll end up feeling bad about that too," Carmen said. "How about some tea or a glass of wine?"

"Okay." Jewell's reply was limp.

"Yeah! You've only got two more nights of single sisterhood. We've had true confessions. Now for the bachelorette party! I'll get the wine." Regina squeezed Jewell's hand. "I can't think of anything you could do that would make me not love you, Bijoux." She hopped off the bed, grabbed her purse and made a detour to the bathroom before heading to the kitchen.

The wine helped Jewell get through the night without a smoke. "I'll miss this place. It's so bright." She looked around her apartment. "Dwight's house is elegant, but it hardly gets any sun."

"Guess you'll have to wait till you and Dwight move into the White House," Regina said.

And Jewell whacked her with a pillow and sent them off to bed. After sharing the load she'd been carrying for years, she actually got some sleep. So when Dwight called in the morning, bright and chipper, to say he'd meet her at the church at 6 o'clock sharp, she was glad to hear his voice.

Vivian met the threesome at Chez Prince and their appointments began and ended on time. Regina supplied champagne and kept the party in stitches and Carmen kept Jewell calm.

Jewell's face brightened when she saw Dwight waiting outside the church for her before the rehearsal. He helped her out of the car, greeted her with a kiss. "Right on time," he said. "I can't wait until tomorrow."

For all the hoopla, the ceremony was relatively simple. Carmen and P.J. were the only attendants so there wasn't a crowd of people to supervise. Regina talked to them about logistics—how much time was allotted for the receiving line, punch and cake, photos and then the ride to the sit-down dinner. "We all want tomorrow to run on time," she said, eyeing Dwight. Jewell stifled a laugh. "So when I come get you, be ready to move out."

And when Jewell practiced her walk down the aisle she looked directly at Dwight. His unwavering gaze assured her that their future together was secure.

Unlike the spectacle Regina had arranged for tomorrow, Jewell wanted the rehearsal dinner to be a time where she and Dwight could chat with friends and family in a way she suspected wouldn't happen the day of the wedding. And by the time they arrived at the Water Club, Jewell felt sure they were back on track. The flickering fireplace and spectacular view of the city lights gave the Club Room the atmosphere Jewell wanted for the small party. It was an easy, casual cocoon beside the East River and the bride and groom to be—sometimes together, sometimes separately—moved easily among their guests. With Forestina at her side, Jewell even managed to smile at King—and wonder if she should have invited Ted.

"I've got a few words for that nephew of mine before the big day. I'm not very motherly, but I guess I'm all he's got."

"I'll find him for you. They're probably in the bar smoking cigars or some other 'farewell to bachelor life' ritual." Jewell smiled at Forestina.

Jewell was at the top of the stairs, on her way to the lounge when she heard Dwight's distinctive chuckle from down the hall. She could see him adjusting his bow tie after he laughed, a habit he denied he had. She followed his voice.

"*...can't go wrong with her. She's got her own goddamn following—the downtown crowd as well as our own folks uptown. That can get you over the hump at the polls. And the sisters—man, they love it! 'He didn't get him no almost-white girl.*'" Dwight's voice rose to a mocking falsetto. "*And sisters vote!*" He laughed again, the laugh that had drawn her to this spot outside the door of the small room. She couldn't believe what she heard. She wanted to put her hands over her ears, block out the conversation, but she couldn't.

And Dwight was on a roll. "*You know how they talk about us successful black men. But she blows that debate right out of the water. This is a gen-u-wine-sho-nuff black woman.*"

"*The berry is black. I bet the juice is pretty sweet too.*" Another voice laughed.

Jewell stepped into the doorway so Dwight could see her.

When he looked into her face, he knew she had heard. He didn't know how much, but he knew it had been enough.

P.J. and Dwight's other friends receded into the background as he moved toward her.

"Jewells," he smiled. "You caught us right in the middle of—"

"Boys will be boys!" P.J. called from the back of the room. "That's a great dress, Jewell."

Dwight shot P.J. a look. "—the middle of a story about an old friend—from camp. He's mounting a senate campaign in Maryland." Dwight came and put his arm around Jewell. "But P.J.'s right about the dress. Of course you look good in anything! I am a lucky man. Aren't I fellas?"

Jewell realized she hadn't spoken. "Aunt Tina asked me to find you." She walked out of the room, Dwight right behind her.

"Whatever you think you heard wasn't about you, Jewells."

Jewell stopped and looked at him. "Is that what I am to you? A walking, talking billboard for your next election?"

"You know you mean the world to me." Dwight pulled her to him. "And you're going to make me the happiest man in New York City when you walk back up that aisle as my wife."

Jewell wanted to believe him. He was a good man who would do the right thing. She believed in him. Didn't she? Claiming fatigue, Jewell found Carmen and Regina, who were spending the night again, and left the party shortly after she delivered Dwight to his aunt. They dropped Vivian at her hotel on the way.

"I'll be there first thing in the morning." Vivian kissed her on the head.

Jewell just nodded, afraid she'd be sick if she spoke.

"Okay, it's now or never," Regina said as soon as they pulled off. "Last chance to find us some trouble, before you're an old married lady."

Jewell rested her head on the seat back. "Think I'll pass."

"What's up? It was a great party," Carmen said.

"Got a lot on my mind."

"Thought we lightened that load last night," Carmen said. "Do we have a part two?"

Jewell shook her head. She couldn't look at her, afraid it would all spill out. "I just need to go to bed."

They sat around in pajamas and sipped a glass of champagne from the bottle Regina smuggled from the reception.

"When was the first time we sat around like this?" Regina asked.

"What if I'm making a mistake?" Jewell blurted.

"You're probably not the first person who thought that the night before her wedding," Carmen answered. "But you haven't made it yet."

"We could make a break for the border," Regina proposed. "Canada or Mexico?"

But the only break Jewell made was for her bedroom, where she was taunted by the lacy, delicate wedding gown, the one she chose to please him. It hung on a rolling rack in the middle of the floor, an effigy of who she had allowed herself to become.

22
"Duty and curtain calls?"

Like the tape from a day's shooting, Jewell's night passed in a stream of images that told her story with Dwight—their first meeting, first dinner, her awful first encounter with King, the proposal on the Capitol steps. Instead of sleep, she rewound, paused, fast-forwarded, searching for favorite scenes, a nuance or phrase she may have missed. But the audio stayed the same. "*That can get you over the hump at the polls*." By morning, film littered the cutting-room floor, but the story hadn't changed and now it was showtime. A standing-room crowd would assemble to see her take her vows. *I can get through this*. But the harder Jewell tried to avert her eyes, the more it was beginning to look like a mistake. *Then what?*

"Jewell—delivery." Regina knocked at the bedroom door. "You alive in there?"

"Fine. Be right out." Jewell dragged herself out of bed and emerged to find two dozen red roses.

"The man's got taste." Regina eyed the enormous blossoms. "I mean besides marrying you. What's the card say?"

"For my Jewells, Happy Valentine's Wedding Day, Love Dwight." *Love Dwight?*

In short order Jewell's apartment felt like a set, bustling with all the people it took to get the bride and her party ready for this production and she was grateful for the distraction. Carin, Jewell's makeup artist from *TIA* arrived, followed by the photographer, who started snapping the second he came in the door. "It's all a part of your special day," he told Jewell. "You'll want to remember every moment." The Prince of Hair showed up with a trunk full of equipment and transformed Jewell's thick mane into an ethereal froth of curls and ringlets to which he secured a delicate band of pearls and crystals, and her veil. When she was done, Carmen, who was already coiffed and powdered, followed Jewell to her bedroom.

"You look like you need to talk," Carmen said once they were alone.

Jewell sat on the edge of her bed staring at her wedding dress. "I don't know. All of a sudden I'm not sure I'm doing the right thing, but it's kinda late. How's Malcolm?" She abruptly changed the subject.

"Great. He'll be there this afternoon." Carmen redirected. "Did something else happen?"

"No—not exactly." Jewell paused. *If I say white, he says black.* She could hear King's awful pronouncement, and now she wondered why Dwight didn't speak up for her right then.

"It's still not too late to change your mind, Jewell."

"That's crazy." The steady look in Carmen's eyes, the composure in her voice cut through the background noise, as if there was no hubbub outside the door. But in the end Jewell came to the same conclusion. "There'll be a thousand people sitting in that church who won't agree with you, and I wouldn't do that to him."

"Him?!" Carmen huffed. "What about you?! I haven't seen the Jewell I know since she became the soon-to-be Mrs. Dwight Dixon—and I miss her."

A quiet tap on the door stopped the conversation. Vivian peeped in. "Ready to get dressed, darling?"

Regina joined them for the spectacle. "It's hot as hell in here." She fanned herself with a magazine. "Anybody else hot?"

"I've been freezing," Jewell said as she peeled out of her robe, revealing her lacy white underwear.

"Actually, I'm just right." Carmen worked at unfastening the gown.

"Guess that makes you Goldilocks," Regina cracked.

"That would be your department, Miss Living Color."

Regina adjusted the headband that covered her overdue dark roots. "I forgot, some of us gave up *living* when we moved to the boonies." She cut her eyes at Carmen and jumped to the next subject. "Doesn't it take a committee to dress the matador for a bullfight? Does that make Dwight el toro? I guess only Jewell would know for sure if he's full of bull—"

"Re-*Gina!*" Carmen snapped.

"Lighten up, Carmen. This is a wedding, not a funeral," Regina replied.

At least Regina's ribbing allowed Jewell to keep her chin up and a smile on her face, although there was no light in her eyes. When she stepped in her gown it felt like it weighed a ton and as Carmen fastened each pearl button up the back Jewell felt a little more trapped.

"You look breathtaking, my darling." Vivian arranged Jewell's hair on her shoulders.

But Jewell never looked in the mirror, didn't want to see the woman it reflected back.

And a little before two, it was time to get the show on the road. "We'll be a little late," Regina said. "Bride's prerogative."

Jewell had to chuckle. "In Dwight's book that might be grounds for divorce."

Regina's nonstop commentary on traffic, pedestrians and especially the VIP guest list kept everyone in the vintage Rolls, including the driver, laughing and allowed Jewell's silence to go mostly unnoticed. Carmen held Jewell's hand, offering a reassuring squeeze now and then.

Jewell stared through the tinted windows at Saturday crowds bustling along city streets in fast-forward. She wanted to hit stop, pause, anything to slow this down so she could separate *what* she was doing from *why*, and see if it added up to a life she wanted forever and ever, amen.

But now the car had stopped and she was startled to be in front of the church, a few people still filing into the sanctuary.

"Duty calls! You guys wait here and I'll see what's up." Regina climbed out.

Duty calls. How many times have I said that? Jewell watched Regina hike up the skirt of her tea-length ruby velvet dress as an usher helped her up the stone steps. *Is that what I'm in for with Dwight? Duty and curtain calls?*

In a few minutes Sydney knocked on the window. "They're ready for you, Mrs. Prescott. There's a Mr. Perlman waiting for you inside."

"I asked Leonard to sit with me. He's such an old friend. I didn't think you'd mind."

"Why would I mind?" Jewell smiled at Vivian's continued charade, the first real smile of the day.

The driver came around and opened Vivian's door, but before she stepped out she gave Jewell a kiss. "Darling, I hope you'll always be as happy as you are today."

Jewell knew it was meant as a blessing, but right now it felt like a curse.

"You okay?" Carmen asked when Vivian had gone.

Jewell nodded. *I can't embarrass him on our wedding day.* She blinked back tears. *If it doesn't work I can get a—I can fix it later.*

In a few more minutes Regina came back to the car to get them. "There's no space in there to breathe. All that's missing is the bride." She led them to the back of the sanctuary and the strains of Pachelbel's Canon signaled time for Carmen to start the processional. From an alcove, away from the view of the guests, Jewell watched the minister, Dwight and P.J. take their places. In the tradition of a formal daytime wedding, he wore a cutaway coat, striped trousers, pearl gray waistcoat, and a gray-and-black-striped four-in-hand tie. *Just like he's ready for his inauguration.*

Regina fluffed out Jewell's full skirt, Carmen spread out the long, lacy train and gave her a quick kiss before she flipped the pearl-edged veil over her friend's face and smoothed her own claret velvet dress. Then she looked up at Jewell. "I love you whatever you do," she whispered.

Jewell gave her an "all's well" smile and Regina shooed Carmen through the door.

Carmen floated down the aisle, gave a quick eye to Malcolm who sat with the Fosters, then took her place. Clarke's Trumpet Voluntary urged the congregation, except those already standing along the walls and around the back, to rise.

"Knock 'em dead, Bijoux." Regina blew a kiss and opened the sanctuary doors.

And despite Dwight's objections—"Isn't there an uncle or somebody who can fill in?" Jewell walked down the aisle alone. She had bristled at the notion of being "given away" and it was a point she had won, but now Jewell stood alone, unsure of the path she was about to travel and whether her legs would carry her. *One foot, then the other*. The flashbulbs started with her first step and in seconds all she could see was the lingering flare of the cameras, just like onstage or in an arena when she was part of the show. But this wasn't entertainment, this was for real. She couldn't find her mother or see Carmen. But thankfully the lights blinded King from her view too. She couldn't even tell if Dwight was at the end of the aisle until she felt him take her hand.

"You look absolutely perfect, Jewells," he whispered as he guided her to his side.

Those were the words she had hoped for when she picked out the dress, but Jewell looked at him and wondered why perfect was so important. What would happen because she wasn't?

"Dearly beloved," the preacher began, "we are gathered together here in the sight of God to join this man and this woman in holy matrimony; which is an honorable estate." His baritone, tinged with a Tennessee twang, boomed to the last pew, and up into the balcony.

Jewell focused on each word to keep herself grounded. "I require and charge you both, as you will be called to answer on the day of judgment, when the secrets of all hearts shall be disclosed, that if either of you know of any impediment, why you may not be joined together in marriage, you should now confess it…" He had them join hands.

"*…secrets of all hearts shall be disclosed…*" The room fell away and Jewell felt like she stood there alone. He didn't ask what she thought, or what she hoped. He didn't ask what seemed safe, or looked like a perfect union.

The minister asked what was in her heart, and for all these years, since Billy and the baby, Jewell had ignored her heart.

"…Dwight Randolph Dixon, wilt thou take this woman…"

"I will." Dwight's voice was so sure and strong it caught Jewell off guard.

"Jewell Anne Prescott…wilt thou love, comfort, and honor him all the days of your life?"

I can't. The voice was so small Jewell tried not to hear it, tried to overrule it and speak her vows, but then she heard it louder, knew she had ignored the voice of her heart when she was fifteen and she regretted it to this day. Jewell didn't know how long she'd been standing there mute, but finally she heard coughs and cleared throats filling the uncomfortable vacuum, and looked through the gauzy veil into Dwight's puzzled face. "I can't." She spoke so softly only those people in the front pews could hear. "I can't spend the rest of my life with you."

"Jewells—" Dwight's voice was even lower than hers and he squeezed her fingers until their bones met. "What are you doing?"

"Let's be real, Dwight. You don't have a friend running for office in Maryland. And I need to mean more to you than extra votes, or proving your father wrong."

"Jewell, you're just tired."

"I'm not tired." She pulled her hand from his grip. "I like what you stand for, but I don't believe I like who you are." She took off his mother's ring, held it out to him, her hand shaking. "I loved who I thought you were, but I don't love you, and that's not fair to either of us. I'm sorry I didn't know that until now."

Dwight didn't move to take the ring. He was coiled tight like he was ready to spring and his eyes had a diamond-hard edge like his father's. "This is crazy. We can work it out," he hissed. "You will not do this to me."

Jewell lifted the veil from her face, placed the diamond cluster on the chancel rail. "You'll want this." Then she turned and headed back up the aisle. She heard King's chuckle as she passed his pew. *They have the same laugh.*

The frenzied buzz reached the back of the church before Jewell did. Carmen was right behind her. She mouthed, "I'll see you later," when she passed Malcolm. Vivian patted Leonard's hand and hurriedly followed them out. Jewell couldn't decide if the clicks of camera shutters and the accompanying flash pops sounded like applause or gunfire. Either way she wanted out.

What have I done?

"We better get in the car." Carmen checked out the photographers following them, looped her arm through Jewell's and guided her out.

Regina caught up with them on the steps. "You really know how to make an exit. Couldn't have happened to a nicer guy."

"Sorry to leave you with such a mess." Jewell looked at her friend.

"Piece a cake—and there sure as hell is plenty of that. Call me later." Regina waved.

"Let's go!" Vivian instructed as the three of them scrambled into the back of the car, startling the driver who was reading the paper, sure he had a good long wait.

"Where to, ma'am?" he asked as he started the engine.

"Away from here for a start," Vivian replied.

As the car sped off all three caught their breath, then Carmen broke the ice. "Told you it wasn't too late," she grinned. "What are you going to do now?"

Jewell looked from one face to the other. "Damned if I know," she said and burst out laughing, until her belly ached and her mascara ran. A warm flush passed over her body. That's when she realized how cold she'd been all day.

When Jewell settled back Vivian handed her a tissue. "I don't need to know why you walked out, but I'm certain you had an excellent reason." She took her daughter's hand. "You were very brave. It takes a lot of courage to admit a mistake, especially before you make it."

Jewell looked at her mother and where she would have expected indignation and embarrassment, she saw compassion and understanding. "I don't know—I—"

"You'll sort it out. I don't have to leave tomorrow, you know."

"I'll be fine, Mom. Carmen won't let me do anything else crazy. Will you?"

"You have my word, Mrs. Prescott," Carmen said.

"The Stanhope," Jewell instructed the driver. "And tell Leonard I said thanks for coming."

"I—uh—all right. If I see him later."

"It's okay, Mom. I've known for years."

Vivian smiled sheepishly and this time it was Jewell who did the hand patting.

When they reached the hotel, Vivian was hesitant to get out. "You could come home with me, you know."

"I know." They hugged. "But I have to figure this out. I'll call you in a day or so."

When Carmen and Jewell walked into her apartment, the phone was ringing. Jewell took one look at the message counter on her answering machine and knew the deluge had begun. "They're not gonna leave me alone. I know I'll have to say something but I can't do it now." She looked around the living room at the leftover pre-wedding, pre-move chaos. Her lease was up in a month, so she had planned her transition to Dwight's house to be a leisurely one. "I guess I can cancel the movers, huh?" Jewell plopped on an ottoman and her layers of lace and tulle made her look like a giant cupcake. "What did I just do?" Her eyes filled with tears.

"You realized you still had a choice. Your mom was right. I think it was pretty brave too," Carmen said. "I don't know if I could've done it." The phone rang again. "You can't stay here. This'll drive you nuts," Carmen said. The machine picked up and they listened as a reporter from the *New York Post* pleaded his case and left six numbers for Jewell to call him back.

"Maybe I'll get in the car and drive—not off a bridge," Jewell added, noticing Carmen's worried look. "Just out of the spotlight for a while. I'm off for ten days. I may as well use them."

"Come home with me. Who'll look for you in New Jersey?"

"You'd be surprised. They're bounty hunters and they won't stop until they get their—"

The phone rang again and Carmen went over to unplug the answering machine.

"Jewell? It's Michael."

Jewell signaled to Carmen to wait.

"What a show! Look, I'm guessing you want to lay low for a while. I've got a little house on Sanibel Island. It's yours for as long as you need. I'm at the Plaza. Call me."

"I thought about going on to Maui, like we'd planned, but I guess that's the first place they'd look, huh?" Jewell stood up. "I can't think in this dress." Carmen unbuttoned and Jewell stepped out, leaving the lacy carcass in the middle of the floor. In less than five minutes she returned wearing slacks and a sweater and found that Carmen had shed her wedding regalia as well. Jewell sat at the dining table, removing hairpins from her mountain of curls. "I'm already packed for warm weather. Maybe I will call Michael. Why don't you and Regina come? I've been trying to get you guys to take a trip with me for ten years."

"I don't know about Regina, but I can't take the time off right now. Flu season's got us short at the hospital and this is my last rotation. Can't blow it now."

Thirty minutes later the deed was done. Jewell left a message for Regina, slipped her doorman a hundred-dollar bill. "You haven't seen me. And believe me, you're gonna be asked." Then she and Carmen climbed into the back of a waiting car.

"Call me when you get there," Carmen said when Jewell got out at Teterboro Airport. "Just so I know you're okay."

"Will do." Jewell waved and headed to the waiting SkyFleet jet Michael had chartered.

Just after midnight Jewell reached into the bill of the cast-iron pelican in front of the banana plant for the key to the front door. Jewell decided to wait until morning to call Carmen. Too exhausted to explore the house, she stopped in the first bedroom she came across, crawled under the covers and it was just right. Twelve hours later, curled in the same position she'd fallen asleep in, Jewell awoke, smiled at the warm sunlight that filled the room. It was only as her eyes traveled over the unfamiliar surroundings that she remembered where she was and why.

She reached for the telephone and dialed Carmen, who answered on the first ring.

"Sorry I didn't call last night. I was so exhausted—" Jewell looked at her arm and realized she was still wearing the bracelet Dwight had given her.

"Have you seen a paper?"

"No. I just woke up." She sat on the side of the bed and looked through the wall of windows out onto the sea.

"It's worse than we thought. Regina called around six to see if you knew."

"What could be worse than 'Soap Star Skips Ceremony,' or 'Daytime Diva Dumps Dixon'?"

"He told them—or somebody did—about the baby."

Jewell felt the blow from twelve hundred miles away. *He didn't. He wouldn't.* "I—I—" Jewell struggled to find her voice. She realized it didn't matter whether it had been Dwight or King. She had dished it out and one of them was going to make her take it. *Why didn't I see this coming?* "Do me a favor and call my mom. I'll call you later."

Suddenly the room was too bright, too white, too cruel. The sky and the sea were too blue, too cool. In the bathroom she turned on the water, hot as she could stand it and let the six shower heads pelt her like hailstones. She shampooed and scrubbed over and over, until her skin was tender, rubbed until the tears flowed and she cried for the mistakes she'd been running from. She cried for the love she lost, for the baby she never touched or smelled. She cried for the hole Dwight's absence should have left in her heart, but didn't, and for the friends who loved her anyway. Jewell sank to the marble bench and let her tears come until the stream ran dry. Then she wrapped herself in a towel and sat out on the deck until the sun was swallowed by the Gulf of Mexico and the moon was high in the sky.

Gianni had said it. "*Why would you think you can hide from your past? It is your life, you take it with you wherever you go*." But it was only now she believed it.

For the next two days Jewell slept late, watched the big boats in the bay and the manatees and dolphins in the gulf. She strolled on the beach, collected shells, tossed them away again and wondered if Billy had seen the paper. She sat on the dock in the rain then waited for the rainbow. She ate fruit for breakfast, cookies for lunch and bacon burgers for dinner. Jewell fed her body, her spirit, her soul and on the third day, when she didn't feel empty or hungry any longer, she picked up the phone. First she spoke to Vivian, assured her she was fine and that Michael's "little house" was anything but. She checked in with Carmen but couldn't catch up with Regina—no answer at home and not in at the office so Jewell left her an "all's well" message in both places. And by day four, she placed a conference call to Michael and Leonard. She knew she would need both her agent and her lawyer to help draft a statement to release to the press, one that acknowledged giving up a baby for adoption when she was fifteen and made clear her honest regret for any embarrassment she'd caused Dwight and his family with her decision not to go through with the wedding. No excuses, no explanations, no revelations. Michael told her that her personal drama wasn't a total loss—*Through It All*'s ratings had jumped dramatically and the producers wanted to start new negotiations even though she still had a year left on her contract.

On day five Jewell jogged to the lighthouse, watched the bright pink spoonbills feed. On her way home, she stopped for a bottle of champagne which she took out on the deck along with a glass, the telephone and a handful of notes signed, "I love you Jewlee Dew."

23
"...nothing to lose and worlds to conquer."

"Don't do this to me, Luc." Regina circled the edge of the Afrique playpit, trailing behind the owner. "How much money have I brought in here, huh? Every freakin' week!" She had to get him to stop moving and listen, because this was no joke. Regina grabbed his arm. He slapped her hand, stared down his pointed finger in warning.

At night, bathed in green light, saturated in sound, the club was a jungle paradise, crawling with exotic, pleasure-seeking creatures. But lights up, five in the afternoon it looked like a decrepit dump, garishly decorated with plastic vines and foliage, papier-mâché bluffs and canyon walls marred with gouges and carved initials. A layer of greasy dust clung to every flat surface, and the upholstered tiger, zebra and leopard chairs, sofas, bar stools, and the pit were scarred by cigarette burns and spotted with stains she'd rather not identify. But Afrique had caché and it was a straight shot from Radio City, making it the primo spot for Ty's Grammy night bash.

"You already pulled Monday from me for some dumb-ass private party. Do not tell me you canceled me Grammy night!" She stomped the floor, feeling like she could go all the way through, and come out where? Anyplace but the hellhole she had dug this time. "I confirmed the same freakin' day as the nominations!" At the time she couldn't believe she'd have another colossal event so soon after Jewell's wedding, but that was the way it had to be. Regina kicked over a bar stool as she passed. "You know I'm good for it! You'll have the money first thing tomorrow."

"Do not sob to me, Regina. You were supposed to have a check here last week, but you tried to blow some story up my ass, and what did I say?" Luc stopped abruptly and she almost walked into him. "Cash in my hand, before two o'clock." Luc yanked a loose section of flame-retardant plastic thatch from the bar hutch and threw it to the floor. "Your Fundays are getting tired. You're getting tired, and I am not in business to have fun. I do this to make money." Luc stood next to the wide slide dressed as a shimmering waterfall—for those daring, drunk or high enough, the express route between floors. “By three o’clock I had another record company’s cash. They didn’t screw with me. They win.” He sat on the slide and made a hasty trip downstairs.

“Fuck you Luc! All right!” She felt like her brains would shoot out of her ears. Regina knew Ty had written that check in plenty of time. It had become part of her floating slush fund. Now the invitations were out, security, transportation—all the details had been arranged, except there was nowhere to party and there was no way she could tell that to Ty. A sickening wave came over her. *I have to get some air*. She sat on the slide, but lost her balance in the first big swoop and careened sideways down the chute with her skirt hiked up to her waist. She scrambled to her feet, adjusted her clothes. “Just fuck you!” The yell scraped her throat. A knobby fake baobab tree stood to one side of the entrance. Regina pulled the lowest limb until it broke off and flung it across the coat-check counter, sending hangers clattering to the floor, then stormed out.

Icy air shocked the sweat on her skin. She had planned to deliver the cash by two o’clock, but she got to the bank and found the Regina Foster Productions accounts had been levied by the IRS. “This tax thing is a mistake. You don’t understand. I need my money,” she had yelled at the teller. “Ma’am, there is no money.” She got so loud the guard escorted her to the bank manager who checked her accounts but came up with the same fat zero. “Okay. A loan. I need a loan—right now.” But the banker informed her there was nothing she could do to get funds today. And the whole time she watched the clock, minutes vanishing in batches, her time running out.

Regina called her accountant from a pay phone, screaming so loudly that people on the sidewalk swung wide around the booth assuming she was another New York nut case. When he told her there was nothing he could do right now she bounced the receiver off the Plexiglas wall.

Desperate, Regina bogarted a cab from two bag-laden shoppers who had hailed it first and badgered the driver to cut faster through the snarled traffic as she raced to DeVille. “You gotta do this for me, Reuben. I swear I’ll pay you back tomorrow.” She hadn’t figured out how yet. She wouldn’t ask Carmen for spit; the prospect of endless lectures on the virtues of thrift and hard work made the interest rate too high. Jewell was still in Florida going through her own hell, but if push came to shove she was sure Jewell would wire the cash; she was too nice to say no. If push came to a gigantic leap off a cliff she’d call her parents, not that she knew what she’d tell them. Certainly not “*I screwed up so bad I don’t know what else to do*,” because she hadn’t swallowed that truth yet. “I need this money bad.” Regina had followed

Reuben through the empty restaurant, her desperation reflected to infinity in the wraparound mirrors.

"I never bet more than I plan to lose, angel and I'm already in the red with you." Her Network Hook-ups had become barter to pay down her cocaine debt since she always bought from him. That way it stayed their little secret, and in her mind she wasn't really doing drugs if she never had contact with a real dealer, only an elfin senior citizen who still knew how to party.

"Okay. What'll this get me?" Without a first thought much less a second, she yanked off the ruby ring Ty had given her, shoved it in Reuben's hand.

"Fiery stone, probably Burmese." He twirled the ring under his desk lamp. "Not enough for your deposit, but if you need more pixie dust we can arrange a deal." He batted his lashes.

"It's worth more than that, you freakin' dwarf," she blurted, too upset to hold her tongue.

"Temper doesn't suit you." Reuben held the ring out to her. "Take it or leave it, angel."

She needed the deposit, but her stash was gone too. If she was going to get out of this she had to think clearly and she didn't feel sharp without a boost. So Regina got a noseful in his office for courage and left DeVille with a full lipstick tube and some extra on the side—Reuben's consolation prize—then made the mad dash to see Luc. She figured she was only a little late—a few hours was no time between friends, but she'd figured wrong and her time had run out.

"You all right?" A man wearing a camouflage jacket and fingerless gloves stooped low enough to look into Regina's face. She was doubled in half, propped against the brick front of a building around the corner from Afrique, lost in her nightmare.

She straightened up. "I'm okay." But when she had stepped out of the club and felt the empty spot where Ty's ring used to be, she was overcome with the harsh reality of having to deal with him. Imagining the look in his eyes made her sick with dread. *I can't do it.*

Ty had looked so happy for the few moments Regina saw him after Jewell's wedding unraveled. In between fielding questions, alerting the hall that the evening's affair was a no-go, and figuring out what to do with cake and punch for a thousand, Ty snuck in a smooch. "I was hoping you'd catch the bouquet," he had said. That had been Regina's exit cue because she was not looking for a proposal. Nobody lived happily ever after, not even Princess Jewell.

But Ty had been in great spirits for the last year. CD sales were slamming, and although he hadn't produced a movie yet, he had opened a video production division. Then the Grammy's came along and put him in orbit. His business was in order, his star on the rise. Regina had been at this as long as he had, and it ate at her that he was so together on all fronts while she was still at loose ends and those were unraveling. Regina's mega-style had been right on eighties' time, and it carried her into the nineties', but however good it looked on the outside, she never had patience for the numbers, so she just made them look good too, except one and one was less than zero and she was doing her best to outrun the fear that her whole show was about to come crashing down.

But right now Regina had to keep moving so she started to walk, decided to go to the office to work out a plan. She called to make sure Sydney and Glenda were gone because she wasn't interested in brainstorming—this had to be a solo effort. The machine picked up. *Excellent.*

Sitting at her desk, door locked, she felt safe. Safe enough to breathe. Safe enough to take a hit from her lipstick tube to stop the idle chatter in her head. First she blew her nose, collected a wad of blood in her tissue—no biggie, it happened sometimes. She closed her eyes and snorted enough to feel her brain come alive like a string of white lights. *I got the power.*

By the ghostly light of her desk lamp Regina wheeled in dizzy circles around the office in her chair, looking for the answer. She knocked over a wastebasket, sent a philodendron crashing to the floor, which seemed hilarious, so she rolled through the dirt making squiggles and footprints. Then it came to her. *Find another club.* To her it was so simple but genius that she laughed aloud.

DeVille was out of the question—much too small, besides Ty wasn't hot on Reuben, and after tonight she wasn't either—but all the other clubs Regina knew were in the running. Boots off, feet on the desk, she sat with her Rolodex, calling for her salvation. Her buzz wore off by the H's, so she took another hit to make it to the P's, but Z still stood for zero. "Grammys, baby. We're booked." No matter how breezy the conversation, that was the bottom line. She kicked the phone from her desk after her last good-bye and it crashed like cymbals, echoing in her ears.

I gotta get out of here. She would go home, get some sleep, let the morning bring fresh thoughts. Regina dipped in her stash, just for enough energy to get her there because suddenly her legs felt brittle, but she got her boost, headed outside. The streets seemed empty except for the slice of moon that followed her. It became a game—dipping around corners, dashing to the dark side of the street, trying to hide from the moon. After a two-mile chase Regina abruptly ran out of steam at Ninety-seventh and Fifth. She drooped on a bench, feeling lost, ready to let the high tide carry her out to sea. Just before she went under, she jumped up, flagged a cab. "A Hundred-and-tenth…"

"No. Sorry. I'm going off duty. That's too far uptown."

"TAKE ME HOME GODDAMMIT!" She perched on the edge of the seat, pounding on the safety partition. "TAKE ME HOME!" Regina yelled louder and longer so he turned off Fifth, shot up Madison like there was nothing between them and kingdom come. In what seemed like seconds they stopped in front of her building. Regina shoved money through the slot, staggered up to 5D and headed directly for the chaise, but even with the expansive view she felt the walls closing in. *Ty's gonna kill me.* She moved to her bedroom, but the clutter was suffocating so she grabbed her purse, headed to the bathroom and traced coke lines on a cracked hand mirror, but after they vanished up her nose she was face-to-face with herself and the fact she had no money and no solution. The paychecks she'd written Sydney and Glenda would be bouncing by morning. *How many checks did I write?*

Regina stared at the phone, picked it up, put it down, didn't know who to call or why. *Carmen. She has to give me money. She owes me.* Regina punched speed dial, but hung up when she heard Carmen's voice because money was beside the point. Talking to Ty was all that mattered, but by 3 A.M. nothing had changed. *I gotta get some sleep. This'll make sense tomorrow*, except her eyelids felt nailed to her brows so she flipped on the kitchen light, ignored the roaches diving for cover and went for the vodka under the sink. She chugged a tumblerfull, no ice, to bring her down, then went back to the lounge and sat drinking and rocking until her body felt liquid and she slipped from consciousness.

The ring of the phone brought Regina halfway back from the state she'd passed into and she struggled to make sense of the voice coming from the answering machine. "*Sydney here. It's one o'clock. Where are you? Somebody vandalized the office last night. Nothing seems to be missing, it's just a mess, but we called the police. Also, Quick Run said their check bounced twice and they cut us off. We really need them. And I've got Big Bang details to discuss. Call me.*"

Regina's mouth tasted like turpentine and pain darted behind her eyes so she slugged more vodka to numb it. There was nothing she could think of to say to Sydney and she was so tired—of running to stay ahead of her lies, of being afraid, of feeling alone. She slipped back into a dead, alcohol-drenched sleep, but was jarred by the phone at irregular intervals, sometimes Sydney, sometimes Glenda. Jewell even called. Regina clutched the phone to her chest, but couldn't answer, afraid that if she tried to talk her words would be drowned in tears and that would get her nowhere.

It was Ty's voice that got Regina moving. "*Just tryin' to hook up with you. I'm leavin' tomorrow for LA, in case you don't remember.*" She shot straight up, her heart thudding slow and hard. *I gotta get myself together.*

In the bathroom she splashed water on her face, drizzled drops in her dry eyes. When she got out her stash she was shocked by how much she'd gone through, but she had to have more. Before the jolt hit her brain, the buzz of the intercom froze her in place. *They're coming for me.* She wasn't sure who "they" were, but she wasn't ready to be found. Still wearing yesterday's clothes, she grabbed her coat and purse, dashed out the door and ducked in the stairwell where she was met by the stench of dead mice and used condoms. Regina kept the fire door open a crack, watching her apartment and in a few minutes Glenda and Sydney showed up. Regina let the door ease closed, listened to them knocking and muttering to each other. After a while they left, but then Regina didn't know what to do. Would they come back? Were they outside waiting? She stayed in the semi-dark hall so long she couldn't taste the smell anymore. Finally she scooped a couple of hits with her fingernail, got the courage to creep to the lobby. At the mailbox the wafer-thin man with a dent in his left temple said, "Two girls was lookin' for you. Couple 'a hours ago."

Regina nodded and hurried out the door, knowing she couldn't come back, not until she had an answer. She checked her watch. Seven thirty on a Thursday. That meant there should be a buzz at the bar at DeVille, but there would be no networking for her tonight. Instead she saw the M4 bus and ran for it. She rummaged in her purse and pockets for exact change, then huddled in a window seat in the last row and rocked, trying to trace a line from where she started out to this moment now, trying to figure out how she ended up here. After a while her gentle rocking turned to a jittery shake and she couldn't sit on the bus another second. *Ladies' room. I need to find a ladies' room.* She pushed the exit buzzer impatiently, stumbled down the aisle of the bouncing bus and jumped off at the next stop to find herself at 34th Street among the late-night shoppers carrying bundles and pink Conway bags. Regina felt like they all knew how much trouble she was in, but she fought the urge to run and fell in step. At least she knew where to find a bathroom so she could clear her head again.

Slipping in the side door at Macy's, Regina ducked up the old wooden escalators and into the rest room where the stalls were fenced in like cages. She pounded the last particles into her palm, traced inside the lipstick tube with her pinkie. It was enough to make her feel normal for now, but this was the last up and she couldn't see far enough ahead to figure out what came next.

Leaving the store, Regina merged into the flow of pedestrians, let herself be carried up Seventh Avenue until she reached the theaters in Times Square and decided she could hide out and think in a movie. She bought a ticket for the next thing showing. On screen, men in fedoras fired tommy guns from the windows of bulky cars, but all she could think of was Ty. He was the last person in the world she wanted to disappoint, but somehow she kept doing it. *I can't make him look like a fool on his big night.* She could see his gap-toothed grin, feel his hands, rough the way they used to be. Ty had never been her type, but he was the one, had been from the start. She'd never had the nerve to say she loved him, even after he did, but love wasn't enough to fix this. *I gotta tell him.* Just the thought catapulted her out of her seat, back into the night.

In a musty liquor store on Eighth, Regina bought a pint of vodka. Next door at the deli she got a carton of orange juice, poured it in the gutter and replaced it with booze and a straw, then descended into the nearest subway, heading nowhere in particular. She rode through the tunnels under the city in a haze, working up the nerve to go see Ty, then chickening out, changing trains. By four in the morning her mind was putty, she still had no solution, both her stash and her pint were gone and she needed to take her head either up or down, at this point it didn't matter which, because she was ready to peel out of her skin.

At West Fourth Street, she ended her train ride to nowhere, headed aboveground in search of an after-hours club she'd been to a few times—never with Ty. Regina hadn't ever bought drugs from anyone except Reuben but she knew that in the grimy tan brick building the music played straight through to noon, and she knew she could find a quick fix, no questions, no hassles. By the time she came upon the old garage she was running on fumes, but the guy on the door said she needed a membership card. Before she had the chance to argue, three men in tight jeans and cropped jackets came up behind her. The one with black eyeliner and a pencil-thin mustache wrapped an arm around her. "Girlfriend's with us."

The heat hit Regina as soon as she walked through the door. "Love Is the Message," pounded from the speakers, taunting her because the message she had to deliver wasn't about love anymore. Before she could decline, her "host" pulled her to the dance floor where she was sucked into the swell of music and bodies writhing, touching, living for the moment, but her own sweat felt like bugs crawling over her skin and Regina couldn't keep moving for long. She meant to say "excuse me" to her partner, but she just walked away in a daze, had to find air, a place to cool down. She made her way upstairs to the bar, discovered they served only fruit juice and she knew that would make her gag so she found the bathroom, slurped cold water from the faucet, splashed some on her face and neck, felt more alone than she ever had in her life.

"Not your song?" Regina's dance partner appeared in the doorway.

"Know where I can buy some coke?" She was past being startled, beyond pleasantries and coy conversation.

"Guess you don't mean in a can." His hips twitched to the beat of the music.

All Regina could do was shake her head no.

"I got somethin' that'll make you feel righteous." He reached in his jacket, pulled out a Wonder Woman PEZ dispenser and flipped her neck. "One of these and you'll be in heaven." He held a little white pill in his palm.

Regina had never taken pills beside aspirin and vitamins, but at this moment it didn't matter. She took the pill in her fingers, tossed it to the back of her throat and swallowed with her own spit chased with tap water. "Come on, let's dance." She led the way back to the pulsating throng, eager to dive in and lose herself, to be free of the noose tightening at her neck.

"*Ain't no stoppin' us now. We're on the move*." The DJ dug out a disco oldie that took Regina back to her yesterdays. She balled up her coat, dropped it on the floor at her feet and danced, her partner egging her on, but he didn't matter. Alone in her own space, she remembered how happy she used to be when she and Ty had nothing to lose and worlds to conquer. The blood in her veins slowed and flowed like warm syrup from the center of her body out to her fingers and toes. Regina closed her eyes, let the colors and the sound swim in her head, free her mind. Hot hands caressed her body, she didn't know whose. It didn't matter. She finally felt happy.

I'm freezing. Regina forced herself into semiconsciousness, shivering, head pounding. Eyes still closed she reached for covers, but felt only slick mattress fabric against her naked skin. *Where are my clothes?* The pulse of music was still a faded echo in her ears, but the room was quiet. There was nothing in her memory beyond the dancing and the music—*and the guy in the bathroom with the little white pill*. A sliver of fear wedged in her throat. *Where the hell am I?* Scared to open her eyes, she patted beside her, found a tangle of sheets and clutched them to her. Then the pain began to blossom, the ache in her jaw, her legs, her ribs, the tenderness beneath her eye, the searing throb between her legs and behind her, up inside. Trapped in a nauseating spin, like circling the drain and trying not to vanish down the void again, she needed to lock onto something, to see what was really there.

Regina opened her eyes a slit, then wider. It was dark, but she didn't know if that meant it was the same night or the next one. The dresser, the heap of clothes—*My room?* Her heart galloped. *How did I get here?* Regina slid her fingers over her thigh, along her cheek, felt the sticky, crusty residue. *What did I do?* Except she already knew the sickening answer, but she didn't know with whom. Or when. Or what day it was now. *Is somebody still here?* She blinked to clear her thoughts and her vision, strained to hear, to remember. Regina lay still a long time, holding her breath, wanting to scream, wanting to drown, to run away, to turn back time—a day, a week, a month, a year. Anything but now. And then her teeth started chattering, not from cold, but from overwhelming horror and shame, from all she drank, snorted, swallowed and from the fear of being lost in a maze of her own creation, not knowing where to turn to get out.

She stayed that way a long time, until she felt as though she would never get up if she didn't do it now, so she eased herself to the edge of the bed, avoiding the dried blood, wrapped herself in the top sheet, steadied herself in the darkness with a hand on the wall. In the front room, brightened by pale light from a hazy moon, she dropped to her knees by the phone, but stopped, not knowing who to call. She wouldn't call Ty, couldn't bear for him to see her like this. She couldn't go through this with her parents either, but she couldn't be alone. With nowhere else to turn, Regina hit speed dial, gripped the receiver with both hands, praying for an answer.

"Carmen—" Regina's voice trembled. "I need you—you have to—please come help me."

"I'm on my way." Carmen didn't hesitate.

It was 2:37 Saturday morning, but she was wide awake when she got the call. Nobody else who knew Regina was asleep either. They'd all been worried since Sydney called Lonnie and Al on Friday to say Regina hadn't been heard from in two days. Carmen left the hospital early and Malcolm drove her into the city but there was no sign of Regina in 5D. Then Carmen called Ty, sure Regina was safe with him, but found out he was in LA. She even went by DeVille, but Reuben was no help. "She seemed a little rattled when I saw her Wednesday. Business problems, man problems, I'm not sure. I don't ask." And that had been that, until now.

"Please don't bring my folks or anybody, okay?"

Carmen had never heard Regina sound that way. She wouldn't say what happened, but Carmen knew it must be bad or Regina would never admit she couldn't handle it, certainly not to her, so she alerted everyone that Regina had surfaced, but she drove to the city alone.

Frightened when she found Regina's silver 5D key ring still dangling in the lock, Carmen crept inside, wary of what might be waiting. "Regina!"

"In here."

The voice was puny, stripped of the wisecracking brashness. She found Regina sitting on the chaise, in the dark, still wrapped in her sheet. Regina looked hollow, like the life had been drained out of her, and as she got closer Carmen could see her left eye was bruised, her lips and jaw swollen, but she didn't react, didn't want to upset Regina more than she already was.

Regina dissolved the moment they saw each other. "I messed up bad, Carmen."

The words came through blubbering sobs, and although the position was unfamiliar, Carmen held her, comforted her, remembered what it was like when Regina and Jewell picked up her pieces, or at least gathered them until she could pick them up herself. They stayed that way through the fits and starts of Regina's story, as much of it as she remembered.

When Regina had calmed down enough, Carmen examined her face and neck for serious injury. "Are you hurt anywhere else?"

Regina looked down at her body and her shoulders started to heave. "I don't know. It hurts. There's—there's blood on my bed."

As a friend, Carmen listened, keeping her judgments in check, steadying the distress that came up for her at the thought of being violated. Regina didn't need to hear about Randy now. Maybe she would later. As a doctor she put together as many facts as she could find and came up with a course of action. "We need to get you to a hospital, get you checked out. They'll collect evidence so maybe the police—"

"I don't want any police." Regina pulled away.

"They're really understanding. They're trained to help you with—"

"I don't know what happened, Carmen. I was drunk. I was high. I don't know what I did. Somebody could have followed me, but I could have brought them here if they promised to give me more drugs." Regina's agitation grew. "I can't identify anybody. I don't know anything and I don't want to know—"

"Okay. Okay." Carmen could see this was only making her more upset. "Let's get you dressed and we'll go."

"Can't you examine me?" Regina asked, horrified at repeating all this to a stranger.

"It's not a good idea Reg, but I'll take you to my hospital. I know the doctor on duty, and I'll stay as long as you need me." Carmen held Regina's hand. "I promise."

AIDS? Pregnancy? What have I done? The doctor had gone, but Regina still sat on the edge of the examining table in a pale blue hospital gown, bare legs dangling, trying to grasp the enormity of what she'd been told. The appalling reality was a cold, sobering slap. The doctor had collected semen samples for a rape kit and Regina promised to report it to the police back in New York. But she didn't know if she'd been raped, or if she'd said or done something to suggest she wanted to be treated like that. Carmen assured her that if she didn't say yes, it was rape, but that was more than Regina could process right now. In seven to ten days she would find out if she was pregnant—but not by who. She'd been tested for the garden variety sexually transmitted diseases, but it was three months before she could take her first AIDS test, to find out if she could look forward to dying like Milton. That was just the clinical reality, but there was no procedure to eradicate the effects of the coke, the vodka, the pill or restore the memories she'd lost, no prescription to cure what she had done to Ty.

"Let's get you out of here." Carmen opened the door, got her dressed, took her home.

Back at Carmen's, Regina curled up on the sofa, drinking coffee like a fiend, trying to tolerate the vibration in her hands and fight the urge to find the things she knew would make it stop. She worked to find the courage to call Ty, but she couldn't muster it.

"Ty needs to know what's happening, and not happening. He deserves that," Carmen said.

Regina knew he deserved much more than that, but she couldn't give it to him today, so she sat in the kitchen with water running while Carmen went in the living room and made that call. As soon as Carmen opened the door Regina asked, "What did he say?" She expected him to be furious. She'd earned that.

"He wanted to make sure you were safe. Asked if you needed anything."

And that broke Regina's heart.

Jewell had flown home early and arrived by Saturday night, in time to reassure Regina that her parents wouldn't disown her.

"They love you Regina, no matter what you think," Carmen said.

"They might not understand, but that won't stop them from doing whatever they can to help you," Jewell added.

On Sunday Regina was glad to have Carmen and Jewell by her side when she went to face her parents. Black eye, swollen lip and all she admitted she needed help, their help, which meant she had to admit it to herself. The pieces of her heart that were left were pulverized when her mother hugged her, too upset to speak, and her father said, "You'll have whatever you need."

And on Tuesday, before the Grammys aired, Carmen and Jewell drove Regina to the Carson Institute, a rehab facility in Pennsylvania, to begin the journey she would have to take alone.

24
"Love feels a whole lot better."

"Your parents are the sweetest people." Carmen hung her coat in the hall closet and headed for the living room. Last year Malcolm had invited her to Atlanta for Thanksgiving with his folks. She declined—she didn't have the holiday off and for once that came in handy since she wasn't ready for a parental encounter. This time he had sprung them on her last minute, told her they were coming up for a visit and made dinner reservations with her schedule in mind, so she didn't have much time to be nervous. As soon as she met Marian and William Wyatt she realized there was no need for jitters; they were as wonderful as Malcolm made them sound.

Malcolm's dad was a gifted storyteller and after a career filled with talking to some of everybody from plumbers to bank presidents as a conductor on the train from New York to Trenton, he had them howling with tales Carmen was sure Malcolm and his mom had heard a thousand times. It was easy to see what Malcolm meant when he told her about his parents' relationship. From a gentle touch, or an intimate glance, the love they shared was obvious.

"They remind me of Regina's folks. You know, even when we were in school I used to want to shake her. She gave them such a hard time, but she's lucky to have them, especially now."

"Sometimes you can't see what's staring you right in the eye 'cause it's too close to your face." Malcolm zoomed in, eye-to-eye, gave Carmen a kiss. "Now, I recognize I'm lucky to have you. And since you say I look just like my dad, consider tonight a preview of me for the next century. All in all he's a good-looking old dude so my prospects are good."

Lucky to have me? When he said things like that it made Carmen nervous, like it was a jinx.

She liked the way Malcolm included her in the time he spent with his friends and family, and when they were tramping through the woods, or eating pizza, or having dinner tonight and she was relaxed and laughing, she felt like one of the people in those commercials she used to think were so fake. The ones full of smiling, happy people, but they were over in thirty seconds. "Well, thanks for the scenes from coming attractions." A change of direction seemed in order. "And dinner was great too. My paella was delicious. I haven't had any since Jewell tried to make it once in college. It didn't taste like that though."

"You think that's good, wait till I make you some." Malcolm came up behind Carmen, massaged her shoulders. "These are like rocks. I can take care of that for you."

Carmen patted his hand, slipped out of his grip. "You have so many talents. Teacher, chef, massage therapist—"

"You haven't even begun to scratch the surface." He sat on the sofa arm, pulled her into a kiss, light at first, then slower, deeper. "I'd be happy to, ah, demonstrate some of my other skills, but I need an assistant."

"So you're a magician too? Is this the part where you saw me in half?" Carmen backed up, flipped on the light, needed to get away before this went any further. "I'm gonna make some tea. Do you want—"

"Why do you always do that?" Malcolm threw up his hands, walked across the room. "Do I have BO? Am I not your type—"

"It's not that. It's not you." Carmen had been dancing around what Malcolm meant to her for months. She resisted giving it a name, afraid that if she called it something, it could be called away, but when it was time to look for a post-residency position, it became clear that Malcolm was someone she didn't want to do without. To her surprise, most of the jobs she applied for resulted in offers from all over the country: hospitals, clinics, private practices. As she weighed the pros and cons of locations, benefits and her future, she realized she didn't want to leave where she was. The more time they spent together, the more she wanted him around. "I've been sort of freaked out, about what happened to Regina, you know?" Carmen sat on the couch. "Malcolm, she looked so awful, beat up and bruised, there was blood on the sheets, I can't imagine what happened." Except she could, and Carmen hadn't been able to strike that image from her mind. In the dark, when there were no patients or charts to distract her, it would sneak up and lead her directly back to that elevator on Montgomery Street and Randy.

Malcolm sighed, sat down next to her. "Regina's doing okay, isn't she?"

"I haven't heard anything definite. Nobody can visit for the first two weeks. I can't imagine how she's liking the isolation."

"It's not about liking it. That's not what rehab is for. In fact, she's supposed to hate it so much she won't ever want to go through it again." Malcolm rested his elbows on his knees, looked at his hands. "Look, I know you're upset for your friend. Drug problem aside, nobody deserves what happened to her, but that's not the only thing that's going on between you and me." He looked over at Carmen. "I don't push. You're busy, you're tired. Okay I'm a reasonable man. I can handle that. And I'm not saying being physical is my top priority. If that was the case I'd have skipped out a while back, but I don't understand what's going on here."

Carmen leaned against the sofa back, stared at the ceiling. It had to come up sooner or later. Until Malcolm, sex in general and Randy Dale in particular had been relegated to a footnote in her life story, but now it had all been moved up to the top of the page. She knew that hanging on to what had gone wrong in her life wasn't worth risking what was so right. She just hadn't figured out what to say to him, how he would look at her afterward, how she would feel. A tear slid down her face, dribbled onto her neck. "When I was a kid there was this guy who hung around with Z. This guy named Randy..." She couldn't look at Malcolm while she spoke or she would never have been able to finish. "After that I didn't let a guy anywhere near me, so Milton was my one and only experiment in dating, if you can call it that. When it didn't work, I washed my hands. I obviously didn't understand how all that stuff worked, I wasn't good at it and there was never going to be another man I trusted that much again, so I removed it from my plan. Then you showed up."

Carmen realized she trusted Malcolm months ago when the standard family fiction she had told him felt more and more like a lie. So one afternoon while he was teaching her how to play chess, she had given him the unabridged version of the Webb family legacy, complete with her father's murder, her mother's mental illness and disappearance, her brother's brutal hostility and abandonment, Jewell and Regina's rescue. If her twisted lineage was going to freak him out, it was better for her to know up front so she could cut her losses, but he never wavered. "To come out of that with your head screwed on straight makes you even more special than I already knew you were," he had said. Now she had revealed the last secret in her closet, and she was afraid to turn and look at him because she didn't know what she would do if he didn't understand. Then she felt his fingers on her face, wiping at the tears that continued to fall. She rolled her cheek into the palm of his hand.

"I can't imagine what you've been through, or how that makes you feel. I'm sorry sounds lame, but I don't know how else to put it," he said quietly. "I won't tell you I'm not interested in you that way, but what I feel for you is not about some jacked-up power trip. What I want to share is from my heart, but you be my guide. Right now a hug just means I want to hold you, and a kiss won't lead anyplace you don't want to go."

Carmen leaned into his arms, her head on his chest, comforted by the steady beat of his heart. They stayed that way a long time, until he said good night. After he left she made tea, feeling like she'd been trapped in a cave for most of her life and now somebody had rolled back the rock. *Thank you Milton*. She wished he was still in his hammock, enjoying the sunset, but he had given her a precious gift. He told her to go get a life, and she was beginning to feel she finally had.

The next morning Carmen called Malcolm early. She could tell by his voice he wasn't awake yet, wondered what he looked like while he was sleeping. "I recognize it too," she said.

"What?" Malcolm asked, his voice still foggy from sleep.

"How lucky I am."

A week later, Carmen went to see Regina, unsure of what to expect. When Regina appeared at reception to meet her, Carmen was pleasantly surprised by how different she looked. Not just from that night, but different than she had in a long time. There was still a hint of greenish, purplish bruise on her jaw, but her face was free of makeup and some of the fullness was back in her cheeks. Her hair was brushed back into a ponytail and enough of the latest red had grown out to reveal the natural soft brown for the first time since sophomore year. In jeans and a sweater she no longer looked like a caricature. She looked like herself, and talked fast as ever.

"I assume you've been searched and are free of mouthwash, hair spray and all other contraband." Regina took a swig from her paper cup. "Let's go to the cafeteria. It has all the comforts of public school, but the coffee's hot."

Carmen wasn't quite sure what to say. "How are you?" suddenly seemed like a loaded question. "You look good."

"A helluva lot better than our last get-together." Regina refilled her cup, avoided Carmen's eyes. They sat at benches on opposite sides of a lunch table. "This is a nice change of pace from scrubbing pots. That's my chore this week, which is a promotion. Last week I had to mop the hallways. Do you have any idea how many this freakin' place has?"

Regina always talked fast, but today it seemed nervous, embarrassed. "My mother is coming at the end of the week." She took a sip, looked off toward the woods outside the window. "Scrubbing toilets was easier. I don't know what to say to her."

"Your dad's not coming?"

"He's coming later. Barry, my very own counselor, has decided I have issues with my mother." Regina rolled her eyes. "I know you think she's perfect but—"

"Nobody's perfect, Regina."

On the drive home from Carson, Carmen thought a lot about Regina and her mother. They still didn't know how to talk to each other, but at least they could still try. As a practicing physician, Carmen understood that when Geraldine walked out, she couldn't have helped herself. And since Carmen had safely passed through her early twenties, the period by which the symptoms usually showed up, she had begun to believe she had been spared her mother's illness. But she still wondered if Geraldine ever found help, found someone to save her from herself and that still nagged Carmen.

After hemming and hawing and trying to figure out what to say, Carmen asked one of the social workers at Mid-Jersey to make some inquiries for her, but New York Department of Social Services didn't have any information on a Geraldine Webb or Geraldine Martin, her maiden name—no shelter assignments, no hospitalizations—mental or otherwise. Carmen decided it was time to do her own research so she started at the beginning.

"No birth certificate unless the party's dead, even if it's your mother." An officious clerk at the Health Department said, and just like that, pointed Carmen down the hall toward the death records, like he was showing her to the corn flakes on special in aisle three. She followed the clerk's directions to the records room, a suitably dismal, institutional gray box with long wooden tables. She found the section she needed and began plowing through a stack of ledgers, starting with 1974, the year Geraldine disappeared. Carmen scanned the random assortment of names, organized by date, occasionally remarking a very long life, or a very short one, until she hit 1987. And there, waiting on the page, was Zachariah Webb Jr.—March 18. It was a gunshot wound that caught up with him. Carmen slammed the book closed, like that would change what she'd seen. Z. She opened it again to the same page, snuck up on the entry. It wasn't a common name. The birthdate matched. *Of course it's him. Probably messed with the wrong person.* It just never occurred to her she might find her brother's name in the book of the dead.

Carmen waited for some emotion to surface. The only one she'd felt for years was hate, and now she sat under the buzzing overhead fluorescents, realizing she'd spent all that time and energy hating someone who was already gone. She copied the pertinent facts in case she needed them one day, then returned to her search for Geraldine, but after she turned the last page of the last book she had found nothing more. She left with the same questions that brought her there.

"His address on the death certificate was right down the block from our old address." Carmen moved the salt shaker in wide circles on the kitchen table. "If I'd stayed in the neighborhood I'd have run into him—at the post office or the subway."

"Haven't you ever been back?" Malcolm had five classes' worth of midterms to grade, but he'd come over as soon as he got her message.

"For what? To revisit the scene of the crime? I barely got out the first time."

"Maybe your mother is around there too," Malcolm said.

"She's just as likely to be on the moon."

"I can't drive you to the moon, but my car goes to Brooklyn."

At first Carmen dismissed the idea as a waste of time and gasoline, but after years of avoiding her father and her past, even Jewell had found some answers there.

"That's where they found my dad, dead in his cab." Carmen showed Malcolm the spot as they drove past Lincoln Terrace, but she felt disconnected, like it was a stop on somebody else's personal history tour. She pointed out a parking space by the old car dealership that was now a funeral parlor. "We're a couple of blocks from my building, but we might not find one closer."

"That's a space?" He backed into the small slot between a battered van and a Seville with blacked-out windows.

Carmen had been tempted to stop on Eastern Parkway, see if her old boss was still overseeing the special sauce, but she decided to pass. White Castle was still at East New York, the fried-chicken place across the street had changed names, but the air still smelled like greasy batter and salty French fries. In the twelve years since she'd last walked up the steep hill of Utica with her shopping cart and her fears, the stores along the avenue had changed awnings, but the street was still clogged with double-parked cars and on a Saturday afternoon folks hurried about their business or somebody else's. Malcolm draped an arm across her shoulder as she led the way. For as much as the neighborhood looked familiar, walking through it didn't bring the dread she expected, but she was also sure that visiting the old neighborhood would not become a regular activity.

When they got to the corner of her block, Carmen was disappointed to see that steel gates shuttered the windows of the old dry cleaners. Only a faded ONE HOUR MARTINIZINGsign identified what it had once been. "Mr. Willis used to sweep in front every morning and every night." The sidewalk was now littered with debris, blown by gusts of March wind. "When he heard I was going to college he gave me twenty-five dollars, right out of the register, said it was for my first textbook. Until then, I didn't know I had to buy them." She had hoped to see him, show him his investment had paid off, ask him if maybe he had seen Geraldine anywhere.

Carmen's old building looked much the same as she remembered with weathered red brick and turrets at the corners that made her think it was a castle when she was young enough for fairy tales. The glass front door had been replaced with a gray metal one with a foot-square glass window embedded with wire mesh. The buzzer system had been replaced since she lived there although the apartment numbers had no names next to them, not that she expected to know anybody. A new crop of men probably played dominos and drank beer out front in the summer. When two guys in North Face parkas came out, Malcolm grabbed the door. "Want to go in?"

Want to was not exactly how Carmen felt about it, but she'd come this far.

Carmen's skin tingled as she got into the elevator and she squeezed Malcolm's hand tight. She could feel what happened there, but it wasn't happening now. She was safe and she wasn't alone. When they got off on her floor, the apartment doors looked like they'd had a fresh coat of paint. It was the same green as she remembered, and as she stared at the one that had been hers, the anger that always bubbled up when she recalled her past seemed to leak away, replaced by a budding thankfulness that for all that had happened, she had been strong enough to survive.

"You okay?" Malcolm asked.

"Yeah. Let's go."

While waiting for a light to change, Carmen told Malcolm about the adventure of walking all the way to the Carvel with her dad on a summer night and trying to make her cone last all the way back home. "It's probably only half a mile from here but I used to think—"

"Yo, Li'l Bit. Is that you?"

Carmen recognized the voice immediately and anger shot up and out of her mouth, bypassing any fear. "Don't you dare call me that." Hands balled into fists, she turned to face him and there she stood, eye to eye with Randy in his motorized wheelchair. She would have passed right by him if he hadn't called out. Frowsy cornrows had replaced the Jheri Curl, and where he had been big and round before, even in his quilted Bulls jacket he was narrow with a face that looked older than she knew he was. Carmen could feel Malcolm's body tense beside her.

"No harm. Just ain't seen you in a oooh-wee long time. What are you, like some big-time doctor or somethin' now? You was always smart. As you can see I'm not doin' too good. Got shot a few years back—dude mistaked me for somebody else."

Carmen could not believe he was rattling on like they were old buddies catching up on the glory days. “What happened to Z?” She figured he’d at least know that.

“Man, he tried to take off this liquor store, up on St. John’s.” Randy shook his head at the sad memory. “Dude blew him away.”

Carmen had a feeling Randy was closer to that event than hearsay, but she’d found out all she needed to know from him and now she had a few things to say. “What you did to me in that elevator was disgusting, Randy.”

He wiped at his half smirk with his hand. “Aw wait now, see—”

“Shut up and listen to her,” Malcolm barked.

Carmen had never heard that tone of voice from him or seen that hard expression. “Guess you thought it was big fun then too, call yourself teaching me some kind of lesson. But you were weak and pathetic, and you didn’t bring me down, Randy. You didn’t win.” Carmen looked at him squarely, with unblinking eyes until he looked away, then she marched blindly across the street.

Carmen didn’t say a word once they got in the car. She had said so many already, ones she never expected to get the chance to voice. Her hands stayed balled in her lap until they crossed the Brooklyn Bridge, then she began to let them uncurl, to release the tension in her shoulders, to take off the armor, to feel some peace.

“Want me to stay or would you rather be alone?” Malcolm asked when he got her home.

“Stay. Please.” Carmen didn’t hesitate.

“How about a fire?”

“Sounds nice.” Carmen usually protested that it was too much trouble, but tonight she wanted to watch the flickering golden flames, let them soothe her. She nestled on the end of the sofa and watched him work. In a short while Malcolm had built a respectable fire, not from the instant logs she kept handy and unused. He went out to the deck for the cherry wood he had stacked at the beginning of winter and the former Boy Scout built a real blaze from kindling up, one that looked like it might burn for the next three days. He brushed his hands on his jeans, joined her on the couch. “Pretty good huh?” He draped an arm around her shoulders. “You want the afghan? Some tea?”

Carmen rubbed her hands together, held them toward the heat. “No. This is great.” She thought about relaxing into the curve of his arm, and as if he sensed her ambivalence, Malcolm pulled her close, her back against his chest. He idly rubbed her arm while they watched the fire and after a few minutes she let a deep sigh escape.

Malcolm kissed the top of her head. "You're beautiful by firelight."

"Excuse me?" She looked up at him.

"If you don't know that I've been falling down on the job."

"Yeah, right."

"Okay. I have obviously been derelict in my duties, so here's something else you need to know." He continued to stroke her arm. "You know I love you, right?"

He said it matter-of-factly like, "the sun is shining," or "today is Saturday." Simple, but stunning. Words Carmen hadn't heard in a very long time. She knew he meant it. She'd just been afraid that it was asking too much to have a life so full and this kind of happiness too. She leaned her head against his chest to collect herself before she looked up at him. "I love you too." And she was sure she did, today more than ever before.

They lounged by the fire with no agenda or timetable, and when Carmen awakened, still in the shelter of Malcolm's arms, only smoldering embers remained. He had pulled the afghan over, tucked it around her. She lay still, letting the feel good seep in, wanting to snuggle closer, but she didn't want to wake him yet. She glanced around the room, letting her eyes settle on the photo Milton had taken of her with Regina and Jewell. All three of them were smiling, but now Carmen noticed the emptiness behind her eyes. *Why didn't I see that before?* All the other photos of herself showed the same sad void.

Malcolm stirred. Carmen held her breath. He adjusted his hold on her, slipped back into sleep. She continued to think about the girl in the pictures, what she had been through, how hard she'd worked to hold herself together, how much of herself she'd shut down to do it, and for the first time she was able to feel compassion for herself, feel that happiness wasn't too much to ask.

Slowly, Carmen turned around until she was facing Malcolm. He looked so content. She smoothed the stray lock that flopped across his brow, even in sleep and his eyes fluttered open.

"I love you," Carmen smiled.

"That's better than good morning." He lowered his head toward her, and she lifted hers to meet his kiss. They shared tender, early morning nuzzles at first, Malcolm staying within the lines. But then Carmen wrapped her arms around his neck, embraced his body with hers and opened up to accept his love and trust.

Malcolm pulled back, let his gaze ask the question. Carmen knew this was the moment, this was the man she wanted to share it with, and she answered.

He held her face in his hands. This was important and Malcolm wanted all the choices to be hers. "Do you want to go upstairs?" This was a first for him too. He'd been around some, had girlfriends before, but he'd never been given this key.

"No. Let's stay here." Carmen willingly suspended her clinical knowledge of bodies and let Malcolm guide her. This first time she expected some pain—that's what she'd heard, read, learned, explained to patients, but it was overshadowed by the fulfillment of their union. He held her, kissed her, touched her, not shaming, but embracing her and she buried her face in his hair, his neck, his scent. It felt like home. Malcolm had given her a keepsake, a forever memory to replace the old one and Carmen felt different, special. She wanted to walk around, show it off, but instead she lay there, happily wrapped in cozy comfort.

25
"...jumping off a building feels like flying till you hit bottom."

There's more oatmeal stuck to this freakin' pot than they slopped in all the stupid bowls. Regina was the last one left in the kitchen. She'd dragged her feet getting to KP, her assigned chore for this week at the "detox depot," as Carson was called by "guests" who realized it was their last stop on a fast train with no brakes and a short track. *But it beats cleaning toilets*. She shook off the memory of week one's choice assignment. At least this didn't smell funky and it distracted her from her 10 A.M. session. *Keep scrubbing*.

She'd been dreading this particular first day of the rest of her life since Barry, former crack head and her counselor, scheduled the one-on-one. Regina stretched to reach the bottom of the huge vat, counted the strokes she made with her wadded-up scouring pad. Nineteen was the same as the number of days since she'd arrived. That left nine more until she got out. *Seventy-one till judgment day, part one*. That's how she'd come to think of the HIV test which was her first waking thought in the morning, the last thing on her mind when she finally fell asleep at night, and occupied every other minute in what felt like endless days lived in a black-and-white horror flick where all the monsters were you. *At least I'm not knocked up*. That was the best news she'd gotten in three weeks, but she was quietly terrified that her luck would run out.

Regina wiped a splatter of pink soap foam off her chin with the sleeve of her UMDNJ sweatshirt, one of the hand-me-downs she'd inherited from Carmen's closet since Regina's wardrobe had been left behind in 5D. The day after the rescue the two of them had packed a Kmart cart full of Wranglers, anklets, three-packs of pastel cotton panties and other essentials. For once in her life, Regina didn't care what any of it looked like. Wearing shades and gripping the cart like it was the only thing that would keep her standing, she'd followed Carmen up and down the aisles and fought the urge to find a drink, a snort, even a pill, anything to still her agitation and obliterate the wreckage she'd left in her wake, because cleaning that up seemed impossible. "It feels like you're getting me ready for summer camp,"

Regina had joked nervously, but as soon as she arrived at Carson she realized it was more like boot camp, or freshman year for screw-ups.

On admission day, after Carmen and Jewell hugged her and had to walk away, Regina was required to check her money, charge cards and pride at the door. Her bags were searched and she was relieved of aspirin, hair spray, mouthwash, any substance she might think would get her high in a pinch. Then she was ushered into an exam room for a physical, capped off with a bend-over-and-spread-'em body search. "You're kidding, right?" The doctor and nurse were nice, but it was clear this was no joke. She wanted to leave, right then. No treatment was worth giving up her self-esteem. Then she caught sight of her black eye in a mirror and knew she'd surrendered that a while back. Besides, where was she going? She'd pretty much used up her free passes. They turned their backs politely while Regina stripped off her paper gown. And there she stood, bare brown feet on cold tile floor with none of the things she had achieved or bought, none of her triumphs or big deals to shield her from the latex-gloved indignity of fingers probing her ears, mouth, everywhere she might hide a last-exit-before-toll drug hit, like any other junkie, but Regina was clean. Her final high hurrah scared her, but she wished she hadn't gone so far that now she had to give up the highs to avoid the lows in order to do what? Live in the beige and boring middle?

After she got dressed, Regina was issued a Carson rule book that was stricter than her parents' regulations had ever been. In rehab Regina had to get up pre-dawn and from 6:30 in the morning until 9:30 at night her day was structured. There were no TVs, phones, books or magazines because she wasn't there for entertainment. It was just her and her addictions, 'round the clock. She had assigned duties, an assigned roommate—a fragile soul with empty eyes who was addicted to Percocet and reminded Regina of Melanye, her morose freshman roommate, the catalyst for Regina's party machine. The one who never made it back sophomore year. The good thing was she didn't talk much. Some of the people at Regina's assigned cafeteria table yapped endlessly about their inner demons and their codependent relationships. One afternoon she got so disgusted she picked up her tray after two bites of an eggplant Parmesan hero. "What the hell did you people talk about before you found out you were addicts?" She dumped the tray and walked out, convinced she wasn't that pitiful.

There were no locks on her door, not even the bathroom. She had to fold her clothes, make her bed, lights out by ten, and there were inspections with extra tasks and restricted privileges handed out for infractions and Regina hated every minute of it. "You have to manage the details before you can manage your life." The zealously recovered Barry said it enough to make her gag, but truth was some days the details were all the challenge she could handle.

"Ow!" Regina jumped back from the pot, the index fingernail she'd snapped in half still attached at the corner. The sharp pain made her eyes brim with tears, but she'd spent a lot of the last three weeks crying. She went through wads of tissues and countless cups of coffee during the daily marathon group-counseling sessions intended to force the addict—a new and disturbing definition of herself—to take responsibility for the choices they'd made. She thought the strip search was bad but at least she could get dressed and be done with it. Here they prodded, poked, and probed every day until she was raw, then came the salt. No topic was off limits and Regina was routinely stunned by the litany of perils recounted by others in the support circle—violent partners, sadistic pimps, parental abandonment, sexual-predator siblings—all temporarily numbed with self-prescribed potions. Some days she wished she was high so at least it would be funny. Most of the time Regina felt like she was crashing the party, but this show-and-tell had mandatory participation. So she talked about her family, the high life in New York, everything but that last night and what she had done to Ty. That was none of their business. But if she got too quiet, somebody would go digging in her dirt. Edward, the photographer who'd put his chemistry know-how to use operating a crystal-meth lab, generously sampling the product, had dubbed her the "scratch-and-sniff party doll." "I've seen a ton of girls like you, so lovely, so misunderstood." Regina hated the nickname and the condescending tone, as though her problems were meringue on a sunny lemon pie. She had eyed his bald head, pierced eyebrow and mutton chops. "Like you'd have any clue what it's like to be the only one who's not perfect in your whole freakin' family!" Edward had laughed at her. "Party doll, nobody's perfect."

Regina bit off the hanging tip of her nail, spat it into the trash and rinsed the last pot. She punched through the swinging doors, spied the clock above the dayroom entrance. *Nine fifty-four. Six minutes to showdown.* She wanted to keep walking—outside, into the woods, off the edge of the planet. Last week Carmen had been her first visitor and Regina was overjoyed to see somebody from her real life. The one she hoped to go back to in 216 hours, certainly not to pick up where she left off, but to try again. *If I live long enough for it to matter.*

After she and Carmen had settled in the cafeteria and got through the nervous, nice-nice talk, Regina asked, "Do you know what happened with the party for Big Bang?" From the moment she could put two thoughts together that didn't concern herself, she wanted to know how things worked out—or didn't. Carmen told her Sydney averted a Grammy night fiasco by arranging to hold the party in the gym of Misha's old high school. After she won the award the unconventional celebration, complete with cheering students, 'round-the-way fans and soda and juice for all, got big media play, including a clip of Ty, raising his glass of root beer and orange juice to toast the singer. "Ty's been calling—to see how you're doing." The fact that he was concerned about her welfare added another heaping shovelful of guilt to the freight Regina already carried, and there was another shipment of emotional cargo heading her way.

Regina got a fresh cup of coffee, checked her reflection on the urn and headed for the psycho suite, another Carson euphemism. During counseling, Regina's hostility toward Lonnie had come up. That's why Barry had scheduled a mother-daughter session. Barry was at his desk, wearing one of what seemed to be a lifetime supply of plaid short-sleeved shirts which revealed furry forearms. A coordinated knit tie was knotted at his neck. "Right on time. Have a sit down."

Lonnie was already seated in one of the two chairs opposite the desk, hands folded in the lap of her blue suit. They hadn't seen each other since Regina's rampage and she could feel her mother looking her over. "So, am I up to par?" She slid into the other chair.

"Must you always be sarcastic with me?" Lonnie's tone was sharper than Regina expected.

Barry had them turn their chairs to face each other, so close their toes almost touched. It didn't take long to strike a nerve.

"Regina's told me some about growing up, her life at home. I'd like to hear your impressions, Lonnie—what that time was like for you."

"I've been so blessed. Al and I knew right away we were meant to be together. It was crazy in the beginning, trying to finish school, pay the rent and then the babies came along."

"Came along? What? Like the stork brought them?" Regina slumped in her chair. "Guess he visited one time too many."

"What on earth are you talking about, Regina?"

"I was standing in the hall outside your bedroom. I heard you say you were sorry you didn't get your tubes tied before me." All the hurt of that confused little girl wavered in Regina's voice. "You and Daddy and your boys—you were a whole freakin' perfect family until—"

"Did I *ever* treat you like I didn't want you?" Lonnie gripped the seat to steady her hands. "Parents are not machines. Sometimes we get tired, and no, we sure as heck weren't planning on another child, but you were my gift, my girl. How could you not know you were special?"

"How was I *supposed* to know?" Regina shot back. "How could I compete with my genius, Eagle freakin' Scout, Ph.D. brothers? The latest in a long line of—"

"It wasn't a competition, Regina." Lonnie sat up straighter, looked directly at her daughter. "You never had to be anyone but you. That was more than enough. And I always praised you, but you never wanted to hear it. That was "way too boring," for you. Frankly, after a while you had very little use for anything I had to say and I didn't know what I'd done to deserve that." The hurt flickered in her eyes, but she quickly steadied herself. "So I will support you in whatever you're going through here, and I will still love you, but you will not blame this on me."

After their hour was up and Barry called a truce, Lonnie's hurt expression haunted Regina as she walked the path through the dense ring of trees that corralled the grounds. "*You never had to be anyone but you.*" She'd always felt she had to *do* something to make herself unique among the fine, upstanding Fosters. *I certainly succeeded at that.* It was like making her mother the enemy had given Regina a reason to fight, something to overcome, a way to tell if she was winning. *It wasn't a competition, Regina.* She pulled her coat collar up to shield her neck against the damp cold and searched for signs of spring. During her second week in captivity, when she was finally allowed outside—at first only with her group, eventually unsupervised—Regina had begun to equate her recovery with the green fuzz of buds on the branches or purple and yellow crocuses peeking out of the dirt. That would make it easier to feel hopeful.

A week and a half later, when Jewell and Carmen arrived to pick Regina up, it was still blustery March—long, hard and spiteful, a lot like the last twenty-eight days. "I really appreciate this." Regina leaned forward between the bucket seats of Jewell's car.

"That's what friends do." Carmen adjusted her seat belt so she could turn and talk to Regina. "Isn't that what you and Jewell told me a hundred years ago?"

"I guess." But she also remembered being annoyed at Jewell for inviting Carmen to intrude on their friendship. "I've been a pretty crappy friend."

"You've got plenty of time to make up for it." Jewell switched the wipers to a faster speed as the rain picked up.

"Let's hope so." By the end of her rehab stay, Regina knew it would take more than a crash course in "Why I Screwed Up My Life" to voice all her questions or understand the answers, but she'd learned that a drink or a snort only made matters murkier. She looked out the window, grateful her friends had saved her from this four-hour car trip with her parents—their disappointment and confusion, and her shame additional passengers along for the ride.

"Next month I'm going to Vegas to do a benefit and to see my father." Jewell glimpsed Regina in the rearview mirror. "It wouldn't have happened if you hadn't meddled, so thank you."

"Glad I didn't screw that up too," Regina bowed her head. "So Five D's finally history huh?" She felt embarrassed that Jewell and Carmen had settled her back rent and moved her out. This was her mess, but her friends were giving her so much help cleaning it up.

"Your stuff is at Carmen's. The rest we left for my nightmare almost-father-in-law King and his minions to clean out."

"A small price for Nine twenty-four Parkview Real Estate Management to pay since they were glad for the empty apartment," Carmen said. "In a couple of years it'll be a luxury co-op, like the one our Jewell is buying on Central Park West."

"But the chaise is in storage until my place is ready so at least that will always be with us," Jewell said. "And my keys will still be on a Five D key ring."

"Speaking of which—" Carmen dug in her purse. "These are yours." She handed Regina the keys to her town house, still on their silver 5D ring.

Regina jangled them like bells. "Thanks." When Carmen asked Regina if she'd like to move in after rehab, she jumped at the offer. Her father had eagerly suggested the holding cell, but then he had looked lost during his Carson visit, like he wanted to put a bandage on her booboo and send her back out to play. Regina felt she needed some distance in order not to lose the perspective she was slowly gaining, so she was glad for another option. Going back into the world, avoiding the very things that landed her in Carson wouldn't be easy, and dealing with her parents was a hurdle, but only one of those Regina faced. *Sixty-two days until judgment day.* She hadn't told her parents the sex with a mysterious stranger episode. Aside from her doctors, only Carmen and Jewell knew that part of the nightmare. Regina couldn't burden her folks with the worry that she might have contracted AIDS on top of all the other worries she'd heaped on them, including footing the bill for her stint in Carson because she'd let her health insurance lapse. *I can't have AIDS. I can't afford to have AIDS.*

As they sped along the highway, sheets of rain streaked the glass and Regina was having a hard time fighting off gloom and doom. "*If your first HIV test is negative, you'll need a second in three months to assure you're free of the virus*." And three more months felt like an eternity.

"Anybody need to stop?" Jewell asked. "Snacks? Bathroom?"

"Nope." Regina knew that five weeks ago she would already have asked for a rest stop, maybe two. *Those days are over. They have to be.* The party, such as it was, had ended.

And by the time they got to Carmen's house, the sun was trying to show its face.

Which is more than could be said for Regina during the next few weeks. Just getting out of bed required her to fight the urge to curl in a ball and play dead. Once she'd conquered that obstacle, gotten dressed and made her bed, Regina brewed coffee, which she now drank by the bucket. Before she'd finished her first cup, she'd bump up against the colossal mess she had made of all she'd worked so hard to achieve. That's when she wanted two fingers of vodka, or a few pinkie nails of coke—anything to smooth out the rough places, give her a little of that old sparkle, when she felt like she could take on the world. Once she'd even left the condo, walked up the road toward the liquor store before she made herself turn around. She locked herself in the bathroom until she heard Carmen's car pull in the driveway.

So nibbling became a distraction. Savory, salty, spicy, sweet—didn't matter. The flavors dissolved on her tongue and allowed her to feel something besides panic for brief intervals. Slowly the pounds that had gone the great white way came back and then some. There were no other temptations in Carmen's house—no frosty champagne flutes or cute cocktails—and right now the thought of a drink or a line made Regina sick. She didn't even think she needed to attend her weekly meeting anymore, but she did anyway. The extra support couldn't hurt.

By the time Carmen got home, Regina would be watching television in the second bedroom, her room, where they had moved the futon and TV from 5D. Carmen had put white roses there to greet her, but Regina didn't miss the irony. She was the stray this time.

After a couple of weeks Regina got up the courage to tally what she owed. The number was daunting but Jewell loaned her enough to cover her IRS debt and make good on the checks she had bounced, including payroll for Sydney and Glenda. Regina promised to pay Jewell back. "If I don't make it, can you write it off as a bad investment?" She tried to joke, but most subjects led to the HIV test looming in her future. That's when she'd think of Hemp trotting beside her on campus, telling one of his corny jokes. It reminded her she never got herself together to call him because she couldn't accept that he was dying and might like to hear from an old friend. Then he was gone. She hated herself for that.

When Jewell called they discussed safe topics like Adrienne's shenanigans which Regina watched daily because it let her get lost in someone else's drama. They also teased Carmen about Malcolm, who came by often, cooked and sometimes stayed the night. At first, Regina asked if Malcolm felt awkward with her there, but Carmen assured her he was fine. Regina was glad because she truly liked Malcolm and thought they made a good couple.

And then she'd wonder about the stranger who'd been in her apartment, in her bed, in her body. Did she invite him or was she forced? Was it him, or them? Somebody from the club or the building? She still had no memory, but that didn't negate the feeling of violation, of stupidity, the sickening knowledge that she had been lucky so far. She wasn't pregnant and she wasn't dead.

Time crept slowly, weeks whittled down to days and finally the time arrived for Regina to enter round one of "does she or doesn't she?"

"Sure you don't want me to go with you?" Carmen asked.

"I'm sure." Regina waved Carmen off. She'd found a clinic in Newark, a place she didn't know anybody and hopefully neither did her parents. Her plan was to get there early and be done with it, but when she arrived the waiting room was jammed, filled with people a lot like the ones she ignored on her way in and out of 5D. With no windows and grim lighting, the room felt oppressive. Regina huddled in a chair in the corner, unnerved by those who were gaunt and gray, obviously already sick, agitated by the wait and her inability to shut off the memory of what had brought her there. Four hours later, she went into the tiny examination room, answered a few questions, the doctor drew blood, assigned her a case number, told her when to call for results. The whole thing was over in ten minutes.

Carmen found her in a limp bundle on the couch.

"I don't deserve to complain. I brought this on myself. Every bit of it." She picked at the edges of the tape that held the gauze over the spot where her blood had been drawn. "It's like I've got something disgusting oozing inside me and I want it out. They wanted us to talk about all this crap in counseling, but I didn't know those people. What was I gonna say, 'I got so high I don't know who I had sex with or what they gave me'? Right. There's a nice topic of conversation."

Carmen sat next to Regina. "Keeping it in is worse." Wind chimes tinkled on the patio.

"Worse than what?" Regina asked.

"I understand how you feel. Better than you think." Carmen thought opening up to Malcolm had been enough but this wasn't for her, it was for Regina. "Remember how scared I was when we got stuck in the elevator in Butler Library?"

"Sorta. That was a hundred years ago. What the hell does that have to do with anything?"

Carmen took a deep breath and told Regina about Randy. "I'd just turned twelve—"

"Why didn't you tell us?" Regina was horrified.

"I didn't know how, and my stuff was already so raggedy. It was like that would make me the official freak of Five D, but after I finally got it out, I realized that not only had he violated my body, he had changed who I let myself be. That's the worst scar."

Carmen's plain talk gave Regina the courage to lay herself open as well. Carmen listened as Regina talked for hours about those hellish last days and about the years that led up to them. "Before we rented Five D, Jewell said this thing about taking charge of your life. 'Flying solo' she called it. It sounded so cool. What I didn't understand is that jumping off a building feels like flying—until you hit bottom. You gotta know the difference."

To start taking charge of her life, Regina made lists of things she would do if the results were negative, *when* the results were negative. There were people like Sydney, Glenda and Jean Luc she needed to call. Ty was really at the top of that list, but she couldn't even write his name yet. She needed to come up with something to do for money because she couldn't stay with Carmen forever, and she had so many debts to pay. And she had to figure out how to approach her parents, especially her mother.

She knew Carmen gave her parents progress reports. Regina had even worked up the nerve to go by the house one evening because she promised her dad she'd try his latest creation—a white chocolate cheesecake with a raspberry swirl. She walked in on her mother in the family room first. Lonnie got up from the couch, let her hand rest briefly on Regina's shoulder. "I'll get your father," she said and disappeared. Regina wanted call after her, say she was sorry, but she couldn't make the words come out and then Lonnie was gone.

Regina sat on the sofa, picked up the photo album her mother had been browsing. Regina was surprised to find it filled with pictures of her—baby pictures in pink blankets and bonnets, birthday parties, pony rides and party dresses, photos she hadn't thought about in years. There was one of her standing in the beautician's chair, proudly displaying the shiny curls of her first beauty-shop hairdo, next to one of her and her troop mates, hands raised, solemnly taking the Girl Scout oath. Regina turned another page and there she was at ten, proudly hovering over her fifth-grade sugar-cube-igloo diorama—the one she'd accused her mother of forgetting. She wanted to crawl behind the sofa and bawl. Instead she'd rushed through her dad's cake, and left before Lonnie reappeared.

Eleven days later Regina stared at the wall phone in the kitchen. The bulletin board jammed with notes, snapshots, coupons, reminded her of her mom. She felt the tears rise, cleared her throat, gulped her coffee. Yesterday she spent hours working up the nerve to call the clinic. Five minutes before closing time she dialed. After being on hold for what seemed light years, she was told her results weren't back yet. Call tomorrow. Now tomorrow was today, and Regina knew the answer, whatever it was, existed at the other end of a wire that snaked its way from Carmen's tidy redwood-and-brick house to a storefront clinic in Newark.

Carmen sat at her desk in the kitchen pretending to sort bills. Regina sucked down coffee and dialed. "Free Clinic," a chirpy woman answered and the humiliation that had become so familiar draped Regina in its creeping warmth. *Like I don't know where I called.* She gave her the number—no names at this clinic.

Carmen dropped her head and said clumsy prayers while a blue jay squawked outside.

Regina twirled the spiral phone cord, counted business cards on the bulletin board, green tiles on the floor. If you asked her how long she'd been on hold she would have said forever, but in truth it was just under sixty seconds, the longest minute of her life.

Never could she imagine that the word "negative" would give her such a euphoric swell. Regina danced around the kitchen, tackled Carmen in a hug, happier than she'd been since she was a kid on Christmas morning, only this was the best present. Her life. "One down. One to go."

"Okay, enough is enough. Now you have to go to the hairdresser," Carmen said. "You used to rag on me about my hair, but yours has been looking like raccoon roadkill." Carmen looped her arm through Regina's. "Your mom and I used to go together, every other month. I still make the appointment, but mostly I can't keep it. Edie works me in when I can get there. It's coming up on Tuesday. Sometimes your mom and I would go out to eat after."

Regina knew she was right about her hair and about taking another step toward her mother.

Lonnie was in Edie's chair waiting to be set when Regina walked in. "Hey, Mom." Regina bent and gave Lonnie a quick kiss. She hadn't kissed her mother in years. She'd forgotten how soft her skin was, and catching a whiff of Lonnie's favorite after-bath splash almost made her cry. Looking past the surprise on her mother's face, she continued. "Know someplace we can grab a bite when we're done?"

Lonnie hesitated a moment. "Sure."

Regina and Lonnie didn't talk much in the shop. They weren't in the same place at the same time, but after Lonnie was combed out, she waited. Her old bouffant had been modernized into a sleeker style.

Regina's hair was still red, but a quieter tone, cut into a chin-length pageboy. It looked better than she expected from the hometown salon. She followed her mother to an Italian place, the kind of chain that Regina would have pooh-poohed as too ordinary, but the setting wasn't important. They hadn't been alone across a table in ages.

At first they perused their menus, exchanging comments about favorite dishes and likely choices. After they ordered, Regina selected a red crayon from the glass on the table and drew squiggles on the paper spread over the tablecloth.

"Whatcha making?" Lonnie asked.

"I don't know." Regina looked up at her mom. *I do look like her. Same nose, same eyes*. She drew a tic-tac-toe grid, and smiled, inviting her mother to play the way they used to at the kitchen table.

Lonnie chose a blue crayon, drew an X in the center square. "Edie did a nice job."

Regina put an O in the top right box. "Yours too. Looks hip."

Lonnie's X went in the lower right box. "How are you?"

"I feel like I should be in detention for life." Regina's O in the top left box blocked Lonnie's X's.

"I don't love your brothers more than I love you." Lonnie looked at Regina, didn't mark her box. "I never have."

"I'm so sorry, Mom." Regina reached across the table, lifted her mother's hand, pressed it to her cheek. There were many more knots to unravel, but at least they'd found a beginning to this ball of yarn.

After lunch Regina went home and waited for her dad. Her presence was enough for him. She could see his relief at his two best girls standing side by side and talking.

Three days later Regina sat in Marylou Porter's office at POWERTemps. Regina's déjà vu wasn't exact, but it was close enough to be scary. She was thirty-one years old and praying to get the same kind of job she could have gotten the day she graduated from high school.

"Word processing will raise your base pay two dollars an hour. Which programs do you know?" Marylou asked. "WordStar? WordPerfect?"

Word what? Regina knew they had something to do with computers. *Glenda always took care of that stuff.* She had to shake off the thought, let go of the fact that not long ago she had her own business, even hired a few temps herself. "Uh…yes. Both."

"We have a diverse group of businesses we serve—pharmaceutical companies, technology, manufacturing—I'm sure we'll have something for you soon."

"There's one I'd prefer not to be sent to. My father works there." Regina couldn't face even one day at the company where her dad had been a pioneer, the first black chemist.

Regina left with a POWERTemps folder full of time cards, pay schedules, holidays, suggested attire, and benefits she'd be eligible for in a year. She got in the car, the one her mother offered for "as long as you need it honey," after a sudden decision to buy a new one. "They never give you what it's worth on a trade-in." Lonnie turned over the keys, registration and insurance papers. Regina drove back to Carmen's and cried for an hour, but she pulled it together, made a pot of coffee and spent all day teaching herself word processing on Carmen's computer.

Marylou called the next morning at seven and dispatched Regina to a six-week stint as a receptionist for a company that printed lottery tickets. At first she found it awkward, being around so many strangers, trying to act normal when she felt like she had a sign that said SCREW-UP taped to her back. But after the first week, she settled in and when her assignment came to an end, her boss offered her a full-time position. Regina thanked him, said she'd happily accept a future placement, but she couldn't make a permanent commitment yet. Not until after her last HIV test. She'd started thinking of it that way, and had begun to contemplate the weeks and months beyond August.

In fact, Regina felt so positive she wanted to do something special for Carmen and Jewell, who'd be down later, something to say thank you. It was Friday, not Tuesday, and in all the years they'd known each other Regina had never cooked more than toast, but she decided to resurrect the international dinner and surprise them. *How hard can it be?* Even Carmen could make a few dishes. From the time she was a kid, Regina had spent as little time as possible in the kitchen. She had been the take-out queen, but now her budget was tight so she swung into the supermarket, confident she too could pull off a simple dinner.

Up one aisle, down the other, Regina examined produce, perused cans of artichokes and peaches, eyed steaks and chops, feeling like she'd landed on an alien planet. *What the hell is spaetzle?* Then rounding a towering display of snack crackers she ran into her answer. *Spaghetti! Mom made it all the time.* She grabbed two boxes of pasta, chose jars of sauce whose labels bragged they were better than homemade, and tossed in a container of grated Parmesan, the kind her mother always used. She snapped up a package of ground beef on the way to produce for salad stuff and onions, garlic and peppers, because even she knew you had to doctor-up jar sauce.

And on the way home, she stopped for a bottle of Chianti. *No reason they shouldn't have it, just because I can't.* Jewell and Carmen rarely had more than a glass of wine anyway, but the past few months, they wouldn't even do that around her. Regina appreciated their concern, but she didn't even want a drink these days. Besides, she couldn't spend the rest of her life avoiding people and places because somebody might have a cocktail.

She unloaded her bounty on the kitchen counter. *Cool. Directions right on the box!* She filled the biggest pot Carmen had with water, put it on to boil. Whatever she was making, Regina remembered Lonnie always minced onions and garlic first. So Regina clumsily chopped with a small paring knife, the process hampered by teary, burning eyes. She wiped them on the back of her hand, glanced at the label on the sauce. "Add meat if desired, toss with your favorite pasta." *No biggie.* Waiting for the water to boil, she made salad, set the table, put the bottle of wine in the center, sighed. So much of her social life had revolved around clinking glasses. It was hard to imagine being the life of the party with ginger ale in her glass. *But that's the new me.*

Back in the kitchen she dumped the spaghetti into the rolling water, set the timer for eight minutes, like it said on the package, but when the buzzer sounded and she checked the pot she thought more of the water would be gone so she let it cook a little longer. *That didn't help much.* But she shrugged and added the meat, onions and sauce anyway. And she waited, nervously lifting the lid every few minutes to check. *It still looks too soupy.* After another ten minutes, there hadn't been any improvement and Regina started to feel panicky. *Any idiot can make spaghetti, but me!* She thought about the Chianti, wondered if it might help the sauce—or her.

"It smells like food in here!" Jewell came in the back door. "You guys ordered already?"

At least it smells like food. Regina quickly put the lid back, afraid to reveal her offering. "No, I'm cooking." She stood defiant, hands on hips, hoping her sauce was thickening up.

"You?" Jewell grinned. "Is there a blizzard coming? I know it's June—"

"Ha ha. I'm learning all sorts of new skills, so if you don't mind, go make yourself comfortable—in the living room. There's a bottle of wine on the dining table." Regina caught the look on Jewell's face. "Unopened. I swear, not a drop." She crossed her heart, pretending the temptation hadn't crossed her mind.

"Okay Reg." Jewell nodded and headed down the hall. "What are we having?"

"Spaghetti." *I hope*. Regina lifted the lid on a pink, swirling mess. *It's not even red*. She found ketchup in the pantry, emptied in the whole bottle which made the mixture a slightly rosier pink. *I can't screw this up too*. She took a deep breath, tried to think of what to do next. *Mom always puts flour in stuff to make it thick*. Regina didn't know how much to use, so she added a couple of scoops which became golf ball-sized lumps.

"What do we have here?" Carmen dropped her keys in the basket by the door.

Regina slammed the top back on the pot. "I wanted to make dinner." She tried to stop them, but her eyes welled up. "You cook, Jewell cooks, Malcolm cooks. I thought I would do it for a change." Her voice got thinner and the tears spilled over. "I had a great day. I got paid and I wanted to do something for you guys."

"Did you hear we have a guest chef—What's wrong?" Jewell got to the kitchen and was surprised by the change in the weather.

"I screwed it up, like everything else!" Regina lifted the lid. "Look at this!"

Jewell headed for the stove. "It's probably not that—what the—" She covered her mouth with her hand, but couldn't keep down the laugh.

"Let me see." Carmen peeked, tried to keep a straight face. "Did you drain the water?"

"Drain?"

The laugh exploded before Carmen could help it.

Regina's look changed to indignation. "The directions didn't say anything about draining." She got the empty box out of the trash, shoved it at Carmen. "See."

Carmen got hold of herself long enough to examine it. "'Step four—Remove from heat. *Drain well*.'" Then she was laughing again.

"I thought it was like rice," Regina said in her defense, which only made them laugh harder.

Jewell wrapped an arm around Regina's shoulder. "Don't be mad. When have we laughed this hard?"

"Yeah, lighten up. Remember the stuff Jewell used to try on us, like the duck? Crispy on the outside, raw on the inside."

Jewell doubled over, recalling that disaster.

And Regina's gloom broke as she gave in to the memory. "Don't forget that orange sauce."

By the time they composed themselves they all felt better. It had been ages since they laughed together. They drained the pinkish mess down the disposal on their way out to dinner.

"Hold on a sec." Regina disappeared back inside and returned with the Chianti. "Take this home with you," she said to Jewell. "Think of it as a consolation prize."

Jewell looked at Regina a moment. "Thanks." She took the bottle without any questions.

Regina's next job was a week-long stint in a dental office calling neglectful patients to remind them they were overdue for a cleaning. She expected the dental delinquents to be annoyed by the intrusion. Instead, most of them seemed thankful for being reminded to do something they should have taken care of without prompting. Each pleasant response reminded Regina of her own negligence, the calls she had yet to make—like to Sydney and Glenda, for starters.

While Regina was in rehab, Carmen found out that Sydney took over the other events on the RF Productions docket, closed up the office, took Glenda and moved into her own space. So after her last day at Dr. Murdock's office, Regina went home and dialed Mayfield Associates. A surprised Glenda answered and chatted amiably with Regina before transferring the call to Sydney, who graciously accepted Regina's apology. The conversation was light, no anger or recrimination passed between them and they ended their chat with an optimistic promise to do lunch. When she hung up, Regina felt relieved of some of the load she'd been carrying. Right after that she called Rutgers for an application and catalog for part-time study. As much as she still hated the idea of sitting in a classroom, finishing school was part of her new game plan. The difference was that this time she knew what she wanted—the know-how to run the fiscal side of a business as well as the creative side. A few days later she called Luc, who refused to come to the phone. *Guess I'll have to write him a letter.*

It was Ty who still weighed heavy on her heart, but she couldn't call him yet. Not before her last test results. *Either I'll feel clean enough to face him, or I'll be in the express check-out line and it won't matter.*

More than anything, Regina needed Ty's forgiveness. She had treated him the worst. He told her the truth and she didn't believe him. She lied to him and he took it as gospel. He tried to help her in every way he knew how. She ignored his advice and discounted his experience. He gave her a ruby ring. She traded it for enough cocaine to fuel her final rampage. Ty showed her again and again that he loved her. And the worst offense of all, Regina loved him but never let him know it. No, she wasn't ready to see him yet.

Regina's test in August didn't send her off the deep end. By then she was feeling positive, thinking positive. This time she was home alone when she called the clinic, watched chipmunks chase across the deck while she awaited the result. She was startled when the voice came back on the other end. "Yes, that's my number." And when she heard him say negative, she felt like she'd been given a whole new life. "Thank you." A life she'd take better care of this time.

By October Regina had saved enough to get her own place, the next step in rebuilding her life. She moved into the high-rise in downtown New Brunswick with her clothes, the futon and the TV. It wasn't much but at least she was on her own again. "It's downtown, in the mix." Carmen gave her a skeptical look. "Not *that* in the mix," Regina explained. "All I'm into is coffee and cola." But she still craved more than squirrels and solitude. Her place was within walking distance of Rutgers and the train to New York when she was ready to take it. Her window overlooked Buccleuch Park instead of Central Park, and now her own keys were on her 5D key ring. She had finally cleared enough of the underbrush in her life to see a path, even if she wasn't sure exactly where it led.

Jewell called to see if she wanted the red chaise. "Think I'll start fresh," Regina said. Jewell also had Dwight news. Tenants from 924 and several of King's other buildings had protested outside of Dwight's office to call attention to deteriorating conditions and tenant harassment. "Couldn't happen to a nicer guy." Regina was gleeful. "Hope this sends his congressional campaign down the toilet, 'cause it was pure shit anyway."

Mid October Regina sat in the cafeteria of Kemp Foyle, an investment firm that managed pension funds, picking sprouts from a salad. She was taking better care of herself, but she drew the line at sprouts. Sandy, from HR, Regina's latest lunch pal, pulled up a tray.

"I'm going to choke my future mother-in-law." Sandy sipped her diet soda. "Bridal magazines give me a headache. I thought all I had to do was pick a day and a dress."

Regina's antennae started wiggling as she listened to Sandy's dilemma. The wedding she had in mind was small compared to the events Regina used to handle. *I could tell her about planning Jewell's wedding. That ought to impress her. I could do this on the side and still have time to*—She stopped herself mid-thought. *Who are you kidding? You can hardly keep your clothes hung up*. Working and getting back into school were her priorities. She knew she wasn't ready to start juggling again.

At Thanksgiving Regina stayed in the kitchen long enough to learn what went into her mother's special stuffing. And at dinner, after her father said the blessing, she surprised everyone, herself included, when she told her family how thankful she was for their love and support. "Okay, don't get all mushy. Who's going to be the first to try the stuffing? I helped make it, you know."

That left one more task to accomplish before she could welcome 1995. So on a warm December day Regina took the train into the city, her first trip in since her last trip out. New York could be a very small town, especially in certain circles and she had been afraid of who she might run into, but she realized it didn't matter who knew she'd crashed and burned. It was the truth, and she was getting better every day. If somebody couldn't be happy about that then screw 'em. Some part of her wanted to see Reuben, but she decided that was pointless too. What could she say, "Thank's for screwing up my life?" Of course, all he had done was ask the question. She was the one who said yes.

But today Regina set out to see Ty. She was surprised to turn down West 20th Street and see the Big Bang logo suspended from the roof of his building like a giant mobile, surrounded by brushed aluminum stars. He'd bought the whole building and the reception area on the ground floor had banks of monitors playing music videos of Big Bang's ever-expanding roster of talent. Regina took a deep breath and approached the burgundy-haired girl behind the shiny black-rimmed steel circle. "Regina Foster to see Ty Washington." She called yesterday to make sure he'd be in.

"Do you have an appointment?"

"No. But I think he'll see me." Regina smiled. "I don't mind waiting."

The receptionist cocked her head, picked up the phone, mumbled too low for Regina to hear. "You can go up. Twelfth floor."

The rickety elevator had been replaced by a spiffy new one and a pretty young woman met her when the doors opened. "Right this way. Ty says you're old friends?"

Regina was glad he still spoke of her as a friend. "We go back a ways." They reached a set of frosted glass doors which stood open. He was on the phone, back to her, silhouetted against the southern skyline of the city.

"He'll be off in a sec. Can I get you anything? Water? Coffee? Juice?"

She wanted coffee in a serious way, but she had to do this without even her substitute stimulant.

Ty finished his call and faced her. He stared a long time, taking her in, head to toe.

Regina's heart thumped in her ears, threatened to gallop right out of her chest. She didn't want to look as uncomfortable as she felt. Ty looked good, the same but better.

"Hey." He smiled enough for her to see the gap was still there.

"I should have come before now, but I couldn't face you." She wanted to look out the window, at her boots, anywhere but in his eyes, but she forced herself to. "I'm sorry—"

"Regina—"

"Please let me finish. Then you can say what you need to." She rubbed the inside of her coat pocket between her thumb and forefinger. "I could list all the hateful things I've done to you, or at least the top ten, but you're a busy man." She felt that empty spot on her finger. "Mostly, I'm sorry for lying to you. I got caught up in—" *No excuses Regina*. "Doesn't matter what I got caught up in. I'm ashamed of the way I treated you. You deserve the best because you are the best, Ty. Quality you always called it. You're the one who's quality." She took a breath. She wanted to say "I love you Ty. I always did." But knew she didn't have the right to. That time had passed. "That's all." She waited to take her lumps.

Ty scruffed up his chin. "It's good to see you looking like your old self." He got up and walked toward her, close enough for her to notice he still wore the same cologne. Close enough for her to take a step back, away from the heat she knew she'd feel if he came any closer. "If you need anything—"

"Don't you hate me?"

"Uh-uh. No. I was mad and I was hurt." He paused a moment, finding the words. "But more than that, I was disappointed."

Regina was prepared for his wrath, but disappointing Ty felt even worse.

"I'm still rootin' for you though," Ty said.

Regina had to drop her eyes. She couldn't watch his kindness. Being with him made her ache for what she'd thrown away. "Thanks for seeing me, Ty. I really mean it I know you're a busy man."

"Never too busy for an old friend. You remember that, hear?"

"I will."

He started toward her again, but stopped, like he couldn't handle being too close, needed to keep a safe distance between them. "You take good care of yourself."

Regina smiled. "Merry Christmas Ty." Hand on the knob, she turned back. "And thanks—for everything." She got all the way outside, in front of a Salvation Army Santa before she broke down. He stopped clanging his bell. "You need some help, Miss?"

"No. Just taking my medicine."

26
"...what-iffing won't change a thing."

April 21, 1996
Somerset, NJ

"Will the food be ready on time?" Carmen surveyed the table.

"You have my personal guarantee." Malcolm basted the tenderloin. "But even if it's not, they'll wait. It's not a shuttle launch. It's Sunday dinner." He closed the oven door. The savory aroma of butter, thyme and rosemary wafted through the house. "Hey, spring has sprung. My folks are here. You have a new job. All perfectly good reasons to celebrate." Malcolm winked. In January Carmen left the clinic where she'd been working since she finished her residency last July and took a position in Sandrine Hawley's new wellness practice. As a resident, Carmen had always gotten along with Sandrine. So she visited the office, liked the vibe in the all-female setting and after talking it over with Malcolm, accepted the offer. She and Sandrine were the family practitioners, in addition to two ob/gyns, childhood and adolescent pediatricians, a psychologist and two nurse practitioners. Carmen had only been there a few months, but she enjoyed the regular hours and a camaraderie that made work fun.

"I'm just a little nervous. Parties always made me that way anyway." Carmen moved a stack of plates to the other end of the table. "Before Regina's crazy parties or Jewell's Tuesday Food-for-Alls, I always thought something would go wrong—we'd have a power failure and couldn't cook and people would be hungry and mad." She examined the table from another angle.

"You probably had a gas stove so you could still cook in the dark."

"Very funny." Carmen moved the basket with the silverware next to the plates. Today was special. She wanted it to look special. For weeks, ever since they planned this day, she would swipe women's magazines from the waiting room, sneak into her office between patients and pour over place settings and table decor. "What I used to worry about most was that nobody would come."

"Baby, the power's on. Food will be great, if I do say so myself. And trust me, they're all showing up." Malcolm came and put his arms around her. "It's our first dinner for our family and friends. They'll be happy just to be here." He kissed the tip of her nose. "It's under control. And I didn't even use every pot in the joint this time." He grinned, knowing his messiness was one of her pet peeves. "I'm gonna get cleaned up and pick up my folks and Dr. Summers from church. Back in an hour." He took the dishtowel from his waist and chucked it on the counter. "Ready?"

Carmen nodded. He blew her a kiss and was out the back door. Although it had taken her a while to believe it, she knew he'd be back. Carmen looked around. The table was lovely and inviting, white roses as a centerpiece and on the mantel. Diamond prisms from the April sun slanting through the windows reflected off the chandelier and pranced on the walls. She opened the windows, let the warm breeze in. *Perfect. It looks perfect.*

An hour later, Carmen met Malcolm, his parents and Reverend Dr. Summers at the door.

"You look lovely dear!" Marian Wyatt said. "It's so nice of you to have us over."

"My pleasure, Mrs. Wyatt. Nice to see you again, Dr. Summers." Carmen shook his hand.

"I've known these good folks forever." Dr. Summers nodded toward the Wyatts. "I'm honored to be included." He smiled, clasped Carmen's hands.

"We'll all have to thank your son for dinner," Carmen said to Mr. Wyatt.

"That boy can cook. Sometimes I think he's better than his mama." He winked at Carmen.

"Humph." Marian gently elbowed her husband. "He's still a mess in the kitchen though, isn't he? I was glad to get him out of mine."

Carmen saw Jewell pull up and waited at the door. "It is a top-down kind of day isn't it, California girl!" She waved as Jewell got out of the convertible, shook her hair free from her baseball cap. "Right on time, as always." Carmen hugged her. "Let's see how late Reg is. She said she was coming from the library—working, going to school and studying on a Sunday! Can you believe it?"

"You know her. Don't hold dinner. Wow, you look great!" Jewell exclaimed as she checked out Carmen's silk shantung suit. The fitted pale gold dress and jacket shimmered in the afternoon light and cast a warm glow on Carmen's honeyed complexion. Her hair was pulled up loosely with wisps framing her face. "You said Sunday dinner, not a state occasion. I might have tried a little harder." Jewell threw up her arms in mock exasperation, not that she was a slouch, in a pink sweater set over cream pants, the cardigan tossed casually over her shoulders.

"Right. You always make the rest of us look like the runners up."

Carmen's bronze leather sling backs caught Jewell's attention before she thought of a comeback. "You? Heels?! I have to mark this day on the calendar!"

"You do that, hear." Carmen laughed, put her arm through Jewell's and they walked into the living room together. "Mr. and Mrs. Wyatt, I want you to meet my friend—"

"Oh my goodness!" Marian grabbed Jewell's hand. "I can't believe it's really you. In person! Wait till I get back to Atlanta. My lunch bunch will just die!" She turned to her husband, "Bill take a picture of us! You did bring the camera, didn't you? Is it okay to take a picture?" Mrs. Wyatt asked Jewell. "I'm sorry. I guess I sound like a silly old woman. I'm just so excited!"

Jewell posed with Marian, chatted up Malcolm's dad. Carmen heard her ask Dr. Summers what kind of medicine he practiced before she left to see how Malcolm was doing in the kitchen, but didn't hear his answer. Malcolm shooed her out. "I can't concentrate with you standing there looking like that." He took her in from head to toe. "Um um um. Now go!"

Carmen felt herself blush. "Why Mr. Wyatt. I believe you're being fresh! And with your parents in the next room! Shame on you!" Carmen did a credible Southern belle for a girl who'd hardly been any farther south than where she was right now.

"You should have heard some of the stuff they did while I was in the next room!"

"Time for me to go. I don't need to hear this!" She stood on tiptoes, lifted his locks and planted a kiss behind his right ear.

"You better run girl." She did and found that almost everyone had arrived. Lonnie and Al, Malcolm's friend Clay and his girlfriend. Then last but not least, Regina burst through the door.

"You didn't eat everything did you?" She surveyed the room, then kissed her parents. "Hey y'all! Man, if I'da known it was a party I'da dressed up." She wore jeans and a red pullover. "Look at you two!" Regina watched Carmen help Malcolm into the jacket of his navy suit. "Can you believe I'm getting A's?"

"It does boggle the mind, considering," Carmen said.

"You know what they say about better late…" Regina joked. "I need a Coke."

"Could you wait a sec Regina?" Malcolm slipped an arm around Carmen's waist. They stood in front of the fireplace.

"Sure. I guess so. What's up?" Regina plopped down on the arm of the sofa.

Malcolm cleared his throat. "We're very happy all of you are here." He gave Carmen a squeeze. "It's not easy to get the folks we care about in the same place at the same time—"

Carmen picked up. "—And now that we have you captive, there's a little business we want to take care of before dinner."

"What? You want to take attendance?" Regina asked and everyone laughed.

"No. But I would like you and Jewell to be my attendants, maids of honor, best women—"

"Are you serious?!" Regina hollered. She grabbed Jewell's arm. "They can't be serious!" She watched them, waiting for the punch line. "When's the wedding?"

"Dr. Summers?" Malcolm called the minister up. "We didn't want a big fuss. We'd have done it sooner, but I couldn't get my folks up here until I could promise it wouldn't snow."

"Now?! You're getting married right now?!" Regina was beside herself, but everyone was in an uproar since no one knew aside from the good reverend, who had promised to keep their secret. "You didn't even tell me you were engaged."

Malcolm had asked Carmen to marry him on New Year's Eve. They were bundled up against freezing temperatures, watching midnight fireworks in the park downtown along the river. Carmen was just happy to be out on a holiday, one of the benefits of being in private practice. Suddenly, he dropped to one knee, sat her on the other one like it was a bench. He spoke before she could open her mouth. "There's nothing that would make this year and the rest of my life happier, than if you would do me the honor of becoming my wife." Carmen felt like one of the spiraling flashes of light they had just watched had gone off in her body. There was nothing in her life that had ever felt so instantly right.

"Surprise!" Carmen sang. "We wanted to share this day with the people who are closest to us, and you're all here." Carmen beamed. Looking at Regina and Jewell she added, "Thank goodness. Because I couldn't keep the secret from you two much longer."

"But where are the bouquets, the doves, the—?" Regina asked.

"That's exactly why I didn't tell you." Carmen wagged her finger at Regina.

"You'll pay for this, Doc!" Regina hugged Malcolm. "But I'm glad he'll be sticking around."

Jewell could see that this was how people who loved each other were supposed to look, how they were supposed act with one another. "This is the best surprise!" She hugged them, and ignored her own sadness that she and Dwight never even came close to what Carmen and Malcolm had. The best she could say about her ex-fiancé is that he got her to stop smoking.

Malcolm took Carmen's hand. "Let's get it on."

"Amen!" added Dr. Summers. And there, in front of the fireplace, before God and the family she had made for herself, free from the cloud of doubt that had followed Carmen her whole life, she made peace with her past and trusted her heart to Malcolm. But she kept her own name—Dr. Webb-Wyatt was more than a mouthful.

Their honeymoon on St. John was Carmen's first real vacation and their room had a balcony facing the pristine beach only a short walk away. They watched brilliant sunrises and glowing sunsets, laughed till it hurt watching each other try windsurfing—Malcolm actually got the hang of it after a few days. Carmen took tennis lessons and enjoyed them. They hiked through the nature preserves, rode the ferry to St. Thomas for some nightlife and a little shopping. Malcolm bought her earrings, big, iridescent sea pearls, since she didn't want an engagement ring. "I'd never get to wear it. My hands are always in soap and water." They spent entire afternoons on the beach, under an umbrella. They'd start out on separate lounges, but would end up together, Carmen resting against Malcolm's chest, secure and happy feeling him behind her.

When they got back, everyone talked about her glow. She said it was the sun, but she knew the glow came from inside, from Malcolm.

He moved into her place, put his condo on the market and they planned to look for a house when his place sold. Carmen imagined a big old one with a wraparound porch and a gently sloping yard out back for snow angels. "And volleyball and a basketball hoop…" Malcolm had a whole list and he had moved enough gear—skis, hockey skates, bats—into her basement to supply a sporting goods store. "Don't you have any clothes?" she teased. He did, but he had more cookware than sweaters. "I love you baby, but your pots and pans need some serious help." Carmen didn't have a problem making room for his pasta pentola. It was a bit tougher to integrate the leather recliner and weight bench, but they worked it out.

In October they fell in love with a house that was so much like Carmen's dreams it was almost spooky. From the road, the spacious white frame colonial beckoned them. Out front there was a huge Norway spruce, taller than the house by half, and the owners left the big birch rockers on the porch, said they belonged there.

"This is where we'll sit when we're old ladies." Jewell pointed to the porch chairs as Carmen showed them the house the next weekend.

"You two can get old if you want to," Regina said. "I'm not having it!"

"Fine. We'll rock and talk about you!" Carmen parked in the driveway.

"If you put it like that, I guess I'll have to join you just to defend myself," Regina said.

Carmen ignored Regina's comment. "And you can't see it from here, but there's a huge yard out back. Malcolm's already talking about swing sets and sandboxes." Carmen folded her arms over the steering wheel. "It feels kind of weird, you know? I had my career thing figured out a long time ago, but I never saw any of this personal stuff for myself—and here I am. *Thank you Milton*. It's a lot to take in. Sometimes I have to pinch myself."

"You deserve every bit of it!" Jewell said.

"Yeah. Actually you do," Regina added. Carmen looked at her, waiting for the smart remark. "Really. I mean it."

"When do you close?" Jewell asked.

"Things are moving fast. Hopefully we'll be in by Christmas."

And in mid December, as Carmen waited for Malcolm and the movers to arrive, she remembered the day she left Montgomery Street with only what fit in a shopping cart.

Before the boxes were all unpacked, Malcolm was dropping hints about a baby. "Not that I'm in a hurry or anything, but we do have five bedrooms to fill," he said.

"We don't have to fill them all up tomorrow!" But she was less afraid of starting a family than she thought she would be. Before Malcolm, Carmen had resigned herself to being childless. It was easy to decide not to pass on whatever strange genes and tragic predisposition seemed a part of her family legacy. But Malcolm had helped her believe in a future she looked forward to sharing with their children.

Like most marriages, adjusting to living together had its challenges. Carmen wrote checks on the first and fifteenth religiously. Malcolm had more of an "I think it's due tomorrow so I'd better write a check and take it to the post office," accounting system. Carmen was orderly to a fault and returned tools and pens and tape to their places. Malcolm was more free form. Before he left in the morning he usually had to find something—keys, wallet, the messenger's sack he carried to school. He wasn't as much of a whirlwind as Regina, but Carmen had gotten so used to her neat solo world that some days his messiness drove her nuts. But so far, that was the worst of it and considering the pluses, how much was right in her life, she could make room for a minus or two.

The holidays passed in a flurry of festivities. And before it seemed possible, Carmen and Malcolm's first anniversary rolled around. It was a Monday, a workday, but Carmen got up extra early and treated him to breakfast in bed—the same breakfast he had fixed for her the morning she called him back into her life. And by the middle of May, Carmen had good news. She was convinced she knew exactly when it happened—right after the grits and eggs. An anniversary present. They hadn't been trying, but they hadn't been not trying either.

"Have you got plans for next January tenth?" Carmen asked casually while Malcolm sat on the floor between her knees and she retwisted his locks.

"Of next year? I don't even know what I'm doing next week."

"Well I'm glad I caught you before you scheduled something else, because we're having a baby and—"

He jumped up like a rocket, scooped Carmen off the sofa and danced around the living room with her in his arms. She'd never seen anyone more elated.

After Malcolm, Carmen had to tell Jewell and Regina. She had the receptionist at the office hook them up on a conference call. As Adrienne became a true love/hate icon on daytime TV, Jewell's *TIA* schedule and appearances at soap conventions all over the country—a concept Carmen didn't completely understand—became more hectic. And with Regina in school four nights a week and working every day, the three of them hadn't seen each other in weeks.

"You beat me to it." Jewell sat in the makeup chair in her dressing room. "I was going to call you guys tonight."

"About what?" Regina asked from her current mauve cubicle, high above East Brunswick.

"I got a call from Barnard," Jewell responded. "They've asked me to give a speech—they have this distinguished alumna series. Can you believe it's almost ten years since graduation?"

"Correction. Only for some of us. Others are still matriculating," Regina grumbled.

"If I could get a word in, you might find out why I called," Carmen said.

When she shared her news they were ecstatic. "Already?! Man, there are gonna be little Wyatts running all over town before you know it," Regina said. "A house full of 'em."

"I can't believe we'll be aunties." Jewell was thrilled. Carmen's baby would be like her sister's child, if she had a sister. She felt attached already. "I have to see you."

"I'm not showing yet. There's nothing to see."

"But I might miss something," Jewell insisted.

"You are gonna be sickening," Regina groused, but they made arrangements to get together in two weeks.

By the weekend Carmen hit a bump in her yellow brick road. She sat, her back against their headboard. "What if the baby gets the gene from my mother for bipolar disorder—"

"Woman, what-iffing won't change anything. It'll just worry you to death." He kissed her hand. "And I don't want you to worry." He pointed at her belly. "He doesn't like it either."

"Oh, it's a he, huh?"

"Intuition." Malcolm smiled. "Men have it too, you know. That, and he told me."

At the office, word spread quickly and her colleagues offered winks, smiles and plenty of advice. Sandrine gave her a box of Saltines. "Stick these in your desk. You may need them later."

Carmen swung her legs gently off the edge of the examination table waiting for her first pre-natal exam from Eleanora Vasquez, one of the OB/GYNs in the practice. Elly had already taken a history, not that there was much to go on. Carmen's parents hadn't been around long enough to provide her much useful medical information. "So, we'll start with what we know, which is that you're preggers, in good health, and I'll meet you in room two soon as I can."

Sitting in a pink rough-dried gown, open to the front, Carmen read and reread the stages of pregnancy chart, still having trouble believing all that was going on inside her right now.

The door swept open. "Here we go." Elly charged in, washed her hands. Short and round, like a Ping-Pong ball, she was just as active, always in motion. "I'll have you out of here in a few."

Carmen slid and scooted so Elly could do the internal. "My daughter was born in January. The good thing is you get through the summer before you get too big. I had a hard time with coats though. Slide back for me."

Carmen stared at the acoustic tile ceiling, hand behind her head while Elly mashed and circled her breasts. Carmen hadn't thought about the weather, or which bedroom would be the baby's, or what they were going to do for child care. And she wasn't paying attention to the fact that Elly's search had narrowed to a small circle near the bottom of her left breast.

"You can get dressed. I'll meet you in my office."

Before long Elly scurried in, sat down and leaned over her desk. "I'm sending you upstairs to Fred for a mammogram and sonogram—"

"What?" Carmen didn't realize she had stood up, couldn't feel her feet.

"It's a precaution, and don't worry about the baby. They'll shield you, but I felt a mass on the lower outside left breast. I want him to take a look at it. He can take you at two."

Carmen had never paid much attention to her body. It was something she carried around to support her mind. And she'd certainly payed little attention to her breasts. They were no bigger than bee bites—definitely not noteworthy. She resisted the urge to reach under her shirt, feel for what Elly had found. *Stop what-iffing*. She repeated Malcolm's instruction. *It's probably a swollen lymph node from that cold I had. Maybe an infection. Elly's just being cautious*. For the next two hours, Carmen concentrated all her energy on her patients, the way she did when she was an exhausted resident but had to keep going. She wouldn't have seen a hippo in front of her if he didn't have a chart, but the sharp focus made her perceptions keener and the time zip by.

It almost seemed too soon when Daniella, the receptionist, knocked gently on Carmen's office door. "Time for your appointment with Dr. Falconer."

Upstairs Carmen slipped into her second gown for the day, this one white with navy piping. After carefully shielding her abdomen, the technician pulled, smushed and squeezed, making sure she got the necessary angles. Carmen recalled all the "boobs in a vise" jokes she'd heard. It was uncomfortable, but it was also over quickly. The X-ray technician went off with the film, came back before Carmen had browsed beyond page ten in a travel magazine.

"I need to get another picture," the technician said.

"Problem with the first ones?" Carmen was planning to joke, ask if she should smile for the next one, but she couldn't.

"No. He just wants another view."

The technician's cool response made the hair on the back of Carmen's neck stand up, but after it was done she had no choice but to head down the hall with her magazine to wait for her sonogram. Although she couldn't really see what was in front of her, flipping the pages was something she could do and still feel sane.

The lubricant for the sonogram was gooey and cold and this time the technician, eyes glued to the monitor, apologized for how hard he had to press the steely ball of the wand into her breasts, across the bone, but it didn't take long either. Carmen dressed quickly, wanting the protection of her clothes, her lab coat. She'd been on the patient side of the table too long.

Carmen knew Fred Falconer from the hospital and always thought his name suited his small, pointy, birdlike features. Fred skipped the introductory patter, got right to the point. Carmen held her breath—watched his mouth as he talked, waiting for the words to spill out one by one, wanting to grab them, pull them out faster so she could find out where this was leading.

"Your sonogram shows a number of cysts, pretty typical, nothing out of the ordinary." Then with no warning, he popped the film of her left breast on the viewer. "But there's a solid mass right here." He pointed to the area with his pen. "We're going to need a biopsy, check for malignancy." He said it with the same even tone that Carmen herself used to inspire confidence and circumvent alarm. "Doorbell." "Paperweight." "Malignancy." They could sound equivalent if you weren't paying attention, but it hadn't slipped past her.

The alarm clanged in her head, but she nodded anyway, said, "Sure," like her brain wasn't melting. Like she didn't want to scream. Falconer called the surgeon, scheduled the biopsy for the next morning, wrote the information on a prescription blank. *It's nothing*. Suddenly Malcolm's "whatiffing won't change anything" had a whole new meaning. *If the mass is malignant, nothing will change that either*. Carmen didn't remember the walk downstairs to her office but she ended up at her desk, clutching the neatly folded script with the name and address of her next doctor.

"Need anything before your four o'clock?" Daniella poked her head in the door, saw Carmen staring into space. "Dr. Webb is something wrong?"

"Huh?" Carmen finally looked up. Her face drained, pale—eyes glazed over, shiny but unfocused. "Sorry. How long have you been standing there?" Her voice sounded strange—distant, like she was speaking from the end of a long tunnel.

"Not long. But you don't look so good. Can I get you anything?"

Carmen stared blankly for a few seconds, tried to compose herself, find her real voice. "I hate to do this to you Daniella, but I need you to cancel the rest of my day—I know I'm on till eight but—" She turned the paper around and around. "See if someone can cover." Carmen reached for the phone, lifted the receiver. "If nobody can do it, then reschedule everybody, okay?" She started to dial, then stopped. She couldn't have this conversation with Malcolm on the phone. She needed to go home, to their house, to their life—the one she'd finally gotten for herself.

Carmen knew she probably shouldn't be driving, but home was only fifteen minutes away.

"I was just starting to think about dinner," Malcolm said when she came in the door. "You're early." He took one look at her, left the chicken in the sink.

Carmen let herself collapse in his arms. There was no dinner and not much sleep that night. "It's not fair!"

She cried as Malcolm held her, curled himself around her, trying to shield her from what pain and worry he could. "We don't even know what 'it' is yet, but we can handle it together."

"But what if we can't? What about the baby?" She tried not to believe this was some punishment for getting too much. The price she had to pay for happiness. "*Everything costs something*," Jewell used to say.

"We can handle it. I know we can. We just have to take this one step at a time."

The next morning, Malcolm went with her to the surgeon. The biopsy was a routine procedure and once again, it didn't take long. She knew it was silly, but somehow Carmen felt that something that could affect her life so dramatically, so permanently, should take more time. Of course, they wouldn't have the results for several days.

Regina and Jewell were coming for lunch on Saturday—the get-together was already planned, so Carmen waited to tell them in person. Originally they were going to eat—she would fill them in on her first pre-natal exam and after lunch Jewell had lobbied for a preliminary shopping expedition to check out baby clothes. But what was supposed to be an afternoon full of glad gab and nursery colors, became a stunned vigil instead. On the sunny May afternoon they sat on the back deck, under their own cloud, taking turns being hopeful and terrified. Malcolm busied himself with yard work, staying near enough to be close, always in sight, but far enough away to let them talk.

"If I had never met Malcolm, maybe this wouldn't have happened." Carmen watched him weed a flower bed. "My life was fine. I didn't need all this." She looked around at her friends, her husband, her home then let her hand rest gently on her belly. "It was too much—"

"Are you sure that tumor isn't in your brain?" Regina snapped. "'Cause that's the stupidest thing I ever heard you say. What?! Like you have some kind of quota? Oops! You're Carmen Webb aren't you? We're sorry but you've exceeded your allotment of happy and now you must be penalized?"

"Look at it this way," Jewell added. "If you hadn't met Malcolm you might not have found the tumor until later, so it looks to me like he showed up right on time." She tried to sound positive, optimistic but she knew that any one of them could have been walking around, feeling great while the seeds of destruction multiplied quietly inside. And it seemed so unfair; just when Carmen had finally found the pleasure in her body, she might have to forfeit so dear a part of it.

Later the next week, Carmen's partners in the wellness group came together to share the pathologist's report with her and Malcolm. "Infiltrating ductal carcinoma." Fred Falconer said it. Carmen had been expecting the worst anyway. Malcolm squeezed her hand, but she wouldn't look at him.

"Staging will be tricky since you're pregnant," Elly Vasquez explained.

Carmen knew that many of the usual tools were off-limits because they might harm the fetus, as would the treatments.

"There's no accurate way to gauge how fast your cancer is growing unless—" Sandrine started.

"You're still in the first trimester," Elly said. "You could terminate the pregnancy and then your cancer could be treated aggressively."

"Stop it!" Carmen snatched her hand away from Malcolm's, jumped to her feet. "Don't you think I know all of this?!"

"Carmen," Malcolm said quietly. "No one thinks you don't know or understand—"

"No? Well I'll tell you what I think. I don't think any of you understand at all." Suddenly she didn't feel supported by their presence, she felt surrounded. "You don't have a clue what I'm going through, so don't sit there giving me your concerned, 'keep the patient calm' faces and bedside manner. There are two things growing inside me—" Carmen looked around the room at all of them. "And you want me to choose!" Her eyes settled on Malcolm and she saw his worry. "I can't do that."

So began a round of consultations. Carmen saw her mentors and associates, esteemed medical faculty and friends, oncologists in New York, New Jersey and Pennsylvania. But her choices were few. If she wanted to continue the pregnancy, a mastectomy was recommended, with an axillary lymph node dissection, to determine if the cancer had spread. Radiation was out of the question until after the birth, but she could begin chemotherapy after the beginning of the second trimester, when it was deemed less hazardous to the fetus.

The fetus, her baby, their baby.

Whenever she put on the examination gown, and lay on the table with her left breast exposed, the clinical, objective part of Carmen's brain shut down and she was overwhelmed by the awareness that it was *her* left breast they were diagnosing. Her life and her baby's that were being discussed.

Carmen knew what chemo meant. Enough chemicals to poison the tumor, and whatever else got in the way, but after all the opinions and advice, after hours of agonizing, talking with Malcolm, she couldn't choose that for their baby.

Malcolm pleaded with her. "We'll get you better. There's plenty of time for another baby." He called Regina and Jewell to talk to her. They tried, but they knew that once she'd made up her mind, changing it was pretty much a lost cause. For once, Regina had no plan, no scheme—all she could do was listen to Carmen's arguments. Jewell understood Carmen's position. She felt a connection to this baby from the moment she first heard about Carmen's pregnancy. This was a baby she could love, see grow up, but she knew her bond couldn't compare to what Carmen felt.

Early in June, Carmen waited on the porch in her rocker, watching fireflies blink on and off, soaking up the warmth. End of term tests and grading brought Malcolm home late. He trudged up the front steps, sat in the other rocker, reached for her hand.

"My medical training taught me to make decisions for other people, not for myself or my family," Carmen said after a while. She looked at Malcolm, knowing her connection to him was stronger than their grip. "I can give up my breast. If that's all that's standing between you and me and living long enough to be Mommy, I can make that choice. Can you?"

Malcolm didn't hesitate. "Whatever they have to do to keep you healthy—keep you here—is fine with me. Surgery won't change who you are, or what you mean to me."

And she believed him.

So Carmen's left modified radical mastectomy was scheduled. They talked with the doctor about whether to have reconstructive plastic surgery done at the same time, but deciding that filling out her clothes was not as important as saving her life, Carmen declined.

The day before her operation, Carmen saw patients. Sitting home waiting would have driven her crazy. Malcolm made an early dinner, but she only picked, crunching crackers instead to ease the nausea which for her came in the evening, not morning. She resented the weeks that had been taken away from what should have been nine months of joyful anticipation, but that was how this deal worked. Take it or leave it.

The enormity of what was about to happen to her set in around eight that night. Carmen neatened her desk, his desk, his dresser drawers, anything she could think of to keep busy. She had pre-natal instructions, pre- and post-surgical instructions, but no one had given her instructions for tonight and she was afraid to stop moving, afraid she'd go to pieces. This was her last night whole. She'd seen clinical photos of mastectomies, but they hadn't been her body. Today she had two breasts. Tomorrow, she'd have one. She couldn't imagine what it would be like to look down at the asymmetry of her chest, look in a mirror. What it would be like for Malcolm to see, to touch. Then she started laughing. *Like my whopping A cups attracted him in the first place.*

Malcolm came up behind her, wrapped his arms around her shoulders. "How about a bath? I already ran the water."

Carmen almost never took baths—too much time. Showers were efficient, but tonight, she thought about the warm water, Malcolm's hands, and abandoned sock and paper clip organization.

Their bathroom was old fashioned—small white tiles, a claw-foot tub. He had run the water, clear, no bubbles, and lined the windowsill and vanity with candles. Looking at him in the golden light broke Carmen's self-enforced, resolute concentration. This moment would never be again. She cried silent, hot tears as he undressed her, helped her into the tub. He took off his clothes, knelt beside her. He ran his hand over her hair, then kissed her, soft, sweet, true.

Carmen traced a wet finger down his chest, smiled. She watched him lather her washcloth and as he rubbed the creamy foam over her shoulders, down her arms, a feeling of calm washed over her. He held each hand as he washed between her fingers, and there were tears in both their eyes as he eased the cloth across her breasts, cupping each one, let his hand come to rest over her heart.

"I love you, Carmen."

"I know. I love you, Malcolm."

He wrapped her in a towel and carried her to bed. She thought they would make love, but instead they lay together, Carmen on top, their arms encircling one another, not talking, just there holding on to their life.

The next morning, Carmen took a quick shower, looked at herself, her breasts in the mirror and made peace with the inevitable. *This is a small price to pay to enjoy the rest of my life with my family. My family.* She knew from personal experience how hard it was when parents left their children, even unintentionally. She was determined to stay around as long as she could.

Jewell and Regina met them at the hospital. There weren't any words when the attendant came to take Carmen to surgery. They hugged her, Jewell, Regina, and finally Malcolm, for a long time. "See you in a few hours," he said.

As they wheeled her into the OR, Carmen prayed, thought about the three people waiting for her, loving her. And for the first time in a while she felt blessed.

Carmen heard the voices, knew they were talking to her. It took a minute before she could get her eyes to open, a few seconds longer before she focused on the recovery room nurse, her flowered top. The procedure could have taken three minutes or two days, she couldn't tell how long she'd been out.

"How ya feelin'?" she asked.

"Like a mummy." Carmen was aware of the binding wrapped tightly around her chest. She slipped her right hand over her baby, feeling relieved, like the threat was gone, at least for now.

Two days later Carmen went home, drains still attached. She knew what they'd done, knew the steps—skin, fat, fascia, muscle, cut, sew—but her training hadn't prepared her for the hot diagonal swathe from her armpit to the center of her chest, the ache in her arm. Lonnie came by every day, Malcolm was in right after school, changed her bandages, emptied the drains. Regina came the nights she didn't have school and Jewell called at least twice a day for updates, showed up on the weekend loaded down with bags from Zabar's and Baby Gap.

The tumor was the size of a marble, and there were three lymph nodes involved. After more consultations with her pathologist and oncologist, they decided she would undergo both chemo and radiation right after she gave birth.

But Carmen didn't look at the incision for two weeks, until it was mostly healed. Holding Malcolm's hand she let her fingers trace the length of it without looking, then slowly opened her eyes. She thought it would look crueler. "It's not so bad," she whispered. But she was terrified of how it looked through his eyes.

Then Malcolm kissed her scar. "No, it's not."

It took Carmen longer than she expected to get back to work. The surgery made her tired, the pregnancy made her even more so. She had to strengthen her left arm. She wanted it all to go faster, but for once, it wasn't in her control. Her body called the shots and she had to follow. Malcolm didn't want her to go back at all, but she started slow, seeing just a few patients and work became like therapy. For at least part of the day, she could pretend her life was normal—make referrals, write prescriptions and give in to her pistachio ice cream cravings. Her coworkers kept her spirits up during the day. Malcolm, Regina and Jewell rallied her the rest of the time. That only left the nights she couldn't sleep to be alone with her thoughts. She worried they didn't get all the cancer. She worried the chemo and radiation wouldn't work. She worried the baby would be affected. But for all the tumult in the beginning, Carmen's pregnancy was relatively routine. She had some edema, a little heartburn. She and Malcolm took birthing classes. Baby Wyatt was active and nocturnal—but she didn't mind the kicks that bounced under her shirt. Sometimes Malcolm would watch "belly-vision," as he called it. "Football player," he would say. "Ballerina," she would counter.

Jewell supplied her with all variety of creams and lotions to minimize the stretch marks, but they weren't on Carmen's worry list. Regina called her growing stomach something new every time she saw her—Bud, Winifred, Sylvester, Etheljean. "You are definitely not on the name committee," Carmen told her.

Despite Malcolm's objections, Carmen was still working in her ninth month. "I see my doctor every day. Is there a better place to be?" In December Elly suggested a C-section to save Carmen the stress of labor, but she wouldn't have it. She wanted to feel every contraction, squeeze Malcolm's hand, breathe to the rhythm of his coaching. She'd had enough surgery for a while.

The first twinges did come at work, while she was going over the day's appointments. She knew it was too early for anything to happen so she kept the contractions to herself and actually saw four patients before she gave up, told Elly and called Malcolm to come and get her.

"You didn't have to come this soon," Carmen said when Regina burst into her room.

"Are you kidding?" Regina tweaked Carmen's foot which was poking out from the sheet. "And risk missing something?" She dumped her coat over the back of a chair. "Besides it got me out of work. Told 'em my sister was having a baby!" She pecked Malcolm on the cheek.

"That wasn't a lie," Malcolm laughed. "Your other sister should be here soon."

Carmen's contractions were two minutes apart and she had pretty nearly cut off the circulation in Malcolm's fingers by the time Jewell arrived. She and Regina stood sentry on Carmen's right side, taking turns with ice chips, a cool cloth for her forehead. Regina had an ample supply of smart remarks to keep everybody loose, but Jewell was too overwhelmed to talk much. She was so excited for Carmen and Malcolm, and she ached to see the baby, snuggle that hot little body in her arms. Then she'd hit a wave of sadness she'd have to ride out.

Coach Malcolm worked the left side, counting, breathing, panting, wishing he could do more.

For Carmen the pains were like a siren that started low, but swelled with intensity until they were shrill and deafening, almost unbearable, then they'd subside. She moaned, grunted, breathed, focused, whatever it took to get through the moment, because she knew it wouldn't last. More than anything she learned from practicing medicine, or Lamaze, Carmen relied on Lonnie's words about childbirth. "*It's the hardest pain to bear and the easiest to forget.*" And when Samuel Walker Wyatt made his appearance at 3:04 A.M. January 13, 1998, slippery and loud with a head full of curly hair and they laid his warm, whole, healthy body on her belly, Carmen knew exactly what Lonnie meant. Malcolm hovered at her side, down low, looking between her and Sam. Jewell and Regina, tears streaking their faces, hugged each other. Sam's little hands were balled tightly, one of them around Malcolm's finger. Carmen was sweaty, tired and happier than she'd ever been in her life. *It doesn't get any better than this.*

Two weeks later, Carmen held on to that as she sat hooked up to IVs for her first round of chemo.

27
"No need for sorry."

"My hair has started to go this time, Jewell. Eyebrows and pubes too. I find it in my clothes, in the crib. I feel like hell. Some days I don't even want to hold Sam. I hate this!"

It had been torture hearing Carmen say that from three thousand miles away. Now, baseball cap pulled low on her brow, ponytail tucked inside her collar, face hidden by enormous sunglasses, Jewell dashed through LaGuardia. She'd found that if she dressed down and moved like a steamroller, she had a better chance of getting through an airport unnoticed. Normally a week in LA was no big deal, but this trip had seemed endless because she was away from Sam, who in two short months had become the light of her life. From the moment she heard Carmen was pregnant, Jewell had known that this baby would hold a special place in her heart, and being a witness to his entrance into the world sealed the deal. She had been an empath that day, channeling Carmen's pains and contractions, knowing what each one felt like, glad that Carmen would not have to endure the hollow emptiness at the end of her labor for the rest of her life. Sam wasn't a replacement for the baby she never saw or held. He was Carmen and Malcolm's gift; she just got to share.

Head down, collar up, Jewell wheeled her carry-on briskly through the terminal. *What good did this little sojourn do? Nada, unless I count aggravation.* Jewell got plenty of that. It was pilot season, the time when actors are cast for the next crop of series, hoping to be picked up for prime time. The meetings Michael had set up with studios and producers turned into an endless string of trivial nonsense. The exact same trivial nonsense. Adrienne had been married and divorced twice, survived a kidnapping, a corporate raid, and a typhoon. Jewell was looking to stretch beyond the confines of *TIA*, and was in California on the hunt for more challenging work, but every exec she saw had her in mind to play—surprise—a larger than life, vengeful, manipulative bitch. It was like fighting her "I'm not Tonya Gifford" battle all over again, so she'd successfully gone from one straightjacket to another.

Jewell had actually walked out of one meeting with a producer who stretched back in his high-tech, ergonomically designed chair, put his feet on his chrome-and-smoked-glass desk and proudly told her that he could identify with her because he had grown up around black people, and learned many important lessons from his brothers in the "hood"—he'd actually said "hood"—like how to hold his liquor and how to fight. Then he stepped in it with both of his shiny, Ferragamo crocodile lace-ups when he told her he'd always liked black girls because he'd found them to be sexually advanced and naturally free. It had taken every ounce of her willpower not to snatch him by his ankles and bounce his head on the floor. Instead she got up, said "I've heard enough," and walked out, leaving him wondering what had gone wrong. Michael was apoplectic and apologetic. "I'll never do business with him again," but she knew that wasn't true. This was a small town and an even smaller business.

Even her phone conversation with Ted didn't calm her down after her mind-boggling meeting, but it gave her perspective. Jewell had come to respect his longevity in the business and now from time to time used him as a sounding board. He urged her not to let one pompous Hollywood Philistine make her lose sight of the reason for her trip. "Don't take it personally, Jewlee. They'll see you the way it's useful for them to see you. You have to take control. Give 'em something else to see."

Vivian knew the business too, and since the almost-wedding, their conversations had been much freer. She'd even owed up to her relationship with the now-divorcing Leonard. But Ted had a performer's perspective.

Getting to know her father had started out tentatively, testing the possibilities. They each realized right away that it couldn't be about recapturing what they'd lost—Jewell didn't need a daddy the way she did when she was six. But she'd learned more about him than she ever knew. Like he wasn't funny all the time; Ted was quieter than she expected. Jewell had stayed in his home outside of Las Vegas, the same bungalow he bought when he first started making a little money. And even though they talked on the phone often, he continued to write her letters—they were something she could hold onto, and now Jewell wrote back.

A blast of March hit Jewell head-on when the sliding doors opened. *Definitely not LA*. She clutched her jacket tight and trotted to short-term parking. It was more expensive, but the advantages—closer to the terminal, no bus ride "Aren't you…?" questions or autographs to sign—were definitely worth it. Usually she had a car pick her up, but since she was heading straight to see Carmen, she had driven herself.

No, a week wasn't a long time. Not unless your best friend had breast cancer. Not unless your best friend had a brand-new baby who was the joy of *your* life too. Not unless your best friend had started chemotherapy while you had been away. Then a week was a lifetime.

Can't wait to see Sam. She saw him right before she left, but Jewell had already seen how much he could change in two days, much less a whole week. She also worried how much Carmen had changed in that time. She'd talked to Regina and Malcolm and already knew it wasn't good.

Carmen held it together after the surgery which Jewell found amazing, since she got queasy just thinking about that scar. Carmen had shown it to her a few months after, in the dressing room when they were shopping for maternity clothes. It didn't look like it had been done with a chain saw or anything, in fact it was neat and tidy—an eyebrow-shaped tuck where once a neat and tidy breast had been. Jewell still couldn't forgive herself for doing such a poor job of hiding her distress. "You get used to it," Carmen said and Jewell felt awful.

Through the whole pregnancy Carmen never complained about anything. She just kept saying she was grateful they found the tumor. Grateful her little bundle was growing so well. She met every test that had been thrown her way, and passed, but her resolve seemed to dissolve after she got through the nine months and her treatments started. "I didn't feel like I was sick before," Carmen said one afternoon. "They sliced out the bad part, and I was done with it. Case closed. But the chemo is a constant reminder, 'You're not well Carmen. In fact, you could die.' Not a great way to start your day." And Jewell was worried because she knew there were a lot more treatments to come. Some days she felt totally helpless and it became hard to stomach her lines for Adrienne's vain and silly antics, hard to be patient about a lot of day-to-day trivia, because it just wasn't worth the time and energy. Not when someone's life was on the line. There was nothing Jewell wouldn't do for Carmen, but she couldn't take this away. The best she could do was help her carry it.

"How was LA?" Malcolm met Jewell at the door.

"Don't ask." Jewell never had a brother and Malcolm never had a sister, but like her, Regina and Carmen, they'd become family for each other. "How is she?" Jewell whispered.

"Rough day," Malcolm whispered back, shook his head.

"*She's* right here," Carmen called from the den. "You can ask her yourself."

"Sorry," Jewell stood in the doorway and tried to compose herself. Carmen sat in a corner of the couch, bundled in layers of silk, wool and fleece and wrapped in a white chenille afghan to combat her constant chill. Even from a distance Jewell could see that she was smaller, more fragile than she had been a week ago. "I thought you might be resting or something."

"Haven't been doing much 'or something' lately, unless that's slang for radiation."

Jewell made herself walk into the den. "When did that start?"

"Day before yesterday, I think. Sometimes I don't know what today is, but now I have a lovely road map drawn on my chest—in semipermanent ink, thank you very much—pointing to the danger zone. And a husband whose job it's become to route me to the proper medical facility at the proper time, kind of like hazardous materials cargo." Although Carmen's words were sharp, her voice was weak, watery.

"Ouch." Jewell felt her rancor even though she knew it wasn't directed at her.

"Told ya," Malcolm said to Jewell.

Jewell knew radiation treatments were coming. She hadn't expected them to start so soon.

"I'm making dinner. You stayin'?" Malcolm redirected the conversation. He'd been doing a lot of that lately. Especially when Carmen got too negative, predicting the worst that could happen, instead of hoping for the best. He couldn't allow himself to get down, afraid that if he did, neither one of them would get back up.

"What's on the menu?"

"Like it matters. You know you'll love it, no matter what I make." He cooked every day—just in case Carmen felt like eating. Sometimes she'd pick a little but her treatments didn't leave her with much appetite. "Besides, you just got back from the land of grilled baby everything. You could use some grown-up food." He headed for the kitchen. Since Malcolm and Jewell both liked to cook, they had a friendly, ongoing duel for culinary supremacy.

"Speaking of baby everything, how's our boy?" Jewell sat in the leather lounger across from Carmen. "I brought him a present." The day Sam was born she and Regina sent Carmen two dozen white roses along with a card that said "Thanks for *our* boy! Love, his aunties."

"He's great. Perfect really, and finally asleep. And you have to stop bringing him a gift every time." Carmen smiled for the first time since Jewell arrived.

But Jewell could see the strain. Carmen's smile looked too big for her face, her skin drawn too tight across her cheeks, around her lips. The circles that had been under her eyes when they first met, were back. And her hair—she had pulled it back into a thin ponytail, but Jewell could see scalp in spaces where hair should be. She remembered Carmen's scrawny ponytail from college and what it had taken for her to finally get her hair thick and healthy. She couldn't let herself go there. "But this is his first gift from California!" she said, sounding way too happy. Jewell got the foot-long stuffed palm tree from her tote. "And I know he doesn't have a tree yet."

"Now you know Regina will have to top this." The auntie competition had started the first time they saw Sam in Carmen's arms in the hospital. They mugged like fools, seeing who could make him grin first. Now Carmen danced the tree in the air a moment, then put it down, tired from the effort. "Jewell, I can't take this. I feel like a slug. We hired Lena because I can't even take care of my own son. I mean she's great but—" Carmen clouded up, tried to collect herself.

"Carmen, you can get through this—" Jewell had to believe she would.

"How do you know, huh?" Carmen snapped, tears escaping down her face. "I know doctors. Hey! I'm one of 'em. We speak with authority, give you prescriptions, make a prognosis. Five years is the magic number for cancer. If I make it that far, cancer free, I become an official survivor. But five years is a long time. And sometimes what doctors tell you is only to make you feel better because they don't know what else to say." Carmen caught her breath again, reached for Jewell's had. "Malcolm's not supposed to be my nursemaid. And Sam—he's so—I love him so much—he looks just like his daddy. Malcolm knew he was a boy—talked to him all the time before he was born." Carmen slipped in the shifting sand of her emotions and lost her balance. "I'm sorry—"

Jewell got up and sat beside Carmen on the couch. "No need for sorry."

They sat like that for a while, not talking, just being there. Then Carmen said, "You and Regina, you guys have to promise that if anything happens to me—"

"Nothing's happening to you—" Jewell rubbed Carmen's arm.

"You don't know that. I can't breast-feed my son because, hey—" She patted her chest. "I'm one tit short of a full tank. And I feel like poison. And sometimes I can't hold him as long as I want to. Look at me, Jewell! Something has already happened! You have to promise you'll tell him what he needs to know about me, because it's awful when you don't know your parents and—"

"I promise." Jewell had a jagged headache from holding back the tears. She walked to the window that overlooked the backyard. It was dark and she could only see her reflection and Carmen's—small and so far away. The image chilled her unexpectedly and tears welled up, but she kept staring outside until she sent them back to their source. "But you're gonna be around to tell him yourself, and some tasty tidbits about his aunties too."

"You guys want to eat in there?" Malcolm called from the kitchen.

"No we'll come to the table." Carmen got up, steadied herself. "Of course that's a guarantee Sam will wake up." Gingerly, she started toward the kitchen, Jewell beside her.

"That's 'cause he wants my cookin' and can't have any yet."

Sure enough Sam started crying during the salad. Jewell jumped at the chance to tend to him. "You two enjoy your dinner." She grabbed a bottle from the warmer in the kitchen and went to the nursery. Later, Malcolm came in to check on them, thought they were both asleep—Jewell in the blue plaid easy chair, Sam stretched out on her chest, his tiny fist clutching a handful of her hair. Malcolm turned to leave. "I'm awake," she whispered. "I just like the way he feels so I didn't want to move."

"I like it too. He looks so peaceful. No worries."

"Are you okay?" Jewell asked.

"Most of the time." He shoved his hands in his pockets, his shoulders more rounded than usual. "I won't tell you I don't get scared, and some days she is stone disagreeable, but mostly I try to have faith that Sam's mommy will see him grow up, and that he might even have a brother or a sister for company, ours or adopted, doesn't matter. We've got rooms full of love to share."

Jewell inched her way forward, handed Sam to his dad. "I better get out of here. Got an early call tomorrow." She stood up. "Is she still up?"

Malcolm nodded. "In the bedroom."

The door was ajar and Jewell saw Carmen standing in front of the mirror, turning her head, tilting it. "We have a great wig maker for the show. I could—"

"I can't have that conversation now." Carmen held up her hand.

"Okay. Get some rest. I'll see you in a couple of days."

"I know. Tomorrow's Regina's turn. She's taking me for radiation." Carmen sat on the edge of the bed. "You don't have to do this, you know. You're busy."

"Later for you. I'm coming to see Sam." Jewell stuck out her tongue and left.

Which wasn't entirely true, but holding him, feeling his warmth, smelling his milky sweetness sent Jewell home to make the call she'd been thinking about for years. She dialed Leonard's office—it was only six o'clock in Los Angeles and she knew any attorney worth his retainer was still at work. For the first time they talked about the adoption he helped Vivian arrange sixteen years ago. She needed to know if she had any options, any way to find out if her daughter was doing well, to let her know that her mother cared for her, would like to meet her if she wanted to.

Leonard told Jewell she could write a letter stating she was willing to be contacted and have it put in the child's adoption file. Once her daughter turned eighteen she could pursue it, if she was interested.

"You know more than that, Leonard."

"I did at the time. I don't anymore. They were good people, Jewell. Leave it at that."

"I have to do this."

It took many drafts before Jewell got down what she wanted to say. "*I never got to hold you, only heard you cry*," the letter began. "*And all this time I've held you in my heart, and wanted to know you were all right.*" She wondered which combination of her features and Billy's she had inherited. Jewell knew her daughter would not be eighteen for another two years, which still didn't mean she'd want anything to do with the woman who gave her life then gave her up. Jewell mailed the letter to Leonard, wishing there was more she could do, knowing she'd have to keep waiting, but it made her feel like she'd done something.

But there didn't seem to be anything she could do to help Carmen out of her blues. Some days she was tearful, others she was angry and shorttempered. Carmen felt trapped in the house, but neither Jewell nor Regina could get her to go anywhere except to her doctor's appointments and back. Whatever they suggested she had an answer for it. She'd fall asleep in the movies, she was too tired for walks, her skin was too sensitive for massages. "I don't feel like having people see me, all right?" Eventually all her hair fell out, down to the eyelashes. She wore a bandanna around the house. Jewell brought up the wig idea again, but she couldn't convince Carmen they didn't look fake. Regina and Jewell shopped for scarves and turbans, but none of them met with approval. "I look like Zenda the fortune-teller." Carmen couldn't concentrate on reading, didn't want to play games, "Because somebody always loses." She was even indifferent to Malcolm's cooking because at this point, she could only tolerate bland food and then in small doses. Warm applesauce, mashed potatoes and ginger ale had become staples. There hadn't been a shortage of laughs among the three of them since the very beginning, but Carmen seemed to have forgotten how.

"I thought you might not make it. This weather sucks." Regina ducked into Jewell's car two weeks later. "I know you orange blossom girls aren't used to driving in the snow."

"The weather is pretty bad. I passed a couple of accidents on the way. But do you realize I've lived in New York almost as long as I lived in California? Don't I get grandfathered or something?" Jewell pulled away from the curb and joined the clog of cars trying to escape downtown New Brunswick.

"Touché." Regina took off her gloves.

"We promised Malcolm we'd be there."

Malcolm coached the math league at his school and his kids were competing in a tournament in Cleveland. Regina and Jewell were spending the weekend with Carmen, having a pajama party, like the old days—almost.

"I could have done it. You didn't have to drive down here in this." Regina watched the snow collect on the windshield faster than the wipers could remove it.

"And let you have all the fun?" Jewell tossed the hair off her shoulder.

"Puh-leez! I just hate to see her like this. In a way, I know how she feels. It's awful when you're waiting to see if you're gonna make it. I wasn't the sunniest person." Regina played with the gloves in her lap. "I got a reprieve, a free pass. She didn't. You know she started out with more crap to deal with than most of us can imagine. Now this. It doesn't seem fair."

"Because it isn't," Jewell responded. "Sometimes life isn't fair."

Because of the weather, it took twice as long as usual to get to Carmen's. They stomped snow off their boots and left them on the porch. Malcolm had given Regina a key weeks ago, "Just in case," so she unlocked the door. "Yo Mama Carma!" Regina called as they came in the door. "Where's Sam I Am?"

"In here."

They found Carmen in the kitchen looking frazzled, Sam in one arm, a sponge mop in the other. "I kinda made a mess." Carmen's attempt to clean up the spill had only smeared the formula around the wood floor.

Jewell confiscated the mop. "Have a seat. I'll finish that."

"I can't seem to do anything right." Carmen looked exasperated.

"You did this baby boy exactly right. Come here to Auntie Gina."

"Auntie Gina? Where'd that come from?" Jewell asked.

"It's easier to say, and since he's going to say my name first—"

Jewell cleaned up the mess, then rustled up a light dinner. She and Regina did their best comedy routines, but their audience was mostly unresponsive.

The aunties tossed a coin to see who would go up and change Sam. Auntie Gina won—or lost, depending on how you looked at it. She brought him down fresh and clean and joined Carmen and Jewell in the den.

"Man, it's still coming down out there." She spoke with a hair elastic clenched in her teeth. Then she handed Sam off to his mother. "He decided I needed a new 'do while I was changing him."

"Hope he didn't add any extra ingredients." Jewell put her hair behind her shoulders.

"He went for the baby lotion, but I caught him in time."

A sad looked crossed Carmen's face. "For most of the time he's been around, I haven't had any hair for him to play with." She adjusted the blue bandanna she wore over her bald head. "I look like Yoda in a do-rag."

"What about a wig?" Regina asked.

"They look like hair hats," Carmen snapped.

"Not all of them. Some of them are great," Jewell said.

"No thanks. Then I'll just look like Yoda in a wig."

"They use amazing ones on the show. Custom-made. I bet you'd never guess who wears one and who doesn't. I told you before I could talk to our—"

Carmen shook her head. "I'll pass." She looked down, saw that Sam had dozed off. "Can one of you—"

"My turn." Jewell leapt to her feet. "You got the dirty diaper, I get the lullaby!" Jewell winked at Reg. Carmen kissed the top of Sam's fuzzy head and handed him to Jewell who carried her precious bundle up to the nursery.

Thirty minutes later, Jewell came back down.

"We were getting ready to send out search and rescue—" Regina turned around to find Jewell standing in the doorway and for once she had no words.

"He's been cranky at bedtime lately, did he give you a—Oh my God."

There was stunned silence. Carmen found her tongue first. "What did you do to your beautiful hair?!" She clamped her hands over her mouth.

Regina circled Jewell who tilted her head obligingly this way and that. "OH MY GOD!" Regina hollered. "THAT'S YOUR HEAD!"

From Tonya Gifford's perky pigtails, to Adrienne's seductive waves, Jewell always had a sheet of shiny, black hair, but it was gone, and her head, with a dimple at the top and two shades lighter than her face, was her crown and glory. "It's a little chilly, but it feels kinda free." She said it nonchalantly, smoothed her hand over her pate and ignored the sting of the cuts. "Of course your bathroom is a mess and I think Malcolm will need to replace his razor." She came into the room. Sat cross-legged on the floor. "Besides, Yoda needed company. You needed company."

Sam had drifted to sleep and Jewell stopped in the bathroom before she came downstairs. While washing her hands she saw Malcolm's razor on the counter and the impulse came over her before she could reason her way out of it. She had to let Carmen know there was time. Time to feel better. Time to play with Sam. Time to grow hair back. Jewell was so used to the weight of her curtain of her hair. Brushing it off her shoulder, flinging it out of her face. She found a pair of scissors first, and when she had whacked what she thought was enough, she started clumsily, spreading shaving cream on her forehead, not knowing where to make the first slice. She pressed too hard, nicked her scalp.

Tears rolled down Carmen's cheeks. "Why did you do that?"

Jewell knelt at her feet. "It's just hair, honey. A renewable resource." Jewell rested her arms on Carmen's knees. "Mine'll grow back, and so will yours once you stop the chemo. If you want hair now, we'll get you some. I'm sure first thing Monday I'll be ordering a replacement." She tilted her head, rubbed skulls with Carmen. "You won't go anywhere, or do anything—even on days you feel pretty good. I say tomorrow we go out for breakfast. Eggs and noggins, sunny-side up."

"But I'm so scared." Carmen rocked as she cried.

"I know," Jewell said. "Not the way you do, but I see you giving up, and that scares me."

Regina had crawled over to join them. "Jewell's right. It's like you're withering away, a little bit more, every time I see you."

Three heads together, arms entwined, they held each other. It took Regina to lighten the moment. "I mean, Carmen, you know I love you, and I like Mike as much as the next girl." She fluffed her flip, now auburn with copper highlights. "But you got two to do the clean-and-shine look without me."

When they finished laughing, Carmen looked at Jewell. "But what about work? You can't show up like that."

"They'll figure it out. Or they won't. If *TIA* doesn't like it, well—screw 'em!" She grinned at Regina. Jewell wasn't on Monday's schedule, but she wondered what would happen when she got to the set on Tuesday.

"I—don't know how I got so lucky. You two are the best—"

"Why yes we are!" Regina interrupted. "But so are you, Carmen." Regina scooted back on the couch. "And if you think she'll have a problem at *TIA*, wait till His Hairness finds out!"

And next morning after the storm had left a carpet of fluffy snow, they all bundled up, with hats especially for Carmen, Jewell and Sam, and while his mommy held him, his aunties showed Sam how to make snow angels.

"Fantasy sells detergent, fast food, feminine hygiene and diapers." Liz Cantor took a bite of her roast beef on rye as she sat in her office across the desk from Jewell on Monday.

"Show your audience you think they're smart. Don't you think viewers are tired of Adrienne's histrionics?" Jewell leaned forward, flipped hair over her shoulder. *Give them something else to see.* She remembered her father's advice. "She's totally predictable. Nobody's that one-dimensional. I'd like the chance to make her human for a change." The idea came to Jewell on her drive back into the city on Sunday afternoon. She made notes, collected her thoughts and her arguments. As director and head writer for *Through It All* Liz had been through it all with the show—good ratings, cast changes, network support, and fighting for their on-screen life. She was steadfastly opinionated and notoriously resistant to change, especially from actors, but Jewell decided her idea was worth a shot.

"It's melodramatic and maudlin." Liz put down her sandwich and peered at Jewell.

"It's heroic and it's real. What woman couldn't empathize with that kind of crisis? I mean, the threat of losing a breast, that's life or death. That hits home for women. Women who watch us. It's a way to show how terrifying it is, but that you can survive it. Now that's a triumph. And it opens other possibilities for Adrienne. She could have a change of heart—permanent, or temporary in which case she can survive to manipulate another day. Or she can die, friendless and alone." Jewell hadn't planned to add that part. It just came out. "I'm not saying the whole show should be gloom and doom. This is one arc, but I think there's some strong stuff here."

Liz bit into a half sour. "We'll see, Prescott."

"Well just between you and me, I've already shaved my head." Jewell peeled off her wig. "Whether Adrienne does or not is up to you. I just thought you should know—in case you need to fire me."

The next week, Regina took Carmen into the city to meet Jewell and the wig maker. They picked out a short sassy style with wispy bangs that made Carmen look spunky. And by Carmen's last chemo treatment, Adrienne Berrard had just been diagnosed.

28
"…once-in-a-life timing…"

"And our next nominee for outstanding lead actress in a drama series is—Jewell Prescott, *Through It All*." Jewell's face, partly veiled by a curtain of hair from her now chin-length bob, remained serene during her close-up.

Adrienne had survived, and while her bout with cancer humbled her temporarily, it later bolstered her determination to win at whatever cost. The audience viewed a clip in which the character, weak and bald from her treatments, finally unsheathes one of the mirrors she has had covered and confronts herself and the fear of death she's been denying.

Jewell remembered shooting the scene. It had taken her all day to prepare because she needed to do it in as few takes as possible. Carmen's experiences—her fear, anger, sadness, her feeling of being powerless over the disease that had altered her body, and could threaten her life—had been fresh below the surface. And right next to Carmen's crucible, Jewell found Regina and Milton waiting to pull her deeper. So as an actor, she allowed what she had witnessed to lead her to her own fears and she channeled those emotions through Adrienne.

The audience applauded as the lights came up and Carmen, Jewell's date for the evening, squeezed Jewell's hand. Carmen too had survived, through her chemo and radiation, to be cancer free for more than a year. She would continue to be monitored regularly, but in September, three months after her last treatment, she returned to work, sporting her own short, snazzy hair and by Sam's first birthday he was starting to walk and Carmen was back on her feet.

"And the Emmy goes to—"

Jewell didn't hear her name. While the other nominees were being announced she'd gotten lost in recollections of the last year, of her first commercial as a child, of her success as Tonya and the personal journey that had brought her to this seat on this night.

"You won! You won Jewell!" Carmen yanked her to her feet, enveloped her in a hug.

Jewell could almost have heard Regina screaming above the tumult at the *TIA* party across town at Tatou, where she, Vivian, Malcolm, Michael and those who did not fit in the arena waited to celebrate. "I knew she would win! I hope she doesn't have lipstick on her teeth!"

Jewell didn't remember the walk. Carmen had pushed her toward the aisle. The stage lights bouncing off the paillettes of Jewell's vermillion, knee-length dress, sent brilliant shards of light dancing around her that made her dizzy, or maybe it was the moment that had her so off kilter.

Jewell held the statuette and beamed. She hadn't expected to win but she had prepared a "what if" speech. It was only those words, lodged in her brain, that allowed her to speak now. "I thank Liz Cantor for giving Adrienne this incredibly important story and for giving me the words to bring it alive." Jewell paused. "By struggling with breast cancer, a disease fought by millions of women, Adrienne Berrard learned a lesson I learned from my friends a while ago—none of us are in this alone. It's an empty life without the love and support of our friends and families. I thank my mother Vivian Prescott for guiding and protecting me in my career, my father Ted Hampton for the advice he gives me now. I am grateful to the people who started with me in my *Daddy's Girl* days—Michael you're the best; Leonard, what would I do without you?" Jewell looked directly into the camera. "Regina, you were my first best friend. Thanks for choosing *me* to be yours." Then she looked into the third row of the audience. "And I most want to thank my other best friend and sister of my heart, my inspiration—not only for Adrienne's ordeal, but for how to build a life on strength, dignity and love no matter how much or little you start with, Dr. Carmen Webb, who is now one year cancer free." Cameras found Carmen, tears streaming down her cheeks. "I admire you. I love you. Thank you for being my friend."

Jewell's Best Actress win had been a surprise, a brilliant night, a blur of congratulations, but the Emmy hadn't given her the legs she'd hoped would carry her to the next stage in her career. She'd done a TV movie, playing the self-indulgent wife of a small-town police chief who leaves him in the first half hour—which turns out to be his salvation. She'd portrayed a ball-busting defense attorney in a nighttime drama, but, nothing really memorable or challenging had crossed her path. So she and Michael remained on the lookout for projects.

And *Fly Girl* was still on her bookshelf, right behind her Emmy. After all these years, she still loved the story of the first American woman to hold a commercial aviation license. Jewell actually felt she was at a better age to play the part, and that somehow she was supposed to get Bessie's story told. And then she would hear Ted's advice, almost see it scrolling across her mind like a news crawl, "*Give 'em something else to see.*" Jewell would get all wound up, spin her wheels, then come to a screeching halt because the road to Bessie also led to Billy and she still didn't know what to do about that.

Later that Emmy spring, Regina finally took her walk down the aisle—in cap and gown—and received her degree in business administration, with Jewell, Carmen, Malcolm, Sam and her whole family there to cheer. But after fielding job offers, she still wasn't ready to be shackled to her very own desk, in her very own cubicle, so she continued temping—now with medical coverage. "While I work out my business plan. I just have to figure out what business," she said.

And by the end of Carmen's second cancer-free year, Malcolm started work on his Ph.D. in applied and computational mathematics. Carmen was happily back at work and along with Sandrine and her other partners, planning to expand their practice to include geriatrics and a nutritionist. Sam was growing like a weed and had left the terrible twos and entered the trying threes at warp speed.

"It was the two weeks Adrienne spent trapped in the pyramid on her trip to Giza that sent me over the edge. You remember the mummies and the talking hieroglyphs?" Jewell, Carmen and Regina sat on a bench in Central Park on an overcast May Sunday. Three-year-old Sam, exhausted from feeding the pigeons, or more accurately chasing them, snoozed in his stroller, head lolled to one side. Carmen wanted him to be as comfortable in the city as he was in his quiet suburban neighborhood, so Sam's twice-monthly visit to Auntie Jew-ey and "her birds"—in his mind they were pets—became a good reason for them to get together. Free Saturdays were a rarity, but today they'd hit the jackpot and all three of them were available. "I have to try and keep from laughing in our story meetings. Except I keep looking for material and I end up back at *Fly Girl*."

Carmen brushed a stray graham cracker crumb from Sam's cheek. "You've been in love with Bessie's story since we were in school." By now, she and even Regina knew all about the "feisty aviatrix" as Jewell called her—the tenth of thirteen children from Atlanta, Texas, who found the courage to go to France and learn to fly when her efforts were thwarted at home. "So why don't you try it? Either Billy will be interested or he won't but you won't know unless you talk to him."

"And the real deal is *Fly Girl* or not, you need to call him." Regina crossed her legs. "Don't you think he has the right to know he has a daughter walking around on the planet?"

"Yeah, but—"

"But—you've been sitting on yours way to long." Regina cut her off at the pass. "Call him up, see how it goes with the daughter thing and you'll figure out if he's worth talking to. I mean, I'd work with Ty again in a heartbeat. He probably feels like I'm the plague and who could blame him? But if you still want Billy's script you need to find out if you can work together. If you can, go for it. Otherwise, bury the damn thing and look for another bone."

"Regina," Carmen gave her a warning glance.

"Oh come on. He'll hear worse than 'damn' in kindergarten."

"It's really starting to look like rain." Carmen examined the sky. "We should go before—"

"Wait a sec," Regina interrupted. "I've got some news."

"And you waited until it's ready to pour? We've been here for hours," Carmen complained.

Regina ignored her. "I was gonna wait, see how it worked out, but you know I'm lousy with secrets." She smiled mysteriously. "I'm back! Or more accurately RF Productions is back—sort of—I'm doing a wedding. I don't even know how this is gonna work out, considering the last one I handled." Regina winked at Jewell. "It's nothing huge, a hundred guests, reception at a new hotel in Bridgewater, small bridal party, but I'm having fun."

"That *is* news," Jewell said. "Somebody you know?"

"A girl from one of my temp jobs. Her mom died when she was little and she and her dad were lost in the 'I do' details. The more I listened, the more I realized I could whip this thing into shape without breathing hard. She enjoys being a bride and I can get my feet wet again with no overhead. All I need is a phone and a bank account, the way I started." Regina folded her arms across her chest. "So I dazzled her with the clubs where I used to promote parties in the city, dropped a few names. I knew she was a big soap fan, so I capped off my soft sell by telling her I had been the planner for Jewell Prescott's 'Wedding that Wasn't.'" Regina laughed. "That wrapped it up in a basket and closed the deal. Of course, I'm not giving up my temp career yet!"

"That's great Reg," Jewell said. "How does it feel?"

"So far so good. Ask me again after this little extravaganza!"

Thunder rumbled in the distance. "We better head back," Carmen said. "I hate schlepping the stroller in bad weather. All the muck on the street, stuff I never noticed before, it seems too close to Sam." She relied the red laces of his little desert boots. "And traffic will be—well, you know what it will be."

"Ah! But you have me to keep you company!" Regina started to put Sam's toys and snacks back in the carryall.

"And between you and Sam, by exit thirteen I'll want to get out and walk home. You should hear them," Carmen said to Jewell. "They name every car, truck, pole, bird, sign, fence—every single thing we pass. Drives me crazy."

"You love it!" Jewell exclaimed. "Didn't you say you were talking about doing it again?"

"Excuse me?" Regina looked from Jewell to Carmen. "Another baby?"

"We're *thinking* about adoption. I've still got two years before I hit the golden mark."

"Excellent. Have a big ol' family. Takes the pressure off me." Regina got up. "Keith's bachelorhood has no foreseeable end. Michael and AJ's kids are far away. Mom and Daddy have taken to being Sam's Auntie Gramma and Uncle Grampa, like those duckies over there in the water—pretty much the same way they adopted you, kiddo." She poked Carmen in the arm. "I say you and Malcolm keep 'em busy and not worrying about me and my eggs."

"They'll always worry about you, with or without your eggs." Carmen smiled at her.

"I understand it's in the parent handbook," Jewell added.

In front of her building Jewell waved good-bye to Carmen, Regina and Sam, and didn't stop waving until they turned the corner toward the garage on West 72nd Street. Carmen told her that one time after they left, Sam had looked back, didn't seen Auntie Jew-ey standing there and he cried all the way home. Since then Jewell wouldn't go in until they were out of sight.

The moment she got upstairs, Jewell called Michael on his cell phone. She didn't know where he was or what he might be doing, but she was afraid that if she waited until Monday, she'd lose her nerve. Regina was starting over, Carmen was expanding her practice and planning to expand her family. Everyone was moving ahead, changing, making progress, except her and she had to do something about it.

Michael sounded groggy when he answered, but Jewell didn't ask why, she just plowed ahead. "You sent me on an audition for this years ago. I don't know who his representation is, or if he's working as Billy Roland or William Christensen, but I need you to find his agent and see if we can option this screenplay. And I need a meeting with him before we finalize anything." Michael was obviously curious, but she wouldn't tell him why.

Jewell waited until Monday to put in a call to Leonard. She told him about *Fly Girl* and her efforts to talk to the writer. And finally, after all these years, she told him about Billy so Leonard would understand why there were more than the ususal roadblocks in the way.

"It's never simple with you, is it Jewell?" Leonard said.

"If it was I wouldn't need a lawyer, would I?" They both had to laugh at that. "I won't know if this is even possible until I talk with him. But if it's a go, I'm producing, which is likely to meet resistance. If not from Billy, then from somebody else. But that's what I want. I've had this project rattling around in my head for more than ten years. I've got ideas about a director, the cast and I want to put together a package." When Jewell hung up, she felt exhilarated. She had taken charge of what *she* wanted to do with her future. But after the initial euphoria her courage began to wither. Every time she answered the phone or checked her messages she was nervous. Could she really talk to Billy, like the adults they were now? Could she tell him the truth? All of it? What would he say? Would it matter? What was more important—their girl or *Fly Girl?*

Jewell desperately wanted to bring Ted into the loop, to ask his advice, but she decided it wouldn't be fair to tell Ted about his grandchild before she told Billy. The following Thursday, after a long, frustrating day on the *TIA* set, she got home, headed directly to the shower. The phone was ringing when she stepped out.

"Jewell?"

With just one word, she recognized Billy's voice. Jewell took a deep breath, hoped it wasn't audible and wished she wasn't wet and half naked for this conversation. She clutched her terry cloth robe around her, tightened the belt, even though she knew exposure was inevitable. They couldn't move ahead without it. "You've obviously heard from Michael Stander so you know I'm interested in *Fly Girl.*"

"Took you a long time to make up your mind," Billy quipped, a tinge of his Danish accent still there.

Jewell heard him smiling. Saw his eyes sparkle. But she ignored his humor and started her climb to the high board. She had to, before she thought too much about how scary the dive was. "There are a few things I need to clear up if we're even going to consider working together—and we need to talk about them in person. Are you in LA?"

"Just got back from a project in Costa Rica, but I'm around for a while. You want me to come to New York?"

"No. I can be there tomorrow evening. Dinner?" She needed to control as much of this encounter as she could, for as long as she could, because once she told Billy the truth she didn't know what would happen.

"Sure."

They agreed to meet at 8:30 and Jewell made reservations at a posh French-Russian restaurant in West Hollywood. She waited at the table, sitting in the chair rather than the banquette. She wanted an easy escape, just in case.

She didn't want to watch him walk in, watch heads turn as he strode through the room, and most of all she didn't want him to see her waiting, looking as anxious as she was. So she sat with her back to the entrance, staring at an ornate samovar across the room, half listening to the balalaika playing in the background, and trying not to feel like there were ants crawling up her spine. Then she felt a disturbance, the vibration in the room changed and she knew Billy had arrived. She took a deep breath, held on to the edge of the table to keep herself grounded.

"*Dasvidanya.*" Billy's long hair was gone, now just a dusting of fuzz covered his head. As always he seemed completely unaware of the effect he had on people. When they were together in New Orleans, she used to tease him about it. He just laughed it off. "I think that means hello, or good-bye. In any case it's the only Russian I know." He was as arrestingly handsome as ever in his tan leather blazer and black silk slacks, just a bit more weathered—more patina, less shine. He stood there, hesitant about what came next, like he was waiting for instructions.

"Sit. Please. This isn't the principal's office." Jewell noted there was still a gold band on his left hand.

"Not at any school I ever went to." He smiled, sat down. His amber eyes danced, crinkled at the corners as he took her in. "You look as beautiful as always, Jewell."

The purpose of this dinner, this meeting, was not to rekindle an old flame, so Jewell was deliberately understated in her choice of clothing—black dress, pumps, small gold hoops and her hair now fell softly to her shoulders. "Thank you." She tried to sound cool, formal. She didn't want to feel the warm tingle his compliment generated, didn't want to believe he could still affect her that way, not after all these years.

Fortunately their tunic-clad waiter appeared, giving Jewell a moment to regain her composure while they ordered drinks. "I want to do *Fly Girl*," Jewell began. "You already know that and I'm sure Michael and your agent can work out terms that will be agreeable to both of us—but we've got some old business we need to clear up."

"I know about our old business, Jewell," he said softy. "Do you think I don't remember? And if I could change what happened—"

"Please, just let me say this." She inched her way to the end of the diving board. "It's not fair for me, for you, for the project—to try and go forward without addressing this."

"You're talking in riddles, Jewell. I assume 'this' that we need to address doesn't refer to rewrites or special clauses." Billy had been writing and directing documentaries, mostly for public TV and cable. He had found it less irrational than trying to predict the next culture craze a studio might want to finance. When his agent called with Jewell's request, Billy had to dig *Fly Girl* out of the archives. He'd decided long ago that the script, like everything about his relationship with Jewell, had been an exercise in wishing on stars and had forced himself to choose more earthly pursuits. Billy put his hands on the table, as if he was showing her he wasn't hiding anything, he had no tricks up his sleeve. "I know we have history and I know I didn't handle things very well."

Jewell looked at his hands, immediately embarrassed that she could remember exactly how they had felt on her skin. "There's something you need to know before you consider my offer." Jewell paused. *Get on with it.* "Probably before we eat dinner. Food's great here and I'd hate to ruin your meal." She smiled nervously. *Why didn't I do this on the phone?* But it was too late for a dial tone or a hang-up and she was bouncing on the end of the high board now, so she held her breath and dove. "I had a baby, Billy. We had a baby." The clatter and chatter of the room fell away and they were alone in a place only they knew about—alone like they had been in Billy's room in New Orleans—plus one.

Billy looked like he'd sucked down a room full of bad air. "That story was true?" The waiter returned with Jewell's sparkling water, Billy's martini. They each took a drink, Jewell to wet the desert that had taken over her mouth, Billy to fortify himself for what came next.

"I never saw her, I don't know where she is, and no one knows you're her father. I wasn't planning to tell you, ever. But over the past few years I've gotten to know my father and I learned some things about him I should have always known—my mother just didn't think so." Jewell paused. "That's another story. Anyway, I've also got a nephew—my friend Carmen's son, and I've been watching him grow, watching his parents love him. And I decided you had a right to know you have a daughter." Billy sat in silence as Jewell told him the story, including the letter she'd written for her adoption file. The waiter stopped by several times, but they ignored him and he was too polite to interrupt. "You can choose to do the same, or not. You can discuss this with your wife, or not. You can speak to me again, or not."

"Why didn't you tell me before—when you wrote?"

"So you could do what? Come get me on your bike and ride us off into a life of bliss? Besides, I decided you didn't care, and whether you did or not, looking back it was probably for the best." The words came hard, especially since she wasn't convinced she believed them.

"I did care. That's why I left you alone. Oh, my God." He propped his elbows on the table, closed his eyes, ran his hands over his head.

"When you showed up at that casting, I felt like I'd been ambushed. I had to get out of there. It was too soon for me to see you." *And too late*. Or maybe it was just that they had bad timing, or once-in-a-life timing, like a comet that passes the earth every million years. It's brilliant, dazzling, unforgettable, but if you don't catch that one time, there's no second chance.

"Ambushed pretty much describes how I feel right now." Billy opened his eyes.

The dazzle was gone and in its place Jewell could see dismay. "That wasn't my intention, Billy. I didn't know a good way to do this." She thought a public place would make it easier for both of them—that and she didn't want to be alone with him. "Because I don't think there is one. Do you have children?" She wasn't sure why she asked, but of all the thoughts ricocheting through her head, that's the one that came out.

Billy nodded. "Two," he said quietly. "Listen, I don't think I can stay for dinner."

"I understand." Jewell glanced away. The blend of sadness and regret was too potent.

"I'm glad you told me. I'm glad I know." He put his hand over hers. "I need to think."

Jewell wanted to turn her hand over, touch his—palm to palm, fingertip to fingertip, but she fought the urge and before the sensation overwhelmed her, he moved it. "I'll go," she said.

"I'm supposed to say I'm sorry, and I am. For what that must have been like—by yourself. In another way I'm not sorry—"

Jewell pushed her chair away from the table. "I just wish I could see her."

"So do I." He didn't get up. "I'll call you."

Jewell left the restaurant, got into her rental car and drove four hours to Las Vegas. She started to call her mother, but this was a subject they had visited more times than she could count. Jewell needed a new view.

Ted came offstage and found her waiting in his dressing room. "Jewlee, this is some kinda surprise." Sweat glistened on his forehead, his damp silk shirt clung to his chest. "They made me earn my check tonight." He went into the bathroom, came back with a gray velour robe over his pants, swabbing his face and neck with a towel. "To what do I owe this monumental pleasure?"

"I should have called, but—I needed—"

"Whatever it is you needed, Jewlee Dew, I'm glad you came. If you're in a hurry we can talk here. Or you can come out to the house. I'm done for the night, so it's up to you."

"I'm supposed to go back tomorrow. Out of LAX." She had managed to get Liz to shoot around her scenes for two days claiming a family emergency, which in some ways it was. "But yes, going home with you will be great."

Jewell was quiet on the ride and Ted didn't press. They got out of the car in his driveway and she looked up at the inky velvet sky. "Can we stay out here a while?" The night hadn't grown too cool so they sat by the pool, under a canopy of stars, and Jewell told her story to the other man who needed to know.

"You did the right thing. You gave him a gift he didn't know he had. What he does with it…?" Ted shrugged. "You can't judge him either way. He has a family, so this won't be easy news for him to take home—and he may choose not to. But to deny him the knowledge of his daughter, to eliminate the possibility of a future relationship, the same one that exists for you, no matter how remote, would be wrong. If she ever found you and asked about her father, do you want to tell her she didn't exist for him?" Ted looked at Jewell who had no answer. "One of the things that kept me going when I couldn't see you, Jewlee, was knowing I could keep loving you, even if I never saw you again—except on TV." He smiled. "The sad part was I didn't think you'd ever know."

Jewell spent the night in the guest room, her father down the hall. She slept like a baby. On the drive back to her car the next morning he tried to convince her to change her flight, leave from there, but Jewell wanted the drive. Since she had first gotten her license, she'd enjoyed her time alone in the car. Thinking time. She didn't get much of that in New York. "I'll be fine, Dad." It spilled out as if she'd just said it yesterday.

Ted noticed, but didn't comment. "I may not have been there when you were a child, but I'm honored to be around the woman you've become. Your mother did a fine job. You can even tell her I said so." He laughed, tipped the valet who brought her car around and waved her off.

Jewell drove back the way she came, wondering if she'd ever get the chance to tell her daughter she'd always loved her, the way her father had. Wondering if she'd set off a time bomb in Billy's life, which was not her intention, but convinced she had no choice.

"Are you sure no messages came for me?" Jewell asked as she checked out of the hotel. She hoped Billy had called—to say thanks for telling me about our daughter? To say let's make the movie? To say I still love you? She knew it was all ridiculous. But wasn't hope mostly built on wish and folly?

29
"...tempting the Fates."

"*Fly Girl* is yours."

By day ten, Jewell had written *Fly Girl* off as a no go, and was even starting to feel relieved, making plans for the official script burial, as Regina had suggested, perhaps at sea. Billy would go on with his life and she would do the same. The idea of them trying to work together was as preposterous as the notion that they would find their daughter one day, or she would find them and they'd—It was time to move on. But when Michael called her at *TIA* with Billy's answer, Jewell was thrilled. She didn't share the news on the set because she wasn't ready for anyone at the show to know what she was up to until she had enough of the pieces together to shop the project to studios. At that point it would be impossible to keep the secret. The industry grapevine was as swift and indiscriminate as lightning; Liz Cantor, the *TIA* producers and the network would know she'd taken a meeting, with whom, and how long it had lasted before she'd get to argue over who would pay the lunch check.

Full of energy and excited by what lay ahead, Jewell walked home from work making mental lists, savoring this opportunity. She had asked for what she wanted, and got it. Now she was determined to make *Fly Girl* into the kind of movie she'd be proud of. She had a six-month option at a price she thought was fair, to develop the project and find it a home. Michael tried to talk her out of spending her own money for the rights. "Movies get made with OPM," he warned—other people's money. Leonard said the same thing. "I plan to get some of that too," she countered. But right now, this project was *hers*, it felt good spending *her* money and within a week, Fifth Dimension Productions was a legal entity. *Jewell Prescott, Executive Producer. A Jewell Prescott Production of a Fifth Dimension Film.* She liked the way it sounded, but she also knew how much work those titles involved. Jewell hired two eager film students to man and woman phones and messengers in the two-room furnished office she'd leased month to month. Michael and Leonard cautioned her about taking on a screenplay that had been knocking around unproduced, for so long. "That's because nobody has seen it the right way," Jewell told them.

Regina congratulated Jewell on her entrepreneurial spirit. "See? That's my philosophy. Find your spot and call the shots. And remember your friend when you're planning the premiere. Man! What I could do with the Fifth Dimension theme." Carmen was excited too, but worried as well. "What about working with Billy?" she asked.

Jewell had come to professional terms, but personal matters were still unresolved. "Don't know." She wondered if Billy had digested the news about their daughter, found a place for it, but his feelings weren't a priority. "He'll be on set for rewrites, and I'm likely to have more interaction with him as a producer than as an actor, but I'll cross that bridge after I get a green light."

Fly Girl had been put in development twice, but for one reason or another, it never made it to production. Jewell felt like Bessie had been waiting for her to tell the story. This was Jewell's vehicle and she planned to drive it all the way to the finish line. She planned to bypass the feature-film route and focus on TV and cable—it's what she knew, where she had the most contacts. It was also where her audience was. Michael's agency represented a full spectrum of creative talent, including actors and directors and he started sending Jewell tapes of people he thought might be right for the project. Jewell thought about calling Oliver Oakes since he'd been there at the beginning, but decided his lyrical sepia-toned long shots no longer fit in with the vision she now had for Bessie's story. Jewell wanted to tell the historical drama like the fast-paced action adventure Bessie's life had been.

As soon as Jewell signed the contracts from Leonard, it was like somebody flipped a switch, turned on the power. She sent scripts to two of the directors on Michael's list of possibilities, both from the music video world. Their work was sharp, edgy, and they were ripe for a transition to movies. She made a call to a former *TIA* costar who had made the leap to features and had sworn he'd love to work with her again and arranged to get him the material.

Within a month Jewell had her male lead and a commitment from Julian Wright to direct—enough to begin scheduling meetings with network bigwigs, so she broke the news to her *TIA* senior producer. "So you think the grass is greener on the other side of the set?" *What's that supposed to mean?* But it didn't matter—it was in Jewell's contract that she could take time off for other projects. *As Regina would say, screw 'em*. The reaction around the TIA set was mixed. Some of her fellow actors thought it was great, wanted to know how she'd done it and if there was a part for them, others resented her initiative. Much to Jewell's surprise, Liz Cantor was supportive. "You're ready for this. If you need to talk, I'm here."

Jewell had never done a pitch, so before she headed west Michael gave her the drill. "You've got ten minutes, tops. If they're not sold in the first ninety seconds, you're leftovers. Hit the high points, keep it simple. Expect a lot of 'Great to see you, Jewell.' 'Imagine little Jewell Prescott, producing a movie.' 'I've got a film coming up next year you might be interested in.' All of which will be followed by 'I'll run it by my team, get coverage on it and get back to you.' They won't be patronizing but they won't be encouraging either. It's ninety percent BS, but all you need is one bite."

Jewell got a nibble on her fifth meeting. Lois Taylor, a honcho at SRO, a cable network that featured a mix of theatrical release films and their own original productions, was with Jewell from the start of her pitch. "I love it! A female adventure hero who goes from mild-mannered manicurist to international aviator, with a secret husband, powerful admirers, dramatic death, triumphant life! And she's black. Where has this been? It's perfect for February."

At least she's up front. Jewell knew that finding Black History Month programming was the motivation for a lot of movies that otherwise wouldn't get made, but if it brought Bessie to the screen, so be it. Fortunately for her and the project, if it was a go this needed to happen quickly. It was already July so they'd need to be shooting by September to be ready for February airing. A plus in her favor was that Julian Wright thought the screenplay was in relatively good shape. There would need to be some changes to reflect the cable-sized budget, but they wouldn't be difficult, so *Fly Girl* got fast-tracked and Jewell, who had resisted getting a cell phone because she didn't want to be that available, suddenly found one growing out of her ear. She discussed contract points with Leonard and there was lots of crossing out and amending. Her newly acquired laptop also became a constant companion, and her *TIA* dressing room was her office outpost. But after what seemed nonstop negotiating, she had a deal.

Then Jewell's life really got hectic. Normally, when Adrienne was in a featured storyline, Jewell's shooting schedule was four days a week. Fortunately Adrienne's life was currently relegated to back story while J.C. Billings plotted a prison break to free his wrongly imprisoned grandson, which gave Jewell more flexibility to her days. They'd be shooting *Fly Girl* for four weeks in September, so the *TIA* writers had lead time to power down her role even further.

The project was assigned a line producer, the SRO on-site bean counter, to avoid overruns. Jewell shot up to Toronto with Julian, the set designer, the line producer and the location scout. It was cheaper to shoot in Canada where they could easily replicate locales from Chicago and Paris to

Waxahachie, Texas. Jewell wanted to take flying lessons, but the insurance company wouldn't allow it, so she got tutorials on a PT-17 Kaydet, a 1940's biplane, mocked up to look like Bessie's Curtiss JN-4, a "Jenny" as it was called. Jewell was surprised by how vulnerable and flimsy the little plane felt and folding her six-foot frame into the tiny open cockpit was a challenge, one the 5′2″ Bessie wouldn't have had, but with film magic they could make the height difference work. Jewell had been shrunk before to accommodate a costar. This time it was an airplane.

The more the pace quickened, the more energized Jewell became. She always enjoyed being on location. Away from the routines of their everyday lives, the cast and crew became their own universe, where the day could start at midnight or it could be winter in summer. And this time Jewell was the lead, the central character, the one who had to make this movie work, but she was ready, she knew her part, she knew Bessie. Jewell received new sides, revisions Billy had done, reflecting the director's input and the switch from big to small screen via FedEx, but she still hadn't seen or spoken to Billy since May in LA.

At the end of August Jewell had her final fittings for her flight suit, leather bomber jacket and other 1920's attire. Between *Fly Girl* and *TIA* she had been swamped and hadn't seen much of her Jersey family, so before she left for a month in Toronto, Jewell swung down for a visit. She brought Sam a toy biplane and he got a kick out of taking off and landing all over the house, complete with sound effects, until Carmen sent him out to the yard. Malcolm cooked, Al baked a cake with sky blue frosting, that read UP, UP AND AWAY in white icing. Carmen and Regina presented Jewell with a red director's chair that said, BIJOUX across the back.

"Guess you were really serious about flying solo," Regina said.

"Aren't you scared?" asked Carmen as they sat outside on the porch. "I mean those planes look so—so risky. And doesn't she fall out of it at the end?"

"Do you think they'd let her anywhere near the real plane?" Regina cracked.

"My stunt double will do most of that. I've got a few scenes where they take me up and I look like I'm flying, but believe me, somebody else is at the controls."

"Well you be careful anyway. Sam needs his auntie."

"Or one with some sense." Jewell laughed.

"Funny." Regina stuck out her tongue.

Billy was sprawled in a leather cube chair in the lobby lounge of the hotel conferring with Julian when Jewell arrived. And whatever he was saying to the director, Billy was adamant. As she watched him gesture, emphasizing his point, she could feel his intensity and she got the familiar jolt that melted into a warm flutter in her stomach. Until then, she had been so buried in production details and so deep in denial, that she hadn't allowed herself to consider how difficult it might be to see Billy almost daily—to be on location with him, like the first time. Before she could rationalize her way out of her gut reaction, Billy was standing beside her.

"Hey." The greeting was subdued, very un-Billy. "Can we talk after you check in?"

She forced herself to breathe normally. "Sure." In five minutes she was back in the lobby.

"There's a coffee shop around the corner. It's a little more private," Billy said.

They walked this time, no motorcycles, no arms wrapped around waists, no flying.

Billy got to the point as soon as they sat down. "I'd like to know how to send the letter—for her adoption file, just in case."

Jewell wanted to ask him what he felt. Why he'd made that decision and not the other one, if he'd discussed it with his wife, his kids? Were they girls, boys or both? So many questions she wanted to ask. She didn't because they were none of her business, but this was. Their daughter was her business. Jewell cleared her throat, dug in her bag for a pen and paper, wrote down Leonard's information. "He's my lawyer. Send him your letter, he'll get it where it needs to go."

"Do you ever wonder what she looks like?" Billy asked quietly.

"I used to, every day." Jewell paused, leaned back in the booth. "I'd see a girl I thought was her age and wonder how tall she was or if she had pigtails or your amber eyes, but I don't do that so much anymore. Now I just want to know if she's well—happy, having a nice life."

"I've been trying to imagine a daughter, I know she's almost twenty, except in my head she's still a little girl." Billy stirred too much sugar in his coffee.

He always had coffee with his sugar—and beignets at dawn. "Did your family come?" Jewell had to bring the conversation back to the present, too much rummaging around in the past wouldn't be good for either of them.

Billy shook his head. "Never do. I travel all the time, but Beth hates it. She's not—"

"I need to get back." *I don't want to hear about your wife—your marriage—good or bad. I don't want to know about the kids' grades or favorite sports*. She eased to the end of the bench.

Billy reached for her arm. "Listen Jewell, I wasn't going to give you a sob story about how my wife doesn't understand me or some other pathetic tale. That's not me—and I would never do that to you. You deserve better than that from me—from anyone."

"And I wasn't snooping." *I wasn't, was I?* "It's not that I don't care about your life Billy—"

"Let's just leave it alone. Deal?" He left a five on the table, got up, waited for her.

Jewell felt strange walking into the hotel lobby with him. There were clusters of crew at the front desk and in the bar. She felt guilty, like people must know. *Know what? That we were together almost twenty years ago?* No one knew anything except, if they even remembered, that her involvement with somebody had become a tabloid story. There was no reason for anyone to think Billy was more to her than the screenwriter. "See you tomorrow." Jewell left him and went to her room, tired of seesawing between then and now.

Until shooting started Jewell kept busy going over her lines, putting up the pictures of Bessie with her plane, of the White Sox Barber Shop where she worked as a manicurist. Jewell had gathered all sorts of photos from the twenties, to see how people sat, walked, looked at one another. She got out the vintage manicure set and goggles she found at flea markets. She sang in French since Bessie spoke French. Jewell did whatever she could to keep her mind from wandering to Billy. She frequently had to put on her producer hat, joining Julian in decision-making meetings, but most of the time, from early morning on, she was with Bessie—was Bessie.

Their schedule was tight and grueling, but Jewell was used to the grind of TV projects. No waiting for the perfect light or inspiration. No unlimited takes or inspired experiments. They had only four weeks to get this in the can and she was in almost every scene. This was a commando experience, get the shot, make it work, move on. But she had forgotten how off balance she got shooting out of sequence, keeping track of which part of Bessie's life she was living. Just up from Texas, learning to fly in France, living in Chicago, barnstorming back in the States. And then she'd see Billy and feel like her own life was out of sequence too. Jewell tried not to catch him looking at her and he tried not to get caught. They'd been there, done that. Besides he belonged to somebody else now.

At the end of the first week, Jewell gave Carmen a buzz. Carmen was always the worrier of the bunch and with every cancer-free year she passed, her anxiety that it might return seemed to intensify instead of lessen. She worried that Regina's wedding planning venture, which was doing really well, might be too much and she might turn to old habits to keep her going. She worried that pursuing his Ph.D. was putting too much stress on Malcolm, worried about Jewell flying around in old airplanes. "Your husband's not breaking a sweat. He can handle it. And I think we have to trust Regina—she's got to try herself again, see what she can do. And as far as me—they won't let me get far enough off the ground to get hurt." She'd already talked herself dry trying to reassure Carmen about her cancer, so Jewell sent hugs to all and returned to Bessie's world.

No sooner than she hung up the phone rang. "Jewell? Billy. I know it's late and I hate to bother you, but I just got out of a script conference with Julian. He's got some changes I want to run past you before you hear it from him in the morning."

Jewell looked at the clock. *Midnight.* Her call, as an actor, wasn't until noon, but her job as producer was around the clock. "Meet me in the conference suite on my floor." The company had booked several suites specifically for meetings, wardrobe consultations and fittings, hair and makeup prep and storage. Jewell pulled on jeans and a T-shirt and headed down the hall. Billy was waiting. Unshaven, shirttail hanging out of his jeans, Jewell thought he looked tired, a little tense—every bit the screenwriter. "What's up?" She unlocked the door, flipped on the light.

Billy followed her into the suite's living room. "Julian wants me to add a couple of scenes that change the—well they alter the arc of Bessie's life while she's in France."

Jewell plopped on the sofa. "We already changed the scene in the barber shop right before she leaves for France—"

"Julian wants a romance, a love scene."

"A what?" Jewell tucked one leg under the other. "With who?"

"Etienne, her flight instructor." At the other end of the couch he straddled the arm. "Julian thinks you'll go for it. I just wanted to get your input. We've taken license in other—"

"What were Julian's reasons?" Jewell needed reason right now.

"I'm not sure if they're his or the network's. You know they like the footage they've seen so far, but they think adding this dimension to Bessie's life will make the story more uh—human—read marketable. You know, promo with Bessie and Etienne looking longingly into each other's eyes, to add to the ones of you in that flight suit." Billy turned to face her, put his feet up on the sofa cushion. "Sex sells, as they say." He ran a hand over his close-cropped hair, then leaned forward, rested his elbows on his knees.

Jewell wondered if his hair would feel like peach fuzz against the palm of her hand—soft but bristly, a little tickly—like one of Sam's old baby brushes. She felt an urge to lean toward him, meet him halfway. *This is business.* That's the only reason she and Billy were alone in a hotel room discussing a love scene—like it was a completely neutral subject. *That's why he called.* She realized he was giving her as much warning as possible that Bessie's affair in a romantic location with a man she worked with might be more personal to her than anyone but Billy could foresee.

It wasn't until Billy cleared his throat that Jewell realized he was still waiting for her feedback. That's what this meeting was for, wasn't it? "He—they—may be right." Jewell, the producer, tried to look thoughtful as she considered the possibility. "An international, interracial love interest?" To keep from making eye contact she focused on a bad watercolor seascape on the opposite wall. "A little spice never hurts the numbers—and I don't want this to be the first and last Fifth Dimension Production." She walked across the suite, sat on a chair by the window. "She was a woman. She must have loved somebody." Jewell had done some love scenes on *TIA*. There was always a towel, a sheet, nothing that risked revealing her stretch marks, but that secret was out anyway. "It has to feel real, Billy, like there's some caring there. It can't be just a roll in the hanger." She turned to him. "Can we do that?"

Billy met her gaze, held it a moment too long. "I think we can."

Jewell jumped up, went for the door. "Thanks—for the heads up." She had to dissipate the sensation that shot through her when she made the mistake of looking back.

Their exit was an awkward fumble—reaching for the light, then the doorknob at the same time, mumbled "sorry"s and "excuse me"s.

After the next morning's meeting Billy disappeared. Two days later the script girl handed Jewell the new additions, but she didn't look at them until that night, in the privacy of her room. On location she usually stretched out in the middle of her bed with her pad and a red pencil when she broke down her scenes, but she couldn't this time. Reading how Etienne was taken the first time he laid eyes on Bessie, but tries mightily to keep his feelings under control—how Bessie discovers a place in herself she didn't know existed and that no man had reached before, Jewell needed a straight-back chair, the desk, hard furniture to keep her grounded. When Jewell read the lines to herself, it was Billy's voice she heard speaking Etienne's lines to Bessie, to her.

By morning there were no notes on her pad. Jewell didn't need to jot down her motivation or look for some device to spark her performance. She was on those pages and so was Billy, even in their aching good-bye. Jewell knew she couldn't have him on set when they shot these scenes. It would be easy enough to arrange, especially the love scene. It was perfectly within her rights to request a closed set, but she also knew he wouldn't be there, that he couldn't stand to watch.

So the new material was incorporated into the existing script, locations found, wardrobe added and shooting went on uninterrupted—like the affair had been there from the beginning.

Jewell's third week in Toronto, Vivian and Ted flew in—on different days, of course.

Ted was a hit on the set, gracious, but low key, not wanting to stand in Jewell's light. "He doesn't know you know, Dad, but I want you to meet him." Jewell pulled Ted aside before introducing him to Billy.

"That's cool." And Ted shook hands with Billy, the same as everyone else. "Good to meet you, man." Ted gave him a solid pat on the back, talked to Billy a little bit longer.

"You're workin' your show. Good for you," Ted told Jewell after dinner. "Feels good to have the power, doesn't it?" He hugged her, kissed her forehead. "Good night Jewlee Dew."

She was in costume, at the airfield aboard Bessie's Jenny when Ted left the next morning. Jewell always wished she could do the flying scenes without her leather helmet. She wanted to feel the wind in her hair, the way she did in her convertible.

The most daring flying Jewell got to do involved tipping the wing, a salute to Etienne. Her stomach did flip-flops, like on a roller-coaster and she wondered what it felt like to Bessie when she fell out of that plane. Was there a moment when it really did feel like flying?

Vivian breezed in two days after Ted, full of praise for the way Jewell was handling her career. "I guess you did know what you were doing, darling."

The praise from her mother felt good, and Jewell didn't tell Vivian anymore about Billy than that he was John Roland's son, because unlike Ted, with her it would not have been cool.

Shooting stayed on schedule until the beginning of the fourth week when it wouldn't stop raining. On the third day of the monsoon, Jewell spent the morning in her room, making phone calls, praying for the weather to break. She called Carmen, knowing she was at work, but the nanny let her talk to Sam who'd just gotten home from pre-school. She promised to bring him another airplane from Canada. Then she called Regina who was bubbling with a new idea—for a coffeehouse. "It's like New Brunswick got hip since I left so I think there's a customer base there. I can have my party, sans alcohol and the only white powder is Sweet & Low. I could do poetry and music open-mike nights. It'll be like my own salon. There are a couple of great spaces I'm gonna look at. I can't wait to show you." Jewell hung up, glad Regina was getting her sea legs back, but her own forced captivity was making her stir crazy. She peeked out the window at the dreary, gray day, decided rain wouldn't kill her, and getting out would probably do her some good, so she grabbed her purse and umbrella and headed out to the Thai restaurant around the corner. She'd gotten takeout from there and right now she'd rather watch the rain and eat red curry alone than listen to more moaning about how much the rain delay would cost. She already knew. She'd been over it with the line producer, minute by minute all morning long.

By the time she hit the street, the rain had slowed to a drizzle, but the air was so thick Jewell felt like she'd stepped into a steam bath. She passed a toy store down the block and stopped in to look for Sam's plane. She was slated to fly out on the weekend and still hadn't found one—not that she'd had much time for shopping. Almost the moment she walked in she saw the wooden biplane dangling from the ceiling. It turned out to be one he could take apart and put together which was perfect since that was currently his favorite activity. Mission accomplished she continued down the street, but before she got to the next corner, the wind kicked up, the sky opened wide and the water came down in a rush that overwhelmed her little travel umbrella. She ducked in the doorway of a rare book dealer to wait it out. *Serves me right for playing hooky*. Jewell smoothed dripping hair out of her face, peeled her sopping wet shirt away from her skin. During her rain delay Jewell peered through the window of the closed shop, inspecting the display of Victorian garden books. That's when she saw him out of the corner of her eye, dashing up the block, no umbrella, a dissolving white deli bag in one hand. Before she could tuck herself deeper in the shadowy doorway, Billy saw her too.

Just keep going. They had gotten through meetings, bumped into each other at craft service, ran into each other in the lobby or elevator. Except for their conversation in the coffee shop that first day, and their midnight script confab that night, they had managed not to be alone. They had kept enough distance between them to keep from tempting the Fates any more than necessary.

But he did stop. Despite the downpour Billy walked slowly, deliberately to her. "Hey."

"Hey." Squeezed in the small hot space, soaked to the skin, they tried not to touch. Neither spoke, but they knew each other's thoughts had gone back to Prytania Street—running in the rain, hand in hand, laughing—climbing the stairs to Billy's room. She could still feel his wet skin on her hands, their bodies entwined on his twin bed, their sweat replacing the rain. Jewell remembered the teenager she had been, how bold she was with Billy, how gentle he was with her, how much she had wanted that feeling again.

The wind shifted and rain pelted the window, forcing them further back in the tiny doorway. The sultry summer air surrounded them, filled the space between them until they were so close. Closer than she'd been to him since they'd come back into each other's lives. Closer than she'd been since then. "I should go." Jewell looked down at her wet sandals, then out at the curtain of water.

"Don't." Billy's voice was low, husky. "Stay. It'll let up in a minute."

Jewell tried to leave, needed to. But she didn't. She looked at him like she'd been afraid to all month. She examined his face—he'd nicked his chin when he shaved this morning—nice lines, life lines, etched the corners of his eyes. His hair had grown since they'd been on location, no longer peach fuzz, it was starting to curl, not quite the fat curls she used to twirl around her fingers in New Orleans. She could see a sprinkle of silver, wondered if that's why he'd cut it short. The whole time she could feel him looking at her, felt her breath leaving her.

And then Jewell looked back at him, into those eyes and she was lost, the way she had been before. She reached out, touched his chest before she could stop herself. Billy smoothed wet hair off her cheek, tucked it behind her ear and Jewell shuddered, let the bag slip from her hand, let him pull her closer until there was no space between them at all. Jewell sank into him, found the feel of his body still familiar. Then she closed her eyes and gave in to the kiss she'd been fighting, one that felt like a welcome home to a place in her heart that had been empty too long. They clung to each other, found the rhythm of one breath they learned to share a long time ago. But then Jewell felt like her heart would stop if she didn't. Her body went rigid and she jerked away. "We can't Billy—we can't do this."

"Jewell—"

"No. You have to go or I will." The noisy patter of rain filled the silence, brought her back to the world beyond the alcove where they stood—back where she had to go.

"I never stopped loving you. I—"

"Don't." Jewell touched her fingers to his lips. "At least now I know I wasn't a fool. That's enough for me." She moved her hand away, folded her arms between them. "I'm going back to my life. You need to go back to yours. I don't regret what happened, but if we do this, if we let this happen, I will regret it, and I don't want that."

Billy nodded. They stood a long moment, listening to the shush of tires on wet pavement, taking each other in, accepting their truth, sealing a memory. "I wrote the letter."

Jewell nodded. Then Billy turned and ran into the rain. She watched him go, getting no satisfaction from knowing she had done the right thing, and aware that she had added another empty ache to the one already in her heart.

The script for the last several days of shooting had been finalized and Billy made arrangements to leave a few days earlier than planned. They had already said their good-byes.

30
...a life is something you build—

"We missed you, Ms. Prescott."

When Jewell dragged in from Toronto the concierge greeted her with a smile and bundles of mail that had accumulated in her absence. She looked at them, then at him. "Got a match?"

Upstairs she dropped the stack on her desk, took the rubber bands off one of the neat packets. *Who am I kidding?* It had waited this long, it could wait until tomorrow. Worn out from her dual role as star and head honcho, she looked forward to waking up in her own bed with nobody's questions to answer. And reconnecting with her first love had shown her that despite the pain their liaison caused her then, and the emotional hangover it left now, her feelings for Billy had been true. Their timing stunk, and she'd never know if their love would have lasted, but she had learned not to settle for the hollow substitute she pretended was enough with Dwight.

Jewell looked at the phone, but she was too tired to talk, even to Regina and Carmen. She'd catch up with them tomorrow. She showered just long enough to knock off the airport dust, and although it was early, she went directly to bed and was asleep before her head hit the pillow. But a little after three o'clock Jewell's eyes flew open as though somebody had called her name. She lay still, listened for footsteps, a door opening. *Must have been a dream. Or an echo of the line producer. I heard him enough to last the rest of my life.* She nestled back in her pillows, but after twenty minutes she was still awake, so she got up, put on the kettle for tea. *The mail. That'll make me drowsy.* Much of it was mindless nonsense—catalogs, offers for yet another credit card, "you may already be a winner" sweepstakes entries. She could toss that stuff without opening it which would at least put a dent in the piles.

Armed with her mug of chamomile she padded into the office. Her tea was cold and her trash can half full when she saw the letter from California. Jewell stared at the envelope, afraid of what it might or might not contain, then ripped it open, impatient to find out. "Dear Ms. Prescott, this is to verify that you still wish to be contacted by the child you gave up for adoption..."

By the second paragraph the paper rattled in her hand. She laid it on her desk to finish reading. *She wants to meet me. Maybe. Slow down.* But

Jewell felt warm all over, like every cell in her body was vibrating and she couldn't sit still. She started a loop, down the hall to the kitchen, through the dining room and back again, trying to digest the words she'd prayed to hear. She'd have made the call right then except it was after one on the West Coast. By five thirty she had sorted the rest of the mail into neat piles and read the letter from the agency at least ten times, to make sure she hadn't dreamed that too. Jewell couldn't contain herself another second, so she called Carmen, knowing she'd be up. Knowing she could babble, about being happy and scared, about Billy, about why her whole life seemed to want to open to the chapter from New Orleans, like she couldn't move on until she came to terms with that time and made peace with it.

"Are you all right?" Carmen picked up after one ring.

"No. Yes. Sorry, I didn't mean to scare you," Jewell said. "I just got amazing news."

Jewell spoke in unconnected bits of fact and feeling, but she knew Carmen understood.

"Let me know what happens the minute you hear. Page me if you have to," Carmen said.

Next, Jewell called Regina who was starting her mornings much earlier these days.

"Are you freakin' serious?!" Regina said. "Boy, do Carmen and I have stuff to tell her."

"She might not go through with it." It was Jewell's biggest fear. To be so close and still fall short.

"And I might not speak to you again, but I doubt it," Regina said.

Jewell wasn't due back on the *TIA* set until tomorrow, so she filled the rest of the morning puttering, unpacking, watching the clock until she could make the call. On the dot of nine Pacific Time she dialed the phone. After some preliminaries, the woman she spoke with said she would release Jewell's letter to her daughter immediately. "Then it's up to her. Sometimes when they get a response it becomes too overwhelming and they stop."

Jewell couldn't let herself think that. "She can call me anytime. She can write. She can show up on my doorstep." She was jubilant. She wondered whether to let Billy know, but decided he would find out on his own, when it was his time.

Then came the waiting. Jewell went back to *TIA* and Adrienne, who had remained suspended in time in Clearfield. She checked her answering machine obsessively. Her cell phone was always within reach, and she flipped through the mail every night before she even got in the elevator, but October and the rest of life marched on. Post-production work on *Fly Girl* took up much of the rest of her time—editing, scoring, looping, and dubbing had to be rushed to make sure Bessie's story would be ready for its February air date. So far Lois Taylor at SRO was pleased and had already talked to Jewell about doing another project with them.

By late October, even though Regina hadn't settled on a location or a name for her coffeehouse—Reggie's Beanery was a current favorite—Jewell and Carmen agreed to be investors and Jewell was elected CDO—Chief Decorating Officer. In her spare time she began combing flea markets and estate sales for furniture, pitchers, vases, paintings, items that felt like they told a story. "I want it to be cozy, but kinda swank too," Regina had told her. "You know, I want people to feel comfortable, but I also want them to know they're *out* someplace. You pull that off and I'll name some outrageous concoction after you. Dad's already baking samples for the dessert menu." Jewell enjoyed roaming the Pennsylvania countryside, Connecticut consignment shops and New Jersey yard sales, top down when a warm day permitted. One sunny, crisp afternoon Regina tagged along. "You're kidding right?" She said when Jewell started the canvas roof folding back on itself. "It's freakin' cold out here." Jewell had smiled. "That's what the heater's for." Her antiquing junkets took up some time and kept her mind off the news she was waiting to hear.

Jewell had just come in with her latest find, a red porcelain cake stand, and was dicing peppers for a frittata when the phone rang. She tucked the receiver on her shoulder.

"Can I speak to Jewell Prescott?"

"Who's calling?" It was rare for her to hear an unfamiliar voice on the line so she figured it was a new *TIA* production assistant with a schedule change.

"*Tracy Hopkins*." There was a pause, a cleared throat. "*Umm—I'm her daughter*."

"Oh my God, yes." Jewell almost dropped the phone. "It's me." *Tracey*. Jewell had never known how to put a name on all she had missed, and hoped and loved. Now she had one. "I am so glad to hear your voice, Tracey." And to feel the sound of her daughter's name come from her own mouth. *Tracey*. She couldn't move, but she couldn't stand either so Jewell sank to the floor, sat cross-legged on the tile. They had a beginner's chat, full of pauses and easy questions—the basic whos, whats and wheres. It was too early for whys.

Afterward, Jewell went to the living room, sat on the chaise, now re-upholstered in a more muted red. Her view of the park was from a different angle than in 5D, but it still made her feel tranquil, like there was space enough to breathe. *Tracey*. Knowing her daughter's name, and that she loved the people who had become her parents removed a weight Jewell didn't know she had been carrying. She could never make up for lost time. She knew that, but to finally see her daughter, touch her, hug her, it would be like getting back the piece of herself Jewell had lost that September day. And getting to know the person Tracey had become, that would be a privilege.

"She grew up in San Francisco, she's a senior at Berkeley, an art major, can you believe it?" Jewell babbled to Regina and Carmen in a three-way call the moment she found her tongue. They were planning to meet in New Brunswick in a few days to see a couple of spots Regina had scouted out for Drip-n-Sip, the coffee bar's current name, but this wouldn't keep. "Tracey even sounds like me, kind of husky." Jewell couldn't talk fast enough, couldn't stop saying her daughter's name. "She says her parents are great—Glen and Paula—he's an architect, she runs a bookstore." Jewell had sucked up all the details she could in that one phone call and spilled them out for Carmen and Regina, because sharing her news with them helped make it real.

So before the real estate tour Jewell met Carmen and Regina for a bite, although food was the last thing on her mind. "I'd go out there right now, but I have to wait two weekends. She's got exams and right now I can't take off midweek because I've been away from the show so much." Jewell sipped her sparkling water. "I don't know how I'm going to last that long. She told me that when she was little people used to say she looked liked the girl from *Daddy's Girl*, but she never paid them any attention. Funny, huh?!" Jewell was as excited as a nine-year-old on Christmas Eve. "Anyway, she's sending me a picture. And I told her about you guys, that you two know me better than anybody. I also warned her to ignore half the things you tell her about me!"

"What about Grandma Prescott?" Regina asked.

"I'll tell her when I go out there. This doesn't seem like phone news."

"It was with us," Regina said.

"That's different," Jewell replied. At this point in their friendship, the method of communication wasn't relevant, they were connected whether it was across a table, via e-mail or by string and a Dixie cup. Vivian would require answers she didn't have yet, that maybe they'd have to find together.

"Aren't you scared?" Carmen asked. "I mean, if my mother showed up now, I don't know what I'd do."

"It's a little scary, but in a good way." Jewell glowed with the warmth of anticipation. "It'll be like meeting somebody I feel like I've known for ages, but for the very first time."

"Well I can honestly say I don't know if I've seen you happier," Carmen said.

"I'm not sure I've seen anybody this happy, Bijoux," Regina added.

"I probably sound like an idiot babbling like this—"

"No worse than me blabbling about Sam," Carmen said. "Speaking of—" She dug in her bag and produced a much-folded piece of first-grade paper. "This is for you."

Printed in bold letters—capital ones touching the top of the widest line, small letters fitting under the thin line in between—"Thank you fo my ai plane Aunty Jewey. Love, Sam." In the lower right corner he'd drawn a biplane like the one she'd brought him from Toronto.

"The first letter from my boy." Jewell held it to her heart. She was thrilled about Tracey coming back into her life, but that could never diminish the love she felt for Sam.

"We're working on the R's, but you don't know what it took to get him to sit down and write that. He kept saying, 'I told her thank you already, Mama. How come I have to write it too?' Sometimes he makes me crazy, but Malcolm got him to do it. I didn't ask how."

Jewell traced her fingers over Sam's backward R's. "It's great. Crazy R's and all!" Jewell refolded the paper, kissed it and put it in her purse. "Give my Sam a great big hug for me."

"And I'll give him one tomorrow," Regina announced, the auntie competition still in full force. "You still need me to pick him up from school, don't you?" Despite her protestations about boring family life, Auntie Gina was thrilled to be on the list of people authorized to pick him up, or who would be called in case of emergency.

"Yep. Tomorrow is crazy. The baby-sitter's having a root canal. Malcolm has a dissertation conference—the end is in sight, thank God. And we're trying to open a wellness clinic in Newark so I've got a meeting up there. Sam gets out at two fifteen—"

"I know," Regina said. "I'm glad my wedding thing is working out. It kills the weekends, but I don't have the nine-to-five daily grind either. Hey, that's a good name. The Daily Grind."

"You're not well." Jewell signaled for the check. "Let's get out of here and take a peek at these places before you come up with another name."

"Bean, Grind, Drip—they're all still in the pot. Hmm. In the Pot." Regina produced a notepad and wrote the two new names in contention. "Anyway, I'll figure it out before I need a sign."

Regina led the way to the first stop, a former pizzeria across the street. "There's lots of foot traffic, especially during the week. And the Rutgers crowd definitely needs coffee. I know what's in the cafeteria." Nose against the glass, they peered inside. "It's got kitchen facilities too. That's a plus." Then she took them around the corner. "Exhibit 'B' is off the main drag, which makes the rent cheaper. There won't be as many passersby, but a lot happens in this town by word of mouth and as you know I've got a big mouth, so I bet I could make it work. I've been preparing a business plan and making projections."

"Business plan? Projections?" Carmen grinned. "Guess you earned that BS degree."

"You two always said BS was my speciality," Regina joked. "Now I'm certified!"

Jewell rubbed her hands together for warmth. "The furnishings I've picked up would work in either place," Jewell said. "I'm seeing a kind of funky nuevo/retro bohemian atmosphere."

"Do you know what the hell she's talking about?" Regina elbowed Carmen.

"You'll love it. Trust me." Jewell checked her watch.

"Without question, Bijoux." Regina took a deep breath. "Ahh, I can smell the cappuccino already. And if you two busy ladies let me know when you're free, I'll make appointments to inspect these places."

"Will do," Jewell said. "And I hate to leave you in the middle of a caffeine flashback, but I've gotta dash."

"Oh come on, it's early. I know Carmen's got to get home to her guys, but I thought I could talk you into heading to Montclair with me. There's a coffeehouse I heard about and I want to check it out. They do open-mike poetry Mondays, jazz Thursdays, comedy Fridays," Regina said. "Maybe I can steal some ideas."

"No can do. Clearfield awaits, bright and early," Jewell said.

Propelled by gusty wind at their backs they hustled to the garage.

"I don't know, Jewell, you finding Tracey, or her finding you—after all this time. It makes me think that things mostly work out the way they're supposed to and we make ourselves crazy worrying about them." They stopped at Carmen's Volvo wagon in the parking deck.

"Listen, I love y'all too." Regina gave them a sugary smile, crossed her hands over her heart. "But I gotta go before the philosophy lecture. I got poets to hear, coffee to drink—" She waved and headed up the ramp to her car.

"I'm coming." Jewell gave Carmen a hug. "That's not for you—"

"I know. It's for Sam. I'm just the messenger." Carmen disarmed the alarm and ducked in.

Jewell called to Regina. "Taking the turnpike?"

"Yeah. Two exits," she answered. Regina walked backward so she could keep talking. "Driving with the top down tonight?"

"It's a little too cold. Even for me," Jewell called.

The three cars formed a caravan to the cashier's booth. Once out on the street, Carmen tooted good-bye and made a left at the corner. Jewell made a right in her Beamer, heading for the highway with Regina, in Carmen's old Saturn, right behind.

At the toll plaza Regina watched Jewell sail through the EZ Pass lane. *I gotta get one of those.* She said that every time she was stuck behind somebody who didn't pull close enough to the ticket machine, or couldn't find their money. Regina flicked on the radio, tapped the wheel impatiently. *I'll never catch her. I don't even know if she took the car lanes or the truck lanes.*

That dilemma was solved after Regina snatched her ticket and found the truck lanes were closed for construction. *Great, now I'll have freakin' truck butts in my way.* But traffic was light and she scooted easily between the cars and eighteen wheelers until she spotted Jewell's white convertible a little past exit 10. Regina pulled behind her, flashed the headlights. *No, that's not what I meant.* Jewell signaled and moved a lane to the right. *She thinks I'm some lunatic trying to pass her.* Regina eased up next to Jewell, gave a quick toot. She glanced over in time to see Jewell wave.

They drove in tandem a while, but Jewell's driving was too slow for Regina, who used the speed limit as a suggestion—one she followed occasionally. That, and staring at the back of a flatbed loaded with lumber got tired pretty quick. So she honked a farewell, took off around the truck, and sailed on to the next exit, singing along with Luther.

Thirty minutes later, Regina pulled into a parking spot on Bloomfield Avenue. *As slow as she drives, Jewell probably hasn't gotten to the Lincoln Tunnel yet.* Regina approached the address and was surprised to see the windows were dark. *That's weird.* But a handwritten sign on the door explained. "Closed tonight, due to water emergency. For further info—" *Great timing, Regina. Why couldn't they have a flood tomorrow?* She got back in her car, grumbling, and retraced her route, heading south, thinking about calls she needed to make in the morning—to the florist who needed to make a substitution for stephanotis in the bridal bouquet because he couldn't get any in before Saturday. Then there was the bride's father who wanted to change the seating arrangements yet again. She was met by a sea of brake lights as soon as she took the exit for the turnpike. *Why couldn't I have seen this a few seconds earlier? I could have gone the back way.* But she was stuck in traffic, nowhere to go but straight ahead. *What else can go wrong?*

As she inched along the jug handle to merge onto the highway she saw the lights—flashing reds, blinding white spots, running red, white and blue lights erect like goalposts on top of state trooper cars. *Must have been some accident.* She couldn't even tell what side of the road it was on. All the activity was near the center median. *I just drove past there an hour ago.*

The blue Villager was nice enough to let her cut ahead onto the highway. She craned her head, trying to catch a glimpse like everybody else. Then the cold shot through her like ice water in her veins when she saw the crumpled carcass of a white BMW sitting on the bed of a tow truck, its amber lights spinning a somber warning. Regina opened her window and laid on her horn, waving, cutting off buses and whatever else was in her way as she headed diagonally across three lanes of traffic, praying she was wrong as she pulled onto the shoulder by the median ahead of the phalanx of police cars and ambulances. Before she could get out a trooper appeared beside her car.

"You can't stop here, lady. This is an accident investigation—"

"Where is she?" On the other side of the road Regina saw the lumber truck she'd been stuck behind, now resting on its side like an abandoned toy. The load of two-by-fours had spilled out over the road like pick-up sticks. Words were second nature to Regina, but she felt like she'd forgotten how to speak, had to struggle to make herself understood. "That's my friend's car. Is she all right?" The tow truck idled loudly, spewing exhaust and Regina felt sick to her heart. *She's okay. Maybe hurt a little, but she's okay. She has to be okay.* "You have to tell me where she is!"

"I'm sorry, ma'am. All I can tell you is there's been a serious accident and you have to move along."

She pounded the steering wheel. "Just tell me where they took her!"

"Ma'am I can tell you that injured parties were taken to the nearest trauma unit. From this location that would be Robert Wood Johnson in—"

"I know where it is!" Regina snapped, but she didn't know if she could drive, if she remembered what the pedals were for or how to steer. *I need to call Carmen. She'll know what to do. I can't call her. I have to go there. What if she's gone to the hospital?* Regina couldn't keep her thoughts straight, couldn't hold down the frenzy in her head, the rolling waves in her stomach. She got the door open just in time to hang her head out and heave up her soul.

"Dr. Carmen Webb?" The state trooper stood on her front porch.

"Yes, Officer—" She tried to pronounce his name, but decided to pass. She couldn't imagine what he wanted with her.

"Ma'am do you know a Jewell Prescott?"

"Yes?" Carmen's stomach lurched.

"There's never a good way to say this—"

"Say what?" That giant hand reached into her chest and squeezed her heart.

The officer shifted his weight, squared his shoulders. "Miss Prescott was involved in a traffic accident on the New Jersey Turnpike—"

"We just had dinner a little while ago." *This isn't happening*. The talking uniform continued, but Carmen couldn't hear all of the words because of the noise in her head.

"Her vehicle was traveling north on the turnpike…A truck carrying lumber shifted its load…every attempt was made…she was pronounced dead at the scene."

Carmen's mouth opened, but she couldn't speak, couldn't hear Sam crying from upstairs, or Malcolm asking who was at the door.

"…we found this in her wallet." The officer handed her a card that listed emergency contacts. Carmen's name was first, followed by Leonard and Vivian.

Carmen never felt it slip through her fingers as her knees gave way. The first sound she heard when she came to was Regina crying.

"I saw it. On my way home." Regina knelt on the floor, next to the couch where Malcolm had carried Carmen. "They wouldn't tell me how she was." But in the moment she looked in Carmen's desolate face, Regina knew. The cry that came up was like a baby's—head thrown back, mouth wide open, but no sound escaped. With the first gulp of air a thin wail emerged and she clamped her hands to her face to hold it down.

Carmen closed her eyes, lay still on the couch, trying to comprehend the unthinkable. Jewell was dead.

Using sheer will and each other for support, they took turns being the one able to face the horrible reality and deal with necessary details, the first of which was identifying Jewell—they couldn't say "the body." They knew Vivian would be inconsolable and shouldn't be alone when she heard, so Carmen called Leonard who took it from there.

When they got back to Carmen's, Regina held onto her own despair long enough to make the call to Las Vegas. Over the phone she could hear the heaviness settle over Ted, see him sink under the weight and it broke her heart even more.

On his way to Vivian's Leonard called Carmen back. "I want to make sure you're aware that Jewell wanted to be an organ donor. And being a doctor you know time is of the essence."

"Oh." Carmen vaguely remembered a conversation about it, but that had been years ago. It wasn't information she had ever seriously thought about needing.

"I'll call the hospital and let them know he's faxing the papers." Carmen told Regina what Leonard had said. "That's the first step." And they could only manage one step at a time.

Regina looked out Carmen's kitchen window, surprised to find the sun shining on a new day. It didn't seem possible that just ten hours ago, they were leaving the restaurant, laughing, waving good-bye. "It's not fair." Regina pressed her forehead against the cool glass, tears rolled down her cheeks.

"I know." Carmen came and stood next to her, looped her arm through Regina's. They stayed that way for a while, swaying gently, finding comfort in rocking themselves.

Malcolm found them that way when he and Sam came downstairs. "I thought I'd take him out for breakfast, then Lonnie and Al said they'll keep him as long as we need." Malcolm put his arms around Carmen, kissed the top of her head. "Back in a while. Call if you need me."

Jewell had always been organized and through the years and with Leonard's guidance had kept her will updated and spelled out her final wishes. One of them was that she didn't want to be buried in California. Her real life had been lived on the East Coast. Leonard stayed in constant contact with Carmen and Regina since Vivian was under a doctor's care and had abdicated responsibility for the final arrangements to the three of them.

"You know we can't put this off any longer. It'll be in the papers," Carmen said to Regina. They had made calls, set the wheels in motion, but there was one duty they both dreaded.

Tracey. There were no words adequate enough to tell the daughter Jewell had never seen, that she never would. That their planned reunion would never take place.

Both Carmen and Regina were on the line for that call. Tracey was quiet, resigned, like fate had taken away something she never had anyway. She said she couldn't bear to attend the funeral. "But you have to come later," Regina said. "Or we'll come out there," Carmen added. "It won't be the same—nothing will—but when you're ready to know about her, we can tell you almost as much as she could tell you herself—" Regina smiled for the first time since the accident. "Maybe more."

Days passed in a flurry of tasks that seemed absurd. Picking out flowers Jewell would never smell, an outfit no one would see.

The day of Jewell's service dawned bright. When the morning weatherman said the day would be a jewel, Carmen turned off the television. The memorial, held at the Manhattan cathedral just down the street from 5D, was attended by family, friends, the cast and crew of *TIA* which had shut down production for the day, and several actors who'd worked with Jewell from as far back as *Daddy's Girl* and her early commercials and as recently as *Fly Girl*. Some fans stood reverently at the back of the sanctuary. Regina, her parents, Carmen and Malcolm were in the first row on one side of the aisle, Vivian, Ted and Leonard sat on the other. A smiling photo of Jewell stood on an easel and a blanket of white roses covered the gleaming casket.

Carmen and Regina had both worked on the service, helping to choose music, a verse from one of Jewell's favorite poems for the program cover, but the hardest request had come from Vivian. "I want one of you to say a few words about her. Not a eulogy. Just the way she was." At first neither of them could imagine how they could talk that day, especially not about Jewell and what she meant to them. Finally Carmen agreed to try.

So as the organ soared, Carmen sat dreading that moment, but finally it came. The click of her heels echoed through the church as she approached the lectern, but when she turned to face the congregation a peaceful feeling came over her. She took a deep breath.

"It's hard now to even imagine, but when I first met Jewell, back in college, I couldn't stand her, thought she was stuck up and phony. One of the best things that's happened to me over the last two decades, was having the honor and the joy of finding out how wrong I was. I can't imagine my life without Jewell's friendship."

After the service, Carmen and Regina stood with Vivian, Leonard and Ted at the back of the chapel, accepting hugs, handshakes, murmured condolences.

"I know you're Regina and Carmen—though I don't know which is which." The man who spoke was tall, his amber eyes rimmed in red and his curly brown hair flecked with gold and silver. "I'm Billy Roland." He looked from one to the other. "I didn't even know if I should come." He clasped his hands behind his back. "Oh boy." He paused, shook his head, cleared his throat. "Jewell was special, but I don't have to tell you that." He moved on, then ducked out the door.

Regina was just about to get in the limo for the ride to the cemetery when she felt a hand on her arm. She turned and found herself face to face with Ty.

"I'm so sorry Regina." Ty looked somber, mature, in his navy suit. "Is there anything I can do? Something you need?"

She couldn't remember the last time she'd been so happy to see someone. The tears welled up, threatened to spill over. She wanted to collapse in Ty's arms, let him soothe and reassure her that it was going to be all right. That she'd get over this. That he'd help her. Instead, she kissed his cheek. "Thank you for coming. It means a lot." A tear trickled from her eye.

Ty tugged the snowy white square of linen from his breast pocket, handed it to her. She dabbed at her tears, refolded the hankie, offered it to him. "Keep it." Like everyone else here, Ty wore the sadness of the day on his face. "Maybe I can get it some other time." He was tentative, not sure his comment was appropriate or welcome. "I—uh—I better get going." Ty turned to walk away, turned back. "Listen Regina—this is the kind of thing—" He paused, looked at the hearse. "This is what reminds us we have to take advantage of every day. You know what I'm sayin'? I mean it's not like we don't have to think about tomorrow, but a life is something you build—and the tomorrows won't add up to much if we haven't been countin' our todays." Ty reached for her hand. "What I'm sayin' is I'd like to call you—see you—"

"I'd like that—a lot."

Epilogue

And some things never change.

Present Day
North Brunswick, NJ

Carmen looked toward the parked car where Regina still sat. *At least she opened the door*. They hadn't been back here since the funeral. The cemetery seemed like a formality, one that had nothing to do with Jewell or their memories of her. Kneeling on the damp ground, Carmen reached out, ran her fingers over the engraved plaque that now permanently marked Jewell's grave. It still felt strange—phrases like "Jewell's grave," or "before Jewell died." Carmen wondered if she'd ever get used to it because it still felt so wrong, like you tried on someone else's glove or shoe. You could get it on. It was your size, but you could tell right away that it hadn't been molded by the shape of your hand or the path your feet had walked.

This is not how it was supposed to be. They were going to grow old together, sit on the front porch—side by side by side. The first warm day of spring, she'd asked Malcolm to move the rocking chairs—at least for now. They were too painful a reminder of what would never be. Some days Carmen couldn't believe that she'd survived cancer, Regina had made it through drugs, alcohol, her harrowing ordeal—and then Jewell was snatched from their midst by a random accident. She and Regina had relived that night a thousand times. If they had stayed longer at the restaurant…talked longer in the parking deck…if traffic had been heavier…or lighter. But they hadn't, they didn't, it wasn't and nothing could change what happened last November.

Carmen looked up at the cloudless spring sky. *Good day for flying*. She heard the car door close, got to her feet. "Well maybe we will get to the airport on time," she teased Regina.

Carmen looked at the flowers in Regina's arms and remembered the ones Jewell sent her from Rome when she graduated from med school. A tear dropped from Carmen's eye, missed her cheek and landed on her silk blouse. She rested her hand over the small bulge in her tummy. She still had four months to go, but she and Malcolm had already decided if Sam was getting a sister, her name would be Jewell.

"Don't get all drippy. Her life wasn't sad. We can't be sad."

"Hormones," Carmen lied. "You'll see, one day."

"You are delirious."

"I don't know. Ty keeps asking me all kinds of questions about being pregnant. And you should hear him and Malcolm."

"The man is trippin'!" Regina answered. She and Ty had been seeing each other again since the first of the year, but she was taking her time, pacing herself, enjoying him and making sure to let him know how important he was to her. She didn't know if they'd be like her parents forty years down the line, but this time she wasn't going to let fear keep her from finding out. "We still have work to do."

Regina's coffeehouse, 5D Beanery had opened in February, the same week *Fly Girl* debuted on SRO, both to rave reviews. This time Regina was determined to grow her business right, and not let it take over her life. She bent to put the flowers down, fluffed out the heads. Then, hands on her hips, she surveyed the cemetery. "Prettiest flowers here," she announced.

Carmen adjusted a couple of blooms. "You may be right."

"Of course I'm right."

And some things never change. "We'd better get going. Tracey's plane is due in an hour."

"Think she'll find us?" Just back from her fourth loop around the baggage carousel, Regina came to a stop next to Carmen.

"Maybe. If you'd stand still for more than two seconds." Carmen leaned against the luggage cart she'd commandeered.

"Funny. Very funny."

They'd been waiting six months to meet the child of Jewell's heart, to sit and talk with her on that red chaise, now in Carmen's care. They had so much to fill her up with—pictures, stories, memories. They couldn't give Tracey the same kind of love Jewell had had for her all these years, but they could share with her the love they had for Jewell for as long as she wanted. They hoped for a lifetime.

"Man, look at all these people." Regina stood on tiptoes, examining the passengers as they streamed in from the San Francisco flight. "How will we know it's her?"

But they needn't have worried. "There she is." Carmen grabbed Regina's hand and the thrill of the moment passed between them. Head and shoulders above the crowd, they watched Tracey striding toward them. They would have recognized her anywhere.

Here space and time exist in light
the eye like the eye of faith believes.
The seen, the known
dissolve in iridescence, become
illusive flesh of light
that was not, was, forever is.

O light beheld as through refracting tears.
Here is the aura of that world
each of us has lost.
Here is the shadow of its joy.

—from "Monet's *Waterlilies*"
by Robert Hayden

Authors' Note to the Readers

Dear Reader,

When we are touched in some way by a book—it makes us cry, laugh, cuss or maybe just nod our heads in agreement, or shake them in commiseration—we are reminded that we are not alone in our fears, joys and needs. Somebody else has been there too. Thank you for letting us know through your letters and e-mails that our previous books, *Tryin' to Sleep in the Bed You Made* and *Far from the Tree*, have made you feel like you've been there. Writing a novel is a kind of communication, but it's not always two-way. We tried to respond to each of you, but as our deadline drew nearer, the mail went unanswered although not unread nor unappreciated. Know that even if you didn't hear from us, we truly value your feedback.

We appreciate the support we've received from countless book clubs—the ones we've been able to visit in person or by phone as well as the ones who have written or sent us pictures from their gatherings—thanks for making us a part of your circle. We hope this book continues to give you plenty to talk about (and if you'd like a reading group guide for this book there's now one available at www.stmartins.com).

When we began *Better Than I Know Myself*, we realized that in order to discover who Carmen, Regina and Jewell were, and how they got to be that way, we had to roll the calendar back and flip through the pages of our own personal histories. We looked at who we had each been before we went to college, who we tried to become while we were there—or after we left, since neither of us graduated from the schools we first attended (those stories are *way* too long for now), and who we've become since then. For different reasons, those years were turbulent for both of us. And while our books are not autobiographical, our own experiences have made us aware that life is an adventure and nobody gets through it alone. Our friends stick by us because of who we are—and in spite of it.

So hug a friend. Or sometimes bug her about that mammogram she's been putting off—yes it's uncomfortable, but so are most of those cute shoes we all wear. Be a cheerleader when she tries to quit smoking. (Virginia kicked the habit while we were in the middle of writing *Tryin'* which made for some crazy times, but we got through it. The good news is that she's still a nonsmoker.) Go for that exercise walk together. Writing this book was a constant reminder that life is fragile and that it's important to take care of the one we've been given. As we've all probably heard from some wise soul in our lives, tomorrow is not promised.

We hope that *Better Than I Know Myself* got you thinking about those times, those friends "back in the day." Or made you realize that the moments you're living now will be tomorrow's memories. And whether you have a degree from college or the school of life, it's the people we gather and love along the way—some still in a circle around us, others gone, but never forgotten—who make all the difference.

Embrace today,

Hiram Bell

Best friends for forty years, VIRGINIA DEBERRY AND DONNA GRANT first met while working as models, and what should have been a rivalry ended up as a decades-long friendship. Their twenty-year writing partnership has resulted in seven novels: *Tryin' to Sleep in the Bed You Made, Far from the Tree, Better Than I Know Myself, Gotta Keep on Tryin', What Doesn't Kill You, Uptown,* and *Exposures* (as Marie Joyce). *Tryin' to Sleep in the Bed You Made* won the Merit Award for Fiction from the Black Caucus of the American Library Association, the Book of the Year Award from the Blackboard Bestseller List, and the New Author of the Year Award from the Go On Girl! Book Club. Virginia lives in New Jersey. Donna resides in Brooklyn, New York.